MW01257571

ALEXANDER KUPRIN

THE GARNET BRACELET

AND OTHER STORIES

Fredonia Books
Amsterdam, The Netherlands

The Garnet Bracelet and Other Stories

by
Alexander Kuprin

ISBN: 1-4101-0235-1

Fredonia Books
Amsterdam, The Netherlands
http://www.fredoniabooks.com

CONTENTS

MOLOCH

I

A long blast from the mill siren announced a new working day. The deep, raucous sound seemed to come up from the bowels of the earth, spreading low above the ground. The murky dawn of a rainy August day tinged it with melancholy and foreboding.

The signal found Engineer Bobrov drinking tea.

During the last few days he had been suffering more than ever before from insomnia. Although he went to bed with a heavy head and started every moment with a jolt, he managed quite soon to drop off into a restless sleep; but he woke up long before dawn, shattered and irritable. This was doubtless due to mental and physical strain, and to his old habit of taking injections of morphia, a habit which he had recently begun to fight in earnest.

He now sat at the window, sipping his tea, which he found flat and tasteless. Raindrops zigzagged down the panes, and ruffled and rippled the puddles. Out of the window he could see a square pond framed by shaggy willows with bare, stumpy trunks and greyish-green leaves. Gusts of wind sent small waves racing over the surface of the pond, while the leaves of the willows took on a silvery hue. The faded grass, beaten down by the rain, drooped limply to the ground. The neighbouring village, the dark, jagged band of a forest stretching on the horizon, and the field patched with black and yellow showed grey and blurred as in a mist.

It was seven o'clock when Bobrov went out in a hooded oilskin raincoat. Like many nervous people, he felt miserable in the morning; there was a weakness in his body, his eyes ached dully as if someone were pressing them with force, and his mouth had a stale taste. But more painful than anything else was the conflict he had lately noticed in himself. His colleagues, who looked upon life from the most primitive, cheerful, and practical standpoint, would probably have laughed at what caused him so much secret agony; at any rate they would not have understood him. His abhorrence of work at the mill, a feeling that verged on horror, mounted with every passing day.

Considering his cast of mind, his habits and tastes, it would have been best for him to devote himself to armchair work, to professorial activities, or to farming. Engineering did not satisfy him, and he would have left college when he was in the third year but for his mother's insistence.

His delicate, almost feminine nature suffered cruelly under the coarse impact of reality. In this respect he compared himself with one flayed alive. Sometimes trifles unnoticed by others caused him a deep and lasting vexation.

Bobrov was plain and unassuming in appearance. He was shortish and rather lean, but he breathed nervous, impulsive energy. The outstanding feature of his face was his high white forehead. His dilated pupils, of different size, were so large that the grey eyes seemed black. His bushy, uneven eyebrows joined across the bridge of his nose, giving the eyes a fixedly stern, somewhat ascetic expression. His lips were thin and nervous but not cruel, and slightly unsymmetrical—the right corner of his mouth was a little higher than the left; his fair moustache and beard were small and scanty, for all the world like a young boy's. The charm of his virtually plain face lay in his smile. When he smiled a gay and tender look would come into his eyes, and his whole face would become attractive.

After a half a mile's walk he climbed a hillock. The vast panorama of the mill, covering an area of twenty square miles, sprawled below. It was a veritable town of red brick, bristling with tall, soot-blackened chimneys, reeking of sulphur and molten iron, deafened by a never-ending din. The formidable stacks of four blast-furnaces dominated the scene. Beside them rose eight hot-blast stoves for circulating heated air, eight huge iron towers topped with round domes. Scattered about the blast-furnaces were other structures: repair shops, a cast house, a washing department, a locomotive shed, a rail-rolling mill, open-hearth and puddling furnaces, and so on.

The mill area descended in three enormous natural terraces. Little locomotives scurried in all directions. Coming into view on the lowest level, they sped upwards whistling shrilly, disappeared in the tunnels for a few seconds, rushed out again wrapped in white steam, clanked over bridges, and finally raced along stone trestles as if flying through the air, to empty ore or coke slap into the stack of a blast-furnace.

Farther off, beyond those natural terraces, you were bewildered by the sight of the chaos reigning on the building site of the fifth and sixth blast-furnaces. It was as if a terrific upheaval had thrown up those innumerable piles of crushed stone and bricks of various sizes and colours, those pyramids of sand, mounds of flagstone, stacks of sheet iron and timber. Everything seemed to be heaped up without rhyme or reason, a freak of chance. Hundreds of carts and thousands of people were bustling there like ants on a wrecked ant-hill. White, acrid lime dust hung in the air like mist.

Still farther away, close to the horizon, workmen crowded near a long goods train, unloading it. From the wagons bricks slid down planks in an unceasing stream, sheets of iron fell with a crash, thin boards flew quivering through the air. As empty carts moved away towards the train, others came in a string, loaded high. Thousands of sounds merged into a long, galloping hubbub: the clear notes of stone-masons' chisels, the ringing blows of riveters pounding away at boiler rivets, the heavy crashing of steam hammers, the powerful hissing and whistling of steam pipes, and occasional muffled, earth-shaking explosions somewhere underground.

It was an engrossing and awe-inspiring sight. Human labour was in full swing like a huge, complex and precise machine. Thousands of people—engineers, stone-masons, mechanics, carpenters, fitters, navvies, joiners, blacksmiths—had come together from various corners of the earth, in order to give their strength and health, their wits and energy, in obedience to the iron law of the struggle for survival, for just one step forward in industrial progress.

That day Bobrov was feeling particularly wretched. Three or four times a year he would lapse into a strange, melancholy, and at the same time irritable mood. Usually it came on a cloudy autumn morning, or in the evening, during a winter thaw. Everything would look dull and lacklustre, people's faces would appear colourless, ugly, or sickly, and their words, sounding as if they came from far away, would cause nothing but boredom. That day he was particularly irritated, when making the round of the rail-mill, by the pallid, coal-stained and fire-dried faces of the workmen. As he watched their toil while the breath of the white-hot masses of iron scorched their bodies and a piercing autumn wind blew in through the wide doorway, he felt as if he were going through part of their physical suffering. He was ashamed of his well-groomed appearance, his fine linen, his yearly salary of three thousand rubles.

II

He stood near a welding furnace, watching. Every moment its enormous blazing maw opened wide to swallow, one by one, hundred-pound pieces of white-hot steel, fresh from a flaming furnace. A quarter of an hour later, having passed with a terrific noise through dozens of machines, they were stacked in the shape of long, shining rails at the far end of the shop.

Someone touched Bobrov's shoulder from behind. He spun round in annoyance and saw Svezhevsky, one of his colleagues.

Bobrov had a strong dislike for this man with his figure always slightly bent, as if he were slinking or bowing, his eternal snigger, and his cold, moist hands which he kept on rubbing. There was something ingratiating, something cringing and malicious, about him. He always knew before anybody else the gossip of the mill, and he reported it with especial relish to those who were likely to be most upset by it; when speaking he would fuss nervously, touching every minute the sides, shoulders, hands, and buttons of the person to whom he was talking.

"I haven't seen you for ages, old chap," said Svezhevsky with a snigger as he clung to Bobrov's hand. "Reading books, I suppose?"

"Good morning," replied Bobrov reluctantly, withdrawing his hand. "I just wasn't feeling well."

"Everybody's missing you at Zinenko's," Svezhevsky went on significantly. "Why don't you ever go there? The director was there the other day; he asked where you were. The talk turned to blast-furnaces, and he spoke very highly of you."

"How very flattering." Bobrov made a mock bow.

"But he did! He said the Board valued you as a most competent engineer who could go far if he chose to. In his view, we oughtn't to have asked the French to design the mill since we had experienced men like you at home. Only—"

"Now he's going to say something nasty," thought Bobrov.

"Only it's a pity, he says, that you keep away from society as if you were a secretive person. One hardly knows what to make of you or how to talk to you. O yes! Here I am talking about this and that, forgetting to tell you the biggest news. The director wants everybody to be at the station tomorrow for the twelve o'clock train."

"Going to meet somebody again, are we?"

"Exactly. Guess who!"

Svezhevsky's face took on a sly and triumphant look. He rubbed his hands, apparently much pleased, because he was about to give a piece of interesting news.

"I really don't know," said Bobrov. "Besides, I'm no good at guessing."

"Oh, please try. At least name somebody at random."

Bobrov said nothing and made a show of watching a steam crane at work. Svezhevsky, noticing it, became fussier still.

"You couldn't tell, not for the world. Well, I won't tantalize you any longer. They're expecting Kvashnin in person."

The frankly servile tone in which he uttered the name sounded disgusting to Bobrov.

"What's so awfully important about that?" he asked casually.

"How can you ask that? Why, on the Board of Directors he does as he pleases, and everybody listens to him as to an oracle. This time the Board has entrusted him with speeding up construction—that is, he's entrusted himself with it. You'll see the hell that'll be raised here when he arrives. Last year he inspected the mill—that was before you came, wasn't it? Well, the manager and four engineers were kicked out. How soon will you finish putting in the blast?"*

"It's as good as done."

"That's fine. In that case we can celebrate that and the laying of foundations when Kvashnin's here. Have you ever met him?"

"No, never. Of course, I've heard the name."

"I've had the pleasure. You wouldn't come across another character like him, I can tell you. All Petersburg knows him. To begin with, he's so fat he can't join his hands across his belly. You don't believe me? Upon my word. He even has a special carriage with the whole of the right side opening on hinges. And he's tall as a steeple, too, with red hair and a booming voice. But what a clever dog he is! God! He's on the board of all joint-stock companies—gets two hundred thousand rubles just for attending seven meetings a year. When something has to be put over at a general meeting, there's no one half so good as he. He can present the fishiest annual report in such a way that the shareholders will take black for white, and will lay themselves out to thank the Board. The

* Heating a blast-furnace before operation to the melting point of ore, which is about 3,000° F Sometimes it lasts several months —*Author's note.*

amazing thing is that he never really knows what he's talking about, and makes his point by a lot of assurance. When you hear him talk tomorrow you'll probably think that all his life he's done nothing but fuss about with blast-furnaces, and yet he knows as much about them as I do about Sanskrit."

"Tra-la-la-la!" Bobrov sang, out of tune and with a deliberate carelessness, turning away.

"I'll give you an example. Do you know how he receives in Petersburg? He sits in his bath, with just his red head shining above the water, while some privy councillor or other stands before him, bowing respectfully, and reports. He's a terrific glutton and can choose his food, too. Rissoles à la Kvashnin are a specialty in all the best restaurants. As for women—ahem! There was a most humorous incident three years ago."

Seeing that Bobrov was about to walk off, Svezhevsky took hold of his button.

"Don't go," he whispered entreatingly. "It's so funny! I'll make it short. This is how it was. Some three years ago, in autumn, a poor young man came to Petersburg. He was a clerk or something—I can't recall his name at the moment. He was trying to secure a disputed inheritance and every morning, after making his round of the various offices, he dropped into Summer Garden to rest on a bench for a quarter of an hour. Well, then. He did that for three and four and five days, and every day he saw an unusually fat, red-haired gentleman strolling in the garden. They got to talking. Redhead, who turned out to be Kvashnin, learned from the young man all about his circumstances, and sympathized with him. But he didn't tell him his name. Well, then. One day Redhead says to the young man, 'Would you be willing to marry a certain lady and part with her right after the wedding, and never see her again?' The young man was starving at the time.

'I'm willing,' he says. 'Only it depends on how much I get, and, besides, I want the money first.' You'll observe that the young man was not born yesterday. Well, then. They made it a deal. A week later, Redhead made the young man put on a dress-coat, and took him to church out in the country, at the crack of dawn. There was no crowd; the bride was waiting, carefully veiled, but you could see she was pretty and quite young. The ceremony started. Only, the young man noticed that his bride was rather melancholy. So he says to her in a whisper, 'It looks as if you've come here against your will.' And she answers, 'So have you, it seems.' In that way they found out all about it. It appeared that the girl's own mother had forced her into marriage. You see, her conscience wouldn't after all let her give away her daughter to Kvashnin outright. Well, then. They talked like that for a while, and then the young man says to her, 'Let's play a trick, shall we? We're both of us young, and there may yet be good luck in store for us, so let's leave Kvashnin standing.' The girl had a resolute temper and a quick wit. 'All right,' she says, 'let's do it.' When the wedding was over everybody walked out of the church, and Kvashnin was beaming with happiness. Now the young man had made him pay in advance, and a lot of money it was, because for that kind of thing Kvashnin spares no expense. Kvashnin walked up to the newlyweds and congratulated them as mockingly as he could. They listened to him and thanked him and called him their benefactor, and suddenly off they hopped into the carriage. 'What's this, now? Where are you going?' 'Why, we're going to the station to start on our honeymoon trip. Get going, cabbie!' And they left Kvashnin gaping. On another occasion— What? You're going already, Andrei Ilyich?" Svezhevsky broke off his chatter as he saw Bobrov slouching his hat and buttoning his overcoat with the most determined air.

"Sorry, I've no time," Bobrov answered drily. "As regards your story, I think I've heard or read about it somewhere before. Goodbye."

And turning his back on Svezhevsky, who was put out by his brusque manner, he walked swiftly out of the shop.

III

On coming back from the mill Bobrov had a hurried meal and stepped out on to the porch. His driver Mitrofan, whom he had told to saddle Fairway, a bay Don, was straining at the girths of the English saddle. Fairway would inflate his belly and quickly twist his neck several times, snapping at the sleeve of Mitrofan's shirt. Then Mitrofan would shout at him in an angry and unnaturally deep voice, "Stand still, you beggar!" and add, gasping with the strain, "Just look at him."

Fairway—a stallion of middle height, with a powerful chest, a long trunk, and a spare, somewhat drooping rump—stood with graceful ease on his strong shaggy legs, with dependable hoofs and fine pasterns. A connoisseur would have disapproved of the curved profile and the long neck with the sharply protruding Adam's apple. But Bobrov held that these features, which distinguish any Don horse, made up Fairway's beauty in the same way as the dachshund's crooked legs and the setter's long ears made up theirs. And there was no horse at the mill that could outrun Fairway.

Like any good Russian driver, Mitrofan considered it his duty to treat horses severely, never allowing himself or the beast any show of tenderness, and called it names like "convict," "carrion," "murderer," and even "bastard." Nevertheless, in his heart, he was very fond of Fairway. His affection found expression in seeing that Fairway was groomed better and got more oats than Swallow and Sailor, the two other mill horses in Bobrov's use.

"Did you water him, Mitrofan?" asked Bobrov.

Mitrofan did not answer at once. As a good driver he was deliberate and dignified in conversation.

"Yes, Andrei Ilyich, of course I did. Stop fretting, you devil!" he shouted angrily at the horse. "I'll teach you to fret! He's just itching for the saddle, sir, he's that eager."

No sooner did Bobrov walk up to Fairway and take the reins with his left hand than the very same thing happened which occurred almost daily. Fairway, who had long been squinting a big angry eye at the approaching Bobrov, started to chafe and fret, arching his neck and throwing up lumps of mud with his hind feet. Bobrov hopped beside him on one leg, trying to thrust his foot into the stirrup.

"Let go the bridle, Mitrofan!" he cried as he at last caught the stirrup; the next moment he swung himself into the saddle.

Feeling his rider's spurs, Fairway gave in at once; he changed pace several times snorting and tossing his head, and started off from the gate at a broad, swinging gallop.

Very soon the swift ride, the chilly wind whistling in his ears, and the fresh smell of the autumnal, slightly damp earth soothed and roused Bobrov's lax nerves. Besides, each time he set out for Zinenko's, he felt pleasantly and excitingly elated.

The Zinenko family consisted of father, mother, and five daughters. The father was in charge of the mill warehouse. An indolent and seemingly good-natured giant, he was actually a most pushing and insidious fellow. He was one of those who under cover of speaking the truth to everybody's face flatter their superiors agreeably if crudely, inform brazenly against their colleagues, and treat their subordinates in a monstrously despotic fashion. He would argue over the least trifle, shouting hoarsely and refusing to listen to any objections; he liked good food and had a weakness for Ukrainian choral songs, which he invariably sang out of tune. He was unwittingly henpecked by his wife, a little, sickly woman with mincing manners and tiny grey eyes set absurdly close to each other.

The daughters' names were Maka, Beta, Shura, Nina, and Kasya.

Each of the daughters had been assigned a role in the family.

Maka, a girl with the profile of a fish, was reputed to have an angelic disposition. "Our Maka is modesty itself," her parents would say when, during a stroll or an evening party, she effaced herself in the interest of her younger sisters (she was already on the wrong side of thirty).

Beta was considered clever, wore a pince-nez, and they even said that once she had wanted to enter courses for women. She held her head bent to one side, like an old trace-horse, and walked with a dipping gait. She would assail every fresh visitor with the contention that women are better and more honest than men, or say with a naive playfulness, "You're so shrewd—won't you guess my character?" When conversation drifted to one of the standard domestic topics, such as "Who is greater: Lermontov or Pushkin?" or "Does Nature make people kinder?" Beta would be pushed to the fore like a battle elephant.

The third daughter, Shura, had made it her specialty to play cards with every bachelor in turn. As soon as she found out that her partner was going to get married she would pick a new one, subduing her vexation and annoyance. And the game was sure to be accompanied by sweet little jokes and bewitching roguery, her partner being called "mean" and rapped on the hands with cards.

Nina was considered the family's favourite, a spoilt but lovely child. She stood out strikingly among her sisters, with their bulky figures and rather coarse, vulgar faces. Perhaps Mme Zinenko alone could have explained the origin of Nina's delicate, fragile little figure, her nearly aristocratic hands, her pretty, darkish face with its fascinating moles, her small pink ears, and her luxuriant, slightly curly hair. Her parents set great hopes upon her and therefore indulged her in everything; she was free to eat her fill of sweets, speak with a charming burr, and even dress better than her sisters.

The youngest, Kasya, was just over fourteen, but the extraordinary child was already head and shoulders taller than her mother, and had far outstripped her older sisters by the powerful prominence of her forms. Her figure had long been attracting the eyes of the young men at the mill, who were completely deprived of feminine company because the mill was far removed from town, and Kasya received their stares with the naive impudence of a precocious girl.

This distribution of the family charms was well known at the mill, and a wag had once said that one ought to marry all the five Zinenko girls at once, or none at all. Engineers and students doing their practical course looked upon Zinenko's house as a hotel and thronged it from morning till night; they ate a great deal and drank even more, but avoided the meshes of wedlock with amazing dexterity.

Bobrov was rather disliked in the Zinenko family. Mme Zinenko, who sought to bring everything into line with trite and happily tedious provincial decorum, was shocked in her philistine tastes by Bobrov's behaviour. The sarcastic jokes he cracked when in good spirits made all eyes open wide; and when he kept a close mouth for many an evening on end because he was tired and irritated, he was suspected of being secretive, proud, and tacitly ironic; moreover, he was suspected—worst of all—of "writing stories for magazines and picking characters for them."

Bobrov was aware of this vague hostility expressed by lack of attention at table, or by the surprised shrugs of Mme Zinenko, but still he continued to call at the house. He could not tell whether he loved Nina. When he chanced to stay away from the house for three or four days he could not think of her without his heart beating with a sweet and disturbing sadness. He pictured her slender, graceful figure, her shaded languid eyes as they smiled, and the fragrance of her body, which for some reason reminded him of the scent of young, sticky poplar buds.

But he had only to spend with the Zinenkos three evenings in a row to feel bored by their company, by their talk —always the same in the same circumstances—by the banal and unnatural expression of their faces. Trivially playful relations had been established once and for all between the five "young ladies" and the "admirers" who "courted" them (terms used by the Zinenkos). Both sides pretended to make up two warring camps. Every now and again one of the admirers stole some object from his young lady for fun, and assured her that he would never give it back; the young ladies sulked and whispered among themselves, calling the joker "mean" and laughing loudly the while, with a stiff, grating laughter. This sort of thing recurred daily, the words and gestures used being absolutely the same as the day before. Bobrov would return from the Zinenkos' with a headache and with nerves set on edge by their provincial frills.

Thus the yearning for Nina, for the nervous grasp of her always warm hands, alternated in Bobrov's heart with aversion to the monotony and affected manners of her family. There were moments when he was quite ready to propose to her, although he realized that she, with her vulgar coquetry and spiritual inanity, would turn their married life into hell, and that they thought and talked in different languages, as it were. But he could not make up his mind and kept silent.

Now, as he rode to Shepetovka, he knew in advance what they were going to say in this or that case and how, and could even picture the expression on their faces. He knew that when from their veranda they sighted him coming on horseback, the young ladies, who were always waiting for "nice young men," would start a long dispute over who was coming. And when he drew near, the one who had guessed rightly would jump and clap her hands and click her tongue, exclaiming perkily, "Well, now? I guessed it, didn't I?" Then she would run to Anna Afanasyevna. ' Bobrov's coming, Mamma, I guessed it first!" And her mother, who would be lazily drying the teacups, would say to Nina—none other than Nina—as if she were telling her something funny and unexpected, "You know, Nina, Bobrov's coming." And finally they would all be loud in their surprise at seeing Bobrov step in.

IV

Fairway trotted along, snorting sonorously and tugging at the reins. The Shepetovka estate came into view ahead. Its white walls and red roof hardly showed through the thick green of lilacs and acacias. Below, a small pond stood out from its setting of green shores.

A woman was standing on the house steps. From afar Bobrov recognized Nina by the bright yellow blouse which set off her dusky complexion so beautifully, and at once, reining in the horse, he straightened up, and pulled back his feet, thrust deeply into the stirrups.

"Riding your treasure again, eh? I simply can't bear the sight of that monster!" cried Nina in the gay and wayward tone of a spoilt child. She had long been in the habit of teasing him about his horse to whom he was so much attached. Someone was always being teased at Zinenko's for something or other.

Bobrov threw the reins to the mill groom who had run up, patted the horse's strong neck, dark with sweat, and followed Nina into the drawing-room. Anna Afanasyevna, who was sitting by the samovar all alone, affected great amazement at Bobrov's arrival.

"Well, well! Andrei Ilyich!" she cried in a singsong. "Here you come at last!"

She pushed her hand against his lips as he greeted her, and asked him with her nasal twang, "Tea? Milk? Apples? What will you have?"

"*Merci*, Anna Afanasyevna."

"*Merci oui, ou merci non?*"

French phrases like these were common in the Zinenko family. Bobrov would not have anything.

"Then go to the veranda," Mme Zinenko permitted him graciously. "The young people are playing forfeits or something there."

When he appeared on the veranda all the four young ladies exclaimed in unison, in exactly the same tone, and with the same twang, as their mother, "Well, well! Andrei Ilyich! Here's someone we haven't seen for ages! What will you have? Tea? Apples? Milk? Nothing? You don't mean that! Perhaps you will have something, after all? Well, then sit down here and join in."

They played "The Lady's Sent a Hundred Rubles," "Opinions," and a game which lisping Kasya called "playing bowlth." The guests were three students, who kept on sticking out their chests and striking dramatic attitudes, with one foot forward and one hand in the back pocket of their frock-coats; Miller, a technician distinguished by his good looks, stupidity, and wonderful baritone; and lastly a taciturn gentleman in grey, of whom nobody took any notice.

The game was not going well. The men performed their forfeits with a condescending, bored air, and the young ladies refused to perform theirs at all, whispering among themselves and laughing unnaturally.

Dusk was falling. A huge red moon floated up from behind the house-tops of the nearby village.

"Come inside, children!" Anna Afanasyevna shouted from the dining-room. "Ask Miller to sing for us."

A moment later the young ladies' voices rang through the rooms.

"We had a very good time," they chirped round their mother. "We laughed so much!"

Nina and Bobrov remained on the veranda. She sat on the handrail, hugging a post with her left arm and nestling against it in an unconsciously graceful posture. Bobrov placed himself at her feet, on a low garden bench; as he looked up into her face he saw the delicate outlines of her throat and chin.

"Come on, tell me something interesting, Andrei Ilyich," she commanded impatiently.

"I really don't know what to tell you," he replied. "It's awfully hard to speak to order. So I'm wondering if there's some collection of dialogues on various topics."

"Fie! What a bo-ore you are," she drawled. "Tell me, are you ever in good spirits?"

"And you tell me why you're so afraid of silence. You feel uneasy the moment talk runs low. Is it so bad to talk silently?"

" 'Let's be silent tonight,' " Nina sang, teasingly.

"Yes, let's. Look: the sky is clear, the moon is red and big, and it's so quiet out here. What else do we need?"

" 'And this barren and silly moon in these barren and silly heavens,' " Nina recited. "*A propos*, have you heard that Zina Makova is engaged to Protopopov? Going to marry him, after all! I can't make out that Protopopov."

She shrugged her shoulders. "Zina refused him three times, but still he wouldn't give up, and proposed for the fourth time. Well, he'll have only himself to blame. She may come to respect him, but she'll certainly never love him!"

These words were enough to make Bobrov's gorge rise. He was always exasperated by the Zinenkos' shallow, small-town vocabulary, made up of expressions like "She loves him, but doesn't respect him," or "She respects him, but doesn't love him." To their minds, these words fully described the most intricate relationships between man and woman. Likewise, they had only two expressions— "dark-haired" and "fair-haired"—to cover the whole range of the moral, intellectual, and physical peculiarities of any person.

Prompted by a vague desire to goad his anger, Bobrov asked, "And what sort of a man is this Protopopov?"

"Protopopov?" Nina reflected for a second. "He's— well, he's rather tall, with brown hair."

"Is that all?"

"What else do you want? Oh, yes, he's an excise-man."

"And that is all? But can't you really describe a man any better than that he has brown hair and is an ex-ciseman, Nina Grigoryevna? Just think how many interesting, gifted and clever people we come across in life. Are they all nothing but 'brown-haired excisemen'? See how eagerly peasant children watch life and how apt their judgement is. But you, an alert and sensitive girl, take no interest in anything, because you have a stock of a dozen battered drawing-room phrases. I know that if somebody mentions the moon in conversation you're sure to put in 'Like this barren and silly moon,' etc. And if I tell you, say, about an unusual occurrence, I know beforehand that your comment will be, 'A legend fresh but difficult to credit.' It's always like that, always. Believe me, for goodness' sake, that all that is original and distinctive—"

"I beg you not to lecture me!" Nina retorted.

He fell silent, with a bitter taste in his mouth, and they both sat for fully five minutes or so without speaking or moving. Suddenly rich chords rang out from the drawing-room, and they heard Miller start singing in a voice which, though slightly spoiled, was very expressive:

> *Where dancing was loudest and maddest,*
> *In vanity's violent pace,*
> *I saw thee—the saddest of secrets*
> *Look'd out from thy lovely face.*

Bobrov's anger soon subsided, and he felt sorry that he had vexed Nina. "What made me expect original daring from her fresh, naive mind?" he thought. "Why, she's like a little bird: she chirps the first thing that comes into her head, and who knows whether her chirping isn't much better than talk about women's emancipation, Nietzsche, or the decadents?"

"Please don't be cross with me, Nina Grigoryevna," he said under his breath. "I let my tongue run away with me and said a lot of foolish things."

Nina made no reply, but sat looking away at the rising moon. In the darkness he found her hand hanging down and clasped it tenderly.

"Please, Nina Grigoryevna," he whispered.

She suddenly turned to him and responded with a swift, nervous handshake.

"What a bad temper you have!" she exclaimed in a tone of forgiveness and reproach. "You always hurt me, knowing that I can't be cross with you!"

Pushing away his hand, which trembled suddenly, and almost breaking away from him, she ran across the veranda and into the house.

Miller sang with passion and melancholy:

And through unknown visions I rove.
I know not if thee my love glories,
I only know well that I love.

"'I only know well that I love'!" Bobrov repeated in an excited whisper, drawing a deep breath and pressing his hand to his throbbing heart.

"Why, then, do I exhaust myself in fruitless dreams of an unknown, lofty happiness while there is a plain but deep happiness here beside me?" he thought, moved. "What else do I want of a woman, of a wife who is so tender, so fetching, so gentle, and attentive? We poor nervous wrecks can't take the joys of life as they are, but must poison them with our insatiable desire to rake in every feeling and every intention, whether it's ours or somebody else's. This still night, the proximity of the girl I love, her sweet, artless talk, a momentary flash of anger and then a sudden caress—Heavens! Isn't this what makes life worth living?"

When he entered the drawing-room he looked cheerful, nearly triumphant. His eyes met Nina's, and he read in her gaze a tender answer to his thoughts. "She shall be my wife," he said to himself, calmly happy.

They were talking about Kvashnin. Filling the room with the ring of her confident voice, Anna Afanasyevna said that she too was going to take her "little girls" to the station on the following day.

"Vasily Terentyevich may well wish to pay us a visit. Anyway, Liza Belokonskaya—she's a niece of my cousin's husband—wrote me about his trip a month ago."

"Isn't that Belokonskaya the one whose brother is married to Princess Mukhovetskaya?" Zinenko humbly put in the usual comment.

"Yes." Anna Afanasyevna nodded with condescension. "She's also a distant relative on her grandmother's side of the Stremoukhovs, whom you know. Well, she wrote me she had met Vasily Terentyevich at a party and had recommended him to call on us if it ever occurred to him to visit the mill."

"Shall we be able to receive him properly, Anna?" Zinenko asked anxiously.

"The funny way you talk! We'll do our best. But of course we can't expect to impress a man who has a yearly income of three hundred thousand rubles."

"Dear me! Three hundred thousand!" groaned Zinenko. "It gives you the creeps to think of it."

"Three hundred thousand!" Nina echoed with a sigh.

"Three hundred thousand!" exclaimed the other young ladies in an ecstatic chorus.

"Yes, and he spends all of it, to the last kopek," said Anna Afanasyevna. Then, in reply to an unexpressed thought of her daughters, she added: "He's married. Only they say his marriage is a failure. His wife has no personality and isn't distinguished at all. And a wife should give tone to her husband's business activities, whatever you may say."

"Three hundred thousand!" said Nina once more, as if in delirium. "The things you could do with that money!"

Anna Afanasyevna ran her hand over Nina's luxuriant hair.

"It wouldn't be bad to have a husband like him, my child, would it?"

That income of three hundred thousand rubles, which belonged to another man, seemed to have galvanized the whole company. Stories were told, and listened to, with gleaming eyes and flushed faces, about the life of millionaires, their fabulous dinners, their magnificent horses, the dancing-parties they gave, the unheard-of extravagance of their spending.

Bobrov's heart went cold and shrank painfully. Quietly he took his hat and walked stealthily out on to the porch. However, no one would have noticed his departure anyway.

Riding home at a smart trot and recalling Nina's languid, dreamy eyes as she whispered, almost distractedly, "Three hundred thousand!" he suddenly thought of the story which Svezhevsky had insisted on telling him that morning.

"This one's just as capable of selling herself," he whispered, clenching his teeth and furiously laying his whip on Fairway's neck.

V

As he rode up to his flat Bobrov saw a light in the windows. "The doctor must have arrived while I was away, and now he's probably lolling on my sofa, waiting for me," he thought, pulling up his lathered horse. Just then Dr. Goldberg was the only person whose presence he could bear without painful irritation.

He was sincerely fond of the light-hearted, gentle Jew for his versatile wit, his youthful liveliness, and his good-natured passion for abstract argument. No matter what topic Bobrov brought up, Dr. Goldberg would dispute his point with equal interest and unvarying ardour. And though so far they had done nothing but clash in their interminable arguments, they missed each other, and met almost daily.

The doctor was actually lying on the sofa, his feet on its back, reading a book which he held close to his short-sighted eyes. Bobrov recognized Mevius' *Handbook of Metallurgy* at a glance, and smiled. He was familiar with the doctor's habit of reading with equal absorption whatever he came upon, always starting from the middle.

"You know, I had some tea while you were out," said the doctor, throwing away the book and looking at Bobrov over his spectacles. "Well, how's my lord Andrei

Ilyich hopping along? My, how angry you look! What is it? A fresh spell of delightful misery?"

"Life is so sickening, doctor," Bobrov said wearily.

"Why, my friend?"

"Oh, I don't know. It's just that way. Well, how's your hospital?"

"The hospital's all right. I had a most interesting case of surgery today. Really, it was both laughable and touching. A Masalsk stone-mason came to me this morning. Those Masalsk lads are all athletes, without a single exception. 'What d'you want?' I asked him. 'You see, doctor, I was cutting bread for the whole team and scratched my finger a bit, and can't stop the blood nohow.' I examined his finger; it was a mere scratch, nothing to worry about, but festering a little. I told my assistant to bandage it. But the lad wouldn't go. 'Well, what else do you want? You've got your hand bandaged, you can go now.' 'That's right,' he says, 'thank you. Only, you see, my head's kind of splitting, so I thought perhaps you'd give me some medicine for that too.' 'What's the matter with your head? Got a sock on it, I suppose?' He fairly jumped with delight, and started laughing. 'Can't say no,' he says. 'We went on a bust the other day, on Saviour's Day it was'— that would be about three days ago—'and drank a good bucketful of vodka. Well, we started fooling among ourselves. Then—you know how it is in a fight, don't you? —I got a reg'lar crack on my nob with a chisel—had it repaired, sort of. It wasn't so bad at first—it didn't hurt, but now my head's splitting.' I examined his 'nob' and was downright horrified. His skull was smashed right in, there was a hole in it the size of a five-kopek piece, and bone splinters stuck in his brain. Now he's lying unconscious in hospital. I must say they are marvellous people: babies and heroes all in one. I'm quite certain that only the patient Russian muzhik can stand having his skull 'repaired' like that. Anyone else would have given up the ghost on the spot. Besides, what simple good humour! 'You know how it is in a fight, don't you?' he says. God!"

Bobrov was pacing the room, cracking his whip across the tops of his high boots and listening absent-mindedly to the doctor. He still could not shake off the bitterness that had settled on his soul at Zinenko's.

The doctor paused for a moment, and then said sympathetically, seeing that Bobrov did not feel like talking, "I tell you what, Andrei Ilyich. Try to get some sleep, and take one or two spoonfuls of bromide for the night. It'll do you good in your present frame of mind—at least it won't harm you."

They both lay down in the same room, Bobrov taking the bed and the doctor staying on the sofa. But neither could sleep. For a long time Goldberg listened to Bobrov tossing and sighing in bed, and at last he spoke.

"What is it, friend? What's worrying you? Hadn't you better tell me frankly what's on your mind? After all, I'm not a stranger asking questions out of idle curiosity."

These simple words moved Bobrov. Although he and the doctor were on friendly terms, neither had ever confirmed it by a single word: both were keenly sensitive and shrank from the embarrassment of mutual confessions. The doctor had opened his heart first, helped by the darkness and his compassion for Bobrov.

"Everything weighs heavily on me and disgusts me so, Osip Osipovich," Bobrov said softly. "First of all, I'm disgusted because I'm working at the mill and getting a lot of money for it, when I loathe the whole business. I consider myself honest and so I ask myself frankly, 'What are you doing? Who benefits by your work?' I'm beginning to see things clearly, and I realize that, thanks to my efforts, a hundred French *rentiers* and a dozen Russian sharks will eventually pocket millions. And there's no other aim or sense in the work which I've wasted the better half of my life preparing for!"

"But that is simply ridiculous, Andrei Ilyich," the doctor protested, turning to Bobrov in the darkness. "You want a bunch of money-bags to go soft. My friend, ever since the world came into being things have been governed by the law of the belly. It has never been otherwise, nor ever will be. But the point is that you don't give a damn for the money-bags, because you're far above them. Aren't you satisfied with the proud manly consciousness that you're pushing forward 'the chariot of progress,' as they say in leading articles? Damn it, shipping-company shares bring huge dividends, but does that prevent Fulton from being considered mankind's benefactor?"

"My dear doctor!" Bobrov made a grimace of annoyance. "You didn't go to the Zinenkos' today, did you, but somehow you're voicing their philosophy of life. Luckily I shan't have to search far for an argument to refute yours, because I'm going to beat you with your own pet theory."

"What theory do you mean? I'm afraid I can't remember any theory. I really can't, my friend—it's slipped my mind."

"It has, has it? Then who shouted, sitting on this sofa here and foaming at the mouth, that by our discoveries we engineers and inventors quicken the heartbeat of society to a feverish speed? Who compared this life with the condition of an animal sealed up in an oxygen jar? I remember perfectly, believe me, what a terrible list of children of the twentieth century—neurasthenics, madmen, overworked men, suicides—you hurled in the face of those same benefactors of mankind. You said the telegraph, the telephone, trains racing at eighty miles an hour, had reduced distance to a minimum, had in fact done away with it. Time has become so valuable, you said, that they'll soon begin to turn night into day to make day twice as long. Negotiations which used to take months are now finished in five minutes. But even this hellish speed is no longer enough for us. Soon we'll be able to see each other by wire hundreds and thousands of miles away! And yet, only fifty years ago, whenever our ancestors had to make a trip from the country to the provincial centre, they'd hold a service in church and set out with enough time to spare for a polar expedition. And we keep rushing on headlong, stunned by the rumbling and clanking of monstrous machines, dazed by the furious race, with irritated nerves, perverse tastes, and thousands of new diseases. Do you remember, doctor? It was you, a champion of beneficial progress, who said all that."

The doctor, who had been making futile attempts to protest, profited by Bobrov's momentary pause.

"Yes, my friend, I did say all that," he cut in, a little doubtfully. "I will say that again. But then we must adapt ourselves, so to speak. How else are we to live? There are these tricky little points in every profession. Take us doctors. Do you imagine we have no doubts or difficulties at all? Why, we're sure of nothing whatsoever beyond surgery. We think up new remedies and systems, but we completely forget that, among a thousand living beings, no two are alike in blood composition, heart activity, heredity, and God knows what else! We've moved away from real therapeutics—the medicine of wild creatures and quacks—and flooded the chemists' shops with cocaine, atropine, phenacetin, and all that sort of stuff; but we've forgotten that if you give a sick man a glass of pure water and earnestly assure him it's a strong medicine he'll recover from his illness. Nevertheless, in ninety cases out of a hundred, what helps us in our practice is the confidence inspired by our professional sacerdotal self-assurance. Believe it or not, but a fine physician, who was also a clever, honest man, once confessed to me that sportsmen treat their sick dogs more rationally than we do people. Their only medicine is flower of brimstone —it can't do much harm, and sometimes it even helps. A lovely picture, isn't it, my friend? But we, too, do what we can. It's the only way, for in this life we all must compromise. Sometimes you can relieve the suffering of a fellow-man by behaving like an omniscient augur if by nothing else. Thank God for even that much."

"You talk about compromise," said Bobrov gloomily, "but today you extracted the splinters from that Masalsk stone-mason's skull, didn't you?"

"Ah, my friend, what difference does one repaired skull make? Think how many bellies you keep full and how many people you give work to. Ilovaisky says in his *History* that 'Tsar Boris, being desirous of winning the favour of the people, undertook the construction of public buildings in the years of famine,' or something like that. Now try to work out what tremendous good you—"

The doctor's last words seemed to jolt Bobrov, who sat up quickly in bed and swung his bare feet over the side.

"Good?" he shouted frenziedly. "Are you talking to me about good? In that case, if you really want to sum up what's good or bad, allow me to give you some statistics." And he began in sharp, measured tones, as if speaking from a platform: "It has long been known that work in a mine, metal works, or large factory shortens the workman's life by roughly a quarter, to say nothing of accidents or back-breaking toil. As a physician you know better than I do how many workmen suffer from syphilis or drink, or live in appalling conditions in those accursed barracks and mud-huts. Wait, doctor—before you object, try to remember how many workmen over forty or forty-five you've seen in factories. *I* haven't met any. That means the workman gives his employer three months of his life a year, one week a month, or, in short, *six* hours a day. Now listen to this. Our six blast-furnaces will require some thirty thousand men—I suppose Tsar Boris never dreamt of such a figure. Thirty thousand men who burn up, so to speak, altogether a hundred and eighty

31

thousand hours of their own lives every day, that is, seven thousand five hundred days, or—how many years does that add up to?"

"About twenty years," the doctor prompted, after a brief pause.

"About twenty years a day!" cried Bobrov. "Two days of work swallow up one man. Damn it! Do you remember those Assyrians or Moabites in the Bible who offered human sacrifices to their gods? But, really, those brass gentlemen, Moloch and Dagon, would have blushed with shame and mortification at the figures I've quoted."

This peculiar calculation had just occurred to Bobrov, who, like many impressionable people, discovered new ideas only in the heat of debate. Nevertheless, both he and Goldberg were struck by the unusual statistics.

"Hang it all, you bewilder me," said the doctor. "The figures may be inaccurate, though."

"And do you know anything," Bobrov went on, with even greater vehemence, "about another statistical table which enables you to compute with devilish accuracy the price in human lives of each step forward of your damnable chariot, the invention of each paltry winnowing-fan, seeder, or rail-mill? A fine thing is your civilization, whose fruits are figures, the units being steel machines, and the ciphers human lives!"

"But look here, my friend," said the doctor, taken aback by Bobrov's violence, "do you mean to say, then, that we'd better fall back on primitive labour? Why do you consider only the black side? After all, in spite of your statistics, the mill has provided a school, a church, a good hospital, and a low-interest credit society for the workmen."

Bobrov jumped out of bed and began to run about barefoot.

"Those hospitals and schools of yours don't mean a thing! They're no more than sops for humanists like you, concessions to public opinion. I can tell you, if you like, what we actually think of all that. Do you know what a finish is?"

"A finish? Hasn't that got something to do with horses—with racing?"

"That's it. A finish is the last seven-hundred foot spurt before the winning-post. The horse makes it at top speed —it's the supreme effort, and to get the horse to make that effort they lash it till it bleeds. Then, when it's passed the mark, it may die for all anybody cares. We're like that, too. When we've squeezed the last spurt out of the horse and it drops with a broken back and shattered legs, to hell with it, it's no longer good for anything! Your schools and hospitals mean a fat lot to a horse that's breathed its last after the finish. Have you ever watched smelting or rolling? If you have, you ought to know that it takes deucedly strong nerves, steel muscles, and the agility of a circus performer. You ought to know that everyone on the job escapes death several times a day thanks only to his wonderful self-control. And would you like to know how much a workman gets for work of that sort?"

"Still, as long as the mill's there, the workman's sure of a job," Goldberg persisted.

"Don't be naive, doctor!" cried Bobrov, sitting on the window-sill. "The workman depends today more than ever on market demand, on stock-jobbing, on various intrigues. Each big enterprise passes through different hands three or four times before it gets under way. Do you know how our company came into being? A sum of money was put up by a small group of business men. At first the business was planned on a small scale. But a whole gang of engineers, directors and contractors frittered away the capital before the owners could see what was what. Enormous buildings were erected that turned out to be good for nothing. They were scrapped—blown up with dynamite. Only when the concern was sold at ten kopeks to the ruble did it transpire that the whole dirty gang had been acting by arrangement, for which they were paid by a more powerful and astute company. Now the business is being conducted on a much larger scale, but I know very well that the first failure cost eight hundred workmen their two months' wages. That's your safe employment for you! Why, as soon as the shares drop wages slide down too. I suppose you know how shares rise or drop? To bring that about you have to go to Petersburg and whisper in a broker's ear that you want to sell, say, three hundred thousand rubles' worth of shares, adding that it's strictly between you and him and that you'll pay him a nice brokerage if only he keeps his mouth shut. Then you whisper the same to another couple of brokers, and the shares instantly drop by several dozen rubles. And the greater the secrecy the sooner and surer the drop. Safe employment, indeed!"

With a vigorous push Bobrov flung the window open. Cold air rushed into the room.

"Look, doctor!" cried Bobrov, pointing to the mill.

Goldberg raised himself on his elbow and peered into the night darkness outside. The immense expanse spreading out in the distance was alight with innumerable heaps of red-hot lime-stone, whose surface flared up into bluish and green sulphur flames every now and again. Those were limekilns* burning. A blood-red glow wavered over the mill, showing in dark relief the slender tops of the great chimneys, whose lower parts were blurred by grey mist rising from the ground. Ceaselessly those giants belched clouds of dense smoke that merged into a chaotic mass trailing eastwards, with patches like balls of dirty grey or rust-coloured cotton wool. Bright

* A limekiln is a man-high pile of lime-stone, kindled with wood or coal. The pile is heated for a week or so, till the lime-stone turns into quick-lime —*Author's note*

shafts of burning gas trembled and danced above the tall, thin smoke deflectors, making them look like giant torches. The gas flames threw on the smoke cloud above the mill strange, ominous reflections. From time to time, following the sharp clank of the signal hammer, the bell of a blast-furnace would go down, and a whirlwind of flames and soot would hurtle skywards from the orifice of the furnace, roaring like distant thunder. Then, with startling suddenness, the whole mill would flash into view for a few seconds, and the serried row of black round hot-blast stoves would look like the towers of a fabulous iron castle. The burning coke ovens stretched in long, regular rows. Occasionally one of them flared up and blazed like a huge red eye. Electric light added its bluish, lifeless shine to the glare of red-hot iron. There was a continuous clangour and crashing of iron.

In the glow of the mill lights Bobrov's face had taken on a sinister coppery hue, his eyes glistened bright red, and tousled hair hung over his forehead. His voice was piercing and angry.

"There he is—that Moloch who wants warm human blood!" he cried, stretching his thin arm out of the window. "To be sure, this is progress and machine labour and cultural advancement. But, for heaven's sake, think of it—twenty years! Twenty years of human life a day! At moments I feel like a murderer, I swear!"

"Good God, the man's mad," thought the doctor, shuddering. He set about soothing Bobrov.

"Come, come, Andrei Ilyich, my friend. Why worry about foolish things! It's damp outside, and you've opened the window. Go to bed, and take some bromide—here."

"He's a maniac, he really is," he thought, with a feeling of both compassion and fear.

Exhausted by his outburst, Bobrov put up little resistance. But when he got into bed he suddenly broke into hysterical sobs. And the doctor sat by his side for a long time, stroking his head as if he had been a child, and soothing him with what words of sympathy occurred to him.

VI

Next day Vasily Terentyevich Kvashnin was welcomed in grand style at the Ivankovo station. The entire mill management was gathered there by eleven o'clock. Everyone seemed ill at ease. The manager, Sergei Valerianovich Shelkovnikov, drank glass after glass of seltzer and pulled out his watch every moment, only to put it back in his pocket mechanically without glancing at the dial—an absent-minded gesture that betrayed his uneasiness. His face—the handsome, well-groomed, self-confident face of a man of society—remained unchanged. Only a few men knew that as manager of the construction project he was a mere figure-head. The real manager was Andréas, a Belgian engineer of mixed Polish and Swedish ancestry, whose role at the mill none of the uninitiated could make out. The offices of the two managers had a connecting door and Shelkovnikov dared not take decision on any important paper without consulting the pencil tick which Andréas would put somewhere in a corner of the sheet. In urgent cases, when consultation was not possible, he would look worried and say to the solicitor in a casual tone, "I'm sorry, but I positively can't spare a moment for you—I'm terribly busy. Kindly state your business to Mr. Andréas, and he will refer it to me later by special note."

The services rendered to the Board by Andréas were innumerable. He had conceived the brilliantly fraudulent plan to ruin the original company, and he, too, had carried the intrigue to the end with a firm but invisible hand. His designs were distinguished by astounding simplicity and coherence, and were considered the last word in mining. He spoke many European languages and, in addition to his special subject, was well informed in a great variety of other subjects—a rare phenomenon among engineers.

Among those gathered at the station, Andréas, a man with a consumptive figure and the face of an old ape, was the only one who retained his habitual stolidity. He had arrived last and was slowly pacing the platform, his hands elbow-deep in the pockets of his wide, baggy trousers as he chewed his eternal cigar. His light grey eyes, which bespoke the powerful mind of a scientist and the strong will of an adventurer, stared indifferently as always from under the tired, swollen eyelids.

No one was surprised at the arrival of the Zinenko family. Somehow everybody had long been used to looking upon them as part and parcel of life at the mill. Into the cold and gloomy station hall, the young ladies brought their forced animation and unnatural laughter. They were surrounded by the younger engineers, who were tired of waiting. The young ladies at once took up their customary defensive position and began to lavish right and left their charming but stale naïvetés. Anna Afanasyevna, little and flustered, looked like a restless brood-hen among her fussing daughters

Bobrov, tired and almost ill after his fit of the previous night, sat all alone in a corner of the hall, smoking a great deal. When the Zinenko family came in and sat down chirping loudly at a round table, he had two very vague feelings. On the one hand, he was ashamed—a heart-searing *shame for another*—of the tactlessness which he felt the family had shown by coming. On the other hand, he was glad to see Nina, ruddy with the swift drive, her eyes shining with excitement; she was very prettily dressed and, as always happens, looked much more beautiful than his imagination had painted her. His sick, harassed soul suddenly flamed up with irrepressible desire for a tender, fragrant love, with longing for a woman's habitual, soothing caress.

He sought for a chance to approach Nina, but she was busy chatting with two mining students, who were vying with each other to make her laugh. And she did laugh, more cheerful and coquettish than ever, her small white teeth gleaming. Nevertheless, twice or three times her gaze met Bobrov's, and he fancied that her eyebrows were slightly raised in a silent, but not hostile query.

The bell rang on the platform, announcing that the train had left the previous station. There was a commotion among the engineers. Smiling sarcastically, Bobrov from his corner watched twenty-odd men gripped by the same cowardly thought; their faces suddenly became grave and worried, their hands ran for the last time over the buttons of their frock-coats, their neckties and caps, and their eyes turned towards the bell. Soon no one was left in the hall.

Bobrov went out on to the platform. The young ladies, abandoned by the men who had been entertaining them, crowded helplessly round Anna Afanasyevna, near the door. Nina turned to face Bobrov, who had been gazing at her fixedly, and walked over to him, as if guessing that he wanted to talk to her in private.

"Good morning. Why are you so pale today? You don't feel well?" she asked, holding his hand in a firm, tender grasp and looking him in the eyes, earnestly and caressingly. "Why did you leave so early last night, without even saying goodbye? Were you angry?"

"Yes and no," replied Bobrov, with a smile. "No, because I have no right to be angry, have I?"

"I think anybody has a right to be angry. Especially if he knows that his opinion is valued highly. Why 'yes'?"

"Because— You see, Nina Grigoryevna," said Bobrov, feeling a surge of boldness, "last night when you and I were sitting on the veranda—remember?—I had a few wonderful moments, thanks to you. And I realized that if you'd wanted to, you could have made me the happiest man on earth— But why should I be afraid or hesitate? You know, don't you—you must have guessed, you must have known for a long time that I—"

He could not finish. The boldness that had surged over him was suddenly gone.

"That you what? What were you going to say?" asked Nina, with feigned indifference, but in a voice which quivered in spite of her, and casting down her eyes.

She expected a confession of love, which always thrills the hearts of young girls so strongly and so sweetly, no matter whether they share the sentiment or not. Her cheeks had paled slightly.

"Not now—some other time," Bobrov stammered. "I'll tell you some other day. But not now, for goodness' sake," he added entreatingly.

"All right. But still, why were you angry?"

"Because, after those few moments, I walked into the dining-room in a most—how shall I put it?—in a most tender mood, and when I walked in—"

"You were shocked by the talk about Kvashnin's income, is that it?" Nina prompted, with that instinctive perspicacity which sometimes comes to the most narrow-minded women. "Am I right?" She faced him squarely, and once more enveloped him in a deep, caressing gaze. "Be frank. You mustn't keep anything from your friend."

Some three or four months before, while boating with a crowd of others, Nina, excited and softened by the beauty of the warm summer night, had offered Bobrov her friendship to the end of time. He had accepted the offer very earnestly, and for a whole week had called her his friend, just as she had called him hers. And whenever she had said *my friend*, slowly and significantly, with her usual languorous air, the two short words had gone straight to his heart. Now he recalled the joke, and replied with a sigh:

"Good, 'my friend,' I'll tell you the whole truth though it won't be easy. You always inspire me with a painfully divided feeling. As we talk there are moments when, by just one word, one gesture, or even one look, you suddenly make me so happy! Ah, but how can I put such a sensation into words? Have you ever noticed it?"

"Yes," she replied almost in a whisper, and lowered her eyes, with a sly flutter of lashes.

"And then, all of a sudden, you would become a provincial young lady, with a standard vocabulary of stock phrases and an affected manner. Please don't be cross with me for my frankness. I wouldn't have spoken if it hadn't tormented me so terribly."

"I've noticed that, too."

"Well, there you are. I've always been sure that you have a responsive and tender heart. But why don't you want to be always as you are at this moment?"

She turned to face him again, and even moved her hand, as if to touch his. They were walking up and down the vacant end of the platform.

"You never tried to understand me, Andrei Ilyich," she said reproachfully. "You're nervous and impatient. You exaggerate all that is good in me, but then you won't forgive me for being what I am, though, in the environment in which I live, I can't really be anything else. It would be ridiculous if I were—it would bring discord into our family. I'm too weak and, to tell the truth, too insignificant to fight and be independent. I go where everybody else does, and I look on things and judge them as everybody else does. And don't imagine I don't know I'm common. But when I'm with the others I don't feel it as I do with you. In your presence I lose all sense of proportion because—" She faltered. "Oh, well—because you're quite different, because I've never met anyone like you in my life."

She thought she was speaking sincerely. The invigorating freshness of the autumn air, the bustle at the station, the consciousness of her own beauty, and the pleasure she felt sensing Bobrov's loving gaze fixed upon her, electrified her, like all hysterical characters, into lying with inspiration and charm, and quite unwittingly. Admiring herself in her new role of a young lady craving for moral support, she wanted to say agreeable things to Bobrov.

"I know you look on me as a flirt. Please don't deny it—I admit I give you cause to think that. For example, I often chat with Miller and laugh at his jokes. But if you only knew how I detest that oily cherub! Or take those two students. A handsome man is disagreeable because he's always admiring himself, if for no other reason. Believe me, although it may sound strange, plain men have always appealed to me particularly."

As she uttered this charming sentence in her most tender accents, Bobrov drew a mournful sigh. Alas! he had heard this cruel consolation from women more than once, a consolation they never refuse to their ugly admirers.

"So I may hope to appeal to you some day?" he asked in a joking tone which, however, clearly suggested bitter self-mockery.

Nina hastened to make up for her blunder.

"See what a man you are. I positively can't talk with you. Must you fish for compliments, sir? Shame on you!"

She was a little embarrassed by her own gaucherie, and to change the subject she asked in a playfully imperious voice, "Well, now, what was it you were going to tell me in different circumstances? Kindly answer me at once!"

41

"I don't know—I don't remember," Bobrov stammered, his ardour damped.

"Then I'll remind you, my secretive friend. You began by speaking of last night. You said something about wonderful moments, and then you said that I must have noticed long ago—but noticed what? You didn't finish. So kindly say it now. I demand it, do you hear?"

She was looking at him with a smile shining in her eyes—a smile at once sly and promising and tender. For one sweet moment his heart stood still in his chest, and he felt a fresh surge of his former courage. "She knows, she wants me to speak," he thought, bracing himself.

They halted on the very edge of the platform, where they were quite alone. Both were excited. Nina was awaiting his reply, enjoying the piquancy of the game she had started, while Bobrov was casting about for words, breathing heavily with agitation. But just then, following the shrill sound of signal horns, a hubbub broke out on the platform.

"I'm waiting, do you hear?" Nina whispered, walking away from Bobrov. "It's more important for me than you think."

An express train, wrapped in black smoke, leapt into view from beyond a curve. A few minutes later, clattering over the points, it slowed down smoothly, and pulled up at the platform. At its tail end was a long service carriage shining with fresh blue paint, and the crowd rushed towards it.

The conductors hurried respectfully to open the carriage door; a ladder was unfolded instantly. Red with running and excitement, a frightened look on his face, the station master was urging the workmen uncoupling the service carriage. Kvashnin was one of the principal shareholders of the X Railway and travelled on its branch-lines with greater pomp than was sometimes accorded even to the highest railway officials.

Only four men entered the carriage: Shelkovnikov, Andréas, and two influential Belgian engineers. Kvashnin was sitting in an easy chair, his enormous legs thrown apart and his belly thrust forward. He wore a round felt hat, his fiery hair shining under it; his face, shaved like an actor's, with flabby jowls and a triple chin, and mottled with big freckles, seemed drowsy and annoyed; his lips were curled in a contemptuous, sour grimace.

With an effort he rose to greet the engineers.

"Good morning, gentlemen," he said in a husky, deep voice, holding out his huge chubby hand for them to touch respectfully by turns. "How's everything at the mill?"

Shelkovnikov began to report in the stiff language of an official account. Everything was all right at the mill, he said. They had been waiting for Vasily Terentyevich's arrival to blow in the blast-furnace and lay the foundations of new buildings. The workmen and foremen had been hired at suitable rates. The great flow of orders induced the management to start the construction as early as possible.

Kvashnin listened, his face turned away to the window, viewing absent-mindedly the crowd which pressed round the carriage. His face expressed nothing but disgusted weariness.

Suddenly he interrupted the manager to ask, "Look here—who's that girl?"

Shelkovnikov glanced out of the window.

"There, that one with the yellow feather in her hat." Kvashnin pointed impatiently.

"Oh, that one?" With an eager look the manager bent to Kvashnin's ear and whispered mysteriously in French, "She's the daughter of our warehouse manager. His name is Zinenko."

Kvashnin nodded heavily. Shelkovnikov resumed his report, but his chief interrupted him again.

"Zinenko?" he drawled thoughtfully, staring out of the window. "Which Zinenko is that? Where have I heard the name?"

"He's in charge of our warehouse," Shelkovnikov said again respectfully, with deliberate indifference.

"Oh, yes, now I remember," said Kvashnin. "They told me about him in Petersburg. All right, go on, please."

Nina realized by her infallible feminine intuition that just then Kvashnin was looking at her and speaking about her. She turned slightly away, but still Kvashnin could see her face, rosy with coquettish pleasure and showing all its pretty moles.

At last the report was finished, and Kvashnin passed into the roomy glass compartment built at the end of the carriage.

It was a moment which Bobrov thought would have been well worth perpetuating with a good camera. Kvashnin lingered for some reason behind the glass wall, his bulky figure towering above the group that clustered round the carriage entrance, his feet planted wide apart and his face wearing a sullen look, the whole giving the impression of a crudely wrought Japanese idol. The great man's immobility apparently dismayed those who had come to meet him: the prepared smiles froze on their lips as they stared up at Kvashnin with a servility that bordered on fear. The dashing conductors had stiffened into soldierly postures on either side of the door. Glancing by chance at Nina, Bobrov with a pang noticed on her face the same smile as he saw on the other faces, and the same fear of a savage looking at his idol.

"Is this really nothing but a disinterested, respectful amazement at a yearly income of three hundred thousand rubles?" he thought. "If so, what makes all these people wag their tails so cringingly before a man who never so much as looks at them? Perhaps what's at work here is some inconceivable psychological law of servility?"

Having stood above for a while, Kvashnin decided to start, and descended the steps, preceded by his belly and carefully supported by the train crew.

In response to the respectful bows of the crowd, which parted quickly to let him pass, he nodded carelessly, thrusting out his thick lower lip, and said in a nasal voice, "Gentlemen, you're dismissed till tomorrow."

Before reaching the exit he beckoned to the manager.

"You'll introduce him to me, Sergei Valerianovich," he said in an undertone.

"You mean Zinenko?" asked Shelkovnikov obligingly.

"Who else, damn it!" growled Kvashnin, suddenly irritated. "No, not here!" He held the manager by the sleeve as he was about to rush off. "You'll do it at the mill."

VII

The laying of the foundations and the blowing in of the new blast-furnace were to start four days after Kvashnin's arrival. It was planned to celebrate the two events with the utmost pomp, and printed invitations had been sent to the iron and steel mills in the neighbouring towns of Krutogori, Voronino, and Lvovo.

Two more members of the Board of Directors, four Belgian engineers, and several big shareholders arrived from Petersburg after Kvashnin. It was rumoured among the mill personnel that the Board had allocated about two thousand rubles for the celebration dinner, but so far nothing had happened to bear out these rumours, and the contractors had to shoulder the whole burden of buying wines and food.

Luckily the day of the celebration was fine—one of those bright, limpid days of early autumn when the sky seems so intensely blue and deep and the cool air is like exquisite, strong wine. The square pits, dug out for the foundations of the new blower and bessemer, were surrounded by a dense crowd of workers forming a U. In the middle of this living wall, on the edge of the pit, stood a plain, unpainted table covered with a white cloth, on which a cross and a gospel-book lay beside a sprinkler and a tin bowl for holy water. The priest, attired in a green chasuble embroidered with golden crosses, was standing a little way off, at the head of fifteen workmen who had volunteered to serve as choristers. The open side of the U was taken up by engineers, contractors, senior foremen, clerks—a motley, bustling crowd of two hundred-odd people. A photographer was busy on the embankment, with a black cloth thrown over his head and the camera.

Ten minutes later Kvashnin arrived at the site in a troika of magnificent greys. He was all alone in the carriage, for no one else could possibly have squeezed in beside him. He was followed by five or six more vehicles. Instinctively the workmen at once recognized him as "the boss" and took off their caps as one man. Kvashnin stalked past them and nodded to the priest.

The hush that fell was broken by the jarring little nasal tenor of the priest, who chanted meekly, "Bless'd be the Lord, for ever and ever."

"Amen," the improvised choir responded, harmoniously enough.

The workmen—there were some three thousand of them—crossed themselves broadly, doing it simultaneously as they had greeted Kvashnin, bowed their heads, raised them again, and tossed back their hair. Bobrov could not help looking at them closely. Standing in the two front rows were staid stone-masons, all of them wearing white aprons, and nearly all tow-haired and red-bearded; behind them were smelters and forge workers in wide, dark blouses styled after those worn by the French and British workmen, their faces grimy with iron dust which could not be washed off; among them appeared the hook-nosed faces of foreign *ouvriers*; still farther away, behind the smelters and forge workers, you could catch glimpses of limekiln workers, recognizable from afar by their faces, which seemed to be thickly powdered with flour, and by their inflamed, bloodshot eyes.

Whenever the choir chanted in loud unison, "Save Thy servants from calamity, O Lady!" all the three thousand people assiduously crossed themselves with a soft, monotonous rustle, and bowed deeply. Bobrov fancied that there was something elemental and powerful, and at the same time childish and touching, in that common prayer of the huge grey crowd. Next day the workmen would set about their hard twelve-hour toil. Who knew which of them was already doomed to pay for that toil with his life—to fall from a high scaffold, to be scorched with molten metal, or to be buried under a pile of broken stone or bricks? And was it by any chance this immutable decision of fate that they were thinking of as they made deep bows and tossed back their fair locks, while the choir prayed Our Lady to save her servants from calamity? And in whom but the Virgin could they trust, these big children with stout, simple hearts, these humble heroes who came out daily from their dank, cold mud-huts to carry out their habitual feat of patience and daring?

Such, or almost such, were the thoughts of Bobrov, who had an inclination for vast, poetic pictures; and although he had long since grown out of the habit of praying, a thrill of nervous excitement ran down his spine whenever the priest's jarring, distant voice was succeeded by the harmonious response of the choir. There was something powerful, submissive, and self-sacrificing in the naive prayer of those simple toilers, who had come together from God knew what far-away regions, snatched from their homes for hard and perilous work.

The service was over. With a careless air Kvashnin threw a gold coin into the pit, but was unable to bend down with the little spade he held, and so Shelkovnikov did it for him. Then the group started for the blast-furnaces whose black towers rose on stone foundations.

The newly-built Fifth Furnace was going "full blast," to use the technical jargon. A seething white-hot stream of molten slag sent blue sulphur flames darting about as it gushed from a hole pierced in the furnace, about thirty inches above the ground. It flowed down a shoot into ladles placed against the vertical base of the furnace, and there hardened into a thick greenish mass like barley sugar. The workmen standing on top of the furnace kept on feeding it with ore and coal, which went up every other minute in trolleys.

The priest sprinkled the furnace on all sides with holy water and hurried off timidly, with the stumbling gait of an old man. The foreman in charge of the furnace, a sinewy, black-faced old man, crossed himself and spat into his palms. His four assistants did the same. Then they picked up a long steel crow-bar, swung it back and forth for a long time and, with one big gasp, rammed it into the lowest part of the furnace. The crow-bar clanked against the clay plug. The onlookers shut their eyes in nervous expectation, and some of them stepped back. The five men struck for the second, third, and fourth time, and suddenly a dazzling-white jet of molten metal burst forth from where the crow-bar had struck. Then the foreman widened the hole by rotating the crow-bar, and the cast iron flowed sluggishly down a sand furrow, taking the colour of fiery ochre. Clusters of big shining stars came flying out of the hole, crackling and melting in the air. Flowing at a seemingly lazy pace, the metal sent out such an unbearable heat that the unaccustomed visitors kept on moving farther and farther back, shielding their faces with their hands.

From the blast-furnaces the engineers made for the blower department. Kvashnin had seen to it that the visiting shareholders got a full view of the enormous mill bustling with activity. He had calculated with absolute accuracy that these gentlemen would be overwhelmed by the wealth of new impressions, and would later report wonders to the general meeting which had sent them. And knowing very well the psychology of business men, he confidently looked forward to a new issue of stock, which would greatly profit him personally and which the general meeting had so far refused.

And the shareholders *were* overwhelmed, so much so that their heads ached and their knees trembled. In the blower shop, pale with excitement, they heard the air, forced into pipes by four vertical fifteen-foot pistons, rush through them with a roar that rocked the stone walls of the building. Along these massive iron pipes, which were about ten feet in circumference, the air passed through the hot-blast stoves, where burning gases heated it to a thousand degrees, and from there went into the blast-furnace, melting ore and coal with its hot breath. The engineer in charge of the blower department was giving explanations. He bent to the ear of one shareholder after another, and shouted at the top of his voice, straining till his lungs hurt, but the terrific din of the machinery drowned his words and it seemed as if he were just moving his lips, silently and strenuously.

Then Shelkovnikov led the visitors to the puddling-furnace shed, a tall building of such immense length that its far end looked like a barely visible small hole. Along one wall of the shed ran a stone platform with twenty puddling furnaces shaped like railway wagons without wheels. In these furnaces molten iron was mixed with ore and processed into steel, which flowed down pipes and filled high iron moulds—rather like bottomless cases with handles on top—and there hardened to puddles weighing each about three-quarters of a ton. The other side of the shed was laid with rails along which steam cranes moved up and down like obedient, agile animals, with tensile trunks, snorting, hissing, clanking. One of the cranes would seize a mould by the handle and raise it, and a dazzling red bar of steel would slip out. But before the bar could reach the floor, a workman would with extraordinary alacrity sling a wrist-thick chain round it. Another crane would hook the chain, waft away the bar, and put it down next to others on the platform attached to a third crane. The third crane would haul the load to the far end of the shed where a fourth crane, equipped with pincers instead of a hook, would lift the bars from the truck and lower them into the gas furnaces built under the floor. Lastly, a fifth crane would pull them, white with heat, out of the furnaces, put them one by one under a sharp-toothed wheel revolving on a horizontal axle at a terrific speed, and the huge steel bar would be halved in five seconds like a slab of butter. Each half would then go under the twenty-five thousand pound press of a steam hammer, which shingled it as easily as if it were wax. Workmen would at once grab and load the pieces on trolleys and push them away at a run, the red-hot iron sending a wave of glowing heat against all who came that way.

Shelkovnikov went on to show his visitors the rail-rolling mill. A huge bar of red-hot metal would pass through a series of machines, moving from one to another over rollers that were turning under the floor, with only their top parts showing. Squeezed between two steel cylinders revolving in opposite directions, it would force them apart, the rollers trembling with tension. Farther away was a machine with an even smaller space between its cylinders. As it passed through each machine the bar became thinner and longer; after running several times up and down the rail-mill it would take the shape of a red-hot rail, seventy feet long. In control of the complex operations of the fifteen machines was a single man who was posted above the steam engine, on a raised platform not unlike a ship's bridge. He would pull a handle and all the cylinders and rollers would start to turn one way, then he would push it back and they would turn the other way. When the rail had been stretched to its final length a circular saw would cut it into three parts with a deafening scream, throwing up a myriad of golden sparks.

Now the group proceeded to the turnery where mostly wagon and locomotive wheels were finished. Leather transmission belts coming down from a stout steel shaft running the whole length of the ceiling set in motion two or three hundred machines of the most varied sizes and shapes. There were so many belts criss-crossing in all directions that they seemed like one tangled, vibrating network. The wheels of some of the machines were making twenty revolutions per second, while others were turning so slowly that you could hardly notice it. Steel, iron, and brass shavings thickly littered the floor in thin long spirals. Drilling machines filled the air with an unbearable screeching. The visitors were shown a nut-making machine—rather like two huge steel jaws munching steadily. Two workmen were busy feeding the end of a long red-hot rod into the machine, which bit off its tip regularly to spit out a completely finished nut.

When they left the turnery Shelkovnikov, who had been addressing his explanations exclusively to the shareholders, suggested that they should inspect the nine-hundred h. p. "Compound," the mill's pride. By then the gentlemen from Petersburg were sufficiently overwhelmed and exhausted by what they had already seen and heard. Every new impression, far from interesting them, wearied them still more. Their faces were red from the heat of the rail-mill, and their hands and clothes were sooty. They therefore accepted the manager's invitation with apparent reluctance, and only because they had to maintain the prestige of those who had sent them.

The "Compound" was installed in a separate building, very neat and nice-looking, with bright windows and an inlaid floor. Despite its huge size the machine made hardly any noise. Two pistons, each about thirty feet long, moved smoothly and swiftly up and down their cylinders encased in wood. A wheel twenty feet in diameter, with twelve ropes gliding over it, was revolving just as noiselessly and swiftly. Its sweeping motion sent the hot, dry air rushing through the machine room in strong, regular gusts. The machine supplied power to the blowers and rolling mills and the machinery in the turnery.

Having inspected the "Compound," the shareholders felt quite certain that their trials were at an end, but the tireless Shelkovnikov obligingly made a fresh suggestion.

"Now, gentlemen, I'll show you the heart of the mill, its life-centre."

He dragged rather than led them into the steam-boiler house. But after all that they had seen the "heart of the mill"—twelve cylindrical boilers each thirty-five feet in length and ten feet in height—failed to impress the weary shareholders much. Their thoughts had long been centring round the dinner awaiting them, and they no longer asked questions but nodded with absent-minded indifference at whatever explanations Shelkovnikov gave. When he had finished they sighed with obvious relief and heartily shook hands with him.

Bobrov was now the only one left near the boilers. Standing at the edge of the deep, half-dark stone pit where the furnaces were, he looked for a long time down on the hard work of six men, bare to the waist. It was their duty to stoke the furnaces with coal day and night, without let-up. Now and again the round iron doors opened with a clang, and Bobrov could see the dazzling white flames roaring and raging in the furnaces. Now and again the half-naked figures of the workmen, withered by fire and black with the coal dust ingrained in their skin, bent down, all the muscles and vertebrae standing out on their backs. Now and again their lean, wiry hands scooped up a shovelful of coal and thrust it into the blazing orifice with a swift, deft movement. Another two workmen, standing above, were kept as busy shovelling down fresh coal from the huge black piles round the boiler house. There was something depressing and inhuman, Bobrov thought, in the stokers' endless work. It seemed as if a supernatural power had chained them for life to those yawning maws and they must, under penalty of a terrible death, tirelessly feed the insatiable, gluttonous monster.

"Watching them fattening your Moloch, are you?" said a cheerful, good-humoured voice behind Bobrov's back.

Bobrov started and all but fell into the pit. He was staggered by the unexpected coincidence of the doctor's facetious exclamation with his own thoughts. For a long time after he regained his composure he could not stop wondering at the strange coincidence. He was always interested and mystified to hear someone beside him suddenly bring up what he had just been reading or thinking about.

"Did I frighten you, old chap?" said the doctor, looking closely at Bobrov. "I'm sorry."

"Yes—a little. You came up so quietly—it was quite a surprise."

"Andrei Ilyich, you'd better look after your nerves. They're no good at all. Take my advice: ask for leave of absence and go somewhere abroad. Why worry yourself here? Enjoy six months or so of easy life; drink good wine, ride a lot, try *l'amour*."

The doctor walked to the edge of the furnace pit and glanced down.

"A regular inferno!" he cried. "How much would those little samovars weigh? Close to fifteen tons each, I should think?"

"A bit more than that. Upwards of twenty-five tons."

"Oh! And suppose it occurred to one of them to—er—pop? It would make a fine sight, wouldn't it?"

"It certainly would, doctor. All these buildings would probably be razed to the ground."

Goldberg shook his head and whistled significantly.

"But what might cause such a thing?"

"Oh, there may be many causes; but more often than not this is what happens: when there's very little water left in the boiler, its walls grow hotter and hotter, till they're almost red-hot. If you let water in at a moment like that an enormous quantity of steam would form at once, the walls wouldn't be able to stand the pressure, and the boiler would blow up."

"So you could do it on purpose?"

"Any time you wish. Would you like to try? When the water runs quite low in the gauge, you only have to turn that small round lever. That's all there is to it."

Bobrov was jesting, but his tone was strangely earnest, and there was a stern, unhappy look in his eyes.

"Damn it," the doctor said to himself, "he's a fine chap all right, but cranky just the same."

"Why didn't you go to the dinner, Andrei Ilyich?" he asked, stepping back from the pit. "You should at least see what a winter garden they've made of the lab. And the spread—you'd be amazed."

"To hell with it all! I can't bear those engineers' dinners." Bobrov made a grimace. "Bragging, yelling, fawning on each other, and then those invariable drunken toasts when the speakers spill their wine on themselves or their neighbours. Disgusting!"

"Yes, you're quite right." The doctor laughed. "I saw the beginning. Kvashnin was splendid. 'Gentlemen,' he said, 'the engineer's calling is a lofty and important one Along with railways, blast-furnaces, and mines he carries into the remote corners of the country the seeds of education, the flowers of civilization, and—' He mentioned some sort of fruits, but I don't remember which. A super-swindler if there ever was one! 'So let us rally, gentlemen,' he said, 'and bear high the sacred banner of our beneficent art!' He got furious applause, of course."

They walked on a few paces in silence. Suddenly a shadow came over the doctor's face.

"Beneficent art, is it!" he said angrily. "And the workmen's barracks are built of chips. No end of sick people, children dying like flies. That's what they call seeds of education! They are in for a nice surprise when typhoid fever breaks loose in Ivankovo."

"But, doctor! Do you mean to say there've been cases already? It would be dreadful with their barracks crammed the way they are."

The doctor stopped to catch his breath.

"What did you think?" he said with bitterness. "Two men were brought in yesterday. One of them died this morning, and the other's sure to die tonight, if he hasn't died yet. And we have neither medicines, beds, nor skilled nurses. Just wait, they'll pay for it yet!" he added angrily, shaking his fist at someone invisible.

VIII

Busy-bodies had begun to wag their tongues. Even before Kvashnin arrived there were so many piquant stories bandied about the mill that now no one doubted the real motive of his sudden intimacy with the Zinenko family. The ladies spoke about it with ambiguous smiles and the men, talking among themselves, called a spade a spade with frank cynicism. But nobody knew anything for certain. Everyone was agog for a spicy scandal.

The gossip was not wholly groundless. After paying a visit to the Zinenko family Kvashnin began to spend all his evenings with them. About eleven o'clock every morning, his fine troika of greys would pull up at the Shepetovka estate, and the driver would invariably announce, "My master begs the lady and the young ladies to have breakfast with him." No other people were invited to those breakfasts. The food was prepared by a French cook whom Kvashnin always took with him on his frequent trips, even when he went abroad.

Kvashnin's attentions to his new acquaintances were of a most peculiar nature. Towards the five girls he at once assumed the blunt manner of a genial unmarried uncle. In three days he was calling them by their diminutive names, to which he added their patronymic; as for the youngest, Kasya, he often took her by the plump, dimpled chin and teased her by calling her a "baby" and a "chick," which made her blush to tears although she did not protest.

Anna Afanasyevna reproached him with playful querulousness, saying that he would completely spoil her girls. Indeed, no sooner did any one of them express a fleeting wish than it was fulfilled. Hardly did Maka mention, quite innocently, that she would like to learn bicycle-riding when, the very next day, a messenger brought from Kharkov an excellent bicycle, which must have cost no less than three hundred rubles. He lost ten pounds of sweets to Beta, with whom he made a bet over some trifle, and for Kasya, as a result of another bet, he bought a brooch set with a coral, an amethyst, a sapphire, and a jasper, indicating the letters of her name.* Once he heard

* In Russian the name *Kasya* is spelt with four letters, the last corresponding to *ya —Tr*

that Nina was fond of riding. Two days after, there was brought to her an English thoroughbred mare, perfectly broken in for lady riders. The young ladies were fascinated by this kind fairy who could guess, and at once fulfil, their every whim. Anna Afanasyevna had a vague feeling that there was something improper about this generosity, but she lacked both the courage and the tact to make that clear to Kvashnin in a discreet manner. Whenever she obsequiously reprimanded him, he would dismiss the matter with a wave of his hand, saying in his rough, firm voice, "It's all right, my dear, stop worrying about trifles."

Nevertheless, he did not show preference for any one of her daughters but tried to please them all alike, and unceremoniously made sport of all of them. The young men who had once called at the house had obligingly disappeared, but Svezhevsky had become a habitué, whereas formerly he had called no more than twice or three times in all. No one had asked him to come—he came of his own accord, as if at some mysterious invitation, and at once managed to become indispensable to all the members of the family.

However, a little incident preceded his appearance in the Zinenko house. About five months ago he had let fall among his colleagues that he dreamt of becoming a millionaire some day and was sure he would by the time he was forty.

"But how?" they had asked him.

Svezhevsky had tittered and answered, rubbing his moist hands mysteriously, "All roads lead to Rome."

He felt intuitively that the situation at the Shepetovka estate was shaping most favourably for his future career. Anyway, he might be of service to his all-powerful superior. So he staked his all and boldly thrust himself into Kvashnin's presence with his servile titter. He made advances to him as a gay pup might to a ferocious mastiff, both his face and his voice suggesting his constant readiness to do anything, however dirty, at a wink from Kvashnin.

Kvashnin did not mind it. He, who used to sack factory directors and managers without bothering to give the reason, silently put up with the presence of a Svezhevsky. There must be an important service afoot, and the future millionaire was eagerly biding his time.

Passed on by word of mouth, the rumour reached Bobrov's ear. He was not surprised, for he had formed a firm and accurate opinion of the Zinenko family. The only thing which vexed him was that the gossip was bound to brush Nina with its filthy tail. After the talk at the station, the girl had become dearer to him than ever. To him alone she had trustingly revealed her soul, a soul that was beautiful even in its vacillation and weakness. Everybody else knew only her costume and appearance, he thought. Jealousy—with its cynical distrust, with the constantly piqued pride attending it, with its pettiness and coarseness—was foreign to his trusting and delicate nature.

Bobrov had never yet known the warmth of genuine, deep woman's love. He was too shy and diffident to take from life what was perhaps his due. No wonder that his heart had rushed joyfully out to meet the new, strong feeling.

Throughout the last few days he had been under the spell of the talk they had had at the station. He recalled it again and again in minutest detail, each time seeing a deeper meaning in Nina's words. Every morning he woke up with a vague feeling that something big and joyful had entered his soul, something that held out hopes of great felicity.

He was irresistibly drawn to the Zinenkos'; he wanted once more to make sure of his happiness, once more to hear from Nina those half-confessions—now timid, now naively bold. But he was restrained by Kvashnin's pres-

ence, and he tried to set his mind at ease by telling himself that in no circumstances could Kvashnin stay in
Ivankovo for more than a fortnight.

By a lucky chance he saw Nina before Kvashnin left.
It happened on a Sunday, three days after the ceremony
of blowing in the blast-furnace. Bobrov was riding on
Fairway down a broad, hard-beaten road leading from the
mill to the station. It was about two o'clock, and the day
was cool and cloudless. Fairway was going along at a
brisk pace, pricking up his ears and tossing his shaggy
head. At a curve near a warehouse, Bobrov saw a lady in
riding-habit coming downhill on a large bay, followed by
a rider on a small white Kirghiz horse. Soon he recognized
her as Nina wearing a long, flowing dark green skirt,
yellow gauntlets, and a low, glossy top hat. She was
sitting in the saddle with a confident grace. The slim
English mare raised its slender legs high as it carried
her along at a round, springy trot, its neck arched into
a steep curve. Nina's companion, Svezhevsky, was lagging
far behind; working his elbows, jerking and bouncing, he
was tryng to catch the dangling stirrup with the toe of
his boot.

As she sighted Bobrov Nina broke her mount into a
gallop. Coming alongside Bobrov, she reined in the horse
abruptly, and it began to fidget, dilating its fine wide
nostrils, and fretting loudly at the bit which dripped
lather. Nina's face was flushed from the ride, and her
hair, which had slipped out of the hat at the temples, fell
back in long, thin curls.

"Where did you get such a beauty?" asked Bobrov, when
he had at last managed to pull up the prancing Fairway
and, bending forward in the saddle, squeeze Nina's finger-
tips.

"Isn't she? It's a present from Kvashnin."

"I would have refused a present like that," said Bobrov rudely, angered by Nina's careless reply.

Nina blushed.

"Just why?"

"Because—what's Kvashnin to you, after all? A relative? Or your fiancé?"

"Goodness, how squeamish you are on other people's behalf!" Nina exclaimed caustically.

But seeing the pained look on his face, she softened at once.

"You know he can afford it easily. He's so rich!"

Svezhevsky was now a dozen paces from them. Suddenly Nina bent forward to Bobrov, gently touched his hand with the tip of her whip, and said under her breath, in the tone of a little girl confessing her guilt, "Don't be cross, now, please. I'll give him back the horse, you grumpy man! You see how much your opinion means to me."

Bobrov's eyes shone with happiness, and he could not help holding out his hands to Nina. But he said nothing and merely drew a deep sigh. Svezhevsky was riding up, bowing and trying to sit his horse carelessly.

"I expect you know about our picnic?" he shouted from a distance.

"Never heard of it," answered Bobrov.

"I mean the picnic that Vasily Terentyevich is getting up. We're going to Beshenaya Balka."

"Haven't heard about it."

"It's true. Please come, Andrei Ilyich," Nina put in. "Next Wednesday, at five o'clock. We'll start from the station."

"Is it a subscription picnic?"

"I think so. But I'm not certain."

Nina looked questioningly at Svezhevsky.

"That's right—a subscription picnic," he confirmed. "Vasily Terentyevich has asked me to make certain arrangements. It's going to be a stupendous affair, I can tell you. Something extra smart. But it's a secret so far. You'll be surprised."

Nina could not help adding playfully, "I started all this. The other day I was saying that it would be fun to go on an outing to the woods, and Vasily Terentyevich—"

"I'm not coming," said Bobrov brusquely.

"Oh, yes, you are!" Nina's eyes flashed. "Now march, gentlemen!" she cried, starting off at a gallop. "Listen to what I have to tell you, Andrei Ilyich!"

Svezhevsky was left behind. Nina and Bobrov were riding side by side, Nina smiling and looking into his eyes, and he frowning resentfully.

"Why, I thought up that picnic specially for you, my unkind, suspicious friend," she said with deep tenderness. "I insist on knowing what it was you didn't finish telling me at the station that time. Nobody'll be in our way at the picnic."

And once again an instant change came over Bobrov's heart. He felt tears of tender emotion welling up in his eyes, and exclaimed passionately, "Oh, Nina, how I love you!"

But Nina did not seem to have heard his sudden confession. She drew in the reins and forced the horse to change to a walk.

"So you will come, won't you?" she asked.

"Yes, by all means!"

"See that you do. And now let's wait for my companion and—goodbye. I must be riding home."

As he took leave of her he felt through the glove the warmth of her hand which responded with a long, firm grasp Her dark eyes were full of love.

IX

At four o'clock next Wednesday, the station was packed with the picnickers. Everybody felt gay and at ease. For once Kvashnin's visit was winding up more happily than anybody had dared to expect. He had neither stormed nor hurled thunderbolts at anyone, and nobody had been told to go; in fact, it was rumoured that most of the clerical staff would get a rise in the near future. Besides, the picnic bid fair to be very entertaining. Beshenaya Balka, where it was to be, was less than ten miles away if you rode on horseback, and the road was extremely picturesque. The sunny weather which had set in a week earlier enhanced the trip.

There were some ninety guests; they clustered in animated groups on the platform, talking and laughing loudly. French, German, and Polish phrases could be heard along with Russian conversation. Three Belgians had brought their cameras, hoping to take flash snapshots. General curiosity was roused by the complete secrecy about the details of the picnic. Svezhevsky with a mysterious and important air hinted at certain "surprises" but refused to be more specific.

The first surprise was a special train. At five o'clock sharp, a new ten-wheeled locomotive of American make left its shed. The ladies could not keep back cries of amazement and delight: the huge engine was decked with bunting and fresh flowers. Green garlands of oak leaves, intermingled with bunches of asters, dahlias, stocks, and carnations, entwined its steel body in a spiral, wound up the chimney, hung from it down to the whistle, and climbed up again to form a blossoming wall against the cab. In the golden rays of the setting autumn sun, the steel and brass parts of the engine glistened showily through the greenery and flowers. The six first-class carriages stretching along the platform were to take the picnickers to the 200th Mile station, from which it was only two hundred yards or so to Beshenaya Balka.

"Ladies and gentlemen, Vasily Terentyevich has asked me to inform you that he's paying all the picnic expenses,"

Svezhevsky said again and again, hurrying from one group to another.

A large number of people flocked round him, and he gave them further explanations.

"Vasily Terentyevich was greatly pleased with the welcome extended to him here, and he is happy to be able to reciprocate. He's paying all the expenses."

Unable to restrain the kind of impulse which makes a valet boast of his master's generosity, he added weightily, "We spent three thousand five hundred and ninety rubles on the picnic!"

"You mean you went halves with Mr. Kvashnin?" asked a mocking voice from behind. Svezhevsky spun round to find that the venomous question had come from Andréas, who, impassive as usual, was looking at him, hands deep in his trouser pockets.

"I beg your pardon? What was it you said, please?" asked Svezhevsky, his face reddening painfully.

"It was you who said something. '*We* spent three thousand,' you said, and so I assume that you meant yourself and Mr. Kvashnin. If that's the case, it is my agreeable duty to tell you that, while I accept the favour from Mr. Kvashnin, I may very well refuse to accept it from Mr. Svezhevsky."

"Oh, no, no! You've misunderstood me," stammered Svezhevsky. "It's Vasily Terentyevich who's done it all. I'm simply—er—his confidant. An agent or something like that," he added with a wry smile.

The Zinenkos, accompanied by Kvashnin and Shelkovni-kov, arrived almost simultaneously with the train. But no sooner did Kvashnin alight from the carriage than a tragicomic incident occurred that no one could have fore-seen. Since early morning, having heard about the planned picnic, workmen's wives, sisters, and mothers had begun to gather at the station, many of them bringing their babies with them. With a look of stolid patience on their sunburnt, haggard faces, they had been sitting for many long hours on the station steps or on the ground, in the shadow cast by the walls. There were more than two hundred of them. Asked by the station staff what they wanted, they said they must see "the fat, red-headed boss." The watchman tried to send them away but the uproar they raised made him give up the attempt and leave them alone.

Each carriage that pulled up caused a momentary stir among the women, but they settled back the moment they saw that this was not the "fat, red-headed boss."

Hardly had Kvashnin stepped down on the footboard, clutching at the box, puffing and tilting the carriage, when the women closed in on him and dropped on their knees. The young, high-mettled horses shied and started at the noise of the crowd; it was all the driver could do to keep them in check by straining hard at the reins. At first Kvashnin could not make head or tail of it: the women were shouting all together, holding out their babies; tears were streaming down their bronzed faces.

Kvashnin saw that there was no breaking through the live ring in which he found himself.

"Quiet, women! Stop yelling!" he boomed, drowning their voices. "This isn't a market, is it? I can't hear a thing. Let one of you tell me what's up."

But each of the women thought she should be the one to speak. The hubbub grew louder, and the tears flew even more freely.

"Please, master, help us! We can't stand it any more! It's worn us thin! We're dying—children and all! The cold's just killing us!"

"Well, what do you want? What are you dying of?" Kvashnin bellowed again. "But don't shout all at once! You there, speak up." He poked his finger at a tall woman who was handsome in spite of the pallor of her weary face "And let the others keep quiet!"

Most of the women stopped shouting, but continued to sob and wail softly, wiping their eyes and noses on the dirty hems of their skirts.

Even so, there were no less than twenty speaking at a time.

"We're dying of cold, master! Please do something. It's more than we can stand. They put us into barracks for the winter, but how can you live there? They call 'em barracks, sure enough, but it's chips they're built of. Even now it's terrible cold in them at night—makes your teeth chatter. And what are we going to do in winter? At least have pity on our little ones—help us, dear master! At least get stoves built. There's no place to cook our meals —we do our cooking outside. The men are at work all day, soaked and shivering. And when they get back home they can't dry their clothes."

Kvashnin was trapped. Whichever way he turned his path was barred by prostrate or kneeling women. And when he tried to force his way out, they would cling to his feet and the skirts of his long grey coat. Seeing that he was helpless, he beckoned to Shelkovnikov and, when the other had elbowed his way through the dense crowd, he asked him angrily in French, "Did you hear? What's the meaning of this?"

Shelkovnikov was taken aback.

"I wrote to the Board more than once," he mumbled. "There was a shortage of labour—it was summer-time, mowing was on—and the high prices—the Board wouldn't authorize it. It couldn't be helped."

"So when are you going to start rebuilding the workmen's barracks?" asked Kvashnin sternly.

"I can't tell for certain. They'll have to put up with it somehow. We must first make haste about quarters for the clerical staff."

"The outrageous things that are going on here under your management!" grumbled Kvashnin. He turned to the women and said aloud, "Listen, women! Tomorrow they'll start building stoves for you, and they'll roof your barracks with shingles. D'you hear?"

"Yes, master! Thank you so much! Of course we heard you!" cried joyous voices. "That's fine—you can rely on it when the master himself has ordered it. Thank you! Please allow us also to pick up the chips at the building site."

"All right, you may do that."

"Because there are Circassians posted everywhere, and they threaten us with their whips when we come."

"Never mind—you come and take the chips. Nobody'll harm you," Kvashnin said reassuringly. "And now, women, off you go and cook your soup! And be quick about it!" he shouted, with an encouraging dash. "Have a couple of cartloads of bricks delivered to the barracks tomorrow," he said to Shelkovnikov in an undertone. "That'll comfort them for a long time. Let them look and be happy."

The women were scattering in quite a cheerful mood.

"Mind you, if those stoves aren't built we'll ask the engineers to come and warm us," cried the woman whom Kvashnin had told to speak up for the others.

"So we shall!" added another woman pertly. "Then let the boss himself warm us. See how fat and jolly he is. We'll be warmer with him than by the stove."

This incident, which ended so happily, raised everybody's spirits. Even Kvashnin, who at first had been frowning at the manager, laughed when the women asked to be warmed, and took Shelkovnikov by the elbow as a sign of reconciliation.

"You see, my friend," he said to Shelkovnikov, heavily climbing up the station steps with him, "you must know how to talk to those people. You may promise them anything you like—aluminium homes, an eight-hour working day, or a steak every morning, but you must do it with a great deal of assurance. I swear I could put down the stormiest popular demonstration in half an hour with mere promises."

Kvashnin got on the train, laughing heartily as he recalled the details of the women's rebellion which he had just quelled. Three minutes later the train started. The coachmen were told to drive straight to Beshenaya Balka, as the company planned to come back by carriage, with torches.

Nina's behaviour perplexed Bobrov. He had awaited her arrival at the station with an excited impatience that had beset him the night before. His former doubts were gone; he believed that happiness was near, and never had the world seemed to him so beautiful, people so kind, or life so easy and joyful, as they did now. As he thought of his meeting with Nina, he tried involuntarily to picture it in advance, composing tender, passionate and eloquent phrases and then laughing at himself. Why think up words of love? They would come of themselves when they were needed, and would be much more beautiful, much warmer.

He recalled a poem he had read in a magazine, in which the poet said to his sweetheart that they were not going to swear to each other because vows would have been an insult to their trusting and ardent love.

Bobrov saw the Zinenkos' two carriages arrive after Kvashnin's troika. Nina was in the first. Wearing a pale-yellow dress trimmed with broad lace of the same colour at the crescent-shaped low neck, and a broad-brimmed white Italian hat adorned with a bouquet of tea-roses, she seemed to him paler and graver than usual. She caught sight of him from afar, but did not give him a significant look as he would have expected. In fact, he fancied that she deliberately turned away from him. And when he ran up to the carriage to help her to alight, she jumped nimbly out on the other side, as if to forestall him. He felt a pang of foreboding, but hastened to reassure himself. "Poor Nina, she's ashamed of her decision and her love. She imagines that now anyone can easily read her inmost thoughts in her eyes. The delightful naïveté of it!"

He was sure that Nina would herself make an opportunity, as she had done previously at the station, to exchange a few confidential words with him. But she was apparently absorbed by Kvashnin's parley with the women and she never looked back at Bobrov, not even stealthily. Suddenly his heart began to beat in alarm and anguish. He made up his mind to walk up to the Zinenko family who kept together in a close group—the other ladies seemed to cut them—and, taking advantage of the noise which held the general attention, ask Nina at least by a look why she was so indifferent to him.

Bowing to Anna Afanasyevna and kissing her hand, he tried to read in her eyes whether she knew anything. Yes, she clearly did: her thin, angular eyebrows—suggesting a false character, as Bobrov often thought—were knitted resentfully, and her lips wore a haughty expression. Bobrov inferred that Nina had told everything to her mother, who had scolded her.

He stepped up to Nina, but she did not so much as glance at him. Her hand lay limp and cold in his trembling hand as he clasped it. Instead of responding to his greeting she turned her head to Beta and exchanged some trivial remarks with her. He read into that hasty manoeuvre of hers something guilty, something cowardly that shrank from a forthright answer. He felt his knees give way, and a chill feeling came into his mouth. He did not know what to think. Even if Nina had let out her secret to her mother, she could have said to him by one of those swift, eloquent glances that women instinctively command, "Yes, you've guessed right, she does know about our talk. But I haven't changed, dear, I haven't changed, don't worry." But she had preferred to turn away. "Never mind, I'll get an answer from her at the picnic," he thought, with a vague presentiment of something disastrous and dastardly. "She'll have to tell me anyway."

<h1 style="text-align:center">X</h1>

At the 200th Mile stop the picnickers got out of the carriages and started for Beshenaya Balka in a long, colourful file down a narrow road that led past the watchman's house. The pungent freshness of autumnal woods floated to their flushed faces from afar. The road grew steeper and steeper, disappearing beneath a dark canopy of hazel bushes and honeysuckle. Dead leaves, yellow and curled, rustled underfoot. A scarlet sunset showed through the thicket far ahead.

The bushes ended. A wide clearing, flattened and strewn with fine sand, came into view unexpectedly. At one end of it stood an octagonal pavilion decked with bunting and greenery, and at the other was a covered platform for the band. As soon as the first couples came out of the thicket the band struck up a lively march. The gay brass sounds sped playfully through the woods, reverberating among the trees and merging far away into another band that sometimes seemed to outrace, and sometimes to lag behind the first. In the pavilion waiters were bustling round the tables, set in a U shape and covered with white cloths.

As soon as the band stopped the picnickers broke into enthusiastic applause. They had reason to be delighted, for only a fortnight ago the clearing had been a hillside scantily covered with shrubs.

The band began to play a waltz.

Bobrov saw Svezhevsky, who was standing beside Nina, at once put his arm round her waist without asking permission and whirl with her about the clearing.

Scarcely had he released her when a mining student ran up to her, and then someone else. Bobrov was a poor dancer; he did not care for dancing. Nevertheless, it occurred to him to invite Nina for a quadrille. "It may give me a chance to ask for an explanation," he thought. He walked over to her when, having danced two turns, she sat down, fanning herself.

"I hope you've reserved a quadrille for me, Nina Grigoryevna?"

"Oh, my goodness! Such a pity. I've promised all my quadrilles," she replied, without looking at him.

"You have? So soon?" Bobrov said thickly.

"Of course." She shrugged her shoulders, impatiently and ironically. "Why do you come so late? I gave away all my quadrilles while we were on the train."

"So you completely forgot about me," he said sadly.

His tone moved Nina. She nervously folded and opened her fan, but did not look up.

"It's all your fault. Why didn't you ask me before?"

"I only came to this picnic because I wanted to see you. Was the whole thing simply a joke, Nina Grigoryevna?"

She made no answer, fumbling with her fan in confusion. She was rescued by a young engineer who rushed up to her. Quickly she rose and, without glancing at Bobrov, laid her thin hand in a long white glove on the engineer's shoulder. Bobrov followed her with his eyes. After dancing one turn she sat down at the other end of the clearing—no doubt purposely, he thought. She seemed almost afraid of him, or else she felt ashamed in his presence.

The dull, listless melancholy, so long familiar to him, gripped him afresh. All the faces about him appeared vulgar and pitiful, almost comical. The cadenced beat of the music resounded painfully in his brain. But he had not yet lost hope and sought comfort in various conjectures. "She may be cross with me because I didn't send her flowers. Or perhaps she simply doesn't care to dance with a clumsy bear like me? Well, she's probably right. These trifles mean such an awful lot to girls. In fact, they make up all their joys and sorrows, all the poetry of their lives."

At dusk Chinese lanterns were lit in long chains round the pavilion. But it was not enough—they shed hardly any light on the clearing. Suddenly the bluish light of two electric suns, carefully camouflaged in the foliage until then, flared up blindingly at both ends of the clearing. The surrounding birches and hornbeams stood out instantly. Their motionless curly boughs, brought out by the unnatural glare, looked like stage scenery set in the foreground. In the grey-green haze beyond them, the round and jagged tops of other trees were dimly silhouetted against a pitch black sky. The music could not drown the chirping of grasshoppers in the steppe, a strange chorus that sounded like a single grasshopper chirping simultaneously to right and left and overhead.

The ball went on, growing livelier and noisier as one dance followed another, the band being given hardly any respite. The women were drunk with music and the fairy-tale setting.

The smell of perfume and heated bodies mixed oddly with the scent of wormwood, withering leaves, and damp woods, with the remote, subtle fragrance of new-mown hay. Fans were waving everywhere like the wings of beautifully coloured birds about to take flight. Loud conversation, laughter, and the shuffling of feet on the sand-strewn earth blended into a monotonous yet lively hubbub that sounded extra loud whenever the band stopped playing.

Bobrov did not take his eyes off Nina. Once or twice she almost brushed him with her dress. He even felt a whiff of air as she swept past. While she danced her left arm lay on her partner's shoulder, bent gracefully and with seeming helplessness, and she tilted her head as if she were going to put it on his shoulder. Occasionally he caught a glimpse of the lace edging of her white petticoat flying with her rapid motion, and of her black-stockinged little foot, with a fine ankle and steeply curving calf. At such moments he somehow felt ashamed, and was angry with all who could see her.

The mazurka came. It was already about nine o'clock. Profiting by the moment when her partner, Svezhevsky, who was conducting the mazurka, got busy with an intricate figure, Nina ran to the dressing-room, lightly gliding to the rhythm of the music and holding her dishevelled hair with both hands. Bobrov, who saw this from the far end of the clearing, hastily followed her, and placed himself by the door. It was almost dark there; the small dressing-room, built of planks behind the pavilion, was hidden in dense shade. Bobrov decided to wait till Nina came out and to make her speak. His heart was throbbing painfully; his fingers, which he clenched nervously, were moist and cold.

Nina stepped out five minutes later. Bobrov walked out of the shade and barred her way. She started back with a faint cry.

"Why are you torturing me like this, Nina Grigoryevna?" said Bobrov, clasping his hands in an involuntary gesture of entreaty. "Don't you see how you hurt me? Ah! You're making fun of my sorrow. You're laughing at me."

"I don't understand what you want," replied Nina, with wilful arrogance. "I never dreamed of laughing at you."

It was her family traits showing through.

"You didn't?" said Bobrov dejectedly. "Then what's the meaning of your behaviour tonight?"

"What behaviour?"

"You're cold to me, almost hostile. You keep turning away from me. My very presence is disagreeable to you."

"It makes absolutely no difference to me."

72

"That's worse still. I sense that some dreadful change I can't understand has come over you. Please be frank, Nina, be as truthful as I thought you were till today. Tell me the truth, no matter how terrible it may be. We'd better settle the matter once and for all."

"What is there to settle? I don't know what you mean."

Bobrov pressed his hands to his temples in which the blood was pulsating feverishly.

"O yes, you do. Don't pretend. There *is* something to settle. We said loving words to each other, words that were almost a confession, we lived some beautiful moments that wove tender and delicate bonds between us. I know you'll be telling me I'm mistaken. Perhaps I am. But wasn't it you who told me to come to this picnic so that we might talk without being disturbed?"

Nina suddenly felt sorry for him.

"Yes, I did ask you to come," she said, bending her head low. "I was going to tell you—to tell you that we must part for ever."

He reeled as if he had been struck in the chest. The pallor which spread over his face could be seen even in the dark.

"Part?" he gasped. "Nina Grigoryevna! Parting words are hard and bitter. Don't say them!"

"I must."

"You must?"

"Yes. It isn't I who want it."

"Who then?"

Someone was approaching them. Nina peered into the darkness.

"Here's who," she whispered.

It was Anna Afanasyevna. She eyed Bobrov and Nina suspiciously and took her daughter by the hand.

"Why did you run away, Nina?" she said in a tone of censure. "Standing here chattering in the darkness. A fine thing to do, indeed. And here I am looking for you in every corner. As for you, sir," she said suddenly, in a loud railing voice, turning to Bobrov, "if you can't or don't care to dance yourself, you should at least keep out of the way of young ladies, instead of compromising them by *tête-à-têtes* in shady nooks."

She walked off, towing Nina after her.

"Don't worry, madam, nothing can compromise *your* young lady!" Bobrov shouted after her, and suddenly he burst into laughter so strange and bitter that mother and daughter could not help looking back.

"There! Didn't I tell you he was a fool and an impudent fellow?" Anna Afanasyevna tugged at Nina's hand. "You can spit in his face, but still he'll laugh and get over it. Now the ladies are going to pick partners," she added more calmly. "Go and invite Kvashnin. He's just finished playing. There he is, in the doorway of the pavilion."

"But, Mother! How can he dance? He can hardly move."

"Do as I tell you. He was once considered one of the best dancers in Moscow. Anyway, he'll be pleased."

A grey mist swam before Bobrov's eyes. In it he saw Nina run nimbly across the clearing and stop in front of Kvashnin with a coquettish smile, her head tilted to one side in enticing appeal. Kvashnin listened to her, bending slightly over her. Suddenly a guffaw rocked his huge frame, and he shook his head. Nina insisted for a long time, then made a sulky face, and turned to walk away. But Kvashnin overtook her with an agility that contrasted with his size, and shrugged his shoulders as if to say, "Well, it can't be helped. You've got to humour children." He put out his hand to Nina. All the dancers stopped, staring at the new pair with curiosity. The sight of Kvashnin dancing a mazurka promised to be very funny.

Kvashnin waited for the beat and, suddenly turning to his partner with a heavy grace that was majestic in its own way, did his first step with such confident dexterity that everyone sensed in him a former excellent dancer.

Looking down at Nina, with a proud, challenging, and gay turn of his head, he at first walked rather than danced to the music with an elastic, slightly waddling gait. It seemed that his enormous height and bulk, far from handicapping him, added at the moment to the ponderous grace of his figure. As he reached the curve he halted for a second, clicked his heels, swung Nina round, and sped smoothly on his thick, springy legs across the centre of the clearing, an indulgent smile on his face. In front of the spot where he had started the dance, he again whirled her in a swift, graceful movement, and suddenly seating her on a chair, stood facing her with bowed head.

Ladies surrounded him at once, begging him to dance another turn. But the unaccustomed effort had exhausted him, and he was panting as he fanned his face with his handkerchief.

"That'll do, *mesdames*, have pity on an old man," he said, laughing and breathing heavily. "I'm past the dancing age. Let's have supper instead."

The picnickers started to take their seats at the tables, moving the chairs up with a grating noise. Bobrov remained standing where Nina had left him. He was alternately agonized by a feeling of humiliation and by a hopeless, desperate anguish. There were no tears, but he felt a burning sensation in his eyes, and a dry, prickly lump clogged his throat. The music continued to echo in his brain with painful monotony.

"Why, I've been looking for you for such a long time!" he heard the doctor's cheerful voice beside him. "Where have you been hiding? The moment I arrived they dragged me to the card table. I've just managed to get away. Let's go and have some food. I've reserved two seats so that we can eat together."

"Go along yourself, doctor!" replied Bobrov with an effort. "I'm not coming—I don't feel like eating."

"You aren't coming? Well, well!" The doctor gazed

fixedly at Bobrov's face. "But, my dear friend, what's the matter with you? You're quite down in the mouth." He was now speaking with earnest sympathy. "Say what you like, I won't leave you alone. Come along, don't let's argue any more."

"I feel shabby, doctor, I feel terrible," said Bobrov softly as he mechanically followed Goldberg who was pulling him away.

"Nonsense, come along! Be a man, snap your fingers at the whole thing. 'Would your heart be aching sorely, or your conscience put to test?' " he recited, putting his arm round Bobrov in a strong friendly embrace and looking affectionately into his eyes. "I'm going to prescribe a universal remedy: 'Lets have a drink, friend Vanya, to warm our hearts!' To tell you the truth, I've had a fair load of cognac with that man Andréas. How he drinks, that son of a gun! Come, be a man. You know, Andréas is very much interested in you. Come on!"

As he spoke the doctor dragged Bobrov into the pavilion. They sat down side by side. Bobrov's other table companion turned out to be Andréas.

He had been smiling at Bobrov from some way off; now he made room for him to sit down and patted his back affectionately.

"Very glad to have you here with us," he said in a friendly voice. "You're a nice chap—the sort of man I like. Cognac?"

He was drunk. His glassy eyes shone with a strange light in his pale face. Not until six months later was it discovered that every evening this irreproachably reserved, hard-working, gifted man drank himself unconscious in complete solitude.

"I might really feel better if I had a drink," Bobrov thought. "I must try, damn it!"

Andréas was waiting, holding the bottle tilted and ready. Bobrov put up a tumbler.

"Want to use that?" asked Andréas, raising his eyebrows.

"Yes," replied Bobrov, with a meek, melancholy smile.

"Good! Say when."

"The glass'll say."

"Splendid. One might think you'd served in the Swedish Navy. Enough?"

"Keep pouring."

"But, my friend, don't forget this is Martel of the VSOP brand—real, strong old cognac."

"Keep pouring—don't worry."

"Well, suppose I do get soaked," he said to himself with malice. "Let her see it."

The glass was full. Andréas put down the bottle and curiously watched Bobrov who gulped down the liquor at a draught, and shuddered.

"Is anything eating you, my child?" asked Andréas, looking earnestly into Bobrov's eyes.

"Yes." Bobrov shook his head dolefully.

"Gnawing at your heart?"

"Yes."

"Humph! Then you'll want more."

"Fill it," said Bobrov, sadly submissive.

He guzzled cognac with disgust, trying hard to dull his pain. But, strangely enough, the liquor had not the least effect on him. In fact, he felt sadder as he drank, and tears burned his eyes more than ever.

Meanwhile the waiters passed champagne round. Kvashnin rose from his seat, holding his glass with two fingers and peering through it at the light of the high candelabrum. A hush fell. All that could be heard was the hissing of the arc lamps and the tireless chirring of a grasshopper.

Kvashnin cleared his throat.

"Ladies and gentlemen!" he began, and paused impressively. "I believe none of you will doubt the heartfelt gratitude with which I drink this toast. I shall never forget the warm welcome I have been given at Ivankovo, and I'll always recall tonight's little picnic with especial pleasure, thanks to the charming kindness of the ladies who attended it. To your health, *mesdames!*"

He raised his glass higher, discribed a sweeping semi-circle with it, and took a sip.

"It's to you, my associates and colleagues, that I address myself now," he went on. "Don't censure me if what I'm going to say sounds like a lecture; I'm an old man compared with most of you here, and old men must be allowed to lecture."

Andréas bent to Bobrov's ear.

"Look at the faces that rascal Svezhevsky's making," he whispered.

Svezhevsky was trying to express the most servile and profound attention, and when Kvashnin mentioned his age he protested with both his hands and his head.

"I must repeat an old, battered expression used in editorials," Kvashnin continued. "Let us hold our banner aloft. Don't let us forget that we're the salt of the earth, that the future belongs to us. Haven't we criss-crossed the globe with railways? Don't we lay open the bowels of the earth and transform its treasures into guns, bridges, locomotives, rails, and huge machines? Don't we, by applying our genius to almost incredible enterprises, set thousands of millions of capital in motion? You should know, ladies and gentlemen, that wise Nature bends her creative energies to bring a whole nation into being for the sole purpose of moulding from it two or three dozen of the elect. So have the courage and strength to be the elect, ladies and gentlemen! Hurrah!"

"Hurrah!" the picnickers shouted, Svezhevsky's voice ringing loudest of all.

They all rose and walked over to Kvashnin to clink glasses with him.

"An infamous toast," said the doctor under his breath.

The next to speak was Shelkovnikov.

"Ladies and gentlemen!" he shouted. "To the health of our esteemed patron, our beloved preceptor, and at the moment our host, Vasily Terentyevich Kvashnin! Hurrah!"

"Hurra-a-ah!" the picnickers shouted in unison, and once more they went to Kvashnin to clink glasses with him.

An orgy of oratory ensued. Toasts were offered to the success of the enterprise, to the absent shareholders, to the ladies attending the picnic, and to ladies in general. Some of the toasts sounded ambiguous and playfully indecent.

The champagne, consumed by the dozen bottles, was telling already; the buzz of voices filled the pavilion, and each speaker had to bang for a long time with a knife on a glass before he could begin his toast. On a small table set apart, handsome Miller was making hot punch in a large silver bowl. Suddenly Kvashnin rose again; a sly smile played on his face.

"I'm very happy to say, ladies and gentlemen, that tonight's celebration coincides with a family event," he said with charming courtesy. "Let us congratulate and give our best wishes to a betrothed couple—let us drink to the health of Nina Grigoryevna Zinenko and—" he faltered because he had forgotten Svezhevsky's name and patronymic "and our associate, Mr. Svezhevsky."

The shouts which greeted Kvashnin's words were all the louder as the news was completely unexpected. Andréas, who had heard beside him an exclamation that sounded rather like a painful groan, turned to look at Bobrov, and saw that his pale face was distorted with suffering.

"You don't know the whole story, my dear colleague," he whispered. "Just listen to the nice speech I'm going to make."

He rose with confidence, overturning his chair and spilling half his wine.

"Ladies and gentlemen!" he cried. "Our highly esteemed host didn't finish his toast out of a magnanimous discretion that is easy to understand. We must congratulate our dear associate, Mr. Svezhevsky, on his promotion: beginning with next month, he will assume the high office of business manager of the company's Board of Directors. The appointment is to be a sort of wedding present to the young couple from the highly esteemed Vasily Terentyevich. I see a look of displeasure on the face of our venerable patron. I must have inadvertently given away a surprise he held in store, and so I offer my apologies. Still, prompted by friendship and respect, I cannot but express the hope that our dear associate, Mr. Svezhevsky, may at his new post in Petersburg continue to be as energetic a worker and as beloved a comrade as he is here. But I know, ladies and gentlemen, that none of you will envy him"—he paused to glance ironically at Svezhevsky—"because we all wish him good luck so earnestly that—"

His toast was interrupted by a clatter of hooves. A hatless rider on a lathered horse dashed out of the thicket, his face frozen into a ghastly mask of horror. He was one of the foremen working under the contractor Dekhterev. He left his mount, which was trembling with exhaustion, in the middle of the clearing, ran over to Kvashnin, and began to whisper in his ear, bending familiarly over him. A deathly silence fell in the pavilion, except for the hissing lights and the grasshopper chirring importunately.

Kvashnin's wine-shot face went pale. Nervously he put down the glass he held in his hand, spilling the wine on the table-cloth.

"What about the Belgians?" he asked hoarsely.

The foreman shook his head and began once more to whisper in Kvashnin's ear.

"Damn it!" Kvashnin exclaimed, rising from his seat and crumpling his napkin. "What a mess! Wait, you'll take a telegram to the governor this very moment. Ladies and gentlemen," he said in a loud, shaking voice, "there is rioting at the mill. Something must be done about it and —I think we all had better break up at once."

"I knew it was coming," said Andréas contemptuously, with a calm anger.

And while everyone started up in a flurry, he slowly took a fresh cigar, felt in his pocket for the match-box, and filled his glass with cognac.

XI

There began a flustered, crazy bustle. Everyone got up and started to scurry about the pavilion, pushing, shouting, stumbling over fallen chairs. The ladies with trembling hands were hastily putting on their hats. To make things worse, someone had ordered the electric lights to be switched off. Hysterical women's cries rang out in the darkness.

It was about five o'clock. The sun had not yet risen, but the sky had brightened visibly, its grey, monotonous hue heralding a rainy day. In the dismal twilight of daybreak, which had so unexpectedly succeeded the brightness of electricity, the general confusion seemed still more terrible and depressing, almost unreal. The human figures looked like ghosts from a weird, nightmarish fairy-tale. The faces, crumpled after a sleepless night, were horrible. The supper table, stained with wine and littered with plates, glasses, bottles, suggested some monstrous feast broken off all of a sudden.

The hurry-scurry round the carriages was even uglier; frightened horses snorted and reared, starting away from the bridle; wheels caught in wheels, and axles snapped;

engineers called their drivers who were wrangling furiously among themselves. The general effect was that of the dazing havoc wrought by a big night fire. There was a scream—someone had been run over, or perhaps crushed to death.

Bobrov could not find Mitrofan. Once or twice he thought he heard his driver calling back to him from the thick of the tangle of vehicles. But it was quite impossible to get there, for the jam grew worse every moment.

Suddenly a huge paraffin torch flared up in the darkness, high above the crowd. There were shouts of "Out of the way! Stand back, ladies and gentlemen! Out of the way!" An irresistible human wave, driven by an impetuous pressure, swept Bobrov away, almost knocking him down, and wedged him between the rear of one cab and the pole of another. From there he saw a wide roadway form quickly between the vehicles, and saw Kvashnin drive along it in his troika. The flame of the torch wavering above the troika cast a lurid, blood-red light on Kvashnin's bulky figure.

Mad with pain, fear, and fury, and crushed on all sides, the crowd was howling round the troika. Bobrov felt his temples throb. For an instant it seemed to him that the rider was not Kvashnin, but some blood-stained, monstrous and terrible deity like those Oriental idols under whose carriages fanatics, wild with ecstàsy, would fling themselves during religious processions. And he trembled with impotent rage.

After Kvashnin drove past, the crush diminished somewhat, and, turning, Bobrov saw that the pole butting into his back was that of his own phaeton. Mitrofan stood by the box, kindling a torch.

"Quick, to the mill, Mitrofan!" he shouted, climbing in. "We've got to be there in ten minutes, d'you hear?"

"Yes, sir," replied Mitrofan sullenly.

He walked round the phaeton in order to get on to the box from the right, as befitted a respectable driver, and picked up the reins.

"Only don't blame me if we kill the horses, master," he added, half-turning.

"Oh, I don't care!"

Cautiously and with great difficulty, Mitrofan wound his way out of the huddle of horses and carriages. Reaching the narrow forest road, he gave the restive horses a free rein; they pulled hard, and a headlong race began. The phaeton bounced on the long roots stretching across the bumpy road, and careened to left and right, so that both driver and passenger had to balance themselves.

The red flame of the torch was tossing and roaring, and the long, grotesque shadows of trees were tossing round the phaeton with it. It seemed as if a crowd of tall, thin, blurred ghosts were rushing along beside the phaeton in a ludicrous dance. Sometimes the ghosts would overtake the horses, growing to colossal sizes as they did so, and then drop on the ground and, shrinking rapidly as the phaeton rushed on, vanish in the dark behind Bobrov; then they would dart into the thicket for a few seconds, only to jump back into view hard by the phaeton, or they would run together in serried ranks, swaying and starting, as if whispering among themselves. Several times the boughs of the dense brushwood fringing the road reached out like thin hands to lash Mitrofan and Bobrov across the face.

They drove out of the forest. The horses splashed across a puddle, in which the crimson flame of the torch jumped and broke into furrows, and suddenly they pulled the phaeton at a smart gallop to the top of a steep hillock. A black, dreary field spread out ahead.

"Hurry, Mitrofan, or we'll never make it!" cried Bobrov impatiently, although the phaeton was racing on at breakneck speed. Mitrofan grumbled in his booming voice and lashed Fairway who was galloping alongside. The driver wondered what had come over his master who was so fond of his horses and had always spared them.

On the horizon, the glow of a tremendous fire cast its wavering reflection on the clouds trailing across the sky. As Bobrov looked up at the flashing sky, a triumphant feeling of malicious joy stirred in his heart. Andréas' insolent, cruel toast had at once opened his eyes to the cause of Nina's cold reserve throughout the evening, her mother's indignation during the mazurka, and Svezhevsky's intimacy with Kvashnin; he recalled all the rumours and gossip he had heard at the mill about Kvashnin courting Nina. "Serves him right, the red-headed monster," he whispered, seething with hatred and so deeply humiliated that his mouth felt dry. "If only I could meet him face to face now I'd spoil his smugness for him, the filthy old buyer of young flesh, the dirty, fat bag crammed with gold. I'd leave a nice stamp on his copper forehead!"

All that he had drunk had failed to intoxicate him, but it had brought about an extraordinary surge of energy, an impatient and morbid lust for action. He was shivering violently, his teeth were chattering, his brain was working rapidly and chaotically as in a fever. He unwittingly talked aloud, groaned, or laughed jeerkily while his fists clenched of themselves.

"You must be ill, master. Hadn't we better go home?" Mitrofan said timidly.

Bobrov flew into a rage.

"Shut up, you fool!" he cried hoarsely. "Drive on!"

Before long they saw from a hilltop the whole mill wrapped in a milky-pink smoke. The timber storage grounds beyond it were blazing like an enormous bonfire. A multitude of small black human figures were scurrying about against the bright background of the fire. You could hear from afar the dry timber crackling in the flames. The round towers of the hot-blast stoves and blast-furnaces would stand out vividly for a moment and then merge with the dark again. The red glow of the fire cast a terrible shine on the brown water of the big square pond. The high dam of the pond was completely covered by the black mass of a huge crowd that seemed to be seething as it moved slowly forward. And a strange roar, vague and sinister, as of a distant sea, came from the formidable human mass compressed in that narrow space.

"Where the hell are you driving, you fathead! Can't you see the people, you son of a bitch?" The shout came from the road ahead; the next moment a tall bearded man appeared on the road, as if he had darted up from under the horses' hooves; his hatless head was bandaged all over with white rags.

"Drive on, Mitrofan!" cried Bobrov.

"They've set fire to it, master," he heard Mitrofan's trembling voice.

The next instant came the whistling of a rock hurled from behind, and Bobrov felt a sharp pain a little above his right temple. He touched it, and as he took his hand away it was sticky with warm blood.

The phaeton sped on. The glow grew brighter. The horses' long shadows ran from one side of the road to the other. At times it seemed to Bobrov as if he were racing down a steep slope and about to hurtle into a precipice, phaeton and all. He had lost all ability to take his bearings and could not recognize the places they passed. Suddenly the horses stood still.

"Well, Mitrofan, why did you stop?" he cried irritably.

"How can I drive on with people ahead?" Mitrofan retorted with sullen anger.

Hard as he peered into the grey twilight of early dawn, Bobrov could see nothing but a black uneven wall, with the sky flaming above it.

"What people are you talking about, damn you?" Bobrov got down and walked round the horses, which were white with lather.

As soon as he had walked a few paces from the horses he realized that what he had taken for a black wall was a large, dense crowd of workmen that had flooded the road and was moving slowly on in silence. Bobrov walked mechanically some fifty paces behind the workmen and then turned back to find Mitrofan and get to the mill by some other way. But Mitrofan and the horses were gone. Bobrov could not make out whether Mitrofan had driven off to look for him or he himself had wandered away. He started to call the driver, but got no response. Then he decided to catch up with the workmen he had just left, and he ran back in what he thought was the same direction. But, strangely enough, the workmen seemed to have vanished into thin air, and instead of them Bobrov bumped into a low wooden fence.

There was no end to that fence either on the right or on the left. Bobrov clambered over it and began to walk up a long, steep hill overgrown with dense, tall weeds. Cold sweat was streaming down his face, and his tongue felt as dry and stiff as a piece of wood; each breath of air he drew caused a sharp pain in his chest; the blood was throbbing violently against the top of his head; his bruised temple hurt unbearably.

The ascent seemed endless, and he was gripped with dull despair. Still he climbed on, falling down again and again, bruising his knees and clutching at prickly shrubs. Sometimes he fancied he was in one of his feverish, morbid dreams. The panic, the long wandering on the road, the endless climb—they were all as painful and absurd, as unexpected and terrible, as those nightmares of his.

At last the acclivity ended, and Bobrov knew at once it was the railway embankment. From up there the photographer had taken pictures of the group of engineers and workmen during the religious service the day before. He sat down on a sleeper, completely exhausted, and the next instant something strange happened to him: his feet became painfully weak, he felt a sickening, painful irritation in his chest and abdomen, and his forehead and cheeks went cold. Then everything turned before his eyes and rushed away somewhere, into unfathomable depths.

He came to in half an hour or so. There was an unusual, frightful stillness below, at the foot of the embankment, where the giant mill had been working day and night with an unceasing din. He scrambled to his feet and walked towards the blast-furnaces. His head felt so heavy that he could hardly hold it up; his injured temple caused him a frightful pain at every step. Touching the wound, he again felt the warm stickiness of blood on his fingers. There was blood also on his lips and in his mouth: he could taste its salty, metallic flavour. He had not yet recovered full consciousness, and the effort to recall and grasp the meaning of what had happened caused him a terrible headache. His soul was brimming over with a deep sadness and a desperate, pointless anger.

Morning was visibly near. Everything was grey, cold, and moist—the earth, the sky, the meagre yellow grass, the shapeless heaps of stone piled up on either side of the road. Bobrov was roaming aimlessly among the deserted buildings of the mill, talking aloud to himself as people sometimes do after a severe mental shock. He was trying to pull together his straggling thoughts and bring some order into them.

"Well, tell me, please, what I am to do. Tell me for God's sake," he whispered passionately to some *outsider* who seemed to be lurking in him. "Oh, how hard it is! How painful! How unbearably painful! I think I'll kill myself. I can't stand this torture."

But the *outsider* replied from the depths of his soul, speaking *aloud* too, and with rude mockery, "Oh, no, you won't kill yourself. Why pretend? You're much too fond of living to kill yourself. You're too feeble in spirit to do that. You're too much afraid of physical pain. You reflect too much."

"So what am I to do? What?" Bobrov whispered again, wringing his hands. "She's so delicate, so pure—my Nina! She was the only one I had on earth. And all of a sudden—oh, how revolting!—to sell her youth, her virgin body!"

"Stop posing. What's the good of those pompous words from old melodramas?" said *the other* ironically. "If you hate Kvashnin so much, go and kill him."

"I will!" Bobrov shrieked, stopping and thrusting up his fists in fury. "I will! Let him no longer infect honest people with his foul breath! I'll kill him!"

But *the other* remarked with venomous mockery, "No, you won't. You know very well you won't. You lack both the resolve and the strength to do it. By tomorrow you'll be reasonable and weak again."

There were lucid moments in this dreadful state of internal crisis, moments when Bobrov wondered what was wrong with him, and how he had come to be where he was, and what he was to do. And he *had* to do something—something big and important—but he forgot what, and grimaced with pain as he tried to remember. During one of those lucid moments he found himself standing on the edge of the stokers' pit. He at once recalled with extraordinary vividness his recent conversation with the doctor on that very spot.

There was not a single stoker below; they were all gone. The boilers had long been cold. Only in the two furnaces on the extreme right and left was the coal still smouldering with a faint glow. A crazy idea flashed across Bobrov's mind. He squatted, then lowered his feet into the pit, propping himself on his hands, and jumped down.

A shovel stuck out of a heap of coal. He grabbed it and started hurriedly to feed coal into both stokeholes. A minute or two later white flames were roaring in the furnaces, and the water was gurgling in the boiler. Bobrov went on feeding shovelful after shovelful of coal; as he did so he smiled slyly, nodding at someone invisible, and giving senseless exclamations. The morbid, terrible idea of vengeance, which had occured to him on the road, was tightening its grip on his mind. As he looked at the huge humming body of the boiler lit by fiery flashes, it seemed to him more and more alive and hateful.

No one stood in his way. The water was dwindling fast in the gauge. The gurgle in the boiler and the roar in the furnaces were growing more and more powerful and menacing.

But the unwonted toil soon wore out Bobrov. The veins in his temples were pulsating at a feverish speed, and the blood trickled down his cheek. The access of wild energy was spent, and the *outsider* in him was saying in a loud, mocking voice:

"Well it needs only one more move to make! But you won't make it. No, you won't. Why, the whole thing is so ridiculous that tomorrow you won't dare to confess having wanted to blow up the steam boilers."

* * *

The sun—a large blur—had risen above the horizon when Bobrov walked into the mill hospital.

Dr. Goldberg had a moment ago stopped dressing the wounds of injured and maimed people and was washing his hands over a brass wash-stand. His assistant stood beside him, holding a towel ready. On seeing Bobrov the doctor started.

"What's the matter with you, Andrei Ilyich? You're a terrible sight," he said, frightened.

Bobrov did look ghastly. The gore showed in black spots on his pale face, smudged with coal dust. His wet clothes hung in shreds from his arms and knees, his tousled hair fell over his forehead.

"Speak up, man, for God's sake! What happened?" said Dr. Goldberg, wiping his hands hastily and walking up to Bobrov.

"Oh, it's nothing at all," groaned Bobrov. "For goodness' sake, give me some morphia, doctor. Some morphia, quick, or I'll go mad! I'm suffering terribly!"

Dr. Goldberg took Bobrov by the arm, hurriedly led him away into another room, and carefully shut the door behind him.

"Listen," he said, "I can guess what's tormenting you. Believe me, I'm very sorry for you, and I'm willing to help you. But, my dear man"—his voice sounded tearful —"my dear Andrei Ilyich, couldn't you do without it somehow? Just remember what an effort it cost you to get over that nasty habit! It'll be awful if I give you an injection now: you'll never—do you understand?—you'll never be able to give it up again."

Bobrov slumped face downwards on the broad oilskin-draped sofa.

"I don't care," he muttered through clenched teeth, shivering from head to foot. "I don't give a damn, doctor. I can't bear it any more."

Dr. Goldberg sighed, shrugged his shoulders, and took a syringe out of a medicine chest. Five minutes later Bobrov was sound asleep on the sofa. A happy smile played on his pale face, grown emaciated overnight. Dr. Goldberg was carefully washing the wound on the sleeper's head.

1896

OLESYA

1

Yarmola the woodman—my servant, cook, and hunting companion—came into the room, bending under a bundle of wood, crashed it down on the floor, and breathed upon his frozen fingers to warm them up.

"Some wind outside, master," he said, squatting in front of the stove-door. "I must heat the stove well. May I use your lighter?"

"So we shan't go hare-shooting tomorrow, eh? What do you think, Yarmola?"

"No chance of that—hear how it goes on? The hare are lying low now. You won't see a single track tomorrow."

I chanced to spend six long months in Perebrod, a little God-forsaken village in the Volhynian borderland of Polesye, where game-shooting was my sole occupation and pastime. To be frank, I did not imagine, when I was offered to go to the country, that it would be so unbearably dull. Indeed, I was quite pleased to go. "Polesye, an out-of-the-way corner—nature at its best—simple manners—primitive characters," I said to myself on the train. "People I know absolutely nothing about, with strange customs and peculiar speech—and a wealth of poetic legends and traditions and songs, no doubt." You see (having started I might as well go all the way), by then I had had a short story published in a small newspaper, describing two murders and a suicide, and I knew at least in theory that a writer should study customs.

However, either because the Perebrod peasants were distinguished by a special, obstinate sort of unsociability, or because I did not know how to go about it, my relations with them never went beyond the fact that, on see·ing me from a distance, they would take off their caps and, as they came alongside, would mutter sullenly "Speedjue," which was supposed to mean "God speed you." And when I attempted to get into conversation with them they would stare at me in surprise, refusing to understand the simplest questions I asked and trying again and again to kiss my hands, an old custom dating from the time of Polish serfdom.

Before long I had read the few books I had with me. Out of boredom I tried—though at first the idea did not appeal to me—to make the acquaintance of the local intellectuals, to wit: a Polish priest living ten miles from my place, the organist assigned to him, the local *uryad-nik*,* and a clerk of the neighbouring estate, a retired non-commissioned officer; but nothing came of it.

Then I had a go at doctoring the Perebrod people. I had at my disposal castor oil, carbolic acid, boric acid, and iodine. But, apart from the scantiness of my knowledge, I was handicapped by the complete impossibility

* Rural police-officer.—*Tr*

of making any diagnosis, for my patients all had one and the same complaint: "It hurts inside" and "I can't eat or drink."

Along comes, say, an old woman. Embarrassed, she wipes her nose with her right forefinger, takes a couple of eggs from her bosom—I catch a glimpse of her brown skin—and puts them on my desk. Then she tries to get hold of my hands in order to stamp a kiss upon them. I pull them back and admonish her, "Stop it, Grandmother, don't! I'm not a priest, that sort of thing isn't for me. What's ailing you?"

"It hurts inside, master, right inside me—I can't eat or drink."

"When did that come?"

"How should I know?" she asks me in her turn. "It burns and burns. I can't eat or drink."

And no matter how hard I try I fail to bring out any more specific symptoms of her illness.

"Don't you bother," the retired non-com. suggested one day, "they'll get over it by themselves. Like dogs do. You know, I only use one medicine—sal-ammoniac. A muzhik comes along. 'What d'you want?' I ask him. 'I'm ill,' he says. So I poke up a bottle of ammonia to his nose. 'Smell this!' says I. And smell he does. 'Smell some more—harder!' I says. He smells again. 'Feeling better?' I says. 'A bit better, I s'pose,' he says. 'Well, run along in peace,' says I."

Besides, that hand-kissing revolted me—some of my patients even threw themselves at my feet and tried to osculate my boots. What urged them to do so was not an impulse of a grateful heart but a fulsome habit inculcated by centuries of slavery and violence. I looked with sheer amazement on the retired non-com. and the *uryadnik*, who thrust their huge red paws into the villagers' lips with unruffled gravity.

I was left no choice but game-shooting. But late in January the weather grew so bad as to make even that impossible. A violent wind blew every day, and during the night a hard, icy crust would form on the snow, over which the hare would scamper without leaving any tracks. Shut in and listening to the howling wind, I was bored to death. And that is why I took up so eagerly the innocent pastime of teaching Yarmola to read and write.

It began in rather an unusual way. One day as I was writing a letter I felt that there was someone standing behind me. I turned and saw Yarmola, who had walked up, noiselessly as always, in his soft bast shoes.

"What is it, Yarmola?" I asked.

"Oh, I'm just looking. I wish I could write like you do. No, no, I didn't mean like you," he hastened to explain in abashment as he saw me smile. "I meant just my name."

"What for?" I asked in surprise. I ought to note here that Yarmola was considered the poorest and laziest peasant in all Perebrod; he spent his woodman's wages and whatever his crops brought him on drink; his team of oxen was the worst in the neighbourhood. It seemed to me that *he* could have no need for literacy. Doubtfully I asked him again, "What do you want to know how to write your name for?"

"You see, master,' he replied, in an exceedingly bland tone, "nobody in this village can read or write. When it comes to signing some paper, or seeing to some business in the *volost*,* there's nobody can do it. The elder sets the seal, but he doesn't know what the paper says. So it would be lucky for everybody if someone could sign his name."

Yarmola was a notorious poacher, a happy-go-lucky tramp whose opinion the villagers would never have

* Here. a rural district seat —*Tr.*

thought of taking into account; yet somehow his solicitude for the public weal of his native village moved me. I offered to give him lessons. But what a hard job it was trying to teach him to read and write! He knew every path in his forest, with nearly every tree in it, he knew his way about anywhere by day or night, and could tell by their tracks all the wolves and hares and foxes in the neighbourhood; but he could not for the life of him understand why *m* and *a*, for example, make up *ma*. He would sit for ten minutes or more brooding painfully over a problem like that, with the greatest mental strain showing in his deep-set black eyes and his dark lean face, smothered in the coarse black beard and large moustache.

"Come on, Yarmola—say *ma*. Just say *ma*," I would urge him. "Don't stare at the paper, look at me—that's it. Now say *ma*."

Yarmola would draw a deep sigh, put the pointer on the table, and say with sad determination, "No, I can't."

"But why not? It's so easy. Simply say *ma* as I do."

"No, I can't, master. I forget."

Every method, every comparison was defeated by his monstrous dullness. But his thirst for enlightenment did not diminish.

"If only I could sign my name!" he would coax me. "I ask no more. Just my name—Yarmola Popruzhuk—and nothing else."

I finally gave up the idea of teaching him to read and write intelligently, and began to teach him to sign mechanically. To my great surprise the new method proved easier for him, so that by the end of the second month he had almost taken the hurdle of writing his surname. As to his first name, we decided to leave it out altogether to lighten his task.

In the evenings, when he had finished heating the stoves, Yarmola would wait impatiently for me to call him.

"Well, Yarmola, let's study," I would say.

He would sidle up to the table, prop his elbows on it, push the pen between his black, stiff, horny fingers, and ask me with raised eyebrows, "Shall I start?"

"Yes."

He would trace the first letter, P—we called it "a stick with a loop"—rather confidently, then look up, a question on his face.

"Why did you stop? Have you forgotten?"

"Yes." He would shake his head in vexation.

"What a queer one you are! All right put down a wheel."

"That's it—a wheel! Now I know!" He would brighten and carefully draw a figure very much like the Caspian Sea in outline. Then he would admire his work for a while in silence, cocking his head to the left, then again to the right, and screwing up his eyes.

"What's the matter? Go on."

"Wait a bit, master, wait just a moment."

We would ponder for two minutes or so, and then ask timidly, "It's like the first one, ain't it?"

"Yes. Come on."

In this manner we gradually made our way to K, the last letter, which we described as "a stick with a crook and a tail."

"You know, master." he said sometimes, looking with proud, loving eyes at his finished job, "if I studied another five or six months I'd be pretty good at it. What do you say?"

II

Yarmola squatted in front of the stove, stirring the charcoal inside, while I walked up and down in my room. Of the twelve rooms of the big landlord's mansion, I occupied only one, the former "sofa room." The other rooms were locked, and mould gathered on the antique furni-

ture upholstered with damask, the outlandish bronze fix-
tures, and the eighteenth-century portraits.

Outside the mansion, the wind was raging like a shivering old devil, its roar punctuated by groans, screams,
and wild laughter. Towards nightfall the snowstorm grew
worse. Someone seemed to be hurling handfuls of fine,
dry snow against the panes. The nearby forest murmured
and hummed with an unceasing, hidden menace.

The wind would get into the empty rooms and drone
in chimneys, and then the old tumbledown house, shaky
and draughty, would suddenly come alive with strange
sounds, to which I listened in involuntary alarm. There
would be a sigh in the white hall—a deep, broken, mournful sigh. Then the rotten dry floor-boards would give way
and creak under someone's heavy footsteps. The next moment I would fancy that in the passage adjoining my
room someone was cautiously but doggedly pushing the
door-knob, and then he in a sudden fury would start to
race about the house, angrily shaking all the shutters and
doors, or crawling into the chimney and whining there
with a dull, never-ending plaint rising sometimes to a
pitiful scream and then dropping to a beast's snarl. At
times, coming from nowhere, the terrible visitor would
burst into my own room, rush suddenly down my spine
in a cold breath, and shake the flame of the lamp shining dimly under a green paper shade with a scorched top.

I was overcome by a strange, uncertain anxiety. "Here
I am," I thought, "sitting on a dark, stormy winter night
in a ramshackle house, in a village lost in woods and
snow-drifts, hundreds of miles from town life, society,
women's laughter, human conversation." And I had a
feeling that the stormy night would drag on for years
and decades, till my death, and the wind would roar
outside just as dismally, the lamp under the shabby green
shade would burn just as dimly, I would pace my room
just as uneasily, and the silent, brooding Yarmola would

squat in front of the stove in the same way, a strange being alien to me and indifferent to everything on earth: to the fact that his family had nothing to eat, to the raging wind, to my uncertain, corroding melancholy.

Suddenly I longed to have the oppressive silence broken by some semblance of a human voice, and so I asked, "Where do you think this horrible wind comes from, Yarmola?"

"The wind?" Yarmola looked up lazily. "Why, don't you know, master?"

"Of course not. How could I know such a thing?"

"Don't you, really?" Yarmola was roused. "I'll tell you," he went on, a shade mysteriously. "Either a witch has been born, or a wizard's making merry."

I pounced eagerly on this. "Who knows," I thought, "perhaps I may worm out of him some interesting story of magic, hidden treasures, or werewolves."

"Have you got any witches here in Polesye?" I asked.

"I don't know. There might be," he replied with his former indifference, and bent over the stove-door again. "Old folk say there were some once. But perhaps that ain't true."

I was disappointed. I knew how stubbornly untalkative Yarmola was, and I lost all hope of drawing anything else out of him on that interesting subject. To my surprise, however, he suddenly began to speak with his lazy carelessness, as if he were talking to the roaring stove and not to me.

"We had a witch here about five years ago. But the lads drove her away."

"Where to?"

"Why, to the forest, of course. Where else? And they pulled down her house, they did, so that not a chip would be left of her accursed nest. They took her beyond the cherry orchards and kicked her out."

"But why did they treat her like that?"

"She did a lot of harm: she quarrelled with everybody, cast evil spells on houses, plaited the stalks in the sheaves. Once she asked a young wife for a *zloty*.* The young woman says, 'I haven't got one, lay off.' 'All right,' says the witch, 'some day you'll be sorry you refused me a *zloty*.' And what do you think happened, master? The woman's baby fell ill just after that. It was ill for a long time, and then it died altogether. That was when the lads kicked out the witch, blast her eyes!"

"And where is the witch now?" I went on to ask.

"The witch?" he echoed slowly, as he was wont to. "How should I know?"

"Did she leave no kin here?"

"No, she didn't. She was a stranger—a *Katsap*,** or a Gypsy. I was a boy when she came. She had a little lass with her: her daughter or granddaughter. The lads drove both of them away."

"Does nobody go to her any longer—to have his fortune told or ask for some potion?"

"The womenfolk do," he drawled contemptuously.

"Oh, so they know where she lives?"

"I don't know. People say she lives somewhere near Devil's Nook. You know that marsh beyond Irinovo Road? That's where she's living, the accursed hag!"

The news of a witch only a few miles away—a real, live Polesye witch—thrilled and excited me.

"I say, Yarmola, how could I meet her—the witch, I mean?" I asked.

"Bah!" He spat out indignantly. "A fine acquaintance she'd make."

"I mean to see her, fine or not. I'll go to her place as soon as it gets a bit warmer. You'll show me the way, won't you?"

* Fifteen kopeks.—*Tr*.
** A Ukrainian nickname for a Russian.—*Tr*

Yarmola was so struck by my last words that he jumped to his feet.

"Me?" he cried indignantly. "Not for all the gold! I won't go, no matter what."

"Nonsense—of course you will."

"No, master, I won't, not for the world. Me go?" he cried again, overcome by a fresh access of anger, "Me go to a witch's nest? God forbid! And I wouldn't advise you to go either, master."

"As you like, but I'll go just the same. I'm very curious to take a look at her."

"There's nothing curious about it," Yarmola grumbled, shutting the stove-door with an angry bang.

An hour later, when Yarmola had had his tea in the dark passage and was about to go home, I asked, "What's the witch's name?"

"Manuilikha," he replied gruffly.

Although he never showed it I had a feeling that he had become strongly attached to me. That was due to our common passion for game-shooting, to my simple manner towards him, to the help which I gave to his eternally starving family once in a while, but above all to the fact that I was the only person who never censured him for his addiction to drink, something which he hated. That was why my determination to meet the witch put him in an exceedingly bad temper, which he indicated by sniffing hard, and by giving his dog Ryabchik a vicious kick in the ribs when he walked out on to the porch. Ryabchik gave a blood-curdling screech and darted aside, but then immediately ran whimpering after Yarmola.

III

About three days later it grew warmer. One morning Yarmola came into my room very early.

"I'd better clean the guns, master," he said casually.

"What's up?" I asked, stretching myself under the sheets.

"The hare have run about last night—there's a lot of tracks. Shall we have a go at them?"

Yarmola was plainly eager to go to the woods but he tried to hide his hunter's longing by a show of indifference. In fact, his carbine was standing already in the hall, a carbine that had never missed a single snipe, although it was adorned with several tin patches round the lock where rust and powder gases had eaten through the metal.

We had scarcely walked into the forest when we came on a hare track: two footprints side by side, and another two behind, following each other. The hare had come out on to the road, run a few hundred yards along it, and then taken a tremendous leap into a clump of young pine-trees.

"We'll now close in on it," said Yarmola. "It'll be lying doggo now. Master, you go—" he paused to decide by signs he alone knew which way to send me. "You go on to the old pot-house, and I'll come in from Zamlin. As soon as the dog starts it I'll halloo to you."

He disappeared at once, plunging into the dense shrubbery. I strained my ears, but not a sound betrayed his poacher's movement, not a twig snapped under his feet.

I sauntered to the old pot-house, a deserted ramshackle hut, and halted on the fringe of the forest, under a tall tree with a straight bare trunk. It was still as it can be only in a forest on a windless winter day. The heavy lumps of snow weighing down the boughs gave them a wonderful, festive appearance. At times a twig broke off a tree-top, and I could very distinctly hear it strike the branches with a light crackle as it fell. The snow showed pink in the sun and blue in the shade. I was overwhelmed by the quiet magic of that solemn, cold silence, and I thought I could feel Time slipping noiselessly past me.

Suddenly Ryabchik's bark rang out far away in the thicket; it was the distinctive bark of a dog chasing game—a high-pitched, nervous sound close to yelping. Immediately afterwards I heard Yarmola's voice shouting fiercely to the dog, "*Oo-bee*! *Oo-bee*!" The first syllable came in a sharp, long-drawn-out falsetto, and the second in a jerky boom. I did not learn until much later that this hunter's call of Polesye was derived from *oobeevat*.*

Judging by the direction of the barking, I thought the dog must be chasing the hare on my left, and so I ran across the glade to intercept it. But I had not run more than twenty yards when a big grey hare darted out from behind a stump; as if in no hurry to escape, its long ears flat against its head, it crossed the road with a couple of long bounds and disappeared in the undergrowth. Ryabchik shot out on the hare's heels. As he saw me he wagged his tail slightly, snatched up a few mouthfuls of snow, and resumed the chase.

All of a sudden Yarmola glided out of the thicket.

"Why didn't you cut it off, master?" he shouted, and clicked his tongue reproachfully.

"But I was so far from it, a couple of hundred feet or more."

My obvious consternation softened him.

"Never mind. It won't get away. Go on to Irinovo Road—it'll come out there in no time."

I headed for the road, and about two minutes later I again heard the dog chasing the game not far from where I was. Gripped by a sportsman's excitement, I ran with my gun at the ready, breaking through the dense brushwood, and heedless of the cruel blows the twigs dealt me. I ran like that for a while, and I was almost out of breath when the dog stopped barking. I slackened my pace. I imagined that if I kept going straight ahead I was sure to meet Yarmola by Irinovo Road. Soon, however,

* To kill —*Tr*

I realized that while running and by-passing shrubs and stumps without a thought of direction I had lost my way. Then I hailed Yarmola. But he did not call back.

Mechanically I walked on. Little by little the forest thinned, and the ground grew marshy. My footprints on the snow darkened fast and filled with water. Several times I was bogged knee-deep. I had to jump from mound to mound; my feet sank in the brownish moss as in a soft rug.

Before long I came out of the brushwood. Ahead of me was a large, round snow-covered marsh with tussocks showing here and there. The white walls of a hut showed between the trees at the other end of the marsh. "It must be the Irinovo woodman's house," I thought. "I'd better walk over and ask my way."

But it was not so easy to reach the hut. Every moment I was bogged down afresh. My high boots were full of water and squelched loudly at every step; it became more and more difficult to drag them along.

At last I was across the marsh and I climbed up on a small hummock that gave me a good view of the hut. It was rather like a fairy-tale witch's hut. It stood high above the ground, being built on piles, probably because the Irinovo Woods were always flooded in spring. But, sagging with old age, it had a lame and mournful look A few window-panes were missing; they had been replaced by dirty rags bellying outwards.

I pushed the knob and opened the door. It was very dark inside; violet circles were floating before my eyes because I had been looking at the snow for a long time, and I was slow in making out whether anyone was in.

"Is anybody in, good people?" I asked aloud.

Something stirred near the stove. I crossed to it and saw an old woman sitting on the floor. A huge pile of chicken feathers rose in front of her. She picked up the feathers one by one, stripped them of the barbs, and put them down in a basket, throwing the shafts on the floor.

"Why, this must be Manuilikha, the Irinovo witch." The thought flashed upon me as soon as I had had a good look at the old woman. She was quite like a folklore Ba-ba-Yaga*: gaunt, hollow cheeks and a long, pointed chin which almost touched the great hooked nose; her sunken toothless mouth moved incessantly, as if chewing; her bulging eyes, once blue, were faded and cold, and with their short red eyelids looked like the eyes of a strange bird of ill omen.

"Good morning, Grandmother!" I said in as friendly a tone as I could muster. "Would you be Manuilikha by any chance?"

There was a rattling and wheezing in the old woman's chest; from her toothless, mumbling mouth came queer sounds like the croaking of a panting old crow, sounds that at times broke into a husky falsetto.

"Perhaps good people did call me Manuilikha once. But now I've got neither name nor fame. Just what do you want?" Her manner was unfriendly, and she did not stop her monotonous work.

"I've lost my way, Granny. Could I have some milk?"

"No milk here," she snapped. "Too many people like you passing here. Can't feed the whole lot."

"You aren't very hospitable, Granny, I must say."

"That's true, sir, I'm not. No meals served here. You may sit down if you're tired, I don't mind. You know the saying: 'Come and sit by our house and hear our church bells ringing, and as for dinner we'd rather come to you.' That's that."

These figures of speech at once convinced me that the old woman did not hail from those parts, where no one liked or appreciated the slashing language, seasoned with

* Witch —*Tr*

rare words, which the eloquent Northerner is so fond of using. Meanwhile the old woman mechanically continued her work, still muttering to herself something that became less and less audible. I could only catch occasional disconnected sentences: "That's Granny Manuilikha for you— But nobody knows who he is— I'm getting on in years now— Fidgeting and chirring and chattering like a regular magpie—"

I listened to her for a while, and suddenly the idea that sitting in front of me was a mad woman both scared and disgusted me.

Still I had a look round. Most of the space was taken up by a huge chipped stove. There were no icons in the front corner. Instead of the usual pictures of green-moustached hunters with violet dogs and the portraits of generals whom no one knew, the walls were hung with tufts of dried herbs, bunches of wrinkled roots, and kitchen ware. I could spy no owl or black cat, but two grave speckled starlings were staring down at me from the stove with an astonished and suspicious air.

"Can I at least have a drink of water, Granny?" I asked, raising my voice.

"There it is, in the bucket," she said.

The water tasted marshy. I thanked the old woman— she took not the slightest notice of it—and asked her how I could find my way to the road.

She raised her head, gazed fixedly at me with her cold bird's eyes, and muttered hurriedly, "Go on. Go your way, young man. You have no business here. A guest is welcome when bidden. Go, sir."

Indeed, I had no choice left but to go. But it occurred to me to make a last attempt to soften the stern old woman a little. I took a brand-new silver coin from my pocket and held it out to her. My guess proved right; at the sight of money her eyes opened wider, and she stretched out her crooked, knotty, trembling fingers to take the coin.

"Oh, no, Grandmother Manuilikha, you can't have it for nothing," I teased her, hiding the coin. "First tell me my fortune."

The witch's brown wrinkled face puckered into a scowl. She was apparently wavering while looking doubtfully at my fist closed upon the coin. But greed took the upper hand.

"All right, come along," she mumbled, rising from the floor with an effort. "I don't tell anybody's fortune nowadays, sonny. I've forgotten how to. I'm too old now, can't see anything. I'll do it just to please you."

Holding on to the wall, her bent form shaking at every step, she went up to the table, got out a pack of brown cards pulpy with long use, and shuffled them.

"Cut 'em with your left hand—the one close to your heart," she said, pushing the pack across to me.

She spat on her fingers and began to lay out the cards. The cards dropped on the table with a thud, as if they were made of dough, and formed an octagonal star. When the last card lay on a king face downwards, Manuilikha held out her palm.

"Cross it with silver, good sir. You'll be happy, you'll be rich," she whined in the cajoling manner of a begging Gypsy.

I slipped the coin into her palm. She hid it behind her cheek with apish alacrity.

"You'll gain a great deal through a long journey," she began in a habitual patter. "You'll meet a queen of diamonds, and you'll have a pleasant talk in an important house. Before long you'll get unexpected news from the king of clubs. It falls out that you'll have some trouble, then some little money. You'll be in a large company, you'll be drunk. Not that you'll be very drunk, but still there's a carouse in store for you. Yours will be a long life. If you don't die at sixty-seven—"

She paused, and raised her head, as if listening. I pricked up my ears. A woman's voice, fresh, vibrant and strong, was singing a song as it drew near the hut. I recognized the lyric of a melodious Ukrainian song:

> *Is it just a bough in bloom*
> *Bends the rose so red?*
> *Is it drowsiness that weighs,*
> *Weighs my weary head?*

"Now please go, sonny," Manuilikha said, fidgeting uneasily and pushing me away from the table. "You have no business hanging about strangers' homes. Go where you were going."

She even caught hold of my sleeve and started to pull me towards the door. There was a hunted look on her face.

Suddenly the song broke off close by the hut; the iron knob clicked, the door flew open, and a tall, laughing girl appeared in the doorway. With both her hands she was carefully holding up her striped apron, from which three tiny birds' heads stuck up, with red necks and black beady eyes.

"Look at these finches, Granny, they've been hanging on to me again," she cried, laughing heartily. "See how funny they are. They're starved. And I had no bread with me."

Then she saw me and stopped speaking at once, blushing deeply. Her black eyebrows gathered into a resentful frown, and she looked questioningly at Manuilikha.

"The gentleman here—he's asking his way," the old woman explained. "Well, sir," she added, turning to me with determination, "you've been wasting your time more'n enough. You had your drink of water and your bit of talk, now don't overstay your welcome. We're no company for you."

"Look here, my beauty," I said to the girl. "Won't you show me the way to Irinovo Road? I don't think I can ever get out of your marsh by myself."

She was apparently impressed by my gently pleading tone. Carefully she put down her finches beside the starlings, threw on the bench the coat she had taken off, and walked silently out.

I followed her.

"Are your birds tame?" I asked as I overtook her.

"Yes," she replied curtly, without glancing at me. "Well, look," she said, stopping by the wattle-fence. "See that path over there, between those pines?"

"Yes."

"Take it and go straight ahead. When you get to an oak log, turn left. Keep going right on through the forest. That'll bring you to Irinovo Road."

While she was pointing out the way with her outstretched right arm, I could not help admiring her beauty. She was in no way like the local wenches, who wore their kerchiefs in an ugly manner, covering their foreheads from above and their chins and mouths from below, and whose faces looked so monotonously frightened. The girl beside me, a tall brunette between twenty and twenty-five, had an easy, graceful bearing. A wide white blouse covered her young, shapely bosom. Once you had seen the unusual beauty of her face, you could never forget it; but it was difficult to describe that beauty even when you had got used to it. Its charm lay in those large, shining dark eyes, to which the eyebrows, fine and broken in the middle, gave an elusive quality of archness, imperiousness and naïveté, in her olive skin touched with pink, in the wilful curve of her lips.

"Aren't you afraid of living by yourselves in these wild parts?" I asked, halting by the fence.

She shrugged her shoulders indifferently.

"Why should we be? Wolves never come this way."

"I didn't mean only wolves. You might be snowed up, or a fire might break out. Lots of things might happen. You're all alone here, and nobody'd have a chance to help you."

"So much the better!" She made a scornful gesture. "If only they'd left Grandmother and me alone for good, but—"

"But what?"

"Too much knowledge makes the head bald, you know," she snapped. "And who would *you* be?" she asked uneasily.

I realized that both the old woman and the girl feared some sort of persecution from the authorities, and I hastened to reassure her.

"Please don't worry. I'm not an *uryadnik*, clerk, or exciseman—in short I've nothing to do with the authorities."

"You haven't?"

"I give you my word of honour. Believe me, I'm a total stranger here. I've come to stay for a few months and then I'll go back. I shan't tell anybody I was here and saw you, if you don't want me to. Do you trust me?"

Her face brightened a little.

"Well, if you aren't lying, you must be speaking the truth. But tell me, had you heard anything about us before, or did you drop in by chance?"

"I really don't know what to say. I did hear about you, I own, and I even meant to look in at your place some day, but today I got here by chance—lost my way. Now I'd like to know why you're afraid of people. What harm are they doing you?"

She scrutinized me with distrust. But I had a clear conscience, and I withstood her gaze without quailing. Then she spoke with mounting emotion.

"We're having a hard time because of them. Ordinary people are not so bad, but the officials— They always must have some gift—the *uryadnik* and the *stanovoi** and all the others. And that's not enough: they call Grandmother a 'witch,' a 'she-devil,' a 'jail-bird.' Oh, well, what's the use of talking about it!"

"Do they ever molest you?" The indiscreet question came before I knew it.

She tossed up her head with haughty assurance, and there was a flicker of malicious triumph in her narrowed eyes.

"No. Once a land surveyor had a try at me. He wanted to make love, see? Well, I'm sure he still remembers the love I gave him."

These ironical but peculiarly proud words rang with so much crude independence that I could not but think, "Yes, you can see she's grown up in a wild Polesye forest—it certainly isn't safe to trifle with her."

"*We* don't molest anybody, do we?" she went on, with increasing confidence in me. "Why, we don't even ask for company. I only go to town once a year to buy some soap and salt. And some tea for Granny—she loves it. I might as well see nobody at all, if it weren't for that."

"I see you and your Granny aren't exactly hospitable. But may *I* drop in for a moment some day?"

She laughed, and how strangely, how unexpectedly her beautiful face changed! Not a trace of the previous sternness was left on it: of a sudden it had become bright and bashful as a child's.

"But why should you? Granny and I are dull company. You may drop in, though, if you really are a good man. Only I'll tell you what: if you ever come our way, better leave your gun behind."

"Are you afraid?'

* District police commissioner.—*Tr.*

"What's there to be afraid of? I'm not afraid of any-thing." Again her voice rang with confidence in her own strength. "I just don't like the whole business. Why kill birds or, say, hares? They do nobody any harm, and they want to live as much as you and I do I love them—they're so small and silly. Well, I must say goodbye now," she added hastily. "Sorry, I don't know your name. I'm afraid Granny will scold me."

With a light, swift movement she ran back to the hut, her head bent and her hands holding her hair, tousled by the wind.

"Wait a minute!" I shouted. "What's your name? Let's introduce ourselves properly."

She stopped for a second and turned round.

"My name is Alyona. Here they call me Olesya."

I shouldered my gun and set out in the direction she had indicated. I climbed a hillock from which a narrow, hardly visible forest path started, and looked back. Olesya's red skirt, waving slightly in the wind, could still be seen on the steps, a bright spot set off by the even background of dazzling white snow.

Yarmola came home an hour after me. True to his habitual distaste for idle talk, he did not ask me a single question about how or where I had lost my way. He only said, as if casually, "I've got that hare, over in the kitch-en. Shall I roast it, or are you going to send it to some-body?"

"I'm sure you don't know where I've been today, Yar-mola," I said, anticipating surprise.

"Don't I?" he growled. "Called on the witches, of course."

"How did you find that out?"

"It was easy enough. You didn't answer my call, so I walked to your track. You shouldn't do things like that, master!" he added, with reproachful annoyance. "It's a sin!"

IV

That year spring came early and, as always happens in Polesye, with unexpected abruptness. Turbulent, glittering brown rivulets ran down the village streets, frothing angrily round the stones in their way and whirling chips and goose-down; enormous pools mirrored the blue sky with round white clouds that seemed to revolve as they sailed across it; tinkling drops of water fell in a rush from the roofs. The sparrows clustering on the roadside willows twittered so excitedly that they drowned all other sounds. Everywhere you could feel the joyous, hurried stir of rousing life.

The snow melted away, except in hollows and shaded copses, where it lingered in dirty, sponge-like patches. The thaw laid bare the warm, damp earth that had had a good winter's rest and was full of fresh sap, of a renewed craving for motherhood. A light vapour wreathed above the black fields, filling the air with the smell of thawed earth, that fresh, subtle, heady smell of spring which you distinguish among hundreds of other smells even in town. I felt as if a spring-time sadness, sweet and delicate, full of wistful expectations and vague hopes, flowed into my soul along with that fragrance—a poetical melancholy that makes every woman seem pretty and is always seasoned with uncertain regrets of past springs. The nights had become warmer, and Nature's invisible creative labour could be sensed going on hastily in the intense, humid darkness.

Olesya's image never left my mind in those spring days. When alone, I liked to lie down, shut my eyes for better concentration, and continuously call up in my imagination her face, now stern or arch, then beaming with a tender smile, her young body, which had grown up in the freedom of the old forest to be as slender and strong as a young fir-tree, her fresh voice with its unexpectedly low, velvety notes. "There is," I thought, "something noble—in the best meaning of that rather commonplace word—a sort of inborn, elegant moderation about every movement she makes, every word she speaks." What drew me to Olesya was also the halo of mystery that surrounded her, the superstitious fame of a witch living in the forest thicket, in the midst of a marsh, and particularly that proud confidence in her own strength which sounded in the few words she had spoken to me.

No wonder that as soon as the forest paths dried a little I set out for the witch's hut. In case I had to appease the querulous old woman, I took with me a half pound of tea and a few handfuls of lump sugar.

I found both women in. Manuilikha was fussing about the blazing stove, and Olesya was spinning flax, sitting on a very high bench. As I entered with a slight noise she turned round, the thread broke in her hands, and the spindle rolled over the floor.

The old woman eyed me for a while with angry attention, shielding her puckered face with her palm from the heat of the stove.

"Good day, Granny!" I said in a loud, cheerful voice. "I suppose you don't recognize me? Remember I looked in last month to ask my way? And you told my fortune, remember?"

"I don't remember anything, sir," she mumbled, shaking her head with displeasure, "I'm sure I don't. And I can't understand what you may want here. We're no company for you, are we? We're plain, ignorant people. You have no business with us. The woods are large enough—you can take your walks elsewhere, and that's that."

Flabbergasted by her ungracious welcome, I was at a loss, feeling silly and not knowing whether to take her rudeness as a joke, or flare up, or turn and go without saying a word. I turned helplessly to Olesya. She smiled slightly, with a touch of good-humoured mockery, rose from her spinning-wheel, and walked over to the old woman.

"Don't be afraid, Granny," she said in a conciliatory tone. "He's all right, he won't do us any harm. Please sit down," she added, pointing to the bench in the front corner and no longer heeding the old woman's grumbling.

Encouraged by her attention, I thought of using the most effective means.

"How unfriendly you are, Granny! You start scolding a visitor the moment he walks in. And I thought I'd bring you a present." I took the parcels out of my bag.

Manuilikha glanced at the parcels and at once turned away to the stove.

"I don't want your presents," she grumbled, fiercely raking the coals with the poker. "I know the worth of the likes of you. First they win your favour by a lot of blarney, then— What have you got in that little bag?" she asked suddenly, turning round to me.

I handed her the tea and sugar. This had a softening effect upon her, and although she went on grumbling the tone was not so uncompromising as before. Olesya went back to her spinning, and I placed myself beside her on a low, short, and very rickety bench. With her left hand she would rapidly twist the white, silky fibre, while her right hand with a light whirr spun the spindle, letting it go almost to the floor, and then catching it up deftly and setting it twirling again with a short movement of her fingers. She did it—a work so simple at first sight but actually requiring the immense skill and dexterity acquired by man through age-long practice— with great ease. I could not help noticing those hands; work had coarsened and blackened them, but they were small and so beautiful that many genteel young ladies would have envied her.

"You didn't say last time that Granny told you your fortune," said Olesya. And seeing me look back with apprehension, she added, "Never mind her, she's a bit deaf, so she won't hear. It's only my voice that she makes out well."

"Yes, she told my fortune. Why?"

"Oh, I was just wondering. Do you believe in it?" She gave me a swift, stealthy glance.

"Believe in what? Do you mean in what your grandmother told me, or fortune-telling in general?"

"I mean in general."

"Well, it's hard to say. I rather think I don't, but still —who knows? They say sometimes it comes true. Even learned people deal with that in books. But I don't at all believe in what your grandmother told me. Any countrywoman could tell fortunes like that."

Olesya smiled.

"Yes, it's true that she can't do it well any longer. She's old now, and she's afraid, too. But what did the cards tell you?"

"Nothing interesting. I don't even remember now. The things you usually hear: a long journey, a gain through the clubs—I've forgotten, really."

"Yes, she isn't much good at fortune-telling now. She's forgotten a lot of words because she's so old. How could she do it well? Besides, she's afraid. She only does it once in a while, if she's offered money."

"But what is she afraid of?"

"The authorities, of course. The *uryadnik* always bullies her when he comes. 'I could shut you up any day,' he says. 'Do you know,' he says, 'what witches like you get for practising magic? Hard labour on Sakhalin Island, for life.' Do you think it's true?"

"Well, there is some truth in what he says. This sort of thing *is* punishable, but it isn't as bad as all that. And you, Olesya, can you tell fortunes?"

She seemed to falter, but only for a second.

"Yes. But not for money," she hastened to add.

"Would you mind laying out the cards for me?"

"Yes, I would," she said, softly but firmly.

"But why? If you don't care to do it now, do it some other time. Somehow I feel that you'll tell me the truth."

"No. I won't do it. Not for the world."

"Now that's unfair of you, Olesya. For the sake of our acquaintance you shouldn't refuse me. Why don't you want to?"

"Because I have already laid out the cards for you, and I mustn't do it any more."

"You mustn't? But why not? I don't understand."

"No, no, I really mustn't," she whispered with a superstitious fear. "You mustn't search your fortune twice. That wouldn't do. It might find out, might overhear you. Fortune doesn't like to be questioned. That's why all fortune-tellers are unhappy."

I was about to answer Olesya with some joke but could not: there was so much sincere conviction in her words, that when, after mentioning fortune, she looked back at the door with a strange dread, I involuntarily did the same.

"Well, since you won't lay out the cards, at least tell me what you found out last time," I begged her.

She suddenly threw down her spindle and touched my hand with hers.

"No, I'd rather not," she said, and a childishly imploring expression came into her eyes. "Please don't ask. It was bad for you. You'd better not ask."

But I insisted. I could not make out whether her refusal and her obscure hints at fate were affectations of a fortune-teller, or whether she actually believed in what she said, but somehow I felt an uneasiness that was close to dread.

"All right, I'll tell you," Olesya agreed at last. "But remember, a bargain's a bargain, and you mustn't be cross if I tell you something you may not like. Here's what fell out: You're a kind man all right, only you're weak. Your kindness isn't good, it doesn't come from your heart. You don't stick to your word. You like to have the upper hand over people, but you knuckle under to them even though you don't wan't to. You like wine, and also— Oh, well, I'll tell you everything while I'm at it. You're very fond of us women, and that'll get you into a lot of trouble. You don't value money and don't know how to lay it by—you'll never be rich. Shall I go on?"

"Yes! Tell me all you know."

"It fell out that your life wasn't going to be a happy one. You'll love nobody with your heart because your heart is cold and lazy, and you'll cause much sorrow to those who will love you. You'll never get married and will die single. You won't have any great happiness in life, but a lot of dreariness and hardship. A day will come when you'll feel like killing yourself. Something will happen to make you feel that way. Only you won't dare to, you'll just put up with it. You'll be much in need, but towards the end of your life your fortune will change through the death of someone who's dear to you, and that quite unexpectedly. But all that won't come for many years, and as for this year—I don't know just when, but the cards tell me it'll be soon. Perhaps even this month—"

"But what'll happen this year?" I asked her when she paused again.

"I'm afraid to go on, really. A great love falls out for you from a queen of clubs. I can't guess if she's married or single, but I know that she has dark hair."

I glanced at her head.

"Why are you looking at me?" She blushed suddenly, understanding the meaning of my glance with that intuition which some women possess. "Well, yes, about the same as mine," she went on, mechanically smoothing her hair and blushing still more.

"A great love from the queen of clubs, eh?" I said jokingly.

"Don't laugh at me, you mustn't laugh," she admonished me earnestly, almost sternly. "I'm only telling you the truth."

"Very well, I won't. What else was there?"

"What else? It'll fall out very badly for that queen of clubs, worse than death. She'll suffer great shame because of you, a shame she won't forget all her life, a long sorrow. But nothing bad will fall to you through her."

"Look here, Olesya, mayn't the cards have misled you? Why should I be so very unpleasant to the queen of clubs? I'm a quiet, modest man, and yet you've said so many awful things about me."

"That's what I don't know. Besides, it won't be you who'll do it, but the whole misfortune will come through you. You'll remember my words when they come true."

"And it was the cards that told you all that, Olesya?"

She did not answer me at once.

"The cards too," she said evasively, with seeming reluctance. "But I can tell a lot even without them—by a man's face, for instance. If a man's going to die a dreadful death soon, I can read that in his face at once; I don't even have to talk to him."

"But what can you see in his face?"

"I don't know myself. I suddenly feel scared, as if he were standing dead in front of me. Ask Granny—she'll tell you I'm speaking the truth. Last year Trofim the miller hanged himself in his mill. I saw him two days before and I said to Granny right away, 'Mark my words, Granny, Trofim's going to die a horrible death one of these days.' And so he did. Last Christmas Yashka—he was a horse-thief—dropped in and asked Granny to tell his fortune. Granny spread out her cards and started. And he asked in joke, 'Tell me, Granny, what kind of death I'm going to die.' He laughed, but I looked at him and froze to my seat: I saw him sitting there, and his face was dead and green. His eyes were shut and his lips were black. Then, a week later, we heard that the peasants had caught Yashka just as he was trying to steal some horses. They beat him all night. People here are pitiless and cruel. They drove nails into his heels, and broke his ribs with stakes, and by the morning he was gone."

"But why didn't you tell him he was going to get into trouble?"

"Why should I?" she replied. "How can you get away from your fate? He'd just have worried uselessly in his last days. I feel nasty myself because I can see things like that, and I hate myself for it. Only what can I do? It's my fate. My grandmother could foretell death when she was younger, and my mother too, and my grandmother's mother—it's not our fault, it's just in our blood."

She had stopped spinning and sat with bowed head, her hands lying quietly in her lap. Her staring eyes with the dilated pupils reflected some dark terror, an involuntary submission to the mysterious powers and supernatural knowledge that had descended on her soul.

V

Just then Manuilikha spread a clean towel with embroidered ends on the table, and put a steaming pot on it.

"Supper's on the table, Olesya," she called to her granddaughter. To me she added after a momentary hesitation, "Wouldn't you like to join us, sir? You're welcome, but ours is poor food. It's just a plain soup."

She was none too insistent with her invitation, and I was about to decline when Olesya in her turn invited me with such charming simplicity and so friendly a smile that I could not but accept. She herself ladled me a plateful of the buckwheat soup with bacon, onions, potatoes, and chicken—exceedingly tasty and nutritious. Neither grandmother nor granddaughter crossed themselves as they sat down to their meal. At supper I kept watching the two women because I have always believed that when eating people show their characters more clearly than at any other time. Manuilikha was devouring the soup with hasty greed, champing loudly and pushing into her mouth huge pieces of bread that made her flabby cheeks bulge. Olesya, on the other hand, displayed an innate breeding even in the way she ate.

An hour after supper I took my leave of the occupants of the witch's hut.

"Would you like me to walk a little way with you?" Olesya suggested.

"What's this about going with him?" Manuilikha mumbled angrily. "Can't you sit still for a while, you fidget?"

But Olesya had already put on her red cashmere shawl; suddenly she ran up to her grandmother, put her arms round her, and gave her a smacking kiss.

"Granny! Dearest Granny, it'll only take me one minute—I'll be back in no time."

"All right, all right," the old woman protested feebly. "Please excuse her, sir: she's so silly."

From a narrow path we came out on to a forest road black with mud, trampled by horses and furrowed by cart-wheels, the ruts full of water that reflected the blazing sunset. We walked along the roadside covered with the brown leaves of the previous year, still moist after the snow. Here and there large campanulas—the earliest flower in Polesye—stuck up their lilac heads through the dead yellow of the leaves.

"Listen, Olesya," I began, "I'd like very much to ask you something, but I'm afraid you may be angry with me. Tell me, is it true that your grandmother—er—how shall I put it—"

"—is a witch?" Olesya prompted calmly.

"No, not a witch," I faltered. "Well, yes, a witch if you like. People say such a lot of foolish things. Perhaps she simply knows certain herbs and remedies and charms. You needn't answer me if you'd rather not."

"Why not? I don't mind," she replied simply. "Yes, she *is* a witch. But now she's old and can't do what she used to."

"And what could she do?" I asked with curiosity.

"All sorts of things. She could cure people, soothe toothache, stop blood, charm away a bite by a mad dog or a snake, discover treasures—there was nothing she couldn't do."

"You know, Olesya—I'm very sorry, but I don't believe in that sort of thing. Be frank with me, won't you—I shan't tell anybody: all that is just so much pretence to humbug people, isn't it?"

She shrugged her shoulders.

"You may think whatever you please. Of course, it's easy enough to humbug a contrywoman, but I wouldn't dream of deceiving you."

"So you firmly believe in witchcraft?"

"Of course I do! All our family has practised it. I can do quite a lot myself."

"Olesya, my dear, if you only knew how much that interests me. Won't you ever show me anything?"

"Why not?" she answered readily. "Do you want it now?"

"Yes, if I may."

"You won't be afraid?"

"What nonsense. I might be afraid if it were night, but it's still light now."

"All right. Give me your hand."

I obeyed. She quickly rolled up the sleeve of my overcoat and unclasped the stud at my cuff; then she took from her pocket a small dagger about five inches long, and pulled it out of its leather sheath.

"What are you going to do?" I asked, a mean fear stirring inside me.

"Just a moment. You said you wouldn't be afraid!"

Suddenly her hand made a hardly perceptible movement, and I felt on my wrist, slightly above where the pulse is counted, the irritating touch of the sharp blade. Blood oozed out at once along the cut, trickled down my wrist, and dripped fast on to the ground. I could hardly hold back a cry, and I think I went pale.

"Don't be afraid—you aren't going to die." Olesya laughed.

She firmly grasped my arm above the wound, bent her head low over it, and began to whisper rapidly, her hot, fitful breath searing my skin. And when she straightened up and let go my arm I saw nothing but a red scratch where the wound had been.

"Well? Are you satisfied?" she asked with a sly smile, putting away her dagger. "Or do you want more?"

"Of course I do. Only I'd prefer something less horrifying—and no bloodshed, please."

"What shall I show you?" she said musingly. "All right, go ahead of me along the road. Only see that you don't look back."

"It won't be something horrible, will it?" I asked, trying to smile away a fearful anticipation of some disagreeable surprise.

"No, not a bit. Go on."

I started to walk, greatly interested in the experiment and feeling Olesya's tense gaze on by back. But having taken about twenty steps, I suddenly tripped at a completely smooth place and fell on my face.

"Go on, go on!" Olesya shouted. "Don't look back! That's nothing, you'll be as good as new. Hold on to the earth when you fall."

I walked on. After another ten steps I sprawled on the ground once more.

Olesya burst out laughing, and clapped her hands.

"Well? Have you had enough?" she cried, her white teeth flashing. "Do you believe now? Never mind—you went down, not up."

"How did you do it?" I asked in astonishment, shaking off the sprigs and dry grass-blades that had stuck to my clothes. "It isn't a secret, I hope?"

"No secret at all. I'll tell you with pleasure. Only I'm afraid you won't understand. I mayn't be able to explain it properly."

She was right—I did not quite understand her. But if I am not mistaken, the trick was that she walked behind me step by step, keeping pace with and looking fixedly at me, and tried to imitate my every movement, even the slightest, identifying herself with me, as it were. Having walked a few paces, she began to imagine, at some distance ahead of me, a rope strung some ten inches above the ground. The instant I must touch the imaginary rope with my foot she suddenly made a falling movement, and then the strongest man was bound to fall, she told me. A long time afterwards, when reading Dr. Charcot's account of the experiments he had made with two Salpêtrière patients, professional sorceresses suffering from hysteria, I recalled Olesya's confused explanation. And I was greatly surprised to learn that French sorceresses used to resort to the very same stunt as had been performed by the pretty Polesye witch.

"I can do a lot more," said Olesya with assurance. "For example, I could give you a scare."

"What do you mean?"

"I could make you feel scared. You would be sitting, say, in your own room one evening, and all of a sudden you'd feel so terribly scared you'd shake in your boots and wouldn't even dare to look behind you. Only to do that I must know where you live, and must first see your room."

"Oh, well, *that* is quite simple," I tried to scoff. "You'd walk up to my window and knock on it, or shout something."

"No, no. I'd be here in the forest, right in my house. But I'd sit there and keep thinking that I was walking down the street, going into your house, opening your door, walking into your room. You'd be sitting somewhere—let's say at the table—I'd steal up on you from behind—you wouldn't hear me—and I'd clutch your shoulder with my hands and begin squeezing it—harder, harder, harder—staring at you all the time, like this—look."

She suddenly knitted her fine eyebrows and fixed her eyes on my face, with a terrible and luring expression, her pupils dilating and taking on a deep-blue shade. I at once recalled Medusa's head, a painting I had seen at the Tretyakov Art Gallery in Moscow—the artist's name has slipped my memory. Under that fixed, uncanny gaze I was gripped with a chilling terror of the supernatural.

"Stop that Olesya, please," I said with a forced laugh. "I like you much better when you smile—then you have such a lovely, childish face."

We walked on. I thought of Olesya's way of speaking —so expressive and, indeed, so refined for an uneducated girl—and I said, "Do you know what surprises me about you, Olesya? You've grown up in the woods, seeing nobody. And you can't have read much, for all I can say."

"I can't read at all."

"Well, there you are. Yet you speak like a real young lady. Why is that? Do you understand what I'm asking?"

"Yes, I do. It all comes from Granny. Don't judge her by her looks. She's so clever! Perhaps she'll get to talking when you're there, some day when she's got more used to you. She knows everything, absolutely everything you can ask her about. Of course, she's old now."

"Then she must have seen a lot in her life? Where does she come from? Where did she live before?"

These questions did not seem to please Olesya. She did not answer at once.

"I don't know," she said, evasively and reluctantly. "She doesn't like to talk about it. And if she ever says anything she asks me to forget it and never mention it again. It's time I was going back, though," she hastened to add, "or Granny'll be cross with me. Goodbye. I'm sorry, I don't know your name."

I introduced myself.

"Ivan Timofeyevich? Good. Well, goodbye, Ivan Timofeyevich! Please don't shun our house—come once in a while."

I held out my hand, and her small, strong hand responded with a firm, friendly grasp.

VI

From that day on I was a frequent visitor to the witch's hut. Each time I came Olesya received me with her usual reserved dignity. But I always noticed, by the first spontaneous movement she made upon seeing me, that she was glad I had come. Manuilikha continued to mutter something to herself but did not otherwise show any unfriendliness towards me, probably thanks to her granddaughter's invisible intercession. Besides, the presents I occasionally brought her, such as a warm shawl, a jar of jam, or a bottle of cherry liqueur, made her more favourably disposed towards me. As if by tacit agreement, it had become a habit with Olesya and myself that she always walked back with me as far as Irinovo Road. And because we always started a lively and interesting conversation we both tried unwittingly to prolong the walk along the quiet forest borders by slackening our pace as much as we could. After reaching the road I would walk back with her about half a mile, but still, before parting, we would talk on for a long time, standing under the fragrant shelter of pine boughs.

It was not Olesya's beauty alone that fascinated me; I was also charmed by her integrity, her distinctive and free character, and by her mind, clear and yet wrapped in unshakeable hereditary superstition, a mind as innocent as a child's, and yet not devoid of the arch coquetry of a beautiful woman. She was tireless in asking me detailed questions about all that caught and held her primitive, vivid imagination: countries and people, natural phenomena, the structure of the earth and the universe, men of learning, big cities, and what not. Many things seemed to her wonderful, fantastic, impossible. But because I had always been earnest, simple and sincere in my talks with her, she readily and unquestioningly believed whatever I told her. Sometimes, when I was at a loss to explain something which I thought was too complicated for her half-savage mind—or about which I was not quite clear myself—I would say in reply to her eager queries, "I'm afraid I can't explain that to you. You wouldn't understand."

Then she would implore me, "Oh, please tell me. I'll try to understand. Tell me somehow, even if you think it won't be easy for me."

She made me venture on monstrous parallels or cite most audacious examples, and if I floundered for the right phrase she would encourage me by a shower of impatient questions like those you put to a stammerer who has got stuck with some word. And indeed, in the end her keen and versatile mind and her fresh imagination would triumph over my lack of skill as an instructor. I had to admit that, for a person of her environment and education—or lack of education, to be exact—she had extraordinary capabilities.

Once in passing I mentioned Petersburg. She at once asked me, "What is Petersburg? A small town?"

"No, it isn't a small town. It's the biggest Russian city."

"The biggest? You mean the very biggest? And there isn't any bigger one?" she questioned me naively.

"No. All the bigwigs live there. The houses are all made of stone—there are no wooden ones."

"It must be much bigger than our Stepan, I suppose?" she asked confidently.

"O yes, a little bigger—about five hundred times, I'd say. In some of the houses there live twice as many people as in the whole of Stepan."

"Good heavens! What are those houses like, then?" she asked, almost terrified.

As usual I had to resort to a comparison.

"Terrific houses. Five, six, or even seven storeys. Do you see that pine-tree there?"

"You mean the tallest? Yes."

"Well, those houses are as tall as that. And crammed with people from top to bottom. Those people live in small rooms like birds in cages, about a dozen in each, so that there isn't even enough air for them all. And others live down below, under the earth, in damp and cold; some of them see no sunshine in their room all the year round."

"*I'*d never swop my woods for that city of yours," she said, shaking her head. "Even Stepan seems horrible to me when I go to the market there. Pushing and yelling and wrangling all around. I feel such a longing for the woods I could throw up everything and run away. I'd never consent to live in a city."

"But suppose your husband came from a city?" I asked, with a fleeting smile.

She frowned, and her fine nostrils quivered.

"Pshaw!" she said disdainfully. "I don't want any husband."

"You're only talking like that now, Olesya. Almost all girls say the same, but they get married all right. Wait till you fall in love with somebody, and then you'll be willing to follow him to the world's end, let alone to a city."

"Oh, no, please, don't let us talk about that," she insisted, annoyed. "What's the good of it? Please don't."

"How funny you are, Olesya. Do you really imagine you'll never love a man? You're so young and beautiful and strong. Once your blood is up you'll forget any pledge you may have taken."

"What if I do fall in love!" she answered, and her eyes flashed defiantly. "I won't ask anybody's permission."

"So you'll get married too," I teased her.

"You mean in church?"

"Of course. The priest will lead you round the lectern and the deacon will sing *Rejoice, Isaiah!* and they'll put a crown on your head."

She dropped her eyelids and shook her head with a wan smile.

"No, my friend. You may not like what I'm going to tell you, but nobody in our family got married in church: both my mother and my grandmother managed without that. We mayn't even enter a church."

"All because of your witchcraft?"

"Yes, because of our witchcraft," she replied calmly. "How could I dare to turn up in church when my soul's been sold to *him* since I was born?"

"Believe me, you're deceiving yourself, Olesya dear. What you're saying is simply preposterous—it's laughable."

The odd expression of grim resignation to her mysterious destiny, which I had noticed before, came into her face again.

"No, no. You can't understand that, but I feel it. I feel it here"—she pressed her hand to her breast—"in my heart. There's an everlasting curse on all our family. Judge for yourself: Who else is helping us if it isn't *he*? How can an ordinary person do what I can? All our power comes from *him*."

And each time this unusual subject came up our conversation finished that way. In vain did I bring forward all the arguments within her grasp and talk to her in simple terms about hypnotism, suggestion, phychiatrists and Indian fakirs, in vain did I attempt a physiological explanation of some of her experiments, such as charming away haemorrhage, so easily achieved by skilfully pressing a vein; much as she trusted me in everything else, she obstinately rejected all my explanations.

"All right, I'll grant what you say about charming away blood, but where does everything else come from?" she would argue, raising her voice. "Charming away blood isn't all I can do, is it? Do you want me to rid your house of all its mice and roaches in one day? Do you want me to cure the worst fever with plain water in two days, even if all your doctors should give up the patient? Do you want me to make you completely forget some word? And why can I interpret dreams? Why is it that I know what'll happen in the future?"

The dispute always ended in Olesya and myself changing the subject, not without pent-up resentment against each other. There was much in her black magic that my little knowledge could not explain away. I cannot tell whether she possessed even half the secrets she spoke about with so much unaffected conviction. But what I did see often enough, made me firmly believe that she had that instinctive, hazy, strange knowledge, acquired through chance experience, which forestalls science by centuries and lives on in the ignorant masses of the people, a knowledge mingled with ridiculous and monstrous superstitions and handed down from generation to generation as a great secret.

Despite our sharp differences over this one point, we were getting more and more attached to each other. So far we had not exchanged a word of love, but it had become a necessity for us to be together, and often, in those silent moments when our eyes chanced to meet, I saw Olesya's eyes grow moist and the thin blue vein on her temple throb faster.

On the other hand, my relations with Yarmola were spoiled for good. My visits to the witch's hut and my evening walks with Olesya were obviously an open secret to him: he always knew with astonishing accuracy what was going on in *his* forest. He had begun to avoid me. His black eyes watched me from afar with a look of reproach and displeasure whenever I made ready to start for the forest, although he did not speak a word of disapproval. Our comically serious studies had ceased. When I occasionally suggested a lesson in the evening he would dismiss the idea with a careless gesture.

"What's the use? It's a waste of time, master," he would say with lazy contempt.

Nor did we go shooting any more. Whenever I brought up the matter Yarmola found some pretext to refuse: a gun out of repair, a sick dog, lack of time.

"I've no time, master, I've got to do some ploughing," he would say more often than not in reply to my invitation; and I knew very well that he had no intention of ploughing but was going to hang about the tavern all day long, hoping against hope that someone might stand him a drink. His tacit, smouldering hostility was beginning to weary me, and I was thinking of seizing the first opportunity to dismiss him. What made me hesitate was commiseration for his large, poverty-stricken family, whom his wage of four rubles kept from starving to death.

VII

One day when as usual I came to the witch's hut shortly before dusk, I was struck by the dejected spirits of its occupants. Manuilikha sat hunched on her bed with her feet tucked under her, rocking back and forth and muttering to herself, her head clasped in her hands. She ignored my greeting. Olesya responded with her habitual friendliness, but our conversation flagged. She must have been listening abstractedly, for her replies were completely off the point. Her beautiful face was shadowed by inner anxiety.

"I see you're in some sort of trouble, Olesya," I said, and gently touched her hand lying on the bench.

Quickly she turned away to stare out of the window. She tried to look calm, but her knitted eyebrows trembled, and her teeth dug into her lip.

"No, what could have happened to us?" she said tonelessly. "Everything's just as it was."

"Why won't you tell me the truth, Olesya? That isn't fair of you. I thought we were friends."

"There's nothing wrong, I assure you. Just our little troubles—all kinds of trifles."

"No, Olesya, trifles wouldn't make you look like that."

"That's your fancy."

"Please be frank with me, Olesya. I don't know if I can help you, but I may at least be able to give you some advice. And after all, you'll feel better simply because you'll have shared your sorrow with me."

"Oh, it's no use talking about it, really," she replied impatiently. "There's nothing you can do to help us."

The old woman suddenly burst into our conversation with unusual heat.

"Stop being a fool, will you? You should listen when he speaks sense to you instead of sticking up your nose. Think there is nobody on earth cleverer than you? Let me tell you the whole story, sir," she said, turning to me.

The trouble proved to be far more serious than I could have gathered from proud Olesya's hints. The *uryadnik* had dropped into the witch's hut the night before.

"At first he sat down nicely and asked for some vodka," said Manuilikha, "and then he let go. 'You clear out of this house,' he says, 'in twenty-four hours, with bag and baggage. If I find you in here when I come next,' he says, 'I'll have you transported, and no mistake. I'll pack you off to your home with two soldiers, damn you!' he says. Now my home is far away, sir—the town of Amchensk. I don't know a living soul there any more and, besides, our passports ran out a long, long time ago. Anyway they weren't in order from the outset. Oh dear!"

"But he didn't mind your living here before, did he?" I said. "Why must he bully you now?"

"That's just what I'd like to know. He gabbled something, but I couldn't make it out. You see, this hut we live in isn't ours, it's the landlord's. We used to live in the village, and then—"

"I know, Granny, I've heard about it. The peasants got angry with you."

"So they did. Then I went to the old landlord, Mr. Abrosimov, and cried, and he let me have this hovel. But now it seems a new landlord's bought the forest and wants to drain the marsh or something. Only why can't I stay here?"

"Perhaps the whole thing's just a tale, Granny?" I remarked. "The *uryadnik* may simply be wanting you to grease his palm."

"I tried that, my friend, I did. He wouldn't take it! Would you believe that? I offered him twenty-five rubles, and he wouldn't have it. Oh, no! He was so mad I was scared out of my wits. He just kept bawling, 'Get out of here!' What are we going to do now, poor orphans that we are! If only you could help us, good sir, and talk him out of it, the greedy dog! You'd oblige me no end."

"Granny!" said Olesya, with reproachful emphasis.

"Granny what?" Manuilikha returned testily. "I've been your granny for twenty-four years. Do you think we'd better go begging? Don't listen to her, sir. Please help us if you can."

Vaguely I promised to plead for them, although, to tell the truth, there seemed little hope. For the *uryadnik* to refuse a bribe, the thing must be serious indeed. That evening Olesya bade me a cold goodbye and would not walk with me as she usually did. I saw that the proud girl resented my interference, and also that she was a little ashamed of her grandmother's tearful behaviour.

VIII

It was a grey, warm morning. Already there had been several brief showers of large raindrops of the beneficial kind that makes young grass sprout under your eyes and fresh shoots come up. After each shower, the sun would peep out for a moment to shine joyfully down on the rain-washed leaves of the lilacs—still a delicate green —that crowded my front garden; the perky sparrows would chirp more loudly on the loosened kitchen-garden beds; the sticky brown buds of the poplars would give off a stronger fragrance. I sat sketching a forest cottage when Yarmola stepped in.

"The *uryadnik*'s here," he said glumly.

I had quite forgotten that two days ago I had told him to let me know if the *uryadnik* arrived, and so I could not understand what business that representative of the authorities might have with me just then.

"What's that?" I asked in perplexity.

"I said the *uryadnik* was here," Yarmola replied, in that hostile tone which he had been using towards me lately. "I saw him at the dam a minute ago. He's coming this way."

Wheels rattled outside. I rushed to the window and opened it. A skinny, chocolate-coloured gelding with a drooping lip and hurt mien was pulling at a staid trot a high, shaky wicker gig to which it was harnessed by a single shaft, the other being replaced by a stout rope—the local wags claimed that the *uryadnik* was using such a sorry turnout on purpose to prevent undesirable rumours. The *uryadnik* himself was driving, his monstrous form, clad in a greatcoat of expensive grey cloth and taking up both seats.

"My compliments, Yevpsikhy Afrikanovich!" I shouted, leaning out of the window.

"Oh, good morning! How are you?" he responded in the amiable, rolling baritone of a superior.

He reined up the gelding, saluted me, and bent forward with a ponderous grace.

"Could you drop in for a second? I've some little business to discuss with you."

He shook his head.

"I can't. I'm carrying out my duties. Driving to Volosha to inspect a dead body—a drowned man."

But by then I knew his foibles and therefore said with affected indifference, "That's too bad. I've got two bottles of some nice stuff from Count Wortzel's estate, and I thought—"

"I can't. Duty, you know."

"A man I know sold it to me. He'd been hoarding it in his cellar like a family treasure. Perhaps you'll drop in, after all. I'll have some oats given to your horse."

"You mustn't insist, really," he said. "Don't you know duty comes first? What's in those bottles, anyway? Plum brandy?"

"Plum brandy, indeed! It's old vodka, sir, that's what it is!"

"I've already had something, to be frank." He scratched his cheek, grimacing regretfully.

"Of course it may not be true," I went on as coolly as before, "but the man swore it was two hundred years old. It smells like real cognac, and it's as yellow as amber."

"See what you're doing to me!" he exclaimed in comic dismay. "Now who'll take over the horse?"

I actually had several bottles of old vodka, although it was not quite so ancient as I had boasted; but I counted on the force of suggestion to make it a few score years older. Anyway it was real home-made old vodka of a stunning strength, the pride of the cellars of a ruined magnate. The *uryadnik*, who came of a clergyman's family, at once secured a bottle from me against the possibility of what he called illness from a cold. And the snack I offered—fresh radish with newly-churned butter —was highly palatable.

"And what may your business be?" he asked me after his fifth glass, and sat back in an old easy chair, which groaned under his weight.

I depicted to him the poor old woman's plight, mentioned her helpless condition and despair, and made a passing allusion to unnecessary form. He listened to me with bowed head, methodically cutting off the roots of the red, sturdy radish and crunching it with gusto. Occasionally he looked up at me with his impassive, bleared eyes, blue and ridiculously small, but I could read neither sympathy nor protest in his huge red face.

"So what do you want me to do?" was all he asked me when I paused at last.

"What do you mean what?" I replied excitedly. "Can't you see the plight they're in? Two poor, defenceless women—"

"And one of them as pretty as a rosebud!" he put in sarcastically.

"Perhaps so, but that's beside the point. What I'd like to know is why you can't show some sympathy for them. You don't expect me to believe you must evict them so very urgently, do you? You might at least wait a little and give me a chance to plead for them with the landlord. What would be the risk of waiting a month or so?"

"What risk?" He sprang up from his easy chair. "Why, it might cost me a lot, and my job first of all. God knows what that new landlord, Mr. Ilyashevich, is like. He might be a busy-body, one of those who write off to Petersburg the moment they come across some trifle. We get people like that down here all right!"

I tried to calm the irate *uryadnik*.

"Come, now, Yevpsikhy Afrikanovich, you're laying it on a bit too thick. And then, even if there is a risk, there'll be gratitude too."

"Pah!" he exclaimed, and thrust his hands deep into the pockets of his wide trousers. "Talk of gratitude! D'you think I'd stake my job for a measly twenty-five rubles? No, sir, you don't know me if you imagine that."

"Don't take on, Yevpsikhy Afrikanovich. It isn't a question of money at all, it's—It would be an act of humanity."

"Hu-man-it-y?" he repeated ironically, syllable by syllable. "Here's where that humanity weighs on me!"

He vigorously slapped his hand across his powerful bronzed nape overhanging the collar in a hairless fold.

"You're exaggerating, I think, Yevpsikhy Afrikanovich."

"Not a bit, sir. 'It's a scourge of these parts,' to use an expression by Mr. Krylov, the famous fabulist. That's what those two ladies are, sir! Have you read *The Police-Officer*, that splendid book by His Highness Prince Uru-sov?"

"No, I haven't."

"You've missed a lot, sir. It's an excellent and highly edifying work. I suggest that you read it at leisure."

"Very good, I'll read it gladly. But still I don't see what that book's got to do with the two poor women."

"What it's got to do with them? A great deal. Point one" —he bent his thick, hairy left forefinger— " 'The police offi-cer shall watch unflaggingly that every person assiduously attends the House of God, which duty he should not, however, deem to be a burthen.' May I ask you if that woman—what d'you call her—Manuilikha, is it?—if she ever goes to church?"

I made no comment, struck dumb by the unexpected turn the conversation had taken. He gave me a trium-phant look, and bent his middle finger.

"Point two: 'It is prohibited to engage anywhere in false prophecies or false auguries.' See how it is, sir? And now comes point three: 'It is prohibited to make oneself out to be a sorcerer or magician, or to resort to any similar fraudulent practices.' What do you say to that? Suppose all that came out all of a sudden or reached the higher authorities somehow? Who'd be called to account? Me. Who would get the sack? Me again. So there you are."

He sat down again. His eyes wandered vacantly over the walls, while his fingers drummed loudly on the table.

"But if I asked you as a special favour, Yevpsikhy Af-rikanovich?" I began again, in an ingratiating tone. "You are doubtless burdened by complex and troublesome du-ties, but then I know you have an exceedingly kind, a golden heart. You could quite easily promise me not to disturb those women."

The *uryadnik*'s roaming eyes hovered somewhere above my head.

"A fine gun you've got there," he said casually, still drumming. "An excellent gun. Last time when I was here and didn't find you in I admired it so much. A wonderful gun!"

I turned my head to look at the gun.

"Yes, it's all right," I praised it. "It's an old one, you know, made in Europe. I had it refashioned into a centre-fire gun last year. Take a look at the barrels."

"Certainly, the barrels are just what I've been admiring most. A splendid thing. I should say quite a treasure."

Our eyes met, and I saw a faint but meaning smile flutter in the corners of his mouth. I got up, took the gun down from the wall, and walked up to him.

"The Circassians have a charming custom of presenting their guests with anything they admire," I said amiably. "You and I aren't Circassians, Yevpsikhy Afrikanovich, but I beg you to accept this from me as a souvenir."

He pretended to be embarrassed.

"Oh, come, you can't give away such a beauty! No, really, that's too generous a custom!"

But I did not have to press him long. He accepted the gun, stood it gently between his knees, and carefully wiped the dust from the trigger with a clean handkerchief. I was somewhat reassured as I saw that my gun had passed into the possession of a connoisseur. The *uryadnik* rose almost immediately after the transfer, and made haste to leave.

"I've got urgent business to see to but I've been chatting instead," he said, stamping on the floor to get his galoshes on. "You're welcome to my place when you visit our parts."

"And how about Manuilikha, sir?" I reminded him discreetly.

"We'll see," he grunted non-committally. "There was something I wanted to ask you for. You've got wonderful radish."

"I grew it myself."

"It's amazing radish. You know, my better half has a weakness for all kinds of vegetables. So I wondered if you couldn't—just one bunch, you know."

"I'd be delighted to, Yevpsikhy Afrikanovich. I'd consider it an honour. I'll send you a basketful by messenger today. And some butter if you don't mind. I've got butter of rare quality."

"Oh, well, and some butter," he condescended. "And you may let those women know that I'm not going to disturb them for a while. But let them bear in mind"—he suddenly raised his voice—"they won't get off with a thank you. And now, goodbye. Thanks again for the present and the treat."

He clicked his heels in military fashion and walked with the heavy gait of a well-fed man of importance to his carriage, near which the *sotsky*,* the elder, and Yarmola were standing respectfully, cap in hand.

IX

The *uryadnik* kept his word and left the occupants of the forest hut alone for the time being. But there came an abrupt and appalling change in my relationship with Olesya. She now treated me without a trace of her former trusting and artless friendliness, of the vivacity in which

* Rural policeman.—*Tr*

the coquetry of a beautiful girl had mingled so charmingly with the sportiveness of a naughty boy. An insurmountable awkwardness had crept into our conversation. With hurried timidity, Olesya avoided all the lively subjects, which had given such a wide scope to our curiosity.

In my presence she would give herself up to her work with stern, tense concentration, but I could often see her hands drop limply on her lap, while she stared at the floor. If at a moment like that I called her by name or asked her a question, she would start and slowly turn to me a frightened face that reflected an effort to grasp the meaning of my words. Sometimes I felt as if my presence were a nuisance or a burden to her; but this seemed strange after the profound interest which only a few days ago she had shown in every comment I made, every word I spoke. And so I could only think that she would not forgive my pleading with the *uryadnik*—an act of patronage which must have offended her sense of independence. But this conjecture did not satisfy me, either, for how indeed could an ordinary girl, who had grown up in the woods, be so squeamishly proud?

An explanation was certainly called for, but Olesya stubbornly avoided every opportunity for a heart-to-heart talk. Our evening strolls ceased. In vain did I look eloquently and imploringly at her every day as I rose to leave—she made believe she did not understand. On the other hand, the old woman's presence disturbed me, even though she was deaf.

At times I was angered by my own inability to break the habit of going to see Olesya every day. I had no inkling of the strong invisible threads that bound my heart to the captivating, unaccountable girl. I did not think of love yet, but I was already going through the restless period preceding love, a period full of vague, agonizingly sad sensations. No matter where I was or how I tried to divert myself, my mind was taken up by Olesya's image, my whole being yearned for her, and the recollection of her words—sometimes quite insignificant ones—her gestures or her smile would grip my heart with a gentle, sweet pain. Then dusk would fall, and I would sit for hours on the low, shaky bench by her side, feeling, to my vexation, ever more timid, ever more awkward and dull-witted.

Once I spent a whole day sitting like that beside Olesya. I had not been feeling well since the morning, although I did not quite know yet what was wrong with me. Towards evening I felt worse. My head was heavy, there was a ringing in my ears and a dull, persistent pain at the back of my head, as if someone were pressing it with a soft, strong hand. My mouth was dry, and a sluggish, languid weakness pervading my whole body made me want to yawn and stretch all the time. My eyes ached intensely as if I had been staring at a dazzling object.

As I was walking home late that evening I suddenly began to shiver violently. I stumbled on like a drunken man, hardly knowing where I was going, and my teeth chattered loudly.

I do not know to this day who brought me home. For fully six days I shook with the terrible, relentless Polesye fever. During the day the illness would seem to subside, and I would recover consciousness. Completely worn out by the disease, I would crawl about the room, my knees weak and aching; if I moved with any vigour the blood would rush to my head in a hot wave, shutting out everything before my eyes. And at nightfall, usually about seven o'clock, the disease would swoop down on me anew, and I would spend a horrible night, as long as a century, during which I alternately shook with cold under the sheets and burned with a unbearable heat. The slightest touch of drowsiness brought with it painful nightmares, bizarre and crazy, that tortured my heated brain. My visions were full of minute, microscopic details that piled up and clung to each other in an ugly hustle and bustle. I would fancy I was sorting out some coloured boxes of grotesque shapes, taking small boxes out of big ones, and smaller boxes out of the small ones, unable to stop the endless task, which had become loathsome to me. Then long, colourful strips of wallpaper would flit before my eyes at a dizzy speed, and with striking lucidity I would see on them, instead of patterns, veritable garlands of human faces—some of them handsome, kind and smiling, others making fearful grimaces, putting out their tongues, baring their teeth, or rolling their enormous eyeballs. Then again Yarmola and I would engage in an abstract dispute, tangled and exceedingly complicated. The arguments we brought forward would become more and more cunning and profound; certain words and even letters would suddenly acquire a mysterious, unfathomable meaning, and I would be beset more and more by a fastidious terror of the unknown, weird force which drew ugly sophisms out of my head one by one and would not let me stop a dispute that had long become hateful.

It was a seething whirlwind of human and bestial forms, landscapes, objects of the most singular shapes and colours, words and phrases whose meaning I perceived with all my senses. Yet, strange as it may seem, I kept on seeing at the same time a neat circle of light, which the lamp with the green, scorched shade threw on the ceiling. And somehow I knew that in that peaceful circle with its blurred rim there lurked a silent, mysterious and terrible life, more dreadful and oppressive than the frenzied chaos of my dreams.

Then I would wake up, or rather find myself awake all at once. I would almost regain consciousness, and would realize that I was ill and in bed, that I had just been delirious, but still the latent and sinister threat of the bright circle on the dark ceiling would frighten me. Feebly I would reach for my watch, only to find in anguished perplexity that the whole endless succession of my hideous dreams had lasted no longer than two or three minutes. "God! When will daylight come!" I would think in despair, tossing my head on the hot pillows and feeling my own panting breath burn my lips. Then a light sleepiness would overpower me once more, and again my brain would become a plaything for a jumbled nightmare, and again I would wake up two minutes later, a prey to mortal anguish.

Six days later my strong constitution, aided by quinine and an infusion of plantain, overcame the illness. I got up from bed, completely shattered and tottering. I recovered fast. My head, wearied by six days of feverish delirium, was now lazily and pleasantly devoid of thoughts. My appetite came back redoubled, and my body gathered strength hourly, its every particle absorbing health and the joy of living. I felt a fresh urge to go to the lone sagging hut in the forest. My nerves had not yet rallied from the illness, and whenever I recalled Olesya's face and voice I was so tenderly moved that I could have cried.

X

Five more days passed, and I was strong enough to walk all the way to the witch's hut without feeling tired in the least. As I approached the threshold my heart beat in fear. I had not seen Olesya for nearly a fortnight, and now I realized with particular clarity how dear she was to me. My hand on the door-knob, I wavered for a few seconds, hardly drawing my breath. I even shut my eyes for a while in my hesitation before pushing the door open.

It is difficult to make out impressions like those which followed my entrance. Indeed, is it possible to remember the words spoken during the early moments of a meeting of mother and son, husband and wife, or two lovers? The words spoken are very ordinary—in fact, they would have sounded ridiculous if recorded. But each word is fitting and infinitely precious merely because it is spoken by the dearest voice on earth.

I do remember, and very distinctly too, that Olesya quickly turned a pale face towards me and that that sweet face, which seemed new to me, reflected in instant succession perplexity, fright, and loving tenderness. The old woman mumbled something, shuffling about me, but I did not hear her greeting. Olesya's voice came to me like sweet music.

"What happened to you? Were you ill? How thin you've grown, my poor one."

For a long time I could say nothing in reply, and we stood silently facing each other, holding each other's hands, gazing happily into each other's eyes. I consider those few silent seconds the happiest in my life; never before had I felt, nor have I felt ever since, so pure, so complete and all-absorbing an ecstasy. And the things I read in Olesya's big dark eyes—the emotion over the meeting, the reproach for my long absence, the passionate confession of love! I felt that, along with that gaze, she was joyfully giving me her whole being, without any conditions, without wavering.

She was the first to break the spell by indicating Manuilikha with a slow movement of her eyelids. We sat down side by side, and she began to ask me solicitous questions about my illness, the medicines I had taken, the things that the doctor had said (he had come from the town twice to see me). She made me repeat my story about the doctor several times, and occasionally I saw a mocking smile quiver on her lips.

"If only I'd known you were ill!" she cried, with impatient regret. "I'd have had you back on your feet in a day. How can you trust people who don't know anything —anything at all? Why didn't you send for me?"

I faltered.

"You see, Olesya, it came so unexpectedly and, besides, I didn't dare to disturb you. You've been treating me in a queer way lately, as if you were cross with me, or fed up with me. Listen, Olesya," I added, lowering my voice. "We must talk over many, many things, just the two of us—you know what I mean."

She dropped her eyelids in acquiescence, then glanced timidly at her grandmother, and whispered quickly, "Yes, I wanted that myself, only not now—later."

Scarcely had the sun set when she urged me to go home.

"Get ready, quick," she said, pulling me by the hand from the bench. "If the damp gets into you now the illness will come back at once."

"Where are *you* going, Olesya?" asked Manuilikha as she saw her granddaughter hurriedly putting on her grey woollen shawl.

"I'll walk with him a bit," answered Olesya.

She said it with seeming indifference, looking at the window and not at Manuilikha, but in her voice I detected a hardly perceptible shade of exasperation.

"So you are going after all?" said the old woman with emphasis.

Olesya's eyes flashed as she looked at Manuilikha.

"Yes, I am!" she replied haughtily. "We've talked about it quite enough. It's my business, and I'll take the consequences."

"So I see!" cried Manuilikha, irritably and reproachfully.

She had been about to add something, but instead she waved her hand hopelessly, shambled on her wobbly feet into a corner, and got busy with a basket.

I gathered that the rapid, resentful dialogue I had just heard was a sequel to a long series of quarrels.

"Your granny doesn't want you to go out with me, does she?" I asked Olesya as we descended to the forest.

She shrugged her shoulders in annoyance.

"Don't pay any attention to that. Well, no, she doesn't. What of it? Surely I'm free to do as I please!"

Suddenly I felt an urge to reproach her for her former severity.

"So you could have gone out with me even before my illness, but you didn't care to. If only you knew how much pain you caused me, Olesya! Every evening I hoped you would go with me. But you were so cold and dull and cross. Oh, how you tormented me, Olesya!"

"Stop it, please, dear one. Forget it," she begged me, a gentle apology in her voice.

"Well, I'm not blaming you—it just came out. Now I know the reason, but at first I had a feeling—it's funny to think of it, really—I had a feeling that you were angry with me because of the *uryadnik*. And that hurt me a lot. It seemed to me you considered me such a stranger that you found it hard to accept a mere friendly service from me. It made me so unhappy. I had no idea, you see, that it all came from Granny."

Olesya suddenly flushed deeply.

"No, it didn't! I just didn't want it myself!" she cried defiantly.

I looked at her from the side, and saw the pure, delicate profile of her slightly bowed head. Only now did I notice that she herself had grown thinner and that there were bluish shadows under her eyes. She sensed that I was gazing at her, and looked up, but at once dropped her eyes again, and turned away with a bashful smile.

"Why didn't you want it, Olesya? Why?" I asked her, my voice breaking with emotion, and, seizing her by the hand, I made her stop.

We were in the middle of a long, narrow lane, straight as an arrow. Tall, slender pines flanked us on both sides, forming an avenue that ran away into the distance, with a canopy of fragrant intertwining boughs. The bare trunks bore crimson reflections of the dying sunset.

"Why, Olesya? Why?" I asked her again and again in a whisper, tightening my grip on her hand.

"I couldn't. I was afraid," she said in a hardly audible voice. "I thought I could get away from fate. But now—"

She gasped as if for air, and suddenly threw her arms round my neck in a strong embrace, and I felt on my lips the burning sweetness of her hurried, tremulous whisper.

"Now I don't care any more, I don't! Because I love you, my dear one, my happiness, my own!"

She clung to me ever closer, and I felt her robust, warm body quivering in my arms, and her heart racing against my chest. Like strong wine, her passionate kisses went to my head, still weak from the illness, and I began to lose my self-control.

"Olesya, for God's sake, don't—let me go," I said, trying to unclasp her arms. "Now I'm afraid too, afraid of myself. Let me go, Olesya."

She turned up her face, and a languorous smile crept across it.

"Don't be afraid, my darling," she said, with an ineffable look of tender caress and touching boldness. "I'll never reproach you or be jealous. Just tell me if you love me."

"Yes, Olesya. I've loved you for a long time, with all my heart. But—don't kiss me any more. I feel weak and dizzy, I'm not sure of myself."

Once again her lips held mine in a long, tantalizingly sweet kiss, and I guessed rather than heard her say, "Then don't be afraid, and don't worry any longer. This is our day, and nobody can take it from us."

And the whole of that night merged into one enchanting fairy-tale. The moon rose, mottling the forest with grotesque, mysterious colours, casting pale blue spots of light on gnarled stumps, crooked boughs, and the soft, plush-like carpet of moss. The slender white trunks of birch-trees stood out in clear outline, while their sparse leaves seemed to be veiled in silvery gauze. Here and there, where the moonlight could not pierce the awning of pine branches, the darkness was complete and impenetrable, except for a beam of light which had somehow made its way into the middle to catch a long row of trees and lay a straight narrow path on the ground, as bright and lovely as a tree-lined walk trimmed by elves for the solemn march of Oberon and Titania. And we walked arm in arm amid that living, smiling legend, without saying a word, overwhelmed by our happiness and the eerie stillness of the forest.

"Why, darling, I quite forgot you must hurry home," said Olesya suddenly. "How selfish of me! You've only just recovered, and here I am keeping you so long in the woods."

I embraced her, and pushed back the shawl from her rich dark hair.

"You aren't sorry, Olesya, are you?" I asked softly, bending over her ear. "You don't regret it?"

She slowly shook her head.

"No. I shan't be sorry no matter what comes afterwards. I'm so happy."

"Must something come?"

There was a flicker of the familiar mystical terror in her eyes.

"Yes, it must. Remember what I told you about the queen of clubs? *I* am that queen, and it's to me that the misfortune the cards foretold will happen. You know, I was going to ask you to stop coming to our place altogether. But just then you fell ill, and I didn't see you for nearly a fortnight. I felt so terribly lonely and sad I thought I'd give anything on earth just to be with you for one moment. That was when I made up my mind. Come what may, I said to myself, I won't give up my happiness for anything."

"You're right, Olesya. I felt that way too," I said, touching her temple with my lips. "I didn't know I loved you till I had to part with you. It's true, whoever said it, that separation does to love what the wind does to the fire: it puts out a small love and fans a big one."

"What was that? Please say it again," said Olesya, interested.

I repeated the aphorism. Olesya fell to musing, and I could see by her moving lips that she was repeating the words.

I peered closely at her pale upturned face, into her big black eyes with the bright glint of moonlight in them, and a vague foreboding of impending misfortune chilled suddenly my heart.

XI

The naive, fascinating fairy-tale of our love lasted for almost a month, and those blazing sunsets, those dewy mornings so fragrant with honey and lily of the valley, so full of crisp freshness and the resounding hubbub of birds, those lazy June days, so warm and languorous, live on unfadingly in my soul, along with Olesya's wonderful image. Never did boredom, weariness, or the eternal wanderlust, stir in my heart throughout that time. Like a heathen god or a young, strong animal, I revelled in light and warmth, in a conscious joy of life, and in my tranquil, healthy sensual love.

After my recovery old Manuilikha had become so peevish, met me with such frank hatred and, as I sat in the hut, moved the pots about in the stove with so much noisy bitterness that Olesya and I preferred to meet in the forest. And the majestic beauty of the green pines adorned our serene love like a precious setting.

I discovered daily with increasing amazement that Olesya, a girl who had grown up in the woods and who could not even read, in many instances displayed a sensitive delicacy and a special, innate tact. Love in its direct, coarse sense always has certain repellent aspects which cause torture and shame to nervous artistic natures. But Olesya knew how to avoid them, and she did so with such naive chastity that not once did an ugly comparison or a cynical moment insult our relationship.

Meanwhile the day was drawing near when I must leave. In fact, my official duties in Perebrod were finished and I was purposely putting off my return to the city. I had not yet said a word about it to Olesya, and I was afraid even to imagine what her reaction would be to the news of my coming departure. I was in a predicament. Habit had already taken deep root in me. It was more than a necessity for me to see Olesya every day, to hear her sweet voice and her ringing laughter, to feel the delightful tenderness of her caresses. On those rare days when rain prevented our meeting I felt forlorn, as if I had been robbed of what was most important to me in life. Any occupation would seem dull and useless, and all my being longed for the forest, for light and warmth, for Olesya's sweet familiar face.

More and more often I thought of marrying Olesya. At first the idea came into my head only occasionally, as a possible, in the last resort, honest solution of our relationship. There was only one circumstance that deterred me: I did not dare to picture Olesya in a stylish dress, talking in my drawing-room with the wives of my colleagues—an Olesya snatched out of the enchanting setting of the old forest that was so full of legend and mystery.

But as the day of my departure approached I was beset by a deep sadness and a growing horror of solitude. My determination to marry Olesya grew firmer every day, and I no longer saw it as an audacious challenge to society. "After all, there *are* good and learned men who marry seamstresses and housemaids, aren't there?" I reassured myself. "And they live very well together and to their last day bless the destiny which led them to take that decision. I hope *my* luck won't be any worse."

One day in mid-June I was waiting for Olesya as usual at the curve of a narrow forest path winding between hawthorn shrubs in bloom. I recognized from afar her light, quick footfall.

"Good evening, my love," said Olesya, a little breathless as she put her arms round me. "Kept you waiting a long time, didn't I? I could hardly get away. Had a quarrel with Granny."

"Is she still carrying it on?"

"Oh, yes! 'He'll be your undoing,' she says. 'He'll have his fill of fun with you and then throw you over. He doesn't love you a bit.' "

"Meaning me, eh?"

"Yes, darling. But I don't believe a word of it."

"Does she know everything?"

"I can't say for sure. I think she does. I never talk to her about it—she does her own guessing. Oh, well, no need to worry. Come along."

She broke off a hawthorn sprig with a rich cluster of white blossoms and stuck it in her hair. We started on a leisurely stroll along the path, to which the afternoon sun gave a touch of pink.

I had decided the night before that this evening I would speak at any cost. But a strange timidity tied my

tongue. I wondered whether Olesya would believe me if
I told her about my departure and my decision to marry
her. Might she not take my proposal as a mere attempt
to lessen, to assuage the first pain of the wound I was
inflicting upon her? "I'll begin as soon as we get to that
barked maple," I said to myself. We came alongside it,
and, paling with agitation, I took a deep breath to speak,
but unexpectedly my courage ebbed, resolving into a nervous, painful heart-beat and a cold sensation in the
mouth. "Twenty-seven's my lucky number," I thought
a few minutes later. "I'll count to twenty-seven and
then—" And I began counting in my mind, but on reaching twenty-seven I felt that my resolution was not yet
ripe. "No," I told myself, "I'd better count on to sixty—
that'll make exactly one minute, and then I'll certainly
begin."

"Is anything wrong, dear?" Olesya asked me all of a
sudden. "You're thinking of something unpleasant.
What is it?"

Then I did speak, but it was in a tone hateful to myself, with an affected, unnatural carelessness, as though
it were a question of some trifle.

"Yes, it is a little unpleasant—you guessed right,
Olesya. You see, my service here is over, and my superiors want me back in town."

Glancing sideways at Olesya, I saw her face drain
of colour and her lips tremble. But she did not speak a
word in reply. I walked on beside her for a few minutes.
Grasshoppers were chirping loudly, and far off I could
hear the monotonous crake of a landrail.

"Of course you understand, Olesya," I began afresh,
"that I can't very well stay here, and I have no place to
stay either. And then I mustn't neglect my duties."

"No, I suppose not—that's clear enough," she replied,
with seeming calm but in so toneless and flat a voice that

I felt a dread. "Since it's your duty you must go—of course."

She halted near a tree and leaned her back against it, pale as a sheet, with arms hanging limply at her sides, a miserable, painful smile on her lips. Her pallor frightened me. I rushed to her and gripped her hands.

"Olesya! What is it, Olesya dear?"

"Never mind—I'm sorry—I'll be all right. I just felt dizzy."

She made an effort and stepped forward, without taking away her hand.

"You must have thought badly of me just now, Olesya," I said reproachfully. "Shame on you! Do you, too, imagine that I could go and leave you? No, my dear. As a matter of fact, I started this talk because I want to tell your grandmother this very night that you're going to be my wife."

To my utter perplexity, she was hardly surprised to hear that.

"Your wife?" She shook her head, slowly and sadly. "No, Vanya dear, that's impossible!"

"But why, Olesya? Why?"

"No, no. You know yourself it's silly even to think of it. What sort of a wife would I make you? You're a gentleman, you're clever and educated, and I? Why, I can't even read, and I don't know how to behave. You'd be ashamed of me."

"What nonsense, Olesya!" I remonstrated hotly. "You won't recognize yourself in six months from now. You have no idea how intelligent and quick-witted you are. We'll read lots of good books together, meet kind, intelligent people, see the whole wide world, Olesya. We'll be together all our lives, just as we are now, and far from feeling ashamed of you, I'll be proud of you, and grateful to you!"

In answer to my passionate speech she squeezed my hand with feeling, but stood firm.

"But that isn't all! Perhaps you don't know it. I've never told you. You see, I have no father. I'm illegitimate."

"Stop it, Olesya. That's my least worry. What do I care about your kin if you yourself are dearer to me than my own father or mother, dearer than the whole world? It's all nonsense and petty excuses!"

She pressed her shoulder to mine in a gentle, submissive caress.

"My dear one! It would be better if you had never started this talk. You're young and free. Do you think I could bind you hand and foot for life? What if you came to care for another woman afterwards? Then you'd hate me, and you'd curse the hour when I agreed to marry you. Don't be angry, dear!" she cried entreatingly as she saw from my face that I was pained. "I don't want to hurt you. I'm only thinking of your happiness. And you forgot about Granny. Judge for yourself—would it be fair of me to leave her all alone?"

"Well, we'd find room for her too." Frankly, the idea came as a shock to me. "And in case she didn't care to live with us, there are homes in any town—they're called alms-houses—where old women like her get all the rest and care they need."

"Oh, no, that's impossible. She won't go anywhere away from the woods. She's afraid of people."

"Then think how to settle that best, Olesya. You'll have to choose between Granny and me. Only remember that without you life will be torture to me."

"My love!" she murmured with deep tenderness "Thank you just for saying that. You've warmed my heart. But still I shan't marry you. I'd rather go with you as I am, if you'll have me. Only please wait a little—don't rush me. Give me a couple of days to think it over. I must talk to Granny too."

"Look here, Olesya," I said as a fresh idea suddenly occurred to me. "Isn't it again that you're afraid of church?"

I ought probably to have begun from that end. I argued with Olesya almost daily, trying to reassure her about the alleged curse weighing on her family because of the magic powers they possessed. Virtually every Russian intellectual is a bit of an enlightener. It is in our blood, it has been inculcated by Russian literature of the last decades. Perhaps if Olesya had been deeply religious, if she had strictly kept the fasts and had not missed a single service in church, I might have mocked—just a little, because I have always been religious myself—at her piety and worked to develop the critical inquisitiveness of her mind. But, the fact was that, with firm and naive conviction, she confessed her communion with dark forces and her estrangement from God, whom she was afraid even to mention.

My efforts to shake her superstition were futile. All my logic, all my mockery, at times rude and cruel, smashed against her meek faith in her mysterious and fatal mission.

"Are you afraid of church, Olesya?" I asked again.

She silently bowed her head.

"You think God won't accept you?" I went on, with mounting passion. "You think he won't have mercy enough for you? He who, while commanding millions of angels, descended upon the earth and died a terrible, an ignominious death for the salvation of all men? He who didn't disdain the repentance of the lowest woman and promised a robber and murderer that he would join him in paradise that same day?"

There was nothing new to Olesya in all that—we had talked about it before; but this time she would not even listen to me. With a swift movement she pulled off her shawl, crumpled it, and flung it in my face. A playful struggle began. I tried to snatch away her hawthorn blossom. In resisting me she fell and pulled me down with her, laughing happily and putting up to me her sweet moist lips, parted by fast breathing.

Late that night, when we had separated and gone a considerable distance from each other, I heard Olesya calling to me, "Vanya! Wait a moment. I want to tell you something!"

I walked back to meet her. She ran up to me. The indented silvery crescent of the new moon was in the sky, and by its wan light I saw that Olesya's eyes were full of large tears.

"What is it, Olesya?" I asked anxiously.

She seized my hands and began to kiss them in turn.

"Darling! How good you are! How kind!" she said in a tremulous voice. "I've just been thinking how much you love me. And, you know, I want so much to do something very, very nice for you."

"Olesya, my wonderful girl, calm yourself!"

"Tell me," she went on, "would you be very glad if I went to church some day? Only tell me the truth, the real truth."

I pondered. A superstitious thought occurred to me: might that not bring on some misfortune?

"Well, why don't you speak? Tell me, quick, would you be glad, or wouldn't you care?"

"How shall I put it, Olesya?" I stammered. "Well, yes, I suppose I'd be pleased. I've often told you, haven't I, that a man may not believe, he may doubt, or even sneer. But a woman—a woman should be pious without question. I always feel there's something movingly feminine and beautiful in the simple and sweet confidence with which she commits herself to God's protection."

I paused. Olesya made no reply, nestling her head against my chest.

"But why did you ask me about it?" I inquired.

She started.

"Oh, I just wanted to know. Forget about it. Well, goodbye, darling. Be sure to come tomorrow."

She was gone. I peered for a long time into the darkness, listening to the rapidly receding footfall. Suddenly I was gripped by a dreadful foreboding. I felt an irresistible urge to run after Olesya, to overtake her and beg her, implore her not to go to church, or even demand it if necessary. But I checked my impulse, and said aloud as I turned to walk homewards, "You seem to have gone superstitious yourself, my dear Vanya."

Oh, God! Why did I not yield then to the vague impulse of my heart which—I now believe in this absolutely!—never errs in its swift, secret presentiments?

XII

The day after that meeting happened to be Trinity Sunday. That year the feast fell upon the day of Timothy the Martyr when, according to popular legend, signs of crop failure appear. The village of Perebrod had a church but no priest, and the rare services—at Lent and on major feasts—were held by a visiting priest from the village of Volchye.

That day I had to go to the neighbouring town on business, and I set out on horseback about eight o'clock in the morning, when it was still cool. I had long before bought for my trips a small stallion about six or seven years old. It was of an ordinary local breed but had been carefully groomed by its former owner, a land surveyor. Its name was Taranchik. I had taken a great fancy to the likeable beast with its strong, shapely legs, its shaggy forelock under which gleamed an angry and distrustful eye, and its vigorously compressed lips. Its colour was rather a rare and amusing one: it was mouse-grey, except that the rump was dappled with white and black spots.

I had to ride through the village from end to end. The large green square spreading between the church and the tavern was completely taken up by long rows of carts in which peasants from the neighbouring villages of Volosha, Zulnya and Pechalovka had arrived with wives and children for the feast. People were bustling among the carts. Despite the early hour and strict regulations some of them were already drunk. (On holidays and at night, vodka could be got on the sly from the former publican, Srul.) The morning was windless and sultry. The air was humid, and the day promised to be unbearably hot. Not the smallest cloud could be seen in the torrid sky, which seemed to be veiled in silvery dust.

After settling my business in town, I went to the inn for a hurried meal of pike, stuffed Jewish fashion, washed it down with abominable, muddy beer, and started homewards. But as I was riding by the smithy I recalled that Taranchik's left foreshoe had been loose for some time, and I halted to have it attended to. That took me another hour and a half, so that I rode up to Perebrod some time between four and five o'clock in the afternoon.

The square was teeming with drunken, boisterous people. Customers jostling and crushing each other had literally flooded the courtyard and the porch of the tavern; Perebrod peasants were mixed with arrivals from the neighbourhood, sitting on the grass in the shade of carts. Heads tipped back and upraised bottles could be seen everywhere. There was not a single man left sober. The general intoxication had reached the point where the muzhik begins impetuously and boastfully to exaggerate his drunkenness, where he begins to move with a heavy, flabby swing, so that instead of, say, nodding his head he sags from the thighs, bends his knees and, suddenly losing his equilibrium, lurches helplessly back. Children were romping and screaming at the feet of horses impassively chewing hay. Here and there a wailing, swearing woman, who could scarcely stand up herself, tugged at the sleeve of her balking, disgustingly drunken husband, trying to get him home. In the shade of a fence, a group of about twenty peasant men and women formed a close ring round a blind hurdy-gurdy player, whose quaking tenor, accompanied by monotonous humming, came out sharply above the general uproar. I heard the familiar words of a ballad:

> *Ho, the evening sun went down,*
> *The dark night quickly fell.*
> *Ho, the Turkish horde swept down*
> *Like a black cloud from hell.*

The ballad goes on to tell how the Turks, unable to take the Pochayev Monastery by assault, resorted to a ruse. They sent as a gift to the monastery a huge candle stuffed with gunpowder. The candle was delivered by a team of twelve pairs of oxen and the overjoyed monks were about to light it before the icon of the Pochayev Virgin, but God did not allow the heinous crime to be committed.

> *A vision then the lector had—*
> *He was cautioned by Our Lord*
> *To take the candle to the field*
> *And smite it with his sword.*

And the monks did so:

> *Then they took out into the field*
> *And smote the candle down,*
> *And balls and bullets from inside*
> *They scattered all around.*

The hot air seemed to be pervaded through and through by the sickening mixed smell of vodka, onions, sheepskin coats, strong home-grown tobacco, and dirty, sweating human bodies. Carefully threading my way through the crowd and with difficulty holding back the restless Taranchik, I met unceremonious, inquisitive and hostile looks as I rode along. Contrary to custom no one took off his cap, but the noise seemed to subside a little at my appearance. Suddenly a drunken hoarse shout rang out somewhere in the middle of the crowd; I could not make out the words, but it was greeted by subdued laughter. A frightened woman's voice tried to check the shouter.

"Shut up, you fool! What are you yelling for? He might hear you."

"What if he does?" the man cried boldly. "Is he my boss or something? It's only in the woods, with his—"

A long, foul, terrible sentence rent the air, together with a burst of uproarious laughter. I swiftly turned my horse about and clutched the handle of my whip, seized with that mad fury which is blind to everything, which does not reason and fears no one. And suddenly a strange, painful thought crossed my mind: "All this has happened to me before—many, many years ago. The sun was just as hot. The huge square was flooded with a noisy, excited crowd as it is now. I turned about just as now in a fit of frenzied anger. But where was that? When?" I lowered my whip and galloped off homewards.

Yarmola came slowly out of the kitchen. He took over the horse, and said roughly, "There's the steward from Marinovka Estate waiting for you in your room, master."

I fancied that he was about to add something—something very important and disagreeable to me—indeed I thought I saw the shadow of a malicious smirk flit across his face. I lingered purposely in the doorway and looked back at him defiantly. But he was already pulling at the bridle, with his face turned away, and the horse was gingerly following him with outstretched neck.

I found in my room Nikita Mishchenko from the neighbouring estate. He wore a short grey jacket with enormous russet checks, narrow trousers of cornflower blue and a flaming necktie. His greased hair was parted in the middle, and he gave off a fragrance of Persian Lilac. The moment he saw me he jumped up from his seat and began to scrape, doubling up at the waist rather than bowing, with a grin that bared the pallid gums of both jaws.

"My compliments," he chattered amiably "Very happy to see you. I've been waiting for you since mass. It's such a long time since I saw you last that I thought I'd drop in. Why don't you ever come and see us? The young ladies are making fun of you."

And suddenly, remembering something, he burst out laughing uncontrollably.

"Some fun we had today, I can tell you!" he cried, choking with laughter. "Ha-ha-ha! I just split my sides!"

"What do you mean? What fun?" I cut in rudely, making no effort to conceal my displeasure.

"There was a row after mass here," he continued, punctuating his speech with peals of laughter. "Some Perebrod girls—no, by God, I can't! Some Perebrod girls caught a witch in the square. I mean, *they* consider her a witch, the ignorant rustics. Well, they gave her a nice shake-up! They were going to tar her, but she slipped away somehow."

A terrible conviction flashed upon me. I rushed to the clerk and clutched at his shoulder, beside myself with anxiety.

"What are you talking about?" I roared in a frenzy. "Stop laughing, damn you! What witch do you mean?"

He at once broke off his laughter and stared at me, his eyes bulging with fright.

"I—er—I really don't know, sir," he spluttered in confusion. "I think her name's Samuilikha, or Manuilikha—wait a second, she's the daughter of a Manuilikha, it seems. The muzhiks were talking about it, but I forgot what they said, honestly."

I made him tell me from the beginning all he had seen and heard. He spoke stupidly, incoherently, mixing up details, and every moment I interrupted him by impatient questions or exclamations, all but swearing at him. I gleaned very little from his story, and it was not until about two months later that I reconstructed the accursed event in its entirety from what the forester's wife, who had been at mass that day, told me.

Presentiment had not deceived me. Olesya had overcome her fear and gone to church; she had arrived when mass was half finished, and placed herself at the back of the aisle, but all the peasants who were there at once noticed her. Throughout the service the women whispered among themselves and kept on looking back.

Nevertheless, Olesya mustered up courage enough to remain in church till the end of mass. Perhaps she had misunderstood the meaning of the hostile looks, or had ignored them out of pride. But when she walked out of the church, a bunch of women surrounded her by the fence, growing from minute to minute and closing in on her. At first they only stared rudely at the helpless girl, who was casting terrified glances about her. Then came a shower of coarse jeers, salty words, oaths accompanied by laughter, and then the various cries merged into a continuous ear-splitting noise that excited the women to an even greater fury. Olesya made several attempts to break out of the terrible live ring, but she was pushed back into the centre again and again. Suddenly an old woman screeched from behind the crowd, "Tar her, the hussy!" (In the Ukraine tarring, even of the gate of the house in which a girl lives, is a great, indelible disgrace to her.) Almost instantly a pail with tar and brush appeared above the heads of the raging women, and was passed on from hand to hand.

Then Olesya, in a fit of anger, terror and despair, flew at one of her tormentors so violently that she knocked her down. A scuffle ensued, with dozens of women in a bawling, struggling mass on the ground. By some miracle Olesya succeeded in wriggling out of the tangle, and she started to run down the road, her kerchief gone, her dress torn to rags and her naked flesh showing in many places. The crowd swore and laughed and hooted, and hurled stones at her. But she was chased by only a few, who soon fell back. Having run about fifty feet away, Olesya stopped, turned her pale, scratched and bleeding face to the brutal mob, and shouted so loudly that every word could be heard in the square, "All right! You'll remember this! You'll cry your eyes out yet!"

The threat, as the eyewitness told me, was uttered with such passionate hatred, in such a resolute, prophetic tone, that for an instant the whole crowd seemed to freeze with fear; but it only lasted an instant, for the next moment there came a fresh burst of oaths.

I repeat that I did not learn many details of the incident until much later. I had neither the strength nor the patience to hear Mishchenko's story to the end. I thought that Yarmola had probably not had time to unsaddle the horse, and I hurried out into the courtyard without a word to the dumbfounded clerk. And so it was —Yarmola was still walking Taranchik back and forth along the fence. I quickly bridled the horse, tightened the saddle-girth, and galloped off to the forest by a round-about way, so as not to have to go through the drunken crowd again.

My state during that furious race is beyond description. At moments I completely forgot where I was riding and why. I was vaguely aware that something irreparable, something absurd and terrible had happened—an awareness that was like the deep, groundless anxiety that sometimes besets you in a feverish nightmare. And, oddly enough, the broken, thin voice of the blind hurdy-gurdy player kept on echoing in my mind to the rhythm of the horse's clatter:

> *Ho, the Turkish horde swept down*
> *Like a black cloud from hell.*

Having reached the narrow path which led straight up to Manuilikha's hut, I alighted from Taranchik and led him by the bridle. The edges of his saddle-cloth and the parts of his skin covered by the harness were thickly lathered. Because of the intense heat of the day and the swift ride, the blood was rushing through my head as if a huge pump were forcing it relentlessly.

I tied the horse to the fence and walked into the hut. At first I thought Olesya was not there, and I froze inwardly with fear; but a minute later I saw her lying in bed, her face to the wall and her head buried in the pillows. She did not turn her head as the door opened.

Manuilikha, who was sitting on the floor by the bed, struggled to her feet and waved her arms at me.

"Quiet! Go easy, curse you!" she whispered threateningly, and stepped close up to me. Looking straight at me with her faded, cold eyes, she hissed angrily, "Well? See where you've got us, my friend?"

"Look here, Grandmother," I replied sternly, "this is no time for settling accounts and finding fault. How's Olesya?"

"Hush! Quiet! She's unconscious, that's how she is. If only you hadn't stuck your nose into what was no business of yours, if only you hadn't told the girl all sorts of foolish things, nothing would have happened. And I, old fool that I am, looked on and winked at it. I knew there was trouble ahead. I'd known it ever since you almost broke into this hut. Well? Are you going to tell me it wasn't you who talked her into going to church?" she burst out suddenly, her face distorted with hatred. "Wasn't it you, you damned idler? Don't you lie now, don't shift and shuffle like a fox, you shameless cur! Why did you have to get her to church?"

"I didn't, Grandmother. Upon my word I didn't. She wanted it herself."

"Oh, God!" she wrung her hands. "She came back, her face an awful sight, her blouse in rags, her kerchief gone. And when she told me about it all she laughed and cried as if she were mad. She lay down in bed and cried and cried, and then I saw she'd sort of dozed off. I was so glad, old fool that I am, thinking she'd sleep it off and get over it. I saw her arm was hanging down, so I said to myself, 'I must put the arm right or else it'll get numb.' I touched her arm—it was burning hot. She'd got fever, my poor darling. She talked without stopping for about an hour, so fast and so pitifully. She stopped only a moment ago. See what you've done. See what you've done to her!" she cried, in a new surge of despair.

And suddenly her brown face twisted into a monstrous, horrible weeping grimace: her lips stretched and drooped at the corners, all her facial muscles became taut and trembled, her eyebrows rose high, furrowing her forehead with deep wrinkles, and tears as large as peas rolled from her eyes with extraordinary rapidity. Clasping her head with her hands and putting her elbows on the table, she started rocking back and forth with all her body.

"My own li-i-ttle one!" she howled. "My de-ear little gi-irl! Oh, how mis-er-able I a-am!"

"Stop your wailing, old woman," I interrupted her rudely, "you'll wake her up!"

She fell silent, but went on rocking to and fro with the same horrible grimace on her face, while large tears kept dropping on the table. About ten minutes passed thus. I sat by Manuilikha's side and listened in anguish to the monotonous, jerky buzzing of a fly beating against the window-pane.

"Granny!" we suddenly heard Olesya call in a feeble, scarcely audible voice. "Granny, who's here?"

Manuilikha shambled hastily to the bed, and at once resumed her wailing.

"Oh, my dear girl, my o-o-own! Oh, how miserable I am, how wretched!"

"Stop it, Granny, please!" said Olesya, with pitiful entreaty and suffering in her voice. "Who's in our hut?"

I tiptoed to the bed with an awkward, guilty awareness of my good health and clumsiness—a feeling you always have with a sick person.

"It's me, Olesya," I said, lowering my voice. "I've just ridden down from the village. I was in town all morning. Are you feeling bad, Olesya?"

Without taking her face away from the pillows, she stretched her bare arm backwards, as if groping in the air. I understood, and took her hot hand in both my hands. Two huge blue spots, one above the wrist and the other above the elbow, stood out sharply on her white, delicate skin.

"My dear one," Olesya began slowly, spacing her words with difficulty. "I want to—look at you so, but I can't. They've spoiled—my face. Remember—you liked

156

it? You did like it, darling, didn't you? And I was always so glad you did——But now you'll be disgusted—to see me——Well, so I—don't want you to."

"Forgive me, Olesya," I whispered, bending low over her ear.

Her burning hand held mine for a long time in a strong grasp.

"How can you say that? How can you, darling? Aren't you ashamed to think of it? Is it your fault? I brought it on myself, fool that I am. Why did I have to do it at all? No, my love, don't blame yourself."

"Allow me, Olesya——But first promise you'll do what I ask."

"I promise, dear—anything you wish."

"Please allow me to send for the doctor. I beg you! You may do nothing of what he tells you to, if you don't care to. But say yes for my sake at least, Olesya "

"Oh, darling! How you trapped me! No, please allow me not to keep my promise. I wouldn't let a doctor come near me even if I really were ill and dying. And I am not. I was just scared, that's all, I'll get over it by tonight. And if I don't, Granny will give me an infusion of lilies of the valley, or tea with raspberries. Why call a doctor? You are my best doctor. I feel much better now that you're here. There's only one thing I'm sorry for: I'd like to have a look at you, just one look, but I'm afraid."

With tender effort I raised her head from the pillow. Her face was blazing feverishly, her dark eyes shone with unnatural brightness, her parched lips twitched. Long, red scars furrowed her face and neck. She had dark bruises on her forehead and under her eyes.

"Don't look at me. Please don't. I'm ugly now," she whispered imploringly, trying to shut my eyes with her hand.

My heart brimmed over with pity. I pressed my lips to her hand, which lay motionless on the blanket, and

167

covered it with long, gentle kisses. I had kissed her hands before, but she had always snatched them away bashfully. But now she did not resist my caress, and stroked my hair with her other hand.

"Do you know everything?" she asked me in a whisper.

I nodded. I had not made out all that Mishchenko had told me, but I did not want Olesya to upset herself recalling that morning's incident. Yet at the thought of the outrage done to her I was gripped with mad fury.

"Oh, why wasn't I there at the time!" I cried, straightening up and clenching my fists. "I'd——I'd—"

"Please don't. It's all right, really. Don't be angry, dear," Olesya stopped me meekly.

I could no longer hold back the tears that had been choking me and burning my eyes. Putting my face to Olesya's shoulder, I broke into silent and bitter sobs, shaking all over.

"You're crying?" Her voice rang with surprise, tenderness, and compassion. "My darling! Please stop—don't torture yourself, dear. I feel so happy with you. Let's not cry while we're together. Let's be gay these last days, and then it won't be so hard for us to part."

I raised my head in surprise. An uncertain presentiment slowly took hold of my heart.

"The last days, Olesya? Why the last? Why should we part?"

She closed her eyes, and did not speak for a few seconds.

"We've got to part, Vanya," she said with determination. "We'll leave as soon as I feel a bit better. We can't stay here any more."

"Are you afraid of something?"

"No, dear, I'm not afraid of anything, if it comes to that. Only why drive people to crime? Perhaps you don't know. Over there in Perebrod I threatened them—I was so angry and ashamed. Now they're going to blame us for anything that happens. Whether it's cattle dying or a house catching fire, *we* shall be held guilty. Am I right, Granny?" she asked, raising her voice.

"What were you saying, my girl? I didn't hear," mumbled Manuilikha, coming nearer and cupping her hand round her ear.

"I was saying that now they'll blame us for any misfortune that may happen in Perebrod."

"So they will, Olesya, they'll blame poor us for everything. They won't let us live in peace, they'll do us in, they will, the damned fools. And that time they drove me out of the village—wasn't it the same thing? I threatened in anger a silly cow of a woman, and then her baby died. God knows I had nothing to do with it, but they nearly killed me, curse them. They threw stones at me as I ran away, and I only tried to shield you—you were only a child. 'Let 'em hit me,' I said to myself, 'but why should harm come to an innocent child?' They're barbarians, a bunch of heathens fit for the gallows, that's what they are!"

"But where can you go? You have no kith or kin anywhere. Besides, you need money to settle in a new place."

"We'll manage somehow," said Olesya carelessly. "Granny'll dig up some money, she's laid something by."

"Do you call that money?" Manuilikha replied testily, moving away from the bed. "It's just a few measly kopeks soaked in tears."

"What about me, Olesya? You won't even think of me!" I cried, with bitter, unkind reproach.

She sat up and, unembarrassed by Manuilikha's presence, took my head into her hands and kissed me several times on the forehead and cheeks.

"I'm thinking of you more than of anybody else, my love. Only, you see, we aren't destined to be together. Remember I laid out the cards for you? Everything's turned out just as they told me then. That means fate doesn't want you and me to be happy together. Do you think I'd be afraid of anything if it weren't for that?"

"Talking about fate again!" I cried impatiently. "I don't want to believe in it, and I never will!"

"Oh, no, no! Don't say that," she whispered in fright. "It's for you I'm afraid, dear, not for myself. You'd better not start talking about it at all."

I tried in vain to dissuade her, painting her a picture of unruffled happiness that neither fate nor coarse, cruel people would be able to disturb. Olesya merely kissed my hands, shaking her head.

"No, no—I know, I can see it," she insisted. "It would be nothing but sorrow, nothing at all."

Disconcerted and confused by her superstitious obstinacy, I finally asked her, "Will you at least let me know when you're going?"

She reflected. Then a faint smile touched her lips.

"I'll tell you a little story. One day a wolf was running through the wood and he saw a hare. 'I'll eat you up, hare!' he says. 'Have pity on me, wolf,' the hare begged, 'I want to live, my little ones are waiting for me at home.' The wolf wouldn't listen to him. Then the hare said, 'Well, at least let me live three days longer, and then you may eat me up. It'll be easier for me to die that way.' The wolf gave him the three days—he didn't eat him up, just kept an eye on him. One day passed, then another, and at last the third day came. 'Get ready now,' says the wolf, 'I'm going to eat you.' And the hare began to cry bitterly. 'Why did you ever give me those three days, wolf! You should have eaten me up as soon as you saw me. Those three days were worse than death to me!' That hare spoke the truth, dear. Don't you think so?"

I did not speak, overcome by a gloomy anticipation of solitude to come. Suddenly Olesya sat up in bed; she looked very earnest.

"Tell me, Vanya," she said with emphasis, "were you happy while we were together?"

"Olesya! How can you ask?"

"Wait. Were you sorry you had met me? Did you think of any other woman while you were with me?"

"Not for a second! Not only in your presence but even when I was alone, I thought of nobody but you."

"Were you jealous? Were you ever displeased with me? Were you bored in my company?"

"Never, Olesya! Never!"

She put her hands on my shoulders and gazed into my eyes with ineffable love.

"Well, then, my dear one, you'll never think of me unkindly or angrily," she said, as firmly as if she were reading my future in my eyes. "You'll feel unhappy at first after we part, oh, so very unhappy! You'll cry, you won't have any peace. Then it'll pass and be gone. And afterwards you'll think of me without sorrow, but with a light and joyful heart."

She put her head back on the pillow.

"Now go, dear," she whispered feebly. "Go home, darling. I'm a little tired. Wait—give me a kiss. Don't be afraid of Granny—she won't mind. You won't mind, will you, Granny?"

"All right, all right, say goodbye properly," Manuilikha answered grudgingly. "What's the use of hiding from me? I've known it for a long time."

"Kiss me here, and here, and here," said Olesya, putting her finger to her eyes, cheeks, and mouth.

"Olesya! You're saying goodbye to me as if we weren't going to meet any more!" I exclaimed, frightened.

"I don't know, darling. I don't know anything. Well, now go in peace. No, wait one more second. Bend your ear to me. Do you know what I'm sorry about?" she whispered, her lips touching my cheek. "It's that I have no baby of yours. Oh, how happy I'd have been!"

I walked out, accompanied by Manuilikha. A black cloud with a sharply outlined curly rim covered half the sky, but the sun was still shining as it dipped westwards, and there was something sinister about that blend of light and oncoming darkness. The old woman looked up, shading her eyes with her hand, and shook her head significantly.

"There'll be a rainstorm over Perebrod today," she said with conviction. "It may even hail, which God forbid."

XIV

I had almost reached Perebrod when a sudden whirlwind snatched up clouds of dust and sent them rolling along the road. The first drops of rain—few and heavy—came down.

Manuilikha had been right. The rainstorm, which had been gathering throughout that hot, sweltering day, burst above Perebrod with extraordinary force. The lightning flashed almost incessantly, and my window-panes shook and resounded with the peals of thunder. The storm died down for a few minutes towards eight o'clock in the evening, only to begin again with fresh violence. Suddenly something drummed on the roof and against the walls of the old house with a deafening noise. I dashed to the window. Huge hailstones, the size of walnuts, were hurtling down and bouncing off the ground. I looked at the mulberry-tree that grew near the house; it was completely bare, all its leaves knocked off by the battering hail. In the gloom below the window, I saw the dark figure of Yarmola, who had run out of the kitchen, his head and shoulders covered by his coat, to close the shutters. But he was too late. An enormous lump of ice struck against one pane with such force that the glass was smashed to smithereens, and bits of it tinkled on to the floor of my room.

Feeling tired, I lay down on my bed without undressing. I thought I should be unable to sleep that night and should toss in helpless anguish till morning; I therefore decided not to take off my clothes, so that afterwards I might tire myself a little by monotonously pacing the room. But a very strange thing happened. It seemed to me that I had closed my eyes for only a moment; but when I opened them again bright sunbeams were slanting through the chinks in the shutters, with countless golden dust-grains whirling in their light.

Yarmola was standing over my bed, with a look of severe anxiety and impatient expectation on his face. He must have been waiting a long time for me to wake up.

"Master," he said in a voice that sounded alarmed. "Master, you've got to go away."

I swung down my feet, and looked at him in astonishment.

"Go? Go where? Why? You must be crazy."

"No, I ain't," he snarled. "Do you know what the hail did last night? Half the crops are as if they'd been trampled down. One-eyed Maxim's, Kozyol's, Mut's, the Prokopchuk's, Gordy Olefir's——So she did make trouble, the accursed witch! May she wither!"

In a flash I recalled all that had happened on the previous day, the threat which Olesya had shouted near the church, and her fears.

"Now the whole community's up," Yarmola went on. "They've all been drinking since the morning, and now they're yelling. They're shouting some nasty things about you too, master And d'you know what our people are like? If they do anything to those witches it'll serve 'em right—it'll only be fair. But to you, master, I'll say this much: get out as fast as you can."

So Olesya's fears had come true. I must immediately warn her and Manuilikha of the impending danger. I dressed in great haste, splashed some water on my face, and half an hour later was riding towards Devil's Nook at a brisk trot.

The nearer I drew to the witch's hut the greater became the uncertain, painful anxiety I felt. I was telling myself that a new, unexpected sorrow was about to befall me.

I fairly ran along the path winding up the sandy slope. The windows of the hut were open, the door stood ajar.

"My God! What's happened here?" I whispered, my heart sinking as I stepped in.

The hut was empty. Inside was that sad mess which always marks a hasty departure. Rubbish and rags lay in heaps on the floor, and the wooden frame of the bedstead stood bare in its corner.

My heart heavy and welling up with tears, I was about to walk out when my attention was caught by a bright object hung on a corner of the window-frame, obviously on purpose. It was a string of the cheap red beads known in Polesye as "corals": the only thing left to me as a keepsake of Olesya and her tender, generous love.

1898

NIGHT DUTY

The evening roll-call had long been over and the prayers chanted in Number Eight Company's barracks. It was already past ten but the men were in no hurry to undress. The following day was a Sunday, when all but those on duty rose one hour later than usual.

Private Luka Merkulov had just gone on duty. He had to keep awake till two o'clock past midnight, making the round of the barracks in greatcoat and cap, with bayonet at his side, and see that everything was in order—that nothing was stolen, that the men did not go out in underwear, that no outsiders got into the barracks. If a superior came round, he would have to report on the state of the camp and to give an account of everything that had happened.

Merkulov had been put on duty out of turn, by way of punishment, because on the previous Monday, during shooting drill, his rolled-up greatcoat had been tied by a string instead of the regulation strap, which had been stolen. This was the third time in five days that he had had to do extra duty, and always at night, which made it even worse.

He was a poor parade-ground soldier. Not that he was lazy or careless. He just could not master, much as he tried, the difficult art of arms drill, of keeping his toes down on the march, of "thrusting his whole body forward," and of "holding his breath at the right moment when pulling the trigger." Nevertheless, he was known as a serious and proper soldier; he kept his uniform trim, used comparatively little foul language, drank no vodka except what was issued to him on grand holidays, and in his spare time slowly and painstakingly made high boots, never more than one pair a month, but what boots! They called them Merkulov boots—huge, heavy, wearproof.

His rough, grey face, matching the colour of his greatcoat, had that shade of dirty pallor which the air of barracks, prisons and hospitals gives to peasant faces. What struck you as strange and somehow out of place in it was his slightly protruding eyes, of an amazingly delicate and pure colour—kind as a child's and so limpid that they seemed to shine. His thick lips were those of a simplehearted man, especially the upper one with the sparse, brownish down on it lying flat as if it had been wetted.

The barracks were full of uproar. The smoky reddish light of four tin night-lamps, hooked on the wall in the quarters of each platoon, barely illumined the four long adjoining rooms. Two continuous rows of plank beds, covered with hay mattresses, stretched down the middle of the rooms. The walls were whitewashed, their lower part painted brown. Shapely rows of rifles stood in long wooden racks against the walls; above them hung framed paintings and prints crudely representing the whole of soldierly knowledge.

Merkulov walked slowly from platoon to platoon. He was lonesome and sleepy, and he envied these men clamouring and laughing in the heavy gloom of the barracks. They all had so many hours of sleep ahead of them that they did not mind staying up a few minutes longer. But what agonized and galled him most was that half an hour later the whole company would fall silent and drop off to sleep, and that he would be the only one to remain awake, wretched and forgotten, all alone among a hundred men, whom some unearthly, mysterious power would have wafted away into an unknown world.

About a dozen soldiers were huddled together in Two Platoon. They were sitting or sprawling so close to each other on the plank beds that you could not tell at once which arms and legs belonged to which heads or backs. Now and then a hand-rolled cigarette glowed red in the darkness. Sitting cross-legged in the middle of the group was Private Zamoshnikov, or Uncle Zamoshnikov, as he was called in the company. Everybody liked the undersized, lively old soldier, who usually led the singing and was always ready to amuse the others. He was now spinning a yarn, rocking back and forth and rubbing his knees with his palms; he spoke in a steady, deliberate undertone that seemed to have a note of wonderment in it. The soldiers were listening in tense silence. Occasionally one of them, carried away by the narrative and unable to check himself, would burst out into a loud oath of admiration.

Merkulov halted near the group and listened indifferently.

"So that there Turkish Sultan sends him a great big barrel of poppy seed and with it there's a letter: 'Your

Ex'lency, glorious and brave General Skobelev! I gives you three days and three nights to count every seed that's in this here barrel. And let me tell you that I've got as many soldiers in my army as you'll count seeds in the barrel.' Well, General Skobelev read the Sultan's letter and he wasn't scared a bit. Not him! He just sent the Turkish Sultan a handful of pepper pods. 'I haven't got half so many soldiers as you've got,' he says, 'just this little handful here, but you try and chew 'em!' "

"That was smart of him!" a voice commented behind Zamoshnikov's back.

The other listeners chuckled.

"Yes. 'Try and chew 'em,' he says!" repeated Zamoshnikov, loth to part with the lucky phrase. "The Sultan, he sent him a barrel of poppy seed, see, and the general sent him back a handful of pepper. 'You try and chew that!' he says. That's what our Skobelev told him—that there Turkish Sultan. 'I've only got a handful of soldiers,' he says, 'but see if you can chew 'em!' "

"Is that the end of the story, Uncle Zamoshnikov?" asked an impatient listener timidly.

"Don't you be in such a hurry, my lad," Zamoshnikov snapped, annoyed. "I'll take my time, if you don't mind. Telling a story's not the same as catching fleas, you know." He paused to regain his composure, and then resumed the story, "Yes, as I was saying. 'It's only a little handful, to be sure,' he says, 'but try and chew 'em.' So the Turkish Sultan read Skobelev's letter, and wrote him another one back: 'You'd better get that fine army of yours out of my Turkish land,' he says, 'because if you don't, I'll give my soldiers a glass of vodka apiece, and that'll make 'em angry and they'll chase all your army out of Turkey in three days.' But Skobelev had his answer ready: 'O great and glorious Sultan of Turkey, how dare you, you freak-faced Turk, write me words like that? Think you can scare me, do you? "I'll give 'em a glass of vodka apiece!" Well, and I won't give *my* soldiers any grub to eat for three days and they'll swallow you up, you son of a gun, alive, with all your army. And they won't bring you up again, either, so you'll just be reported missing, you dog, you pig-eared beast!' Well, the moment that there Turkish Sultan heard this he started wobbling at the knees and spoke up for peace right away. 'Go along,' he says, 'and take your army with you. Here's a million rubles cash down, please take it like a good fella and leave me alone.'"

Zamoshnikov paused, then said briefly, "That's all, lads."

As the listeners came back to life the group stirred. Gruff exclamations of approval were heard from all sides.

"Showed him up proper, didn't he!"

"One in the eye for him, that was."

"Not half it was. 'I won't give my soldiers any grub for three days,' he says, 'and they'll swallow you alive, you dirty dog.' Was that how he said it, Uncle Zamoshnikov? Eh, Uncle Zamoshnikov?"

Zamoshnikov repeated the sentence word for word.

"They're no good against us!" cried boastful voices.

"Bah! As if they could be, against the Russians!"

"You'd better think twice, old man, before you take us on."

"Yes, and think hard——Before you start a thing like that you'd better have a good pray and eat a lot."

Zamoshnikov reached for the cigarette glowing beside him, and said carelessly, "Give us a pull, mate. I'm dying for a smoke."

He took several strong pulls one after the other, blowing out the smoke through his nostrils in two straight, powerful jets. His face, particularly his chin and lips, would light up for a moment in the red glow, then vanish again into the darkness. A hand reached for the cigarette in his mouth, and a voice begged, "Come on, Uncle Zamoshnikov, leave something for me to smoke."

"Some'll do the smoking and some the spitting," Zamoshnikov replied curtly.

The soldiers laughed.

"That Zamoshnikov—he's always ready with his tongue!"

The encouraged Zamoshnikov went on cracking his jokes.

"You know how a chap offers you a smoke nowadays, don't you? You give the paper and let me have your baccy, and then we'll have a smoke—that's how."

Still he thrust the fag-end into the outstretched hand and spat aside, leaning over someone's back.

"Here's another story, lads," he said. "Perhaps you've heard it. I mean the one about the soldier who put on a pair of iron claws and climbed a tower to see a princess. I'd rather not tell it if you know it already."

"No, we don't——shoot it! Nobody's heard it."

"Well, it starts this way. Once upon a time there was a man, Yashka by name, soldier by fame. And he was an amazing fella, was that soldier."

Merkulov moved listlessly away. At some other time he would have been only too glad to listen to Zamoshnikov's yarns, but now he thought it strange that the others should listen so eagerly to stories which were quite unamusing and, moreover, obviously invented.

"They've forgotten all about sleep, the bastards," he said to himself angrily. "They've got all night to snore."

He walked up to a window. The panes were misted over on the inside, and every now and then a drop of water trickled down. He wiped the pane with the sleeve of his coat, pressed his forehead to it, and cupped his hands round his eyes to keep out the reflected light of the lamp. It was a black, rainy autumn night. The light from the window fell on the ground in a long slanting rectangle and in it he could see a large puddle wrinkling and rippling. Far ahead and below, the lights of the little town glimmered faintly, as if they were on the very edge of the world. His eyes could make out nothing else in the rainy darkness.

After lingering awhile at the window Merkulov made the round of Four Platoon, and wandered slowly on along the windows on the other side. Swinging their feet from the corner of the row of plank beds sat two soldiers, Panchuk and Koval. A small wooden chest with a padlock attached to it by rings stood between them. On the chest lay a loaf of rye bread, sliced up into thick hunks, five onions, a lump of bacon, and some coarse grey salt in a clean rag. Panchuk and Koval were linked to each other by a strange, silent friendship based on an extraordinary voracity. Their bread ration, three pounds apiece, did not satisfy them; every day they bought extra bread from their fellow soldiers, and always ate it together, usually in the evening, without ever exchanging a single word. They both came of prosperous families and received from home a monthly allowance of one or even two rubles each.

Using a narrow knife, so worn by sharpening that its blade had become curved, they took turns to cut off a few slices of bacon, thin as cigarette paper, and neatly spread them out between two pieces of bread, well salted on both sides. Then they silently and slowly set about munching the huge sandwiches, lazily dangling their feet.

Merkulov stopped in front of them and looked dully on. The sight of bacon made his mouth water, but he did not venture to ask for some; he knew they would refuse and jeer at him. Nevertheless, he said in an unsteady, almost pleading voice, "Have a good meal, lads."

"What I eat is my own, and you can stand and look on," Koval replied, without a hint of derision in his voice. Without glancing at Merkulov, he skinned the brown peel off an onion with the knife, cut it in four, dipped one of the pieces into the salt, and started to crunch it with relish.

Panchuk did not say anything but stared at Merkulov's face with drowsy, stupid eyes. He was champing loudly, the knots of muscles on his heavy cheek-bones straining and rolling under the taut skin.

For a few minutes none of the three spoke a word. Finally Panchuk gulped down a big mouthful, and asked in a thick, indifferent voice, "On duty, are you?"

He knew very well that Merkulov was on duty, and he had asked the question for no special reason, without the least curiosity—it just came of itself. And Merkulov, just as indifferently, uttered for an answer a long string of foul words that might have been intended for the two soldiers who could afford to eat their fill of bread and bacon, or equally well for his commanding officer who had put him on extra duty.

He walked away from the two friends, who continued their silent, unhurried eating. The damp barracks filled rapidly with the warmth of human breathing. Merkulov even felt hot in his greatcoat. He made the round of all the platoons several times, listening in boredom to the talk, the loud laughter, the swearing and singing that seemed as if it would never cease. Nothing made him laugh or amused him, but deep in his heart he longed for the noise to go on till very late, possibly till the morning, so that he might not be left alone in the murky stillness of the sleeping barracks.

At one end of Number One Platoon stood a separate plank bed, occupied by Warrant Officer Noga, Merkulov's immediate superior. Noga was a notorious fop and lady-killer, very talkative and well off. The hay mattress on his bed was covered with a quilted blanket, made of coloured squares and triangles. A small, round looking-glass with a crack in the middle was pasted to the wooden back of the bed with a lump of bread.

Having discarded his uniform and boots, Noga was lying back on the magnificent quilt, his hands under his head and his feet up, one of them propped against the wall and the other slung across it. A reed holder with a lighted cigarette in it protruded from the corner of his mouth. Standing in front of him like a huge dispirited ape was Kamafutdinov, a private of his platoon. A pallid, dirty, doltish Tatar who in the three years of his military service had hardly learned a word of Russian, Kamafutdinov was the laughing-stock of the company and the horror and shame of inspection parades.

Noga did not feel like sleeping and was making use of the opportunity to "coach" Kamafutdinov. The mental effort had brought out beads of sweat on the Tatar's temples and the tip of his nose. From time to time he pulled a dirty rag out of his pocket to wipe his swollen, purulent eyes, affected by trachoma.

"You Turkish idiot!" Noga fumed. "You fish-face! What did I ask you? Well? What did I ask you, you block-head?"

Kamafutdinov made no reply.

"You unwashed monkey! What's your rifle called? Tell me what your rifle's called, you Tatar beast!"

Kamafutdinov rubbed his sore eyes, shifting from one foot to the other, but made no reply.

"Why, you—! What am I to do with you! Here, repeat after me." Noga began aloud, pronouncing each syllable with the utmost clarity, "Small-bore, quick-firing—"

"Esmol-boor kick-fie—" Kamafutdinov repeated, with terrified haste.

"Fool! Don't hurry. Say it again: small-bore, quick-firing—"

"Semol-bor—kivick-firy—"

"Ugh! You Tatar monkey!" Noga gave him a terrible scowl. "All right, damn you. Go on, repeat: infantry rifle—"

"Infat rifil—"

"With sliding bolt—"

"Visselidin boolt—"

"Berdan's type, number two."

"Beerdan sipe, numba two."

"Good. Now start from the beginning."

Kamafutdinov fidgeted and got his rag out again.

"Well? Speak up, damn you!"

"Ismolboor—visselidin—" Kamafutdinov blurted out the syllables that occurred to him first.

" 'Visselidin'!" Noga cut in. "Visselidin yourself! I can't be bothered to get up, or I'd polish your mug for you! You're spoiling all the beauty of my platoon. Do you think I'm not told off on your account? I am, my lad, I am indeed! Well, say it again: small-bore, quick-firing—"

At the other end of Number One Platoon, three old soldiers lay sprawling on the plank beds near the iron stove, their heads together. They were singing in an undertone, but with great feeling and apparent pleasure, a peasant song from "back home." The first singer led in the sad melody in a soft high-pitched falsetto, slurring his words and putting in extra vowels for greater sonority. Another singer accompanied him in a husky but pleasant and mellow little tenor, with a slight twang. The third sang an octave below the first, in a flat, colourless voice; occasionally he would fall silent, miss a couple of beats and suddenly chime in again and overtake his partners in a sort of fugue.

> *Goodbye, my love! My life, goodbye!*
> *My eyes will never dry.*
> *My sweetheart now I'll never see,*
> *My own true-oo-oo—*

The first two voices drew it out in beautiful harmony, and the third, which had stopped after the words "never see," suddenly joined in again with a strong and resolute:

> *—true love is leaving me.*

And then all the three sang together:

I'll never see my love come home,
In lovers' lanes we'll never roam.

Having finished one verse, the first singer, who had sung the melody, suddenly struck a terribly high note and drew it out infinitely, his mouth wide open, his eyes closed, and his nose wrinkled with the effort. Then, breaking off abruptly, as if he had finished with it for ever, he made a brief pause, cleared his throat, and began afresh:

All through the ni-ight my eyes are we-et,
A wink of slee-eep I cannot ge-et.
I can't forget, I ca-an't forge-et—

"No, sir, I can't forget!" the third suddenly cut in, in a confident recitative, and the trio continued:

Oh, never now shall I forget
Your loving eyes, your tender gaze,
Your merry talk, your taking ways.

Merkulov had heard the song in his home village and he listened to it with deep attention. He thought how nice it would have been to be lying down undressed, with his greatcoat over him up to his ears, thinking of his village and his folk until sleep gently and caressingly closed his eyes.

The three soldiers stopped singing. Merkulov waited long for them to start again; he liked the vague sadness and self-pity which mournful melodies always aroused in him. But the soldiers lay flat on their bellies, head to head, without moving; they too must have been cast by the plaintive song into silent melancholy. Merkulov drew a deep sigh, scratched his itching chest vigorously with a suffering expression on his face, and walked slowly away from the singers.

Gradually a hush spread over the barracks. Only from Two Platoon did there come frequent bursts of noisy laughter. Zamoshnikov had finished his story about the iron-clawed soldier and was now "performing." He did both the improvising and the acting. His favourite theme, which he was now rendering, was the regimental inspection, as taken by the exacting "General Zamoshnikov." In the course of the show he alternately appeared as a fat general suffering from asthma, the regimental commander, Junior Captain Glazunov, Sergeant-Major Taras Gavrilovich, an old Ukrainian countrywoman who had just come to town and who had "not seen a *Moskal** for eighteen years," the bow-legged, squint-eyed Private Tverdokhleb, a crying child, an angry lady with a lapdog, Kamafutdinov the Tatar, an entire battalion, a brass band, and the regimental surgeon. Each of the listeners must have attended Zamoshnikov's "performances" at least a dozen times, but their interest never flagged, the more so as Zamoshnikov always embellished his dialogue anew with brisk rhymes and a joke here and there, each joke being more of a surprise and more ribald than its predecessor

Zamoshnikov was performing in the passage between the plank beds and the windows, his audience sitting or lying about on the beds.

"Muze-zicians fo-orward!" he commanded in a hoarse, purposely muffled voice, opening his mouth wider than necessary and throwing back his head. He was naturally afraid to shout and used the mimicry to make up in some degree for the regimental commander's deafening bawl.

* A Ukrainian nickname for a Russian.—*Tr.*

"Re-egiment! 'Shun! Present a-a-arms! Band, strike up! Tram-pa-pim-ta-ti-ra-ram!"

Zamoshnikov trumpeted a march, blowing up his cheeks and whanging them with his palms as he might a drum. Then he said in a glib patter:

"Here comes the brave General Zamoshnikov riding on a white horse. He has an eagle eye, and holds his head high. His decorations glitter and put you in a twitter. 'I salute you, my brave men!' 'We salute Your Ex'cy!' 'Well done, men!' 'Doing our best, Your Ex'cy!' And now comes the regimental commander to report: 'I have the honour to report to Your Excellency, the glorious and brave General Zamoshnikov. Everything is in order in the jolly old Nizhny-Lom Regiment. A full thousand soldiers are on the list. A hundred are sick and in bed, a hundred more tight and half dead, and as many away who've fled. Fifty men are propping the fence, another fifty're held for offence, and fifty more drunk—no pretence. Two hundred have gone a-begging, the rest are limp as a legging. They're unshaved and awful hairy, and their faces bruised and scary. For a whole year they took no food—just went on strolls with girls and cooed. There's no regiment on earth merrier'n ours!' 'That's the stuff, men, thank you, my heroes!' 'Doing our best, Your Ex'cy!' 'Any complaints?' 'No complaints, Your Ex'cy!' 'Do you get enough bread?' 'Yes, sir, Your Ex'cy, an awful lot. It sets our tongues clacking and our bellies cracking.' 'Bully for you, men. That's the way. Sing, my men, as hard as you can, keep your chins up and don't ask for grub. Each man shall have a messtinful of vodka and a pound of tobacco, and half a ruble to top it.' 'Thank you ever so much, Your Ex'cy.'

"Then the regimental commander rides up. 'Regiment will march past by companies, at a distance of two platoons. Number One Company, forward march!' Music. Ta-ra-ram-ta-ram. There they go—left right, left right!'

And all of a sudden: 'Halt! Back! As you were!' 'What's the m-matter?' 'Which company is this, colonel?' 'The Tipsy Eighth, Your Ex'cy. 'And who's that wry-faced rooky in the ranks?' 'Private Tverdokhleb, Your Ex'cy.' 'Send him off parade and give him fifty of the best.' "

The soldiers guffawed, and Private Tverdokhleb, nudged in the ribs from every side, laughed louder than anybody. Then there came the usual story of how "General Zamoshnikov" had lunch with the regimental commander after the inspection.

" 'Will you have cabbage or potato soup, Your Ex'cy?' 'Give me both—a lot of both.' 'How about some vodka, Your Ex'cy?' 'Ahem. Yes, I'll have some—a tumblerful.' Then there followed a refined conversation with the colonel's daughter. 'Treat me to a little kiss, dear miss.' 'Oh, no, sir, how could I, with my father about? He might see it.' 'So you can't, eh?' 'Ah! absolutely impossible.' 'In that case kindly grant your tiny hand.' 'Yes, you may take that.' "

But Zamoshnikov had no chance to finish his "performance." The door was suddenly thrown open and the figure of Sergeant-Major Taras Gavrilovich loomed in the doorway with nothing on but his underwear, his bare feet in slippers, and a pair of spectacles on his nose.

"What's the idea of neighing like stallions in a stall?" his angry old man's voice rang out. "When are you going to stop this noise? Want me to lay my fist across your big mouths? Get into bed, and look lively!"

The soldiers scattered, slowly and reluctantly. Quite soon, in about five minutes, the barracks lapsed into silence. Someone whispered a hurried prayer: 'O mighty God, Jesus Christ— Son of God, have mercy upon us— Father, Son and Holy Ghost, have mercy upon us!" Someone else dropped his high boots one after the other on the asphalt floor with a thud. A third coughed a deep, racking cough—it might have been a sheep coughing. Life stopped all at once.

Merkulov continued his round of the barracks. He paced along the wall, mechanically picking chips of paint off it with his thumb nail. The soldiers lay on the plank beds, huddled together under their greatcoats. In the dim, smoky light of the night-lamps the outlines of the sleeping men had lost their sharpness and looked blurred, as if it were not men lying, but monotonous, still, grey heaps of coats.

For lack of anything better to do, Merkulov peered at the men. One of them was lying on his back with his knees in the air, breathing deeply and evenly, his mouth half open; a foolish expression lingered on his calm face. Another was sleeping face downwards, his head buried in the crook of his left arm, while his right arm stretched along his body, with the palm upturned. His bare feet stuck out from under the short greatcoat; the calves were taut, and the toes were contracted as if gripped by cramp. There was the twisted form of Private Yestifeyev, a fellow-villager of Merkulov's and his neighbour in the file. He could hardly have taken a more unnatural posture; his head was thrust deep under the greasy red calico pillow, his knees drawn up nearly to his chin. The blood must have rushed to his head, for long, painful groans came from under the pillow.

Merkulov had an uncanny, oppressive feeling. But a few minutes before, a hundred men had been moving about, laughing, talking, wrangling, and now here they were, all of them, lying motionless, groaning or snoring, overpowered and borne away into *another* life that was quite unaccountable and mysterious. For them there was no longer any military service with its hardships and affected gaiety, the dreary gloom of the barracks, the sleeping men tossing their heads restlessly on each other's chests, Merkulov wandering all alone with his melancholy. And a dark terror crept into Merkulov's heart that made the hair bristle on his scalp and sent cold shivers down his spine.

He stopped in front of the clock hanging in Number Three Platoon under the night-lamp, and stared at it for some time. He was no good at telling the time, but he knew—the man on duty before him had explained that to him patiently and at great length—that when the big hand pointed straight up and the small one formed almost a right angle with it, that would be the time for him to be relieved. It was an ordinary two-ruble clock with a white square dial and little roses painted in the corners; it had two brass weights with a stone and an iron bolt tied to one of them by a piece of string, and a time-battered brass pendulum that looked as if someone had been chewing it.

"Tick-tock, tick-tock," the pendulum counted in the stillness, and Merkulov listened to it attentively. The first tick was weaker and clearer, while the second rang out dully, with an effort, as if something checked it within; and a chain could be heard scraping inside the clock between the two ticks. "Tick-tock, tick-tock."

And Merkulov whispered to the rhythm of the ticking clock, "Tough luck, tough luck." There was a strange spiritual connection between the clock and Merkulov on his night watch, as if both of them—alone in the barracks—had been condemned by some cruel power drearily to mark off the seconds and suffer in long solitude. "Tough luck, tough luck," whispered the pendulum, with weary monotony. It was dull and eerie in the barracks, with the night-lamps hardly giving any light and ugly shadows crammed into the corners, and Merkulov drowsily whispered, together with the pendulum, "Tough luck."

Then he went into the far corner of Number One Platoon and sat down between the stove and a rifle stack, on a high stool with a shiny, time-blackened seat. A faint warmth, mingled with the smell of coal-gas, came from the stove. Merkulov dug his hands deep into his sleeves and pondered.

He recalled the letter he had received from his "homeland" the other day. The letter had been read to him aloud: first by the platoon warrant officer; then by the company's orderly-room clerk, and lastly by all his fellow-villagers who could read, so that by now Merkulov knew the letter by heart and could even prompt readers whenever they reached an illegible passage.

"This letter is for a soldier, an infantryman, and very important. Posted from the village of Mokriye Verkhi, on September 20th this year. From your father.

"Our dear son, Luka Moiseyevich, first we send you our parental blessing and wish you in the name of the Lord speedy and happy success in your affairs, and advise you that your mother Lukerya Trofimovna and myself are, thank God, in good health, which we wish you too. Also, your loving wife, Tatyana Ivanovna, sends you her regards, the respect of a true and loving wife and best wishes with love, and she would have you well and happy in God's name. Also, your dear father-in-law, Ivan Fedoseyevich, with wife and children, sends you his regards and wishes you success in your affairs. Also, your brother Nikolai Moiseyevich, with wife and children, sends you his regards and wishes you all the best in God's name.

"Everything here is all right, thank God, and may it be so with you too. In the village everything is the same as usual. On Lady Day Nikolai Ivanov's house on the highway burnt down. Must have been Matyushka set fire to it; that's what the police said too. Dear Luka, I beg you to please write clearly, I couldn't make out anything in your letter because it was poorly written and nobody could read it. And let me know who wrote it and who wrote the address, nobody can make out the hand, but what we could follow was all, a lot of nonsense that nobody could believe. Hereupon I remain your loving father M. Merkulov, who being illiterate had the letter signed for him by Anany Klimov."

"It's bad, very bad," Merkulov whispered, shaking his head and clicking his tongue sorrowfully. He was thinking that it would be more than two years before he finished "doing his duty for his country," and also how difficult, how hard it was to live far from home; he was thinking of his wife, too. "She's a young woman, gay and pampered. I suppose it isn't easy for her, either, to have to live without her husband four years. A soldier's wife. I know what they're like, those soldiers' wives. Lieutenant Zabiyakin's always ragging me.` 'Are you married?' he asks. 'Yes, sir, I am.' 'Well, wait till you get back from service—you'll find some additions to your family.' Hm. It's all very well for him to laugh. He's sleek and fat. Gets up in the morning and has his tea with a roll. Then his orderly brings him his boots, all polished and shining. And during drill all he has to do is smoke cigarettes. But you, Merkulov, must sit up all night. Ah, it's bad, very, very ba-a-ad!" Merkulov whispered, winding up his last word with a long, deep yawn that brought tears to his eyes.

Never before had he felt such an outcast, so forlorn and wretched. He would have liked to talk to some kindly silent man and tell the plaintive tale of all his sorrows and cares, and he would have liked that kindly silent man to listen attentively, understand everything, and sympathize with him. But where was there such a man? Everybody was taken up with himself and his own cares and worries. "What a life, brother!" Merkulov thought, shaking his head, and then said aloud, drawing out the words in a singsong fashion, "O-oh what a li-i-ife!"

And gradually he began to sing under his breath. At first there were hardly any words in his song. It was something dismal, sad and incoherent, yet it softened and stirred his soul agreeably, "O-o-oh, my-y, wha-at a li-i-ife!" Then the words began to form—soft, touching words:

> *O-oh, my mother dear,*
> *My own mother dear—*

A deep sympathy for the poor, forgotten soldier, Luka Merkulov, filled Merkulov's heart. They kept him on a starvation diet and assigned him to extra duty, the platoon commander rated him, and so did the section leader —sometimes he even punched Merkulov in the mouth— and the drill was so heavy and hard. He might easily be taken ill, break an arm or a leg, or go blind from some eye disease; half the company had sore eyes as it was. Or he might even die far from home. Merkulov felt a bitter lump rise in his throat; there was a pricking sensation in his eyelids, and a drowsy sweet melody surged in his breast. Now the sad words of the improvised song moved him still more, and the tune he was making up seemed to him more and more tender and beautiful.

> *Oh, my mother, mother dear,*
> *Lay me in a coffin,*
> *A pinewood, aspen coffin.*
> *Lay me in the cold, cold ground!*

The air in the barracks had thickened and become unbearably heavy. The soot-blackened night-lamps shone dimly through a steamy haze as in a bath-house. Merkulov sat hunched, his feet twisted round the cross-piece of the stool, his hands deep in the sleeves of his coat. He felt hot and cramped in the coat; the collar chafed his neck, the hooks dug into his throat, and he longed for sleep. His eyelids felt swollen and were itching, there was a continuous dull noise in his ears, and a hollow sticky feeling persisted inside him, somewhere in his chest or stomach. He tried not to give way to sleep, but at times something soft and yet irresistibly strong gave his head a gentle squeeze; then his eyelids would flutter and shut, the hollow feeling would disappear at once, and there would be no more barracks or long night, and for a few seconds he would feel blissfully light and comfortable. He would not notice his head drooping in short jerks, lower and lower down, until suddenly, lurching forward, he would open his eyes in fright, straighten his back and jerk up his head, and again the hollow feeling of sleeplessness would rise in his chest.

In those brief seconds of unexpected half-doze, his memory had clung to his village, and he had been happy and amused because no matter what he thought of, he at once saw it before him, better and clearer than he could ever have seen it in reality. There was his old white gelding, spotty all over, as if it had been strewn with buckwheat. It was standing on the green common, its forelegs crooked, the bones sticking out on its crupper, the ribs showing. Its head hung down, dejectedly motionless, its lower lip with the scant long hair drooped flabbily, and its eyes, a light faded blue, with white eyelashes, gazed at him in vacant surprise.

And just beyond the common there was a broad cartroad. And it seemed to Merkulov that it was now a warm evening in early spring and that the road was black with mud and pitted with hoof marks, and the water in the ruts was pink and amber in the afterglow. The small, narrow river crossed the road, winding its way from under the little log bridge; it lay there as smooth as a mirror, hazy in the distance, looking as if it had been cast between its low but steep emerald-green banks. It reflected in neat, clear-cut outline the rounded tops of the fluffy yellow-green willows on the banks, and the banks themselves that looked even fresher and more intensely emerald in the water. Far off the bell-tower of the church stood out, tall and slender, against the limpid sky, a white wooden tower with pink stripes running down it and a steep green roof. The Merkulovs' kitchen garden was next to the church; you could even see the scarecrow, leaning so that it looked about to fall over, with Father's old cap on its head and its arms in tattered sleeves spread out in a permanent attitude of concentrated determination.

And Merkulov saw himself riding along the black, muddy road on his way home from the field. He sat sideways on his white gelding, dangling his feet and slipping back and forth on the horse's back at each step. The hooves plopped loudly as they came out of the mud. A light wind brushed Merkulov's face, bringing with it the strong, fresh scent of the earth, still moist after the thaw; and Merkulov felt fine and happy. He was tired and worn out after the day's toil, having ripped up nearly three acres of land; his body ached, his arms hurt, he could hardly bend or unbend his back, and yet he sang with all his might, carelessly dangling his feet:

Oh, my orchards, orchards mi-ine!

How wonderful he was going to feel when he lay down in the cool barn, on a heap of straw, throwing out his weary arms and legs!

His head drooped again, almost touching his knees, and again he awoke with that cloying, agonizing sensation in his chest. "Must have dozed off," he murmured in surprise. "Well, well!" He was terribly sorry that he could no longer see the black springtime road, the lovely reflections of the willows in the smooth mirror of the river, that he could no longer smell the good fresh earth. But he was afraid he might fall asleep, and to brace himself he started on a fresh round of the barracks. His feet were numb with the long sitting, and at first he could not feel them at all.

Passing the clock, Merkulov looked at the dial. The big hand stood upright, and the small one had moved slightly to the right of it. "It's past midnight," he guessed. He yawned vigorously, made several times the sign of the cross over his mouth in a hurried manner, and muttered something like a prayer, "O Lord—Holy Mother—two hours and a half to go yet, I reckon——O ye saints—Pyotr, Alexei, Yona, Filipp—our righteous fathers and brethren—"

The paraffin was running out in the lamps, and the barracks were plunging into darkness. The sleepers lay in strained unnatural attitudes; their arms and heads must have grown numb from the hard mattresses. Plaintive groans, deep sighs, unhealthy, choking snores could be heard everywhere. There was something ominous, something depressing and mysterious about those inhuman sounds coming from under the grey, monotonous heaps in the melancholy darkness.

"Shall I go outside for a bit?" Merkulov said aloud to himself, and walked slowly to the door.

It was pitch black outside and a fine drizzle was falling steadily. A row of dimly lighted windows glimmered feebly across the courtyard; those were the barracks occupied by the Sixth and Seventh companies. The rain drummed dully on the roof and pattered on the panes and on Merkulov's cap. Somewhere nearby rain-water was gushing out of a drain-pipe with a hurried gurgling sound and splashing down on some stones. Above the noise of the rain, Merkulov thought he heard strange sounds. It was as if someone were coming towards him along the barracks wall, splashing fast and heavily through the puddles. Merkulov would turn to peer in that direction. The splashing would stop at once. But no sooner did he turn away than he would hear the heavy, hurried splashing again. "I'm just imagining things," Merkulov told himself, and lifted his face to the pattering raindrops. There was not a star in the sky.

Suddenly, close by, the entrance door of the Fifth Company's barracks flew open and the pulley on the door gave a piercing screech. The form of a soldier in coat and cap showed for a second in the faint light of the doorway. But the door was pulled shut again by the screeching pulley, and you could not even tell in the dark where it was. The soldier who had come out stood on the steps—Merkulov could hear him noisily taking in the fresh air and vigorously rubbing his hands.

"Must be on duty, too," thought Merkulov, feeling an irresistible urge to walk over to this one man who was awake and *alive* and look at his face, or at least hear his voice.

"I say, friend!" Merkulov called to the soldier, invisible in the dark. "Could you lend me a match?"

"Mebbe I could," came a low, husky voice from the steps. "Wait a bit."

Merkulov heard the soldier slap his pockets, and then caught the rattle of the match-box found at last.

The two soldiers came together midway between the two barracks, near the well, finding each other by the sound of their boots squelching in the wet, slippery clay.

"Here you are," said the soldier and, since Merkulov could not at once find his outstretched hand, slightly shook the box.

But Merkulov had no need for matches, for he did not smoke; he merely wanted to stay for a moment near a man who was awake and not in the clutches of that strange supernatural force, sleep.

"Thanks," he said, "a couple will do. I've got a box over in the barracks, but no more matches."

They took shelter under the high roof built over the well. Merkulov idly fingered the huge wooden wheel that worked the shaft. The wheel creaked plaintively and swung softly round. The two soldiers leaned on the edge of the well and stared down into the darkness.

"Lord, I'm sleepy" said Merkulov, and yawned aloud.

The other soldier followed suit at once. Their voices and yawns resounded with a pealing echo in the void of the deep well.

"Must be just past midnight," said the soldier from Five Company, in a flat indifferent voice. "How long have you been in the army?"

Merkulov guessed by the changed sound of the voice that the soldier had turned to face him. He turned too, but could not see so much as a shape in the darkness.

"Since eighteen-ninety. What about you?"

"Same here. You come from Orel Province, too?"

"No, I be from the Kromi region," replied Merkulov. "My village is called Mokriye Verkhi. Ever heard of it?"

"No, I come from far away—close to Yelets. I must say it's dull here!" These words he uttered in the midst of a yawn, swallowing them, and they sounded like "Ahmu-hay issdullyere."

They fell silent for a while. The soldier from Yelets spat into the well through his teeth. Ten seconds or so passed. Merkulov listened with curiosity, his head on one side. Suddenly there came from the darkness an unusually neat, clear ping, like two pebbles striking together.

"It's deep down there!" said the man from Yelets, and spat again.

"It's a sin to spit into the water. You mustn't do that," Merkulov remarked censoriously, and at once spat himself.

The long interval between the spitting and the ping which came from the well greatly amused both soldiers.

"Suppose a man jumped down there?" the soldier from Yelets asked suddenly. "I reckon he'd give his head a good banging against the walls before he reached the water?"

"That he would," Merkulov responded confidently. "Make a proper mess of himself too."

"Tur'ble!" said the other, and Merkulov guessed that he was shaking his head.

There was another long pause, and again the two men spat into the well. Suddenly Merkulov spoke up again.

"You know what a funny thing happened? I was sitting in the barracks and—I must have dozed off a bit—I saw such a—such a queer dream."

He was eager to tell his dream with all its charming poetical detail, the wonderful scent of his native soil, of that sweet old life that was so far away. But what he brought out was too plain and colourless and uninteresting.

"I dreamed I was in my own home village. It looked like evening. And I could see everything—I could see it so well it didn't seem like a dream at all."

"Ye-es, things like that do happen," the other put in indifferently, scratching his cheek.

"And I was riding on my horse—my old gelding. We've got a white gelding, about twenty years old it is, I'll bet. It may be dead by now."

"Seeing a horse means a falsehood. Somebody's going to cheat you," remarked the soldier.

"I was riding on my gelding and could see everything. Just like it used to be. It was such a queer dream I saw—"

"Ye-es, a man sees many a dream," the soldier put in lazily. "I'm sorry, though," he added, straightening up. "Our sergeant—damn him—sneaks about at night. Good night to you."

"Good night, friend. What a night, eh! My goodness— it's dark as a pit."

After the fresh air the atmosphere in the barracks seemed unbearable at first. The air was soaked with heavy emanations of the human body, the acrid smoke of coarse tobacco, the sour mustiness of coat cloth and the powerful smell of ill-baked bread. The men were still sleeping restlessly, tossing and groaning and snoring as though every breath cost them a tremendous effort. As Merkulov paced through the quarters of Three Platoon one of the men sat up suddenly in bed. He stared wildly about him for a few seconds, as if in utter bewilderment, making noises with his lips. Then he began to scratch himself furiously—first his head, then his chest; then sleep took him again and he toppled over on his side. Another man hurriedly muttered a long sentence in a stiff, hoarse voice. Merkulov listened with superstitious fear and was able to make out some of the words: "Don't break it off—tie it in a knot. A knot, I tell you!" To Merkulov there always seemed to be something dreadful in these ravings he heard in the dead of night. He imagined that those broken words were not uttered by the man himself but by some *invisible* being who had descended on his soul and taken possession of it.

The clock kept on ticking unevenly, as if delaying the second stroke, but its hands seemed not to have moved at all. The wild, fantastic idea crossed Merkulov's mind that perhaps Time had stopped altogether and that this night would last months, years, an eternity; the sleepers would breathe as heavily and rave in the same way, the dying night-lamps would flicker as dimly, the pendulum would tick as sluggishly and indifferently. This vague, swift sensation, which Merkulov himself could not account for, filled him with helpless anger. And he shook his fist threateningly in the darkness, and whispered through clenched teeth, "You devils! Wait till I get at you!"

Once again he sat down in the same place, between the stove and the rifle stack, and almost immediately drowsiness enclosed his temples in its soft, tender embrace. "What now? What?" he asked himself in a whisper, knowing that it was now in his power to summon something familiar and very pleasant. "Oh, yes. My village—the river——Come on, please, come on—"

And again the little river winds its way in the fresh green grass, now dropping out of sight beyond velvety hills, now showing forth its pure glistening breast, and again the black, rutted road stretches away in a broad ribbon, the thawing earth is fragrant, the water gleams pink in the fields, the smiling breeze fans his face with its warm, caressing breath, and again Merkulov rocks back and forth on the knobbly back of the horse, while a plough, with the coulter turned up, trails along the road behind him.

Oh, my o-orchards, orchards mi-ine!

Merkulov sings at the top of his voice, thinking with pleasure how sweet it is going to be to sprawl his tired body on a heap of fresh straw. Ploughed fields run along the road on both sides, and glossy blue-black rooks stalk gravely about. The frogs in the marshes and puddles croak in a deafening chorus. There is a subtle fragrance of blossoming willows in the air.

Oh, my orchards, o-orchards mine!

The only thing that seems odd to Merkulov is that somehow the white gelding is walking at an uneven, rocking pace, swinging him from side to side. There it goes again. Merkulov all but falls headlong from his mount. He must settle properly in the saddle. He tries to sling his right foot to the other side, but his leg will not move, it feels heavy, as if someone had clamped a strange weight to it. And the horse rocks and sways under him. "Gee up, damn you! Gone to sleep?"

Merkulov topples down from the horse's back, hits his face on the ground, and opens his eyes.

"Sleeping, damn you!" a voice shouted above him.

Merkulov sprang up from the stool and fingered dazedly his cap. Sergeant-Major Taras Gavrilovich was standing in front of him in his underwear, with dishevelled hair. It was he who had roused Merkulov by jabbing his fist in the soldier's cheek.

"Sleeping, eh?" the sergeant-major repeated in a sinister tone. "You son of a—! Sleeping on duty, were you? I'll learn you how to sleep!"

A swift blow caught Merkulov on the cheek-bone and staggered him; he shook his head and muttered hoarsely, "I was all in, Sergeant."

"Ha! All in, were you? Well, you'll go on duty twice more out of turn so you won't be in again. When are you due for relief?"

"At two, Sergeant."

"You've missed relief time, damn you! Now look lively! Wake up the next one. Get going!"

The sergeant left. Merkulov rushed to the plank bed on which the next man to go on duty—the old soldier Ryaboshapka—was sleeping. "Sleep, sleep, sleep," a joyous, exultant voice cried inside him. "Two extra duties? I don't care a straw, that'll come *later*, but now I'm going to sleep!"

"Uncle Ryaboshapka, d'you hear, Uncle Ryaboshapka," said Merkulov in a fearsome whisper, tugging at the sleeper's leg.

"Mrmr—g'way—"

"Get up, Uncle Ryaboshapka, it's relief time."

"Oh, g'won—"

The watch had exhausted Merkulov to such an extent that he had no more patience to wake up Ryaboshapka. He ran to his place on the plank bed, undressed as fast as he could and squeezed himself in between two sleepers, who at once sank back upon him, heavily and lifelessly.

For a second Merkulov recalled the well, the pitch black night, the fine drizzle, the gurgling water running out of the drain-pipe, and someone's invisible feet squelching in the mud. Oh, how cold and grim and creepy it was out there now! A blissful animal joy engulfed him. He pressed his elbows hard to his sides, drew up his knees, dug his head deeper into the pillow, and whispered to himself, "And now—quick, the road—the road—"

Once again the black rutted road winds away neatly before his eyes, once again the delicate green of the willows looks down into the mirror of the stream... And all of a sudden Merkulov hurtled at a frightening but agreeable speed into a deep, soft darkness.

1899

THE WHITE POODLE

I

They were strolling players making their way along
narrow mountain paths from one summer resort to
another, on the south coast of the Crimea. Usually they
were preceded by Arto—a white poodle with a lion cut—
who trotted along with his long pink tongue lolling out
on one side. When he came to a cross-road he would stop
and look back questioningly, wagging his tail. By certain
signs that he alone knew, he would unerringly pick the
right way and go on at a run, his ears flapping gaily.
Behind the dog came Sergei, a boy of twelve, who carried under his left arm a rolled-up rug for acrobatics,

and in his right hand a dirty little cage with a goldfinch, trained to pull out of a box coloured slips of paper telling the future. Old Martin Lodizhkin shamblingly brought up the rear, a hurdy-gurdy on his crooked back.

The hurdy-gurdy was an old one; it gave out croaking, coughing sounds, having undergone innumerable repairs during its long life. It played two tunes: a dreary German waltz by Launer and a galop from "Journey to China," both of which had been in vogue some thirty or forty years ago and were now completely forgotten. There were two treacherous pipes in it. One of them, the treble, did not work at all and as soon as its turn came the music seemed to stutter, limp and stumble. In the other pipe, which played a low note, the valve did not close at once; having begun to boom, it would go on, drowning or jumbling up the other sounds, until it suddenly decided to break it off. The old man was well aware of these shortcomings, and he sometimes remarked jokingly, but with a shade of hidden sadness:

"Well, it can't be helped. It's an ancient instrument, with a cold. When I start it people say, 'Pah, what a nasty thing!' But the pieces used to be nice ones, and fashionable too, only the gentry of today have no admiration for my music. What *they* want is 'The Geisha,' 'Under the Double-Headed Eagle,' the waltz from 'The Bird-Seller.' Then there are those pipes. I took the instrument to a repair shop, but they wouldn't tackle the job. 'You've got to put in new pipes,' they told me. 'And you'd do better still to sell this old wheezer to some museum as a relic.' Oh, well! It's fed you and me so far, hasn't it, Sergei, and let's hope it will serve us some more."

The old man was as fond of the hurdy-gurdy as you can be of a living thing that is close to you, or perhaps even related to you. He had got used to it during the long years of his hard wanderer's life, and had come to see it as something animate, almost rational. Once in a while, as he spent the night at a dingy inn, the hurdy-gurdy, which usually stood on the floor beside him, would all of a sudden give out a feeble sound, sad, lonely and trembling as an old man's sigh. Then Lodizhkin would stroke its carved side and whisper tenderly, "Life isn't easy, is it, my friend? Don't give in."

He was as fond of the poodle and the boy, who went with him on his eternal wanderings, as of the hurdy-gurdy, or perhaps a little more. He had "hired" the boy five years before from a hard-drinking widowed shoemaker, whom he had undertaken to pay two rubles a month. But soon the shoemaker died, leaving Sergei tied to the old man by a sincere affection, and by everyday interests.

II

The path ran along the high, steep shore, winding in the shade of ancient olive-trees. The sea, glimpsed occasionally between the trees, seemed to rise in a calm, powerful wall as it stretched away, and through the pattern of silvery-green foliage its colour showed even bluer and deeper. Cicadas were chirping shrilly everywhere—in the grass, in the cornel shrubs and wild briers, in the vineyards and trees; the air was quivering with their resonant, monotonous clamour. It was a sultry, windless day, and the hot earth was scorching to the feet.

Sergei, who was walking ahead of the old man as usual, stopped and waited for him.

"What is it, Sergei?" asked the old man.

"It's so hot, Grandad Lodizhkin, I just can't stand it! How about a dip?"

With a habitual movement the old man adjusted the hurdy-gurdy on his back and mopped the sweat off his face with his sleeve.

"Nothing could be better," he said with a sigh and a longing glance at the cool blue of the sea. "But the trouble is we'd feel even worse afterwards. A doctor's assistant I know told me sea-salt makes you flabby."

"Perhaps it isn't true," Sergei remarked doubtfully.

"Not true! Why should he have lied to me? He's a serious man, doesn't drink, has a little house in Sevasto-pol. Besides, there's no way down to the sea here. Wait till we get to Miskhor, and then we'll wash our sinful bodies a bit. It's a good thing to bathe before dinner and then take a nap—a very good thing."

Hearing the murmur of conversation behind him, Arto turned back and came running. His mild blue eyes blinked against the glaring sunlight, and his long, lolling tongue trembled with fast breathing.

"Well, doggie my friend? Warm, is it?" said the old man.

The dog yawned tensely, curling its tongue, shook all over and gave a thin whine.

"Yes, my friend, there's nothing you can do. It says 'in the sweat of thy brow,'" Lodizhkin went on, in edifying tones. "Of course you haven't got a brow but still— All right, now, run along, you've no business hanging about here. You know, Sergei, I must say I like it when it's warm like this. It's just that the instrument's a bit heavy, and if it wasn't for the work I'd lie down some-where on the grass, in the shade, with my belly up, and stay there. Sunshine's the best thing for old bones."

The path ran downwards and joined a wide, dazzling white road, hard as stone. This was the beginning of an old park, owned by a count, with beautiful villas, flower-beds, glass-houses and fountains scattered throughout its rich greenery. Lodizhkin knew those places well; every year he made the round of them in the grape-gathering season, when the whole Crimea filled with well-dressed, wealthy and gay people. The colourful luxuriance of southern plants did not move the old man, but there were many things that delighted Sergei, who had never been in those parts before. The magnolias with their hard, glossy leaves that seemed varnished, and their white blossoms the size of large plates; vine arbours hung with heavy clusters of grapes; the huge platans, many centuries old, with their light bark and powerful crowns; tobacco plantations, brooks and waterfalls, and the magnificent fragrant roses that were everywhere—in flowerbeds, on fences, on the walls of the villas—the charm of all this life in bloom kept the boy's simple soul in a state of rapture, so that he was tugging at the old man's sleeve every moment.

"Look at those fish in the founting, Grandad Lodizhkin—they're made of gold! Honest, they are, Grandad, strike me dead if they aren't!" the boy would cry, pressing his face to the iron fence of a garden, with a large fountain in the middle. "And the peaches, Grandad! See how many there are! All on one tree!"

"Go on, you silly boy. Don't stand here gaping!" the old man would reply, pushing him jokingly. "Wait till we get to the town of Novorossiisk and go south again. That's something really worth seeing. There's Sochi, for example, and Adler, and Tuapse, or Sukhum and Batum farther south. Why, you get goggle-eyed looking. Take the palm-tree, for one thing. It's a wonder! It has a shaggy trunk, like felt you'd say, and each leaf is big enough to cover both of us."

"Honest to God?" said Sergei, happily amazed.

"You just wait—you'll see for yourself. There are lots of things! Oranges, for instance, or, say, lemons. You've seen 'em in the shops, haven't you?"

"Well?"

"Well, they grow in the air. Just like that, on a tree, like apples or pears at home. And the people there are quite a queer lot: Turks and Pershings and Circassians, all of them in robes and with daggers. A tough bunch!

And sometimes you see Ethiopians there. I've seen them often in Batum."

"Ethiopians! I know. The ones with horns," said Sergei confidently.

"It's a lie about the horns—they aren't that bad. But they're black as boots, and even shiny. They've got thick and red lips and big white eyes, and woolly hair, like a black sheep's."

"I suppose they're terrible, those Ethiopians?"

"Of course when you aren't used to them you feel a bit scared, but afterwards you see that other people aren't afraid and you get bolder. There are all kinds of things there, my boy. You'll see them for yourself when we get there. The only trouble is fever. It's swamps and rot all around, and besides there's that heat. Those who live there don't mind it because it doesn't do them any harm, but strangers have a hard time. Well, our tongues have been wagging long enough, Sergei. Come on, get in through the wicket. The gentry who live in this villa are very nice people. You only have to ask me—I know!"

But that day brought them no luck. From some places they were driven away the moment they were seen coming; in others, as soon as tne hurdy-gurdy sent forth its first wheezy, twanging notes, people waved them away from balconies with annoyed impatience, in still others the servants told them that "the master" hadn't arrived yet. True, they were paid for their performance at two villas, but it was a niggardly sum. Nevertheless, the old man did not scoff at any reward, however small. As he walked back to the road he jingled the coppers contentedly in his pocket.

"Two and five makes seven kopeks," he would say good-humouredly. "That isn't to be sneezed at, either, Sergei. Seven by seven runs up to a half ruble, and that means a square meal for the three of us, and a place to sleep the night, and a swig of vodka for the weak old man Lodizhkin, because of his many ailments. Ah, but the gentry can't understand! They're too stingy to give us twenty kopeks and too proud to give five, so they tell us to get out. Why not give three kopeks rather than nothing? I don't take offence, I don't mind. Why should I?"

Lodizhkin was a modest man and did not grumble even when he was driven away. But that day his habitual placidity was upset by a beautiful, plump, seemingly very kind lady, the mistress of a splendid villa surrounded by a flower garden. She listened attentively to the music and looked with still greater attention at Sergei's acrobatic feats and Arto's tricks. Then she questioned the boy at great length about his age and his name, about where he had learned his gymnastics and whether the old man was related to him, what his parents had been, and so on. Then she told them to wait, and walked into the house.

She did not reappear for ten minutes or perhaps a quarter of an hour, and the longer she kept them waiting the higher soared their vague but bold expectations. The old man even whispered to the boy, shielding his mouth with his hand, "Well, Sergei, we're in luck, believe me: I know, my boy. She'll give us some clothes or shoes. That's quite certain!"

Finally the lady came out again, dropped a small white coin down into the hat Sergei held up, and was gone at once. The coin turned out to be an old ten-kopek piece effaced on both sides and, moreover, with a hole in it. The old man looked at it for a long time with a puzzled air. When they were out on the road and far from the villa, he still held the coin in his palm as if weighing it.

"Yes, that was a fine trick she played on us!" he muttered, stopping all of a sudden. "I can tell you that. And we fools tried so hard to please her. She'd have done better to give us a button or something. You can at least sew it on somewhere. But what am I to do with this trash? The lady probably thinks the old man'll slip it on to somebody at night, on the sly. Oh, no, you're very much mistaken, madam. Old Lodizhkin will not go in for that sort of thing! No, he won't! Here's your precious ten kopeks! Take it!"

Indignantly and proudly he threw away the coin, which dug into the white dust of the road with a faint tinkle.

In this manner the old man, the boy and the dog made the round of all the villas, and were about to go down to the beach. There was one more villa, the last, on their left. It was shut out of sight by a high white wall above which, on the other side, a serried row of dusty slender cypresses rose like so many long, greyish-black spindles. Only through the wide cast-iron gate, with fretwork of an intricate lace-like design, could you see a corner of the fresh silky-green lawn, the rounded flower-beds and, far in the background, a covered walk smothered in a dense growth of vines. In the middle of the lawn stood the gardener, watering the roses with a long hose. He had put his finger to the nozzle, and the sun picked out all the colours of the rainbow in a fountain of spray.

The old man was about to walk past, but peering in at the gate he stopped in wonder.

"Wait a bit, Sergei," he called to the boy. "I think I can see people in there. That's funny. I've passed here so many times but I never saw a soul. Let's hear what it says, Sergei my boy!"

"*Friendship Villa. No trespassing,*" Sergei read the inscription skilfully engraved on one of the gate-posts.

"Friendship, eh?" echoed the old man, who could not read. "That's it! That's just the right word—friendship. We've had bad luck all day, but now we're going to make up for it. I can scent it like a hound. Here, Arto, you son of a dog! Step right in, Sergei. And always ask me—I know!"

The garden walks were neatly strewn with coarse gravel that crunched underfoot, and bordered with big pink shells. Wonderful bright-coloured flowers filling the air with a sweet fragrance rose from the flower-beds, above a carpet of variegated grasses. Clear water gurgled and splashed in the fountains; creeping plants hung in garlands from beautiful bowls suspended between the trees, and on marble pillars in front of the house stood two glittering ball-shaped mirrors, in which the man, the boy and the dog were reflected head downwards, in ludicrous, distorted shapes.

On the smooth-rolled ground in front of the balcony, Sergei spread out his rug, and the old man, having set up the hurdy-gurdy, was going to start turning the handle when there was a strange, unexpected interruption.

A boy somewhere between eight and ten, screaming at the top of his voice, burst out on to the veranda from inside the house. He wore a light sailor suit, and his arms and knees were bare. His curly fair hair flowed carelessly to his shoulders. Six people ran out after him: two pinafored women; an old fat footman in a tail-coat, without beard or moustache but with long grey side-whiskers; a thin, red-haired, red-nosed damsel in a blue checked frock; a young, sickly-looking but very beautiful lady in a pale blue lace dressing-gown, and lastly a stout, bald-headed gentleman in a tussore suit and gold-rimmed spectacles. They were all waving their arms in a flurry, talking loudly and jostling each other. It was easy enough to guess that the cause of their excitement was the boy in the sailor suit, who had darted out so suddenly.

Meanwhile the boy, who did not stop screaming for a second, flopped down on his stomach on the stone floor, rolled quickly over on to his back and started to kick and to wave his arms in fury. The adults fussed around him. The old footman entreatingly pressed his hands to his starched shirt-front and said plaintively, his long whiskers shaking, "Master Nikolai Apollonovich! Please don't vex your mummy, sir—get up. I beg of you to take medicine, sir. It's very sweet indeed, sir, it's plain syrup. Please, get up."

The pinafored women wrung their hands and chattered away in frightened servile voices. The red-nosed damsel, gesticulating tragically, shouted something very touching but absolutely unintelligible in a foreign language. The gold-spectacled gentleman admonished the boy in a sober boom, cocking his head from side to side and gravely lifting his hands. As for the beautiful, sickly lady, she moaned languidly and dabbed her eyes with a handkerchief of fine lace.

"Ah, Trilly, oh, my God! I implore you, my angel. Mummy implores you. Please take the medicine, please; you'll feel better at once: both your tummy and your head will be all right. Please do it for my sake, my pet! Do you want Mummy to kneel before you, Trilly? Well, here I am kneeling before you. Do you want me to give you a gold coin? Two gold coins? Five gold coins, Trilly? Do you want a real little donkey? A real little pony? Do say something to him, doctor!"

"I say, Trilly, be a man, will you?" boomed the stout gold-spectacled gentleman.

"Aaaaah!" squawked the boy, wriggling on the floor and kicking madly.

Despite his extreme agitation he tried to hit out with his heels at the stomachs and legs of those bustling about him, but they were rather deft in dodging his kicks.

Sergei, who had been watching the scene for a long time with curiosity and astonishment, now gently nudged the old man in the ribs.

"What's got into him, Grandad Lodizhkin?" he asked in a whisper. "Are they going to whip him?"

"Whip him, indeed! Why, he could flog any of them himself. He's just a spoilt brat. Probably sick, too."

"You mean crazy?" Sergei suggested.

"How should I know? Hush!"

"Aaaaah!" the boy yelled, more and more loudly. "Pigs! Fools!"

"Let's start, Sergei. I know!" Lodizhkin commanded suddenly, and began to grind the hurdy-gurdy with a determined air.

The twanging, wheezing sounds of the old galop rang out in the garden. Those on the veranda were startled, and the boy stopped screaming for a few seconds.

"Oh, my God, they'll upset poor Trilly still more!" the lady in the blue dressing-gown cried plaintively. "Oh, send them away, send them away at once! And that dirty dog. Dogs always have such horrible diseases. Well, don't stand like a statue, Ivan!"

In weary disgust she raised her handkerchief to dismiss the three; the red-nosed damsel rolled her eyes, and someone else hissed threateningly. With a quick, soft step the man in the tail-coat ran down the steps and up to the old man, with a terrified look on his face, his arms thrown wide apart.

"W-what's the meaning of this?" he snorted in a hoarse, choking whisper that was at once frightened and angrily overbearing. "Who permitted this? Who let you in? Go away! Get out!"

The hurdy-gurdy gave a dismayed squeak and stopped.

"Allow me to explain, good sir," old Lodizhkin began politely.

"None of your explanations! Go away!" the tail-coated man cried, with something like a hiss deep in his throat.

In an instant his fat face went crimson, and his eyes opened incredibly wide, as if they had come out of their sockets, and rolled round and round. It was so terrible a sight that the old man stepped back.

"Come on, Sergei," he said, hurriedly shouldering the hurdy-gurdy. "We'd better go!"

But they were no more than a few yards away when fresh deafening screams pealed from the balcony.

"Aaaaah! I want it! I do! Aaah! Bring 'em here! Call 'em! I want it!"

"But, Trilly! Oh, my God, Trilly! Bring them back this instant!" the nervous lady groaned. "How brainless you all are! Did you hear what I told you, Ivan? Call those beggars back at once!"

"Hey! You there! Hey, you! Organ-players! Come back!" several voices called from the veranda.

The fat footman, his whiskers flying, bounded like a big rubber ball after the departing players.

"Hey! Musicians! Listen, come back! Back!" he shouted, gasping and waving his arms. "Good old man"—he had at last caught hold of the old man's sleeve—"turn back! The gentry want to see your pantomin. Quick!"

"Well, I never!" The old man shook his head and sighed, but he walked up to the veranda, took down the hurdy-gurdy, and began to grind out the galop from where he had left off.

The tumult on the balcony died down. The lady with the boy and the gold-spectacled gentleman stepped up to the railing; the others hung back respectfully. The gardener wearing an apron came and stopped not far from the old man. The gate-keeper, who had emerged from nowhere, posted himself behind the gardener. He was a huge bearded man with a sombre, pock-marked face topped by a low forehead. He wore a new pink shirt with slanting rows of black dots.

To the wheezing, stuttering sounds of the galop Sergei spread out the rug on the ground, threw off his canvas trousers (they were made of an old sack, and a square trade mark adorned their seat), slipped off his old jacket and remained in his shabby tights which, much mended as they were, looked neat on his thin but strong, lithe body. By imitating adults he had already acquired the style of a genuine acrobat. As he ran on to the rug he put his hands to his lips and then, with a sweeping theatrical gesture, spread out his arms, as if blowing two swift kisses to his audience.

With one hand the old man played the hurdy-gurdy, wringing a wheezy, coughing melody out of it, and with his free hand he tossed various objects to the boy, who nimbly caught them in mid air. Sergei's repertoire was small, but he performed well, doing "a clean job," as acrobats would say, and enjoying it, too. He threw up an empty beer bottle, so that it turned over several times in the air, then suddenly caught it bottom up on the edge of a plate and balanced it for a few seconds; he juggled with four ivory balls and with two candles which he caught simultaneously with two candlesticks; he also played with three objects at a time—a fan, a wooden cigar and an umbrella. They all went up and down in the air, never reaching the ground, and suddenly the umbrella came to be over his head and the cigar in his mouth, while the fan cooled his face with a coquettish swing. In conclusion Sergei himself turned several somersaults on the rug, performed a "frog," did an "American knot," and walked about on his hands. Having exhausted his stock of "tricks," he blew two more kisses to his audience and went panting up to the old man to take his place at the hurdy-gurdy.

Now came Arto's turn. The dog knew that perfectly well; in fact, with a jerky, nervous bark he was already jumping at the old man, who was edging out of the strap. Perhaps what the clever poodle meant to say was that, in his view, it was folly to engage in acrobatic exercises when the temperature was over a hundred degrees in the shade. But with a cunning air old Grandad Lodizhkin brought out from behind his back a thin cornel whip. "I guessed as much!" Arto barked in annoyance for the last time and reluctantly got on his hind legs, his blinking eyes fixed on his master.

"Beg, Arto! Good," said the old man, holding the whip over the poodle's head. "Turn over. Good. Turn over. Do it again—again. Now dance, doggie, dance! Sit up! What? You don't want to? Sit up, I'm telling you. Ha, so there! I'll teach you! Now say 'how d'you do' to the ladies and gentlemen. Well? Arto!" the old man raised his voice menacingly.

"Wow!" the poodle barked with disgust. Then he looked at his master, blinking sorrowfully, and added another two wows.

"The old man doesn't understand me at all!" the disgruntled bark seemed to say.

"That's better. Politeness first. And now let's jump a bit," the old man went on, holding out the whip low above the ground. "*Allez!* Don't you stick out your tongue. *Allez! Houp!* Fine. Now do it again, *noch einmal. Allez! Houp! Allez! Houp!* Wonderful, doggie. I'll give you a carrot when we get home. Oh, so you don't care for carrots? I quite forgot. Then take my top hat and beg the ladies and gentlemen. They may give you something more to your taste."

The old man stood up the dog on his hind legs and thrust into his mouth the ancient, greasy cap which he had so humorously called a top hat. Holding the cap in his teeth, Arto walked up with a mincing gait to the veranda. A small mother-of-pearl purse flashed in the sickly lady's hands. Those around her smiled indulgently.

"Well? What did I tell you?" the old man whispered jauntily, bending to Sergei. "You just ask me—I know, my boy. It can't be less than a ruble."

Just then an almost inhuman shriek came from the veranda; it was so piercing that Arto dropped the cap and skipped to his master, glancing back fearfully, his tail between his legs.

"I wa-a-nt it!" shrilled the curly-headed boy, stamping his feet. "I want the do-o-og! Trilly wants the do-o-og!"

Once again there was a turmoil on the veranda. "Oh, my God! Ah, Nikolai Apollonovich! Master! Calm yourself, Trilly, I implore you!"

"The dog! Get the dog! I want it! Beasts, fools!" howled the boy.

"But don't be upset, my angel!" stammered the lady in the blue dressing-gown. "You want to stroke the doggie? All right, my darling, all right, just a moment. Do you think Trilly may stroke that dog, doctor?"

"Speaking generally, I wouldn't recommend it"—the doctor spread out his hands in dismay—"but if it's thoroughly disinfected, say, with boric acid or a weak solution of carbolic acid, then I should think—er—"

"Get the do-og!"

"Just a second, my own darling, just a second. As you say, doctor, we'll have it washed with boric acid, and then——But, Trilly, don't get so excited! Please bring your dog here, old man. Don't be afraid, you'll be paid for it. Now tell me, it isn't sick by any chance? I mean, it isn't mad? Or perhaps it has echinococci?"

"I don't want to stroke it, I don't!" Trilly screamed, bubbling at mouth and nose. "I want it for my own! Fools, beasts! I want it for good! Want to play with it myself. Always!"

"Listen, old man, come up here," said the lady, trying to make herself heard above the boy's screaming. "Ah, Trilly, you'll kill your mummy with your cries. Why were those musicians let in here at all! Come up nearer—nearer, I tell you! That's it. Oh, but don't cry, Trilly, Mummy will do anything you wish. I implore you. Do calm the child, miss! Please, doctor. How much do you want, old man?"

The old man took off his cap; there was a respectfully wretched expression on his face.

"As much as it may please your ladyship to give, Your Excellency. I'm a poor man and any donation is a boon to me. I'm sure you won't wrong an old man."

"Ah, how stupid you are! You'll get a sore throat, Trilly dear. Try to understand, will you: the dog is *yours*, not mine. How much, now? Ten? Fifteen? Twenty?"

"Aaa! I wa-ant it! Give me the dog, the do-og!" squalled the boy, kicking the footman in the round belly.

"You mean—I'm sorry, Your Highness," stammered Lodizhkin. "I'm a stupid old man. Can't make it out at once and, besides, I'm a bit hard of hearing. What was it you said, please? For my dog?"

"Oh, my goodness! Are you acting a fool?" the lady flared up. "Give Trilly a glass of water, nurse, quick! I'm asking you a plain question: How much do you want for your dog? Do you understand—your dog, the dog!"

"The dog! The do-og!" the boy shrilled, louder than ever.

Lodizhkin put on his cap; he was offended.

"I don't deal in dogs, your ladyship," he said, with cold dignity. "As for this dog here, madam, it feeds and clothes the two of us." He jerked his thumb over his shoulder at Sergei. "And it's absolutely impossible for me to sell it."

Meanwhile Trilly was screaming as shrilly as a locomotive whistle. A glass of water was brought to him, but he furiously splashed it out in the governess's face.

"But listen to me, you crazy old man! There is nothing that can't be bought or sold," the lady insisted, pressing her temples with her palms. "Miss, wipe your face, quick, and fetch my smelling-salts. Perhaps your dog is worth a hundred rubles? Or two hundred? Three hundred? Answer me! Say something to him, doctor, for heaven's sake!"

"Get ready, Sergei," grumbled Lodizhkin. "They want the dog, do they? Come here, Arto!"

"Just a moment, my good man," drawled the stout, gold-spectacled man in a superior boom. "You'd better stop putting on airs, my man, if you'll take my advice. Ten rubles is the most I'd pay for your dog, with yourself into the bargain. Just think, you dolt, what a fortune you're being offered!"

"I thank you most humbly, sir, only—" He shouldered the hurdy-gurdy with a groan. "Only I can't do that—sell it, I mean. Better look for a dog somewhere else. Good day. You go ahead, Sergei."

"And have you got a passport?" the doctor roared suddenly. "I know your kind of riff-raff!"

"Gate-keeper! Semyon! Throw them out!" cried the lady, her face distorted with fury.

The sombre gate-keeper in the pink shirt stepped forward with an ominous look. A terrific uproar arose on the veranda: Trilly was yelling at the top of his voice, his mother was moaning, the nurse and under-nurse were cackling in a patter, and the doctor was booming like an angry bumble-bee. But the old man and Sergei had no chance to see the end of it all. Preceded by the thoroughly terrified poodle, they hurried to the gate almost at a run. The gate-keeper followed close on their heels, pushing the old man on from behind.

"Loafing around here, you tramps!" he said threateningly. "You should thank God you got away with a whole skin, you damned gaffer. But next time you turn up you can be sure I'll give it to you—I'll punch your head and take you to the *uryadnik*. You scum!"

The old man and the boy walked a long way in silence, then suddenly they looked at each other as if by agreement, and broke into merriment; first Sergei burst out laughing, and, then, rather self-consciously, the old man smiled as he looked at the boy.

"Well, Grandad Lodizhkın? You know everything, don't you?" Sergei teased him slyly.

"Ye-es, my boy. We got into a fix, all right." The old man shook his head. "What a vicious brat he is, though. I wonder how they brought him up to be like that. Just think: twenty-five people dance to his piping. I'd certainly give it to him hot if I could have my way. Give me the dog, he says. Why, he might want the moon from the sky next—what then? Come here, Arto, come, my doggie. God, what a day! It's simply amazing!"

"Couldn't have been better," Sergei commented sarcastically. "One lady gave us clothes, another a ruble. You certainly know everything in advance, Grandad Lodizhkin."

"Hold your tongue, you whipper-snapper," the old man growled good-humouredly. "Remember how you scuttled from the gate-keeper? I thought I'd never catch up with you. That gate-keeper isn't to be trifled with, is he?"

The three came out of the park and went down a steep, crumbling path to the beach. There the cliffs receded a little, leaving a narrow, flat strip covered with pebbles, against which the sea now rippled gently. Dolphins were turning somersaults in the water some five hundred yards off shore, showing momentarily their round, glossy backs. Far out on the horizon, where the azure satin of the sea was bordered by a dark-blue velvet ribbon, the sails of fishing boats stuck up trimly, slightly pink in the sun.

"Here's where we'll bathe, Grandad Lodizhkin," said Sergei resolutely. He had already contrived, while walking, to pull off his trousers, hopping along on one leg. "Let me help you with the instrument."

He stripped swiftly, slapped his naked body to which the sun had given a chocolate tan, and flung himself into the water, setting up waves of seething foam.

The old man took off his clothes unhurriedly. He shaded his eyes with his hand and peered at Sergei with an affectionate grin.

"He's growing into a fine lad," he thought to himself. "A bit bony, to be sure—you can see all his ribs—but he'll be a sturdy chap."

"I say, Sergei! Don't swim too far. Look out for porpoises."

"I'd grab it by the tail if I saw one!" Sergei shouted back.

The old man lingered in the sun for a long time, feeling his arm-pits. He then stepped down into the water very gingerly, and before dipping he carefully wetted his bald red crown and his hollow sides. His sallow body was flabby and weak, his legs surprisingly thin, and his back with the sharp protruding shoulder-blades was hunched from carrying the hurdy-gurdy for so many years.

"Grandad Lodizhkin, look!" cried Sergei.

He turned a somersault in the water, and the old man, who had gone in up to his waist, taking little dips with blissful snorts, cried in alarm, "Stop fooling, you puppy. Don't you dare! I'll show you!"

Arto was barking in a frenzy, running up and down the beach. He was worried because the boy had swum out so far. "Why show off?" he seemed to ask. "Here's dry land and that's where you should stay. It's so much safer."

He even ran into the water up to his belly and lapped a little. But he found the briny water distasteful, and the light waves rustling against the beach gravel frightened him. So he scrambled ashore and started barking at Sergei. "Who's interested in those foolish tricks? Why not stay on the beach, beside the old man? Oh, what a nuisance that boy is!"

"Hey, Sergei, come out, will you now—you've had enough!" the old man called.

"Just a minute, Grandad Lodizhkin," the boy replied. "Look, I can swim like a duck. Whoo-oop!"

At last he swam up to the beach, but before dressing he snatched up Arto, went back into the sea, carrying the dog, and hurled him far out into the water. The dog started at once to swim back, snorting offendedly, with nothing but his nose and floating ears above the water. He got out and shook himself, sending a shower of spray at the old man and Sergei.

"Look, Sergei—I think that man's heading our way," said Lodizhkin, staring upwards.

Shouting incoherently and waving his arms, a man was coming hurriedly down the path. It was the sombre gate-keeper in the black-spotted pink shirt, who, a quarter of an hour earlier, had turned them out of the villa.

"What does he want?" asked the old man in perplexity.

IV

The gate-keeper went on shouting as he came down at a clumsy trot, his sleeves flapping in the wind and his shirt-front swelling like a sail.

"Hallo-o-o there! Wait a bit!"

"Curse you and blast you," grumbled Lodizhkin. "It must be about Arto again."

"Let's lick him, Grandad," Sergei suggested bravely.

"Oh, don't be silly. Good heavens, what people!"

"Listen," the gate-keeper gasped, even before reaching them. "Sell the dog, will you? We just can't manage the young master. He just keeps squealing, 'I want the dog, I want it!' The mistress has sent me to buy the dog, no matter what the price."

"That's rather silly of the mistress!" Lodizhkin retorted, feeling much more confident on the beach than he had at the villa. "Besides, who says she's a mistress to me? She may be a mistress to you, but *I* don't care a fig who she is. Please leave us alone, for Christ's sake, and—and lay off."

But the gate-keeper would not give in. He sat down on the shingle, next to the old man, and said, poking his fingers awkwardly in front of him, "But can't you see, you fool?"

"Fool yourself," the old man snapped calmly.

"Wait a second! I didn't mean it that way. How touchy you are. Just think: what's a dog to you? You can pick up another puppy, teach it how to stand up, and there you are again. Well? Am I wrong? Eh?"

The old man was busy tightening the belt round his trousers.

"Keep yapping," he said with affected indifference, in reply to the gate-keeper's persistent questioning. "I'll give you my answer all in one."

"And here they are offering you a whale of a sum right away!" the gate-keeper went on heatedly. "Two or three hundred rubles all at once! Of course I must get something for the trouble I'm taking. But just imagine: three hundred rubles! Why, you could open a grocery."

While talking like that the gate-keeper took a piece of sausage out of his pocket and hurled it to the poodle. Arto snatched it in mid-air, swallowed it at a gulp, and fawningly wagged his tail.

"That all?" asked Lodizhkin briefly.

"There isn't much to be said. Gimme the dog and let's call it a bargain."

"I see," the old man said with a sneer. "So you suggest I should sell the dog, eh?"

"Of course, I do. Why not? The trouble is, the young master's so wild. Once he gets it into his head to have

224

something he'll kick up hell. He just wants it, and that's all there is to it. It ain't so bad when his father's away, but when he's here, holy smoke! Everybody runs about like mad. His father's an engineer—perhaps you've heard the name—Mr. Obolyaninov? He builds railways all over Russia. A millionaire! And the boy's his only son. So he's up to mischief all the time. If it's a pony he wants, he gets a pony. If it's a boat, he gets a real boat. There just isn't a thing he can't have."

"What about the moon?"

"Just what d'you mean?"

"I mean, did he never want the moon down from the sky?"

"Well, now, what an idea!" The gate-keeper was taken aback. "So what do you say, good man? Is it a deal?"

The old man, who in the meantime had pulled on his brown jacket, green with age at the seams, straightened proudly as far as his bent back would let him.

"I'll tell you this much, my lad," he began, with a touch of solemnity. "Suppose you had a brother or, say, a friend, one that you'd known since you were kids. Hold on, don't waste your sausage on the dog—that won't get you anywhere; better eat it yourself. As I was saying, suppose you had a faithful friend since you were kids. How much d'you think you'd sell him for?"

"Some comparison!"

"You asked for it. Tell your master who's building a railway"—the old man raised his voice—"tell him all isn't sold that is bought. Yes! And you'd better stop stroking the dog, that's no use. Come here, Arto, you son of a dog, I'll teach you! Get ready, Sergei."

"You're an old fool, that's what you are," the gate-keeper burst out, losing his temper at last.

"Perhaps I am a fool, but you're a cur, a Judas, a mean sneek," Lodizhkin countered. "Tell your grand lady when you see her that I send her my love and humble compliments. Roll up that rug, Sergei! Oh, my back, my poor back! Let's go."

"So that's how it is!" said the gate-keeper, meaningly.

"Exactly!" replied the old man.

The three plodded along the same seaside road. Glancing back by chance Sergei saw the gate-keeper watching them. He looked preoccupied and sullen. With all the five fingers of one hand he was studiously scratching the red-haired nape of his neck under the cap, which had slipped down over his eyes.

V

Old Lodizhkin had long ago marked a nook between Miskhor and Alupka, beneath the lower highway, where you could have a nice meal. There he now led his companions. A bubbling spring sent its cool water running out of the ground in the shade of crooked oaks and dense hazel bushes, not far from a bridge spanning a muddy, turbulent mountain stream. It had hollowed out in the soil a shallow bowl from which it flowed to the stream in a thin meandering line that glittered in the grass like quicksilver. Every morning and evening you could see at the spring pious Turks drinking the water or performing their sacred ablutions.

"Heavy are our sins and scanty is our food," said the old man, sitting down in the cool shade of the hazel bushes. "Well, Sergei, blessings on our food!"

Out of his canvas bag he took a loaf of bread, a dozen tomatoes, a chunk of Bessarabian cheese, and a bottle of olive-oil. The salt was tied up in a rag of doubtful cleanness. Before starting the meal he crossed himself and whispered for a long time. Then he broke up the loaf into three unequal parts; one of them, the biggest, he held out to Sergei—the boy was growing and had to be fed properly—the second he left for the poodle, and the third, the smallest, he kept for himself.

"In the name of the Father and the Son. The eyes of all look upon Thee, O Lord," he whispered as he fussily distributed the food and poured oil upon it. "Eat, Sergei!"

The three ate their frugal meal, slowly and silently, as real workers always do. All that could be heard was the noise of the three pairs of jaws munching. Arto was eating his share a little way off, sprawled on his belly and holding the bread with his forefeet. The old man and Sergei took turns to dip the ripe tomatoes into the salt, and as they bit into them the blood-red juice ran over their lips and hands; bread and cheese followed each bite of tomato. When they had stilled their hunger they drank from a tin mug, which they held under the running water. The water was crystal-clear and had an excellent taste; it was so cold that the mug dimmed on the outside. The day's heat and the long walk had exhausted them, for they had risen at dawn. The old man could hardly keep his eyes open. Sergei yawned and stretched.

"Shall we take a little snooze, my boy?" asked the old man. "Let me have a last drink. My, lovely!" He took the mug away from his lips with a gasp, and clear drops of water trickled down his moustache and beard. "If I was a king I'd always drink this water—from morning till night! Here, Arto, come here! Well, God gave us a meal with nobody to steal, so we had our food and it was good."

The old man and the boy lay down on the grass side by side, pillowing their heads on their old jackets. The dark leaves of the gnarled spreading oaks rustled overhead, and the serene blue sky showed through them. The brook leaping from rock to rock gurgled monotonously and soothingly, as if trying to charm someone by its lulling babble. For a while the old man tossed and groaned and mumbled, but to Sergei the voice seemed to be coming from some soft and sleepy distance, and the words were as mysterious as in a fairy-tale.

"First of all I'll buy you an outfit: pink tights with gold, and satin shoes, also pink. In Kiev, Kharkov or, say, the city of Odessa—that's where they have real circuses! Lamps as thick as stars, all electricity. Perhaps five thousand people sit there, or even more—I don't know exactly. We must think up an Italian name for you. D'you call Yestifeyev or Lodizhkin a name? It's just trash—no imagination at all. But we'll put you on a poster and call you Antonio, or—here's a nice name—Enrico or Alfonso."

The boy heard no more. A soft, sweet drowsiness overcame him, weakening and paralyzing his body. The old man also fell asleep, losing all of a sudden the thread of his favourite after-dinner thoughts about Sergei's brilliant future in the circus. Once it seemed to him in his sleep that Arto was snarling at someone. A half-conscious recollection of the gate-keeper in the pink shirt flitted across his drowsy mind; yet, overpowered by sleep, fatigue and heat, he was unable to get up. He only called to the dog lazily, without opening his eyes, "Back, Arto! I'll teach you, you tramp!"

But immediately his thoughts tangled and straggled in heavy, shapeless visions.

Sergei's voice roused the old man. The boy was running up and down on the other side of the brook, whistling shrilly and shouting in anxiety and fright, "Here, Arto! Come back! Whew, whe-e-ew! Come back, Arto!"

"What are you yelling for, Sergei?" asked Lodizhkin gruffly, straightening his numbed arm with an effort.

"We've lost the dog, that's what!" the boy retorted irritably. "The dog's gone."

He gave a sharp whistle and called once more, "Arto-o-o!"

"Rubbish! He'll come back," said the old man. But he scrambled quickly to his feet and started calling the dog in an angry, quaking falsetto, husky with sleep, "Come here, Arto, you son of a dog!"

With small unsteady steps he ran over the bridge and up the highway, calling the dog again and again. The smooth, dazzling white road stretched away before him for nearly a quarter of a mile, but there was not a single form, not a shadow, upon it.

"Arto! Arto my doggie!" wailed the old man piteously. Then he suddenly bent down and squatted.

"So!" he muttered in a hollow voice. "Sergei! Come up here."

"What's the matter now?" the boy cried rudely, walking up to Lodizhkin. "Found something you didn't lose?"

"What's this, Sergei? I mean this—what is it? Do you understand?" the old man asked him, almost in a whisper.

He was looking at the boy with miserable, perplexed eyes, while his trembling hand pointed to the ground.

A fairly big gnawed piece of sausage lay in the white dust, with a dog's footprints all around it.

"He's lured away the dog, that ruffian!" the old man whispered in fright, still squatting. "It must be him—it's clear enough. Remember him on the beach feeding sausage to the dog?"

"It's clear enough," Sergei repeated with sullen fury.

The old man's eyes, wide open, suddenly filled with large tears and started blinking. He covered them with his hands.

"What shall we do now, Sergei dear? Eh? What shall we do?" asked the old man, rocking to and fro and sobbing helplessly.

"What shall we do! What shall we do!" Sergei aped him angrily. "Get up, Grandad Lodizhkin—let's go."

"Let's go," the crestfallen old man agreed meekly, rising from the ground. "Yes, let's go, Sergei dear!"

Sergei lost his temper.

"Stop slobbering, will you!" he shouted at the old man as if he had been his elder. "They have no right to lure away other people's dogs. What are you gaping at me for? Am I wrong? We'll go right there and say, 'Give us back the dog!' And if they don't we'll go to the J. P. That's all there is to it."

"To the J. P.—yes, of course. You're right about the J. P.," Lodizhkin muttered with an inane, bitter smile, while his eyes shifted in awkward embarrassment. "To the J. P., yes— Only, we can't go to the J. P."

"Why not? There's one law for all. Why should we be scared?" the boy interrupted him impatiently.

"Please, Sergei, don't be cross with me. They won't give us back the dog, anyway." He lowered his voice with a mysterious air. "I'm worried about my passport. Did you hear what that gentleman said? 'Have you got a passport?' he says. See how it is? Now the passport I've got"—the old man's face took on a frightened look, and he went on in a scarcely audible whisper—"that passport isn't mine, Sergei."

"What d'you mean, not yours?"

"Just that. I lost mine in Taganrog, or perhaps somebody stole it. For two years after that I shifted and hid and gave bribes and wrote petitions. At last I saw I couldn't keep it up any longer, living like a rabbit—being afraid of everybody. I had no peace. One day a Greek popped up in a doss-house in Odessa. 'That's easy,' he said. 'You fork out twenty-five rubles, old man,' he says, 'and I'll provide you with a passport that will last you till you die.' I turned it over in my mind. 'Come what may,' I said to myself. 'Get it,' I says. Ever since then, my boy, I've been using somebody else's passport."

"Oh, Grandad!" Sergei sighed with a sob. "It's such a pity we lost the dog. Such a fine dog, too!"

"Sergei, my own dear boy!" The old man stretched out his trembling hands. "If only I had a proper passport, do you really think I'd be scared because they're generals? Why, I'd grab them by the throat! 'What's this?' I'd say. 'What right have you to steal dogs? There's no such law!' But now we're done for, Sergei. If I went to police the first thing they'd say would be, 'Show your passport! Are *you* Martin Lodizhkin of Samara?' 'Yes, sir.' But I'm not Lodizhkin—I'm Ivan Dudkin, a peasant. God alone knows who that Lodizhkin is. How do I know he isn't a thief or a runaway convict? Or even a murderer? We can't do anything, Sergei, believe me we can't. It's no use."

The old man's voice broke off. Fresh tears rolled down the deep wrinkles on his face, browned by the sun. Sergei, who had been listening in silence, his lips pressed tight and his face pale with emotion, suddenly caught the old man under the arms to raise him.

"Come on, Grandad," he said in an imperious but friendly tone. "To hell with the passport—come on! We can't spend the night out here on the highway."

"You dear, dear boy," the old man murmured, shaking from head to foot. "It's such a clever dog, is our poor Arto. We'll never have another so good."

"All right, all right. Get up," Sergei commanded. "Here, let me brush you. Keep your chin up!"

They did not perform any more that day. Though still a boy, Sergei well knew the fatal meaning of that terrible word, "passport." He therefore did not insist on looking for Arto, going to the Justice of the Peace, or taking any other strong measures. But while he walked to the doss-house beside the old man, his face kept its new, stubborn expression, as if he were planning something big and exceedingly important.

Without previous agreement, but apparently moved by the same secret desire, they purposely made a long detour in order to pass Friendship Villa again. They lingered for a moment at the gate, in the vague hope of seeing Arto, or at least hearing his bark.

But the wrought-iron gate of the magnificent villa was tightly shut, and there was an unruffled, solemn quiet in the shady garden, under the slender, melancholy cypresses.

"Gentry, are they!" hissed the old man, putting into the exclamation all the bitterness that filled his heart.

"That's enough—come on," the boy commanded grimly, and pulled at his companion's sleeve.

"Perhaps Arto will run away from them, Sergei dear?" The old man gave a sob. "What do you think, my boy?"

But the boy made no reply. He was walking ahead with a firm stride. He kept his eyes fixed on the road, his thin eyebrows gathered in an angry frown.

VI

They reached Alupka in silence. All the way the old man groaned and sighed, while Sergei still wore his angry, determined look. They put up for the night at a dingy Turkish coffee-house that bore the splendid name of "Yildiz," or "Star." For night companions they had Greek stone-cutters, Turkish navvies, a few Russian workmen who kept body and soul together by doing odd jobs, and several of the shady tramps of whom there are so many in southern Russia. As soon as the coffee-house closed at the usual hour they all lay down on the benches which lined the walls, and also on the floor; the more experienced took the necessary precaution of putting their clothes, and anything else of value, under their heads.

It was well past midnight when Sergei, who had been lying on the floor beside the old man, rose quietly and began to dress. Pale moonlight poured in through the wide windows; it lay on the floor in a slanting pattern, and in it the faces of the sprawling men looked tormented and dead.

"Vere you koing at zis time of night, boy?" Ibrahim, the young Turk who owned the coffee-house, called sleepily to Sergei.

"Let me out. I must go!" Sergei replied in a stern, business-like tone. "Get up, now, you Turkish clod!"

Ibrahim unlocked the door, yawning, scratching himself and clicking his tongue reproachfully. The narrow streets of the Tatar section were sunk in an intense dark blue shade that covered the roadway and with its jagged edge reached the foot of the houses opposite, whose low walls showed very white in the moonlight. Dogs were barking on the far outskirts of the town. The resounding clatter of an ambling horse came from somewhere on the upper highway.

The boy walked past the white mosque with the green onion-shaped dome, surrounded by a silent group of dark cypresses, and went to the highway down a narrow, crooked lane. He wore nothing but his tights, so as to move more easily. The moon beat down on his back, and his shadow ran ahead of him in a black, strangely short-ened silhouette. From the dark curly shrubs which crouched on both sides of the highway, a bird called monotonously at regular intervals, in a tenuous voice, "Sleep! Sleep!" It seemed as if the bird were obediently guarding some melancholy secret in the still night, trying in vain to overcome drowsiness and fatigue, and sending forth its hopeless plaint, "Sleep! Sleep!" And above the dark shrubs and the bluish tops of the distant forests, the Ai Petri peak thrust its twin prongs skywards, looking as light and clear-cut and airy as if it had been made from a giant piece of silvery cardboard.

Sergei was awed by the majestic silence, in which his steps rang so sharply and audaciously, but at the same time a kind of tickling, dizzy courage filled his heart. As the road curved the sea sprang into view. Immense and placid, it heaved with calm dignity. A narrow, shimmering silvery path stretched to the shore from the horizon; it was lost to sight out at sea, with only occasional spangles flashing here and there, but just short of the beach it spread out like a liquid, glittering metal band, running along the entire shore.

Noiselessly Sergei stole into the park through the wooden wicket. It was quite dark in there, under the dense trees. A restless brook murmured in the distance, and you could sense its damp, cool breath. The wooden floor of a bridge thudded loudly under the boy's feet. The water beneath it was black and terrible. Here at last was the high iron gate, patterned like lacework and entwined by the creeping stalks of wistarias. Cutting through the foliage of the trees, the moonlight glided over the fretwork in feeble phosphorescent spots. Beyond was darkness and a timid, alert silence.

For a few seconds Sergei wavered, feeling almost afraid. But he overcame the sensation and whispered, "I'll get in just the same! It's all one!"

The gate was not difficult to climb. The elegant cast-iron scrolls of the pattern served as dependable supports for his tenacious hands and small muscular feet. A broad stone arch topped the gate at a great height. Sergei groped his way up on to it, then, lying flat on his belly, lowered his feet on the other side, and began to push down the whole of his body, at the same time feeling with his feet for some support. Then he was hanging from the arch, with only his fingers clinging to the edge, but still he found no foothold. It had not occurred to him that the arch over the gate projected much more deeply inside than it did outside, and terror gripped his heart as his hands grew numb and his weakening body heavier.

At last he could hold on no longer. His fingers let go the sharp edge and he hurtled down.

He heard the coarse gravel crunch under his weight and felt a sharp pain in his knees. Stunned by the fall, he stood for a few seconds on all fours. It seemed to him that all the people in the villa were going to wake up, the gloomy gate-keeper in the pink shirt would come running, and there would be a general turmoil. But the silence in the garden was as profound and solemn as before. He could hear only a low, monotonous hum filling the garden.

"Why, it's the ringing in my ears," he guessed. He rose to his feet; the garden, which seemed full of aromatic dreams, was terrible and mysterious and beautiful as in a fairy-tale. Flowers hardly visible in the dark swayed gently in the beds, bending to each other with vague anxiety, as if whispering among themselves and spying on him. The slender, fragrant cypresses slowly shook their pointed tops, with a pensive and reproachful air. And in the dense shrubs beyond the brook, the weary little bird kept on wrestling with drowsiness and repeating its submissive plaint, "Sleep! Sleep! Sleep!"

Sergei did not recognize the place at night, amid the tangle of shadows that lay on the walks. He wandered long on the crunching gravel until he came to the house.

Never before in his life had the boy felt so painfully, so completely helpless and forsaken. The house seemed full of merciless crouching enemies stealthily watching through the dark windows every movement of the small, weak boy, and smiling maliciously as they silently waited for some signal, for someone's angry, thunderous command.

"Not in the house—it can't be in the house," the boy whispered, as in a dream. "It would howl in the house and bother everybody."

He walked round the villa. In the wide courtyard behind it there were several buildings that were less elaborate than the house and were probably occupied by the servants. As in the big house, there was no light in any of the windows, except that the dark panes reflected the moon with a ghastly, uneven shine. "I'll never get out of here, never!" Sergei thought in anguish. For an instant he recalled Lodizhkin and the old hurdy-gurdy, the nights spent in coffee-houses, the meals taken at cool springs. "There won't be any more of that!" he said to himself sadly. But as his thoughts grew hopeless fear gave way in his heart to a dull, grim despair.

Suddenly a thin yelp that sounded like a groan caught his ear. The boy halted on tiptoe, with bated breath, his muscles taut. The sound was repeated. It seemed to come from a stone cellar near where he was standing. Treading on a flower parterre, the boy stepped up to the wall in which there were some crude rectangular glassless holes. He put his face against one of these and whistled. There was a slight noise somewhere below, but it died away at once.

"Arto! Arto!" Sergei called, in a tremulous whisper.

Instantly a frantic, broken barking filled the whole garden, echoing in its every corner. There was complaint and anger and physical pain in it, combined with a joyous welcome. The boy could hear the dog trying to break loose from something that held him in the dark cellar.

"Arto! Doggie! Arto dear!" the boy responded tearfully.

"Shut up, blast you!" came a harsh boom from below. "You damned nuisance!"

There was a thump in the cellar. The dog gave a long, broken howl.

"Don't you dare to beat him! Don't dare to beat the dog, you beast!" Sergei screamed in a frenzy, scratching the stone wall with his nails.

All that happened next Sergei could remember only dimly afterwards, as if he had been delirious. The cellar door crashed open, and the gate-keeper rushed out. Barefoot and with nothing on but his underwear, his bearded face livid in the bright moonlight, he appeared to Sergei as a giant, an enraged ogre.

"Who is there? I'll shoot you down!" his voice thundered in the garden. "Catch the thief! Help!"

But just then Arto darted like a white bouncing ball out of the dark doorway, barking. A bit of cord dangled from his neck.

However, the boy had no time for the dog. The formidable appearance of the gate-keeper had gripped him with a supernatural terror, bound his feet, and paralyzed his small, slight body. Luckily the stupor did not last long. Almost unconsciously, Sergei gave a desperate shriek and, mad with fear, started to run blindly away from the cellar.

He sped on like a hare, his feet suddenly becoming as strong as two steel springs. Arto raced alongside him, barking happily. The gate-keeper, cursing furiously, tore along behind them.

Sergei ran into the gate but instantly sensed rather than realized that there was no way out there. There was a dark narrow pathway between the white stone wall and the cypresses growing along it. Without hesitating, and prompted by fear alone, he ducked, dashed into it, and ran along the wall. The sharp cypress needles, smelling pungently of resin, lashed him across the face. He tripped on roots and fell and bruised his hands more than once, but he rose again and sped on, unaware of the pain, almost doubled up, deaf to his own cries. Arto shot after him.

Thus, like a little animal caught in an endless snare and mad with terror, he scampered along the narrow passage formed by the high wall on one side and the serried row of cypresses on the other. His mouth was dry and each gasping breath pricked his chest with a thousand needles. He heard the gate-keeper's footsteps to the right and then to the left, and, losing his head completely, he now rushed forward, now turned back again, passing the gate repeatedly and plunging afresh into the dark, narrow pathway.

At last he was spent. A cold, mortal anguish, a dull indifference to all danger, took hold of him despite his wild terror. He sat down under a tree, leaned his exhausted body against its trunk, and shut his eyes. Closer and closer crunched the sand under his enemy's heavy feet. Arto was whining softly, his nose on Sergei's knees.

Boughs pushed apart rustled two yards from the boy. He looked up involuntarily, and suddenly bounded to his feet, beside himself with joy. He had not noticed until then that the wall opposite the place where he had been sitting was no more than three and a half feet high. Its top was studded with bits of bottle glass stuck into lime, but that did not stop Sergei. In the twinkling of an eye he seized Arto and stood him with his forefeet on the top of the wall. The clever dog understood perfectly what was wanted. He clambered up on the wall, wagged his tail, and started to bark triumphantly.

Sergei followed him just as a hulking dark figure emerged from the parted cypress boughs. Two lithe forms—the dog's and the boy's—jumped softly on to the road. Savage, foul curses came after them in a filthy torrent.

Whether because the gate-keeper was slower than the two friends or because he was tired chasing about the garden, or because he had lost hope of catching the fugitives, he gave up the pursuit. Nevertheless, the two ran for long without stopping to rest, both of them strong and agile, as if borne on wings by the joy of deliverance. The poodle soon regained his habitual playfulness. Sergei still glanced back fearfully now and then, but Arto leapt up at him in glee, shaking his ears and the bit of cord, and trying hard to lick the boy's face.

Sergei did not recover his calm until they reached the spring where they had taken their meal the day before. Dog and boy put their mouths to the cool fountain and drank long and deeply of the fresh, delicious water. They would push each other aside, raise their heads momentarily to draw breath, the water trickling from their lips, and bend over the fountain with renewed thirst, unable to pull away from it. And when they finally tore themselves away and walked on, the water splashed and gurgled in their overfilled bellies. They were out of danger, all the terrors of the night were gone, and it was a pleasure to walk along the white road bright with moonshine, between dark shrubs that were already drenched with morning dew, their refreshed leaves smelling sweetly.

At the coffee-house Ibrahim greeted the boy with a reproachful whisper, "Vass ze idea of kadding about, boy? Vass ze idea? Iss a bad sing you did, very bad."

Sergei did not want to wake up the old man, but Arto did it for him. Instantly he found the old man among the forms huddled on the floor, and before Lodizhkin knew what was happening the dog, yelping happily, had licked him all over the face. The old man woke up; he saw the cord round the poodle's neck, and the boy lying covered with dust by his side, and he understood. He asked Sergei how it all had come about, but the boy was already asleep, his arms thrown apart and his mouth wide open.

1904

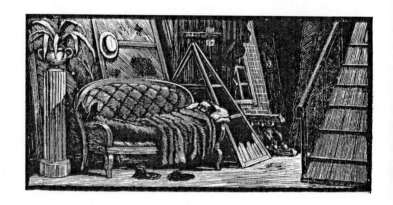

I WAS AN ACTOR

I have this sad and laughable story, which is more sad than laughable, from a friend who had lived a most colourful life and had been both the rider and the horse, as the saying goes, but who, despite the cruel blows of fate, had kept both a kind heart and a lucid mind. It was only the events described in this story that had a rather strange effect upon him, for since they happened he has never been to the theatre again, no matter how strongly urged to do so.

I shall try to relate his story here, though I fear I may not be able to do it in the simple manner, or with the soft, wistful irony, which marked his own narrative.

I

Well, now. Can you imagine a shabby little southern town? In its middle is a huge hole where *Khokhols** from the countryside, waist-deep in mud, sell cucumbers and potatoes from their carts. That is the market-place. One side of it is formed by a cathedral and, of course, Cathedral Street; another, by a public garden; the third, by a row of stalls, with the yellow plaster peeling off, and pigeons perched on the roofs and cornices; and on the fourth side the main street runs into the market-place, with a branch office of some bank, a post-office, a notary's office and the saloon of *Théodore* the hairdresser, of Moscow. On the outskirts of the town, in all sorts of Zaselyes, Zamostyes and Zarechyes,** an infantry regiment is stationed, and in the town centre, a dragoon regiment. There is a theatre in the public garden. And that is all.

I ought to add, however, that the town of S. with its *Duma**** and school, its public garden and theatre, and the cobbles in the main street, owed its existence to the bounty of the local millionaire Kharitonenko, a sugar manufacturer.

II

The full story of how I came to live in that town would take too long to tell. So I shall be brief. I was to meet there a friend of mine—may he rest in peace—a true friend married to a woman who, as is the case with the wives of all our *true* friends, could not stand me. He and I had several thousand rubles apiece, earned by hard

---

   * Ukrainians —*Tr*.
   ** Names of districts: Beyond-the-Village, Beyond-the-Bridge, Beyond-the-River.—*Tr*.
   *** Town Hall.—*Tr*

work; he had been a teacher for many years and at the same time an insurance agent, and I had been in luck at cards for a whole year. Once we hit on a very profitable enterprise in southern lamb and made up our minds to take the risk. I set out first, and he was supposed to follow me two or three days later. As I had long been known for my absent-mindedness it was he who kept all our money in two separate parcels, for he was as precise as a German.

And then came a shower of misfortunes. At Kharkov railway station my wallet was stolen from my pocket while I was eating cold sturgeon with *sauce provençale.* I arrived in S., the town I am talking about, with the small change I had in my purse, and with a poorly filled but fine reddish-yellow suitcase of English make. I put up at the hotel—it was called the St. Petersburg, of course— and started sending wire after wire. The answer I got was dead silence. Yes, "dead" is the word, because at the exact hour when the thief was filching my wallet—imagine the kind of tricks fate plays on us!—my friend and partner died of a stroke while riding in a cab. All his luggage and money were sealed, and for some idiotic reason judicial pettifogging dragged on for six weeks. Whether or not the sorrow-stricken widow knew anything about my money I cannot tell. As a matter of fact, she did receive every one of my telegrams, but obstinately re- fused to answer them, by way of petty, jealous woman's revenge. It is true that afterwards those telegrams stood me in good stead. When the seals had been removed the telegrams chanced to catch the eye of a barrister who had been dealing with the inheritance and was a total stran- ger to me. He reproved the widow and at his own risk remitted five hundred rubles to me, in care of the theatre. This was scarcely surprising, for those were not ordinary telegrams but tragic cries from my soul, each compressed into twenty or thirty words.

III

It was my tenth day at the St. Petersburg. The tragic cries of my soul had completely drained my purse. The hotel owner—a grim, sleepy-looking *Khokhol* with a murderer's face—no longer believed a word of what I told him. I showed him certain letters and papers which I said should make it clear to him ... and so on, but he turned scornfully away and sniffed. Finally a waiter brought my dinner and announced, "The master says this is the last time."

And the day came when all that I had in my pocket was a lone, musty twenty-kopek piece. That morning the owner told me roughly that he was not going to feed or keep me any longer and would take matter to the police. I gathered from his tone that the man meant what he said.

I spent the day wandering about the town. I remember I walked into a transport office and into some other places to ask for work, but I was refused the moment I opened my mouth. Now and then I would sit on one of the green benches placed along the main street, between tall Lombardy poplars. I felt dizzy and sick with hunger. But the idea of suicide did not occur to me for a second. Throughout my tangled life, I had many times toyed with that idea, but a year, sometimes a month, or even ten minutes, would pass and everything would suddenly change, and once again I would be in luck and gay and happy. As I roamed the hot, dull town I kept saying to myself, "It's a fine mess you're in, Pavel Andreyevich."

I was hungry. But some mysterious presentiment made me keep my last twenty kopeks. Night was falling when I saw a red poster on a fence. I had nothing to do anyway. So I walked mechanically over and read the poster, which said that that night *Uriel Acosta*, a tragedy by Gutzkow, would be presented in the public garden, with

such and such a cast. The names of two actors were printed in large black type: those of "Mlle Androsova, an
actress of the Petersburg stage," and "Mr. Lara-Larsky,
the well-known Kharkov actor"; the minor stars were
"Mmes Vologodskaya, Medvedeva, Strunina-Dolskaya,
and Messrs. Timofeyev-Sumskoi, Akimenko, Samoilenko,
Nelyubov-Olgin, and Dukhovskoi." The names set in the
smallest type were "Petrov, Sergeyev, Sidorov, Grigoryev,
Nikolayev, and others." The stage-director was "Mr. Samoilenko," and the managing director, "Mr. Valerianov."

I was inspired with a sudden, desperate decision. I ran
across the street to the hairdresser *Théodore*, of Moscow,
and for my last twenty kopeks got him to shave off my
moustache and small pointed beard. God Almighty! What
a sullen, bare face I saw in the mirror! I could not believe my eyes. Instead of a man of thirty, respectable-
looking if not very handsome, I saw, sitting in the mirror
in front of me, an old, hardened provincial comedian,
draped in a sheet up to his throat, with the marks of all
kinds of vices on his face and, what was more, obviously
drunk.

"Going to work in our theatre?" the hairdresser's assistant asked me, shaking down the sheet.

"Yes," I replied proudly. "Here's your money."

IV

On my way to the public garden I was thinking:

"It's an ill wind that blows no one good. They'll at
once see what a downy old bird I am. These little summer
theatres can always use an odd man. I won't ask much
to begin with. Let's say fifty—no, forty rubles a month.
Afterwards we'll see. I'll ask for an advance payment of
twenty rubles—no, that would be too much—ten rubles
or so. First of all I'll send a strong-worded telegram; five
by five is twenty-five, plus nought, that'll be two fifty,

244

plus fifteen kopeks for delivery, that'll make two sixty-five. I'll live on the rest till Ilya comes along. If they feel like testing me, let them do so, and I'll recite something— Pimen's monologue,* for instance."

And I began under my breath, in a deep solemn voice:

One more event I will inscribe—

A passer-by darted aside in fright. I gave an embarrassed cough. I was now near the public garden. A military band was playing there; slim local misses in pink or blue were strolling hatless along the walks, and local clerks, telegraphists and excisemen dangled after them, laughing without constraint, one hand thrust under their coat lapels and their white service caps cocked.

The gate was wide open. I walked in. Somebody invited me to buy a ticket at the box-office, but I asked carelessly where I could see the manager, Mr. Valerianov. I was at once referred to two clean-shaven young gentlemen sitting on a bench not far from the entrance. I walked over and stopped about two paces from them.

Absorbed in conversation, they took no notice of me, and I had a chance to have a good look at them. One of them, in a light Panama hat and blue-striped flannels, had the affectedly noble countenance and proud profile of a *jeune premier*, and was playing absent-mindedly with his slender cane. The other, dressed in grey, had unusually long legs and arms. In fact, his legs seemed to start right from the chest, and his arms must have hung below his knees, all of which gave the effect of a grotesque zigzag that could easily have been duplicated by means of a hinged yardstick. He had a very small head, with a freckled face and quick black eyes.

Unobtrusively I cleared my throat. Both men turned to look at me.

* From Pushkin's *Boris Godunov.—Tr.*

"May I see Mr. Valerianov?" I asked in a friendly tone.

"That's me," said the freckled man. "What can I do for you?"

"You see, I'd like to"—my voice caught—"I'd like to offer you my services as—er—as, say, a comedian, or—er—a 'simpleton.' I could also play character parts."

The *jeune premier* got up and walked off, whistling and swinging his cane.

"Where were you employed before?" asked Valerianov.

I had only acted once, when I played a comic part in an amateur performance. But I strained my imagination and replied:

"To be frank, I've never been employed by a sound enterprise like yours. But I had a chance to play with small companies in the South-West. They failed almost as fast as they were set up—Marinich's, for example, Sokolovsky's, and some other besides."

"I say, do you drink?" Valerianov demanded all of a sudden.

"No," I answered promptly. "I take something occasionally before dinner, or at a party, but no more than a drop."

Valerianov looked down at the sand, narrowing his black eyes.

"All right," he said after some reflection, "I'll take you on. You'll be paid twenty-five rubles a month, and then we'll see. You may be needed even tonight. Go to the stage and ask for the assistant stage-director Dukhovskoi. He'll introduce you to the director."

I went to the stage, wondering why he had not asked my stage name. He must have forgotten, I thought, or guessed that I had no such name. Nevertheless, as I walked along I invented a surname for myself, just in case: Osinin, a name that was not flashy but simple and pleasant-sounding.

V

I found Dukhovskoi, a fidgety lad with a sallow thief's face, behind the scenes. He introduced me to the director, Samoilenko. Samoilenko was going to play some heroic part that night and so he wore golden armour, jack-boots and the make-up of a juvenile. I managed to observe despite the camouflage that he was fat and moon-faced, with pin-point eyes and a mouth set in a perpetual inane smile. He gave me a haughty welcome and refused to shake hands. I was about to walk away when he said, "Wait a minute. What did you say your name was? I didn't catch it."

"Vasilyev!" Dukhovskoi hastened to prompt, with ser·vile alacrity.

Taken aback, I was going to correct the error, but it was too late.

"Now look here, Vasilyev. You stay here today. Dukhovskoi, tell the tailor to give Vasilyev a coat."

That was how I changed from Osinin into Vasilyev, a name I retained to the end of my stage career, along with "Petrov, Ivanov, Nikolayev, Grigoryev, Sidorov, and others." An inexperienced actor, I did not guess until a week later that, of all those names appearing on the poster, mine alone represented a real person. The accursed assonance did it!

The tailor, a lean, lame man, came in, put on me a long, black calico shroud with sleeves, and basted it from top to tail. Then came the hairdresser. I recognized him as *Théodore*'s assistant who had just shaved me. We gave each other a friendly smile. He put on my head a black wig with lovelocks. Dukhovskoi burst into the dressing-room and bawled, "Make up, Vasilyev!" I dipped my finger into some paint, but my neighbour on the left, an austere man with a grave forehead, snapped at me, "Can't you keep out of somebody else's box? Here are the common paints."

I saw a large box divided into cells that were filled with mixed, dirty paints. I felt dazed. It was all very well for Dukhovskoi to bawl "Make up!" But how was I to go about it? Bravely I drew a white line down my nose and at once took on a clownish appearance. Then I made a pair of cruel eyebrows, put two blue shadows under my eyes, and wondered what else I should do. I screwed up my eyes and drew two vertical wrinkles between my eyebrows. Now I looked for all the world like a Comanche chief.

"Get ready, Vasilyev!" came a voice from above.

I went out of the dressing-room and up to a linen door in the back wall. Dukhovskoi was waiting for me.

"It's your turn now. Lord, what a face! You must go on the moment you hear 'Yes, he will come back.' You'll walk on and say"—he mentioned a proper name that I have forgotten— " 'So-and-so wants a rendezvous,' and then came out again. Is that clear?"

"Yes."

" 'Yes, he will come back!' " I heard someone say, and, pushing Dukhovskoi out of my way, I rushed to the stage. What was that man's name, damn him? I was dumb for a second or two. The audience seemed to be a stirring black abyss. I saw unfamiliar, coarsely painted faces right in front of me, in the glaring light of a lamp. Everyone was staring at me intently. Dukhovskoi whispered something from behind, but I could not make out a word. Then I suddenly blurted out in a solemnly reproachful voice, "Yes! He has come back!"

Samoilenko swept past me like a hurricane in his golden armour. Thank God! I slipped behind the scenes.

I was used in that play twice more. In the scene where Acosta denounces Jewish ritual and then falls, I was to take him in my arms and drag him out. I was assisted by a fireman attired in a black shroud like myself. (Probably so far as the audience was concerned he was "Sidorov.") Uriel Acosta turned out to be the actor whom I had seen sitting with Valerianov on the bench, that is, Lara-Larsky, "the well-known Kharkov actor." We grabbed him rather clumsily—he was muscular and heavy—but fortunately we did not drop him. He only muttered to us, "Blast you both, you numskulls!" We succeeded in hauling him through the narrow door, only the entire back wall of the ancient temple shook and swayed for a long time after.

When I appeared on the stage for the third time, it was to attend mutely the trial of Acosta. There was a little incident when Ben Akiba came in and everyone rose in deference but I remained sitting from sheer absent-mindedness. Someone gave me a painful pinch above the elbow and hissed, "You're crazy! This is Ben Akiba! Get up!"

I got up in all haste. But, really, I did not know it was Ben Akiba. I thought it was just an ordinary old man.

After the performance Samoilenko said to me, "Vasilyev, you'll attend a rehearsal at eleven tomorrow."

I returned to my hotel, but the owner banged the door shut as soon as he heard my voice. I spent the night on one of the green benches set up between the poplars. It was warm and I dreamed of fame. But the cool morning wind and the sensation of hunger woke me up rather early.

VI

At half past ten sharp I went to the theatre. No one had come yet. Here and there in the garden sleepy waiters from the summer restaurant were loafing with their white aprons on. Breakfast or morning coffee was going to be served to someone in a green latticed arbour twined with wild vines.

249

Later I learned that Valerianov, the theatre manager, and Bulatova-Chernogorskaya, a former actress of about sixty-five, who maintained both the theatre and its manager, had breakfast there in the open every morning.

A fresh, gleaming-white cloth was spread on the table; two covers lay on it, and two piles of sliced bread rose on a plate.

Now comes a painful passage. I became a thief for the first and last time in my life. With a swift look round me, I whisked into the arbour, and snatched several slices of bread. It was so soft! so fine! But as I rushed out I ran into a waiter. He had probably come out from behind the arbour. He was carrying a cruet-stand with mustard, pepper and vinegar. He looked sternly at me and at the bread in my hand, and asked softly, "What's the meaning of this?"

I felt a burning, contemptuous pride rise inside me. Looking him straight in the eye, I answered just as softly, "It is that I haven't had a thing to eat since four o'clock the day before yesterday."

He spun round and hurried away without a word. I put the bread in my pocket and waited. I felt at once terrified and elated. "Wonderful!" I thought. "The owner will be here in a moment, the waiters will all gather, they'll whistle for the police to come—there'll be a turmoil, a lot of swearing, and a scuffle. Oh, how splendidly I'm going to smash those plates and this cruet on their heads! I'll bite them till they bleed!"

But the waiter came running back—alone. He was slightly out of breath. He sidled up without looking at me. I turned away too. And suddenly, from under his apron, he thrust into my hand a big chunk of last night's cold beef, carefully salted, and whispered entreatingly, "Please take this."

I grabbed the beef, went behind the scenes and picked a place where it was dark enough. There, sitting amid all sorts of shabby props, I began greedily to tear the meat with my teeth, weeping with relish.

Afterwards I saw the man almost daily. His name was Sergei. When none of the customers was about he would look at me from a distance with friendly, devoted, pleading eyes. But both for his and my own sake I was loth to spoil the original good impression, although, to be frank, sometimes I was as hungry as a wolf in winter.

He was podgy and bald-headed, with black moustaches like the feelers of a cockroach, and kindly eyes shaped like two narrow, glowing semi-circles. And he was always in a hurry as he ran about limping a little. When at last I received my money and my stage bondage was gone like a bad dream, when all the scum lapped in my champagne and fawned on me, how I missed my dear, funny, touching Sergei! I should never have dared to offer him money, of course, for how could such tenderness and affection be repaid in money? I simply wanted to leave him a souvenir. A trinket of some sort. Or to give some present to his wife or children—he had a whole bunch of them, and sometimes they came scurrying to him in the morning, as fussy and noisy as young sparrows.

But a week before my miraculous transformation Sergei was discharged, and I knew why. Captain von Bradke was served a steak that he did not find to his taste.

"Is this the way to serve it, you scoundrel?" he roared. "Don't you know I like it underdone?"

Sergei ventured to remark that it was not his fault but the cook's, and that he would at once have it changed, and even added timidly, "Pardon me, sir."

The apology made the officer quite furious. He slapped Sergei's face with the hot steak and yelled, crimson with rage:

"Wha-at? So you sir me, eh? Y-you sir me? You can't sir His Majesty's staff captain of cavalry! Owner! Call the owner here! Ivan Lukyanich, you'll get this idiot out of here this very day! I won't have him here! You kick him out or I'll never set foot in your tavern again!"

Captain von Bradke used to make merry in a big way, and so Sergei was promptly dismissed. The owner was busy all through the evening appeasing the officer. I could hear for a long time, as I went out into the garden for some fresh air during the intervals, an indignant voice coming in peals from the arbour, "Just listen to that bastard! 'Sir,' he says! I'd have shown him how to sir me if it wasn't for the ladies!"

VII

Meanwhile the actors came gradually together, and at half past twelve the rehearsal began. The play, entitled *The New World*, was an absurd side-show adaptation of Sienkiewicz's novel *Quo Vadis*? Dukhovskoi handed me a sheet of paper with my part lithographed on it. I was playing a centurion of Marcus the Magnificent and had to pronounce such excellent, high-sounding lines as "O Marcus, thy orders have been executed precisely!" or "She will be awaiting thee at the foot of Pompey's statue, O Marcus." I had taken a fancy to the part and was already reciting it in my mind in the courageous voice of a stalwart old warrior, stern and devoted.

But as the rehearsal progressed something strange happened to me: quite unexpectedly for myself, I began to fall into more and more small parts. For example, the matron Veronica finished speaking and Samoilenko, who was keeping an eye on the text of the play, clapped his hands and cried, "Enter Slave!"

Nobody came in.

"Who's the Slave here, gentlemen? See who's the Slave, Dukhovskoi."

Dukhovskoi made a hurried search in sheets of some sort, but discovered no Slave.

"Oh, cross it out—why waste our time!" Boyev suggested lazily. He was the man with the grave forehead, into whose paint I had dipped my finger the day before.

But Marcus (Lara-Larsky) suddenly took offence.

"Oh, no, please. This is one of my spectacular appearances. I won't play this scene without the Slave."

Samoilenko's eyes darted about the stage and fell on me.

"Just a moment. Are you engaged in this act, Vasilyev?"

I stared into my sheet.

"Yes. At the very end."

"Well, then, here's another part for you—Veronica's slave. Read from the book." He clapped his hands. "Quiet, please, ladies and gentlemen! Enter Slave. 'Noble lady—' Louder, they can't hear you in the first row."

A few minutes later they could not find a slave for the divine Mercia (Sienkiewicz's Lygia), and stopped the gap with my person. Then someone else was wanted for the part of the House Manager, and again they used me. Thus, towards the end of the rehearsal, I came to have five additional parts besides the centurion's.

At first I did not get on well. I would come out and speak my first words, " 'O Marcus—' "

Samoilenko would spread his legs apart, bend forward and cup his palms round his ears.

"What's that? What are you mumbling, anyway? I can't make out a thing."

" 'O Marcus—' "

"I'm sorry. I can't hear at all. Louder!" He would walk up close to me. "This is how you should say it." And he would sing out in a throaty billy-goat's voice that could be heard throughout the garden, " 'O Marcus, thy command—!' That's the way to say it. Remember, young man, the immortal maxim of one of the great Russian actors: 'On the stage one doesn't speak—one utters; nor does one walk—one stalks.' " He looked smugly round. "Now say it again."

I did, but worse than before. Then they took turns to coach me, and kept on coaching me till the end of the rehearsal, all of them: proud Lara-Larsky—with a scornful, fastidious air—old, puffy Goncharov, whose flabby, red-veined jowls hung below his chin, the grease-paint owner, Boyev, the "simpleton," Akimenko, with his affected look of Ivan the Fool. I was like a harassed, steaming horse with a crowd of street advisers gathered round it, or a new pupil who had got out of the snug family circle smack into the midst of experienced, sly and cruel schoolboys.

At that rehearsal I made a petty but merciless enemy, who later poisoned every day of my existence. This is how it came about.

I was just speaking one of my endless lines: " 'O Marcus—' " when Samoilenko suddenly rushed up to me.

"Hold on, my friend, hold on. That's wrong. Who are you speaking to? It's to Marcus the Magnificent, isn't it? Well, in that case you haven't the slightest notion of how subordinates in ancient Rome addressed their supreme commander. Look: this is the right gesture."

He put his right foot forward a half pace, bent his trunk at a right angle, and dropped his right arm, shaping his palm into a scoop.

"See how it must be done? Now do it again."

I did, but the gesture turned out so stupid and ugly that I attempted a timid protest.

"I beg your pardon, but it seems to me that a military bearing somehow precludes a bent posture, and the direction here says that he comes out in armour—and you'll agree that anyone wearing armour—"

"Kindly be silent!" Samoilenko shouted in anger, and went purple. "If the stage-director tells you to stand on one leg and put out your tongue it's your duty to obey implicitly. Kindly do it again."

I did. It turned out even uglier than before. But at this juncture Lara-Larsky came to my aid.

"Stop it, Boris," he said reluctantly to Samoilenko. "Don't you see he can't do it? Besides, you know yourself that history gives us no direct guidance on this score. It's—well, it's a moot point."

Samoilenko left me alone with the classical gesture. But from then on he never missed a chance to pull me up, taunt or hurt me. He jealously looked out for every slip I might make. He hated me so intensely that I am sure he must have seen me every night in his dreams. As for me, ten years have passed since, but up to this day I choke with rage the moment I think of the man. Of course, before I left—however, I must leave that till later, or else the continuity of my narrative will be impaired.

Just before the end of the rehearsal a tall, long-nosed, gaunt gentleman with a moustache and in a bowler hat appeared suddenly on the stage. He swayed and knocked against the wings, and his eyes were like two tin buttons. Everyone looked at him with disgust, but nobody made any criticism.

"Who's he?" I asked Dukhovskoi in a whisper.

"Oh, a toper!" he replied carelessly. "Nelyubov-Olgin, our scene-painter. He's a gifted man—sometimes plays a part when he's sober—but a hopeless, irretrievable drunkard. And we've got nobody to take his place; he costs so little and paints the settings so fast."

VIII

The rehearsal was over. We began to disperse. The actors cracked jokes, punning on Mercia's name. Lara-Larsky significantly asked Boyev to go with him "there." I overtook Valerianov on one of the tree-lined walks and said, hardly keeping pace with his long stride, "Victor Victorovich, could you please advance me a little money— a very little?"

He stopped, all but speechless with amazement.

"What? What money? Why? Who for?"

I began to explain my plight to him, but he gave me no chance to finish; he impatiently turned his back on me and walked off. Then he suddenly stopped and beckoned to me.

"I say, what's your name—Vasilyev. You go to that man—your hotel-owner—and tell him to come and see me. I'll be here in the box-office for another half-hour or so. I'll talk to him."

I flew rather than went to the hotel. The *Khokhol* listened to me with gloomy distrust, but he pulled on his brown jacket and sauntered to the theatre. I waited for him. He came back in a quarter of an hour. His face was like a storm-cloud, and in his right hand he clutched a bunch of red pass-checks. He poked them under my nose and boomed, "See this? I thought he was going to give me money, but I got these bits of paper instead. What good are they to me?"

I stood perplexed. But the bits of paper proved of some use. After much coaxing the owner agreed to a bargain: my splendid new English suitcase of yellow leather went to him by way of security, and I kept my linen, my passport and what I treasured most—my notebooks. Before saying goodbye he asked, "Are you going to fool about there too?"

"Yes," I corroborated with dignity.

"Ha! Better look out. The moment I see you I'll yell, 'Hey, where are my twenty rubles?' "

For three days I did not dare to bother Valerianov and spent the night on a green bench, with the bundle of linen under my head. Luckily two of the nights were warm enough; as I lay on the bench I even felt a dry warmth rising from the flagstones of the pavement, heated during the day. But on the third night it drizzled for a long time, and seeking shelter in doorways I got no sleep till morning. At eight o'clock the public garden was opened. I crawled behind the scenes and took a sweet two-hour nap on an old curtain. But, of course, Samoilenko had to catch sight of me, and he took his time pointing out to me in caustic tones that the theatre was a temple of art, not a dormitory or a boudoir or a doss-house. Then I ventured once more to overtake the manager on a garden walk and ask him for a little money because I had no place to sleep.

"I am very sorry," he said, "but that's no business of mine. You're not under age, I think, and I don't happen to be your nurse, either."

I made no comment. His narrowed eyes wandered over the sunlit sand on the walk, and he said pensively, "I'll tell you what, though. Would you like to sleep in the theatre? I spoke to the watchman about it, but he's afraid, the fool."

I thanked him.

"Only remember this: no smoking in the theatre. If you want a smoke you must go out into the garden."

From then on I had guaranteed night quarters with a roof overhead. Sometimes I went by day to the little river two miles away, washed my linen there in a sheltered corner and dried it on the boughs of the willows growing on the bank. That linen helped me a great deal. Occasionally I went to the market to sell a shirt or something else. The twenty or thirty kopeks I made on the sale kept my stomach full for two days. Things were clearly shaping favourably for me. One day I even succeeded in wheedling a ruble out of Valerianov at a propitious moment, and I at once wired to Ilya:

"Starving send telegraphic order Leontovich c/o S. theatre."

IX

The second rehearsal was also the dress rehearsal. On that occasion I was given two more parts: an aged Early Christian and Tigellinus. I accepted them without murmur.

Timofeyev-Sumskoi, our tragic actor, also arrived for that rehearsal. He was a broad-shouldered man about six feet tall, middle-aged, with curly red hair, bulging eyeballs, and a pock-marked face—a veritable butcher or rather hangman. His voice was even bigger than himself, and he recited in the old, howling manner.

> *And like a wounded beast of prey*
> *The tragic actor roared.*

He did not know his part at all—he played Nero—and read it with difficulty from his book, using strong spectacles fit for a very old man. If anyone suggested that he should study his part a little he would reply in a low rumble, "I don't give a damn. It'll be all right. I'll stick to the prompter. This isn't the first time. The audience doesn't understand a thing, anyway. The audience is stupid."

He was having a lot of trouble with my name. He could not pronounce Tigellinus, and called me either Tigelinius or Tinegillus. Whenever they corrected him he snarled, "I don't give a damn. What rot. Why should I stuff my brains with trash?"

If he came upon a difficult figure of speech or several foreign words in a row he would simply mark it in his book with a Z and say, "I'm crossing this out."

However, everyone else did the same. Nothing was left of the play but dregs. Tigellinus' long speech was reduced to one line.

Nero asked, "Tigellinus! In what condition are the lions?"

And I answered, kneeling before him, " 'O divine Caesar! Rome has never seen the like of those beasts. They
are hungry and ferocious.' "

That was all.

The day of the performance came. The open auditorium
was full. A dense mass of ticketless spectators crowded
outside round the barrier. I was uneasy.

Heavens, how abominably they all acted! They might
have agreed in advance to go by Timofeyev's words, "I
don't care, the audience is stupid." Each word they uttered,
each gesture they made reminded me of something
monstrously old, something that people had become tired
of generations ago. I had a feeling that all that those
votaries of art had at their disposal was about twenty in-
tonations learned by heart and thirty studied gestures
like the one which Samoilenko had tried in vain to teach
me. And I thought what moral degradation those people
must have gone through to lose all shame.

Timofeyev-Sumskoi was magnificent. Leaning to the
right of his throne, with his outstretched left leg sprawling across half the stage and his clownish crown set awry
on his head, he would roll his eyeballs at the prompt-box
and roar in a voice that made the boys beyond the barrier
scream with delight. He didn't remember my name, of
course. He simply yelled at me like a merchant in a Turkish bath, "Telyantin! Bring my lions and tigers here.
S-snappy!"

I humbly swallowed my lines and walked off. Marcus
the Magnificent—Lara-Larsky, that is—was by far the
worst, because he was more shameless, unrestrained,
vulgar and self-confident than anyone else. With him
passion became sheer yelling, tender words degenerated
into cloying toffee, and the way he spoke the imperious
lines of the war-like Roman patrician betrayed the Russian trooper that he was. But Androsova was superb.
Everything about her was charming: her face, full of in-

spiration, her lovely hands, her supple melodious voice, and even her long, wavy hair, which she let down her back in the last act. She performed as naturally and beautifully as birds sing.

Through the little holes in the canvas of the setting, I watched her with genuine artistic enjoyment, sometimes with tears in my eyes. But I could not foresee that a few minutes later she would move me in quite a different manner, off stage.

I was so multiform in that play that the management would have done well to add the names of Dmitriev and Alexandrov to those of Petrov, Sidorov, Grigoryev, Ivanov and Vasilyev on the bill. In the first act I appeared first as an old man in a loose white overall with a hood on my head; then I ran behind the scenes, threw off the overall and came back a bare-legged centurion in armour and helmet; then I disappeared once more to turn up again as an aged Christian. In the second act I was a centurion and a slave. In the third, two more slaves. In the fourth, a centurion and two further slaves. In the fifth, a house manager and another slave. Lastly I was Tigellinus, and in the finale a mute warrior who imperiously motions Mercia and Marcus to the arena to be devoured by the lions.

Even the "simpleton" Akimenko patted me on the shoulder and said good-humouredly, "Lord! You have a knack of transforming yourself."

But I had paid dearly for this praise. I could hardly stand on my feet.

The performance was over. The watchman started putting out the lamps. I paced the stage, waiting for the last actors to wipe off their make-up so that I could lie down on my old theatrical sofa. I also longed to get at the piece of fried tavern liver that hung in my corner, between the props room and the common dressing-room. (Ever since the rats had whisked off my bacon I used to hang up all my food on a string.) Suddenly I heard a voice behind me saying, "Good night, Vasilyev."

I turned round. Androsova stood there holding out her hand. Her lovely face looked tired.

Incidentally, of all the company she alone, with the exception of small fry—Dukhovskoi and Nelyubov-Olgin—gave me her hand; all the others disdained to do this. I remember her handshake to this day: frank and tender and strong, as only a real woman and a friend can give.

I took her hand. She looked intently at me and said, "I say, you aren't ill, are you? You don't look well." And she added in a lower voice, "Perhaps you're short of money? Eh? I could lend you some."

"Oh, no, no, thank you!" I interrupted her seriously. And suddenly, inspired by a recollection of the delight I had just experienced, I burst out effusively, "How wonderful you were tonight!"

My compliment must have been unusual in its sincerity. She blushed with pleasure, dropped her eyes, and laughed softly.

"I'm glad you enjoyed it."

I respectfully kissed her hand. But just then a woman's voice called from below, "Androsova! Where are you? Come down, they're waiting to take you to supper."

"Good night, Vasilyev," she said, in a simple and friendly tone; then she shook her head and murmured as she started to go, "Oh, you poor, poor man."

At the moment I did not feel poor at all. But it seemed to me that if, before leaving, she had touched my forehead with her lips I should have died of happiness.

X

Soon I was quite familiar with the entire company. To tell the truth, even before I involuntarily became an actor I had never thought highly of the provincial stage.

But Ostrovsky* had planted in my imagination a host of outwardly coarse but inwardly delicate and generous Neshchastlivtsevs and clownish Arkashkas who were, however, devoted in their own way to art and comradeship. And now I saw that the stage was peopled by shameless men and women.

They all were heartless, treacherous towards and jealous of each other, lacking any respect whatsoever for the beauty and force of creative work—cads and hidebound souls. And what was more, they were surprisingly ignorant and thoroughly indifferent people, hypocrites, hysterically cold liars with false tears and theatrical sobs, obstinately backward slaves, always ready to cringe to their superiors and patrons. Chekhov was right in saying, "Only the police-officer is more hysterical than the actor. See how they both stand at the refreshment bar on the tsar's birthday, making speeches and weeping."

But theatrical tradition was maintained unswervingly. A certain Mitrofanov-Kozlovsky had been in the habit of crossing himself before he went on to the stage. The gesture stuck, and each of our principal actors was sure to do exactly the same, squinting an eye to see if the others noticed it. And if they did they must certainly think how very superstitious and original he was.

One of these prostitutes of art, with a billy-goat's voice and fat hips, had once beaten up a tailor and on another occasion a hairdresser. This had also become a custom. I often saw Lara-Larsky lunging about the stage with bloodshot eyes and foaming mouth as he shouted hoarsely, "Get that tailor here! I'll kill that tailor!"

Then, having slapped the tailor and secretly expecting and dreading a blow in return, he would stretch his arms backwards, tremble and scream, "Stop me! Stop me before I really become a murderer!"

* A Russian classical playwright.—Tr.

For that matter, how impressively they spoke about "sacred art" and the stage! I remember one bright, green day in June. We had not yet started rehearsing. It was rather dark and cool on the stage. Of the more important actors, Lara-Larsky and his actress wife, Medvedeva, had come first. A few young ladies and schoolboys were sitting in the stalls. Lara-Larsky was walking up and down the stage, with a worried look on his face. He must have been mentally studying some new, profound character. Then his wife spoke to him.

"Sasha, please whistle for me that melody we heard in *Pagliacci* last night."

He stopped, looked her up and down expressively, and said in a velvety actor's baritone, squinting at the stalls:

"Whistle? On the stage? Ha-ha-ha!" He laughed the bitter laugh of an actor. "Are you in earnest? Why, don't you know the stage is a temple, an altar on which we deposit our best ideas and desires? Whistle, indeed! Ha-ha-ha!"

Nevertheless, local cavalrymen and wealthy parasites, landowners, frequented that altar—the ladies' dressing-rooms—in absolutely the same way as they did private brothel rooms. We were not at all fussy about that. Often enough you could see a light in the vine arbour and hear a woman's laughter and the tinkle of spurs and wineglasses, while the actor husband walked in the darkness up and down the path like a sentinel, hoping that he might be invited. And a waiter would elbow him out of the way as he swept past with zander *au gratin* held high on his tray, and say drily, "Excuse me, sir."

And if he were invited he would give himself airs, drink vodka mixed with beer and vinegar, and tell smutty jokes about Jews.

But still they spoke of art with proud enthusiasm. Timofeyev-Sumskoi delivered more than one lecture on the lost "classical exit."

"The style of classical tragedy is lost!" he would say gloomily. "How did an actor go off in the old days? This way!" He would stand up to his full height and raise his right hand with clenched fingers, except the forefinger which stuck up like a hook. "Do you see?" And with enormous, slow strides he would start towards the door. "This is what was known as the 'classical exit.' And what have we got now? You put your hands in your trouser pockets and off you go home. That's all."

Sometimes they fancied a novelty, a gag. This was how Lara-Larsky, for one, told us about how he played the part of Khlestakov*:

"Look. Here's how I interpret that scene with the governor. The governor says the hotel room is a bit dark. And I say to him, 'Yes. You would like to read something— *Maxim Gorky, for example*—but you can't! It's so-o dark, so-o dark in here!' And I always get applause!"

Occasionally it was amusing to listen to the older men, such as Timofeyev-Sumskoi and Goncharov, when they were slightly tipsy.

"Yes, brother Fedotushka, the actor's not what he used to be. No, he isn't."

"You're right, Petrusha. He isn't. D'you remember Charsky or Lyubsky? Those were actors for you!"

"The outlook's different now."

"You're right, Petersburg. They *are* different There's no more respect for the sanctity of art. After all, you and I were priests of art, Petrusha, but these people— Ah! Let's have one, Peccatoris."

"And do you remember Ivanov-Kozelsky, brother Fedotushka?"

"Stop it, Petrograd, don't break my heart. Let's have one. The actors of today are a far cry from those of yore!"

* The main character in Gogol's comedy, *Inspector-General* —Tr

"A far cry's the word!"

"Yes, sir, a far cry!"

And there was Androsova, so pure and delicate and beautiful and gifted, who really served art amid this medley of vulgarity, stupidity, cunning, gigoloism, bragging, ignorance and debauchery.

Now that I am older I realize that she was as unaware of this filth as the white, beautiful corolla of a flower is unaware of the black swamp mud that feeds its roots.

XI

We staged play after play with the speed of an express train. Minor dramas and comedies we presented after a single rehearsal. *Death of Ivan the Terrible*, and *The New World* went on the stage after two rehearsals, and *Izmail*, a play by Bukharin, required three rehearsals only because the cast included over forty extras from the local garrison, home guards and fire-brigade.

Owing to a stupid and laughable incident, I remember particularly well the performance of *Death of Ivan the Terrible*. The part of Ivan was played by Timofeyev-Sumskoi. Attired in a long brocade garment and a pointed dog-skin cap, he looked like a moving obelisk. In an effort to impart more ferocity to the terrible tsar he kept thrusting out his lower jaw and turning down his thick lip, rolling his eyes and roaring as he had never done before.

Of course, he did not know the part and recited it in such preposterous rhyme that even those actors who had long believed that the audience were fools who understood nothing were horrified. But he distinguished himself more than ever in that scene where Ivan drops to his knees in a fit of repentance and confesses to the boyars: "Scabs have crusted my mind," etc.

265

Finally he came to the words "like a mangy dog." It goes without saying that his eyes were fixed on the prompt-box. He yelled "like" and paused.

" 'Like a mangy dog,' " the prompter whispered.

"Pike!" roared Timofeyev.

" 'Like a mangy—' "

"Tyke!"

" 'Like a mangy dog—' "

At last he managed to deal with the passage. He showed no sign of confusion or embarrassment, but I, who was standing by the throne at the moment, was suddenly seized by an irresistible fit of laughter. Indeed, that is what always happens: just when you feel you *must not* laugh you are attacked by that shaking, morbid laughter. I at once realized that the best hiding-place was the high back of the throne, behind which I could laugh as much as I liked. I turned and strutted as befitted a boyar, hardly able to restrain a peal of laughter, and went behind the throne; there I found two actresses, Volkova and Bogucharskaya, hugging the back of the throne and choking with soundless mirth. That was more than I could bear. I ran off stage, fell down on a sham sofa—*my* sofa—and started rolling on it in fits of laughter. Samoilenko, who always kept a jealous eye on me, fined me five rubles.

That performance was full of incidents anyway. I forgot to mention that we had an actor by the name of Romanov, a very handsome, tall, portly young man suited for showily majestic secondary parts. He had the misfortune to be extremely short-sighted, so that he had to wear special glasses. On the stage, without his pince-nez, he always tripped on things, toppled pillars, over-turned vases and arm-chairs, caught his feet in rugs and went sprawling. He had long been famous for the time when he was playing the part of a green knight in *Princess Fancy* with another company in another town.

He had fallen and rolled to the footlights in his tin armour, rattling like a huge samovar. But he surpassed himself in *Death of Ivan the Terrible.* He burst into Shuisky's house, where the conspirators were gathered, with such force that he knocked down the long bench with the boyars sitting on it.

Those boyars were quite a sight. They all had been recruited from young Karaite Jews employed in the local tobacco factory. I was the one who had led them on to the stage. I am short of stature, but the tallest among them stood no higher than my shoulder. Besides, half of those high-born boyars wore Caucasian garbs, while the others were fitted out with caftans hired from the local bishop's choir. To crown it all they had boyish faces with black beards tied to them, shining black eyes, mouths gaping with delight, and bashfully awkward movements. The audience greeted our solemn entrance with a roar of laughter.

We staged new plays almost daily, and our theatre was rather popular. Officers and landowners came because of our actresses, and every day a box was reserved for Kharitonenko. He came seldom, no more than twice during the season, but each time he sent us a hundred rubles. The theatre was not doing badly at all, and if the minor actors got no salary it was because Valerianov was as cunning as the cabman who would hang a bunch of hay in front of his hungry horse's mouth to make it go faster.

XII

One day there was no performance, I do not remember why. It was nasty weather. At ten p.m. I lay already on my sofa, listening in the darkness to the rain pattering on the wooden roof.

Suddenly there was a rustle behind the scenes, I heard footsteps and then the crash of falling chairs. I lit a candle-end and went to see who it was: it was Nelyubov-Olgin, drunk and tottering helplessly in the passage between settings and the wall. When he saw me he showed a calm surprise, not fright.

"What the hell are you d-doing here?"

I told him in a few words. His hands in his trouser pockets, he rocked for a while from toe to heel. Then he lost his balance, but steadied himself by taking a few steps forward, and said, "But why d-didn't you come to my p-place?"

"I don't know you well enough."

"Bosh. Come along."

He took my arm, and we went to his home. From that hour until the last day of my actor's career, I shared with him his tiny half-dark room, which he rented from a retired *ispravnik*.* A drunkard and brawler, and an object of the hypocritical contempt of the whole company, he proved to be a gentle, quiet man of great delicacy, and an excellent companion. But there was in his soul some kind of painful, incurable wound caused by a woman. I never quite made out the point of his unhappy love story. When he was drunk he would take out of his hamper the picture of a woman, not very pretty but not ugly, either, slightly squint-eyed, with a little nose turned up defiantly—rather provincial-looking. He would kiss the picture, then throw it on the floor, press it to his heart, then spit on it, put it on the icon in the corner, then pour candle-grease on it. Nor did I understand which of them had left which, or whose children he talked about: his, hers, or someone else's.

Neither he nor I had any money. He had long ago borrowed from Valerianov a large sum to send to *her*,

* A district police-officer —*Tr*

and was now no better off than a serf in bondage, which he was too honest to break. Occasionally he earned a few kopeks by lending a hand to a local sign-painter. But this income was a secret which he carefully kept from the company; Lara-Larsky would never have tolerated such an outrage on art.

Our landlord was an exceedingly good-natured man, stout, with ruddy cheeks and a double chin. Every morning and night, after his family had had its fill of tea, he would send us his refilled samovar, his teapot with tea-leaves, and as much black bread as we could eat. Thus we always had full stomachs.

After his afternoon nap the retired *ispravnik* would go out in dressing-gown and sit with his pipe on the steps of the house. Before leaving for the theatre we would sit beside him for a while. We always discussed the same topic: his misfortunes while he was in the service, the unfair treatment he had had at the hands of his superiors, and the infamous intrigues of his enemies. He was always asking our advice on how to write to the national newspapers a letter which would establish his innocence and have the governor and deputy-governor kicked out of their offices together with the present *ispravnik* and the scoundrel of a bailiff who was in charge of the second district, and who had been the main cause of all his misfortunes. We would give him all the advice we could, but he would only sigh, pucker up his face, and shake his head.

"That isn't what I want," he would say stubbornly. "No, that isn't it. If only I could find a man with a clever pen! If I could lay my hands on a pen! I would stop at no expense."

The rascal really had money. One day I happened to step into his room and found him clipping coupons from dividend warrants. He was a little embarrassed; he got up and hid the slips of paper with his back and the flaps of his dressing-gown. I am perfectly sure that while in the service he must have exceeded his authority and resorted to bribery, extortion and other forms of sharp practice.

At night, after the performance, Nelyubov and I sometimes strolled about the garden. Little white tables stood invitingly everywhere among the green plants, and candles burned with a steady flame in bell-glasses. Men and women smiled and bent towards each other in a way that was somehow festive, coquettish and full of meaning. The sand crunched under light women's feet.

"I wish we could find a mug!" Nelyubov would sometimes boom huskily, with a sly sidelong look at me.

At first that jarred on me. I have always hated the greedy and genteel readiness of garden actors to sponge on other people's meals, those moist, hungry eyes, friendly as a dog's, those unnaturally pert baritones at table, that gastronomic omniscience, that eagerness, that habitually imperious familiarity with waiters. But afterwards, when I had come to know Nelyubov better, I realized that he did not mean it. Though a crank he was proud and very fastidious in his own way.

But there was one amusing and slightly shameful occasion, when a "mug" himself found the two of us. This is how it happened.

One evening we were last out of the dressing-room after a performance, when a certain Altschiller darted out from somewhere behind the scenes. He was a local Rothschild, young but already fat, a ruddy-cheeked Jew of the voluptuous kind, over-free of manner, glittering with rings, chains and pendants. He rushed to us.

"Oh, my God! I've been running about for half an hour now—I'm utterly exhausted. Tell me, for goodness' sake, have you seen Volkova or Bogucharskaya anywhere?"

We had seen the two actresses leave immediately after the performance for a ride with some dragoon officers, and we obligingly informed Altschiller of the fact. He clutched his head and rushed about the stage.

"How mean of them! I've ordered supper! Really, it's beyond me! They gave me their word, they promised! And now see what they've done."

We made no reply.

He whirled about the stage some more, then he stopped, faltered, scratched his temple, smacked his lips thoughtfully, and suddenly said with determination, "Gentlemen, I humbly beg you to have supper with me."

We declined.

But it was no use. He stuck to us like a leech. He dashed from one of us to the other, shook our hands, gazed tenderly into our eyes and hotly protested that he loved art. Nelyubov was the first to waver.

"Hang it all! Let's go. Why not?"

The patron of art led us to the main dais and got busy. He picked the most prominent spot, seated us, and then jumped up again and again to fetch the waiter, waved his arms and, after a glass of *doppeltkümmel*, made himself out to be a terrific rake. He had cocked his bowler to give himself a more jaunty look.

"Pickles? How do you say that in Russian? No food will go down without pickles—right? And how about some vodka? Please eat, eat all of it, I beg you. Perhaps you'd like a *bœuf Stroganoff*? The cuisine here is excellent. Hey, waiter!"

I was drunk on a big chunk of fried meat as if it had been wine. My eyes were closing. The veranda with its lights, its blue tobacco smoke and its whirl of chatter kept floating away past me, and I heard as in a dream, "Please have more, gentlemen. Don't stand on ceremony. What can I do if I love art so much!"

XIII

But the climax was drawing near. The unrelieved diet of tea and black bread had made me irritable, and often I had to run out into some far corner of the garden to check my temper. I had long sold all my linen.

Samoilenko went on tormenting me. You know how a boarding-school teacher comes to hate some puny pupil—for his pale face, for his protruding ears, for his unpleasant habit of jerking a shoulder—and the feeling lasts for years. That was how Samoilenko felt towards me. He had already fined me a total of fifteen rubles, and during the rehearsals he treated me, to say the least, as a prison governor might treat his prisoner. Sometimes as I listened to his rude comments I would drop my eyelids and see fiery circles before me. Valerianov no longer spoke to me and when we met he would stump away as fast as an ostrich. I had been employed for six weeks but had received only one ruble.

One morning I woke up with a headache, a metallic flavour in my mouth and black, unaccountable anger in my heart. I went to the rehearsal in that mood.

I forget what play we were presenting that evening, but I do recall that I had in my hand a rolled-up book. As usual I knew my part thoroughly. Incidentally, it contained the words "I deserve it."

During the rehearsal the moment came for me to say that.

"I deserve it," I said.

But Samoilenko rushed up to me and yelled, "Do you call that Russian? Who ever speaks such Russian? 'I deserve it,' indeed! The right way to say that is 'I deserve *for* it'! You ignoramus!"

I went pale, and held out my book to him.

"Kindly consult my text," I said.

But he roared, "I don't care a tinker's damn for your text! *I* am the text for you! If you don't like it here you may go to hell!"

I looked up quickly. He understood at once; he went as pale as I and swiftly took two steps back. But it was too late. With the heavy roll I struck him a painful smack on the left cheek, then on the right, then again on the left, and again on the right, and kept on hitting him. He did not resist, did not so much as duck or try to escape, but just jerked his head right or left at each blow, like a clown pretending surprise. Finally I hurled the book in his face, left the stage and went into the garden. Nobody tried to stop me.

And lo! a miracle happened. The first person I saw in the garden was a messenger boy from the local office of the Volga and Kama Bank. He asked me who was Leontovich, and handed me an order for five hundred rubles.

An hour later Nelyubov and I were again in the garden, where we ordered a monstrous meal, and in two more hours the whole company was quaffing champagne with me and congratulating me. It was Nelyubov, and not I, who spread the rumour that I had inherited sixty thousand rubles, but I did not refute him. Afterwards Valerianov swore that the company was on the rocks, and I gave him a hundred rubles.

At five o'clock in the afternoon I was taking my train. I had in my pocket, besides a ticket to Moscow, no more than seventy rubles, but I felt like Caesar. After the second bell, when I was climbing into my carriage, Samoilenko, who until then had kept away from me, walked up.

"Please forgive me for letting my temper run away with me," he said theatrically.

I shook his proffered hand and replied amiably, "Please forgive me for doing the same."

They gave me three cheers in farewell. I exchanged a last, warm glance with Nelyubov. The train started, and everything moved away, for ever, irrevocably. And when the last blue huts of Zarechye were dropping out of sight to be replaced by a dreary steppe scorched yellow, a strange sadness clutched my heart. You would say that back there, where I had known anxiety and suffering and hunger and humiliation, I had left part of my heart for ever.

1906

THE GAMBRINUS

I

This was the name of a beerhouse in a bustling seaport town in southern Russia. Situated in one of the busiest thoroughfares, it was, nevertheless, rather hard to find because of its underground position. Even a regular customer, well known at the Gambrinus, often somehow missed that famous establishment, and walked past two or three neighbouring shops before he turned back.

No sign marked the house. Customers went in from the pavement through a narrow door that always stood open. An equally narrow staircase of twenty stone steps, battered and deformed by millions of heavy boots, led down from the entrance. On the wall facing the bottom of the stairs was a painted ten-foot alto-relievo image of King Gambrinus, the famous patron of brewers. It looked as if it had been crudely hewn out of petrified blocks of sponge, and must have been the first creation of an amateur; but the red doublet, the ermine cloak, the golden crown and the tankard raised high and running over with white foam, left no room for doubt: here in person was the great patron of brewers.

The place consisted of two long but exceedingly low vaulted halls. Subterranean moisture was for ever trickling down the stone walls, glittering in the light of gas-jets, which burned day and night because the place had no windows. Traces of droll murals were, however, still discernible. One painting represented a large company of carousing young Germans in green sporting jackets and with pheasant feathers in their hats, their fowling-pieces slung across their shoulders. Facing the hall, they all greeted you with raised tankards, two of them, moreover, holding by the waist two plump wenches—waitresses at the village inn, or perhaps daughters of a goodly farmer. Another mural depicted a high-life picnic in the first half of the eighteenth century; genteel countesses and viscounts in powdered wigs frolicked with lambs on a green meadow, and close by, under a clump of spreading willows, was a pond with swans fed gracefully by ladies and their escorts, who were sitting in a golden shell-like contraption. The next painting showed the interior of a Ukrainian cottage and happy rustics dancing the *hopak* with bottles of *horilka* in their hands. Farther on stood in all its splendour a big barrel with two fulsomely fat, red-faced and thick-lipped Cupids on it, decked with vines and hop leaves, and staring with shamelessly oily eyes as they clinked shallow wineglasses. The second hall, separated from the first by an arch, displayed scenes from frog life: frogs drinking beer in a green swamp, chasing dragonflies among the rushes, playing in a string quartet, fencing, and so on. The painter had obviously been a foreigner.

Instead of tables, heavy oak barrels stood on the floor, which was thickly strewn with sawdust, and small kegs did duty as chairs. To the right of the entrance was a low dais with a piano. There Sashka the musician, a meek, bald-headed Jew of uncertain age, always drunk and gay, looking like a shabby ape, had for many years played the violin every night to cheer and entertain the customers. As the years rolled by waiters in leather cuffs were succeeded by others; so were caterers and deliverers of beer, and even the proprietors of the house. But every day at six Sashka would invariably be sitting on the dais, with his violin in his hands and a little white dog on his knees, and towards one o'clock in the morning he would leave the Gambrinus, groggy with the beer he had drunk, in the company of Snowdrop, the little dog.

However, there was another permanent character at the Gambrinus—Mme Ivanova, the barmaid. She was a stout, bloodless old woman, who, having spent all her time in the damp basement, had come to resemble one of those lazy white fishes that dwell in the depths of sea grottoes. Like a skipper from his bridge, she silently ordered the waiters about from the eminence of the bar and smoked endlessly, holding the cigarette in the right corner of her mouth and screwing up her right eye against the smoke. Few people ever heard her voice, and to all who greeted her with a bow she always gave the same faded smile.

II

The huge harbour, one of the biggest in the world, was always crammed with ships. Giant dreadnoughts, dark with rust, put into it. Yellow, thick-funnelled steamers of the Dobrovolny Line, bound for the Far East, took cargo there, daily swallowing up trainloads of goods or thousands of convicts. In spring or autumn, hundreds of flags from every corner of the globe fluttered in the wind, and orders and oaths in every imaginable tongue rang out from morning till night. Dockers scurried to the countless warehouses and back to the ships over swinging gangplanks. They were Russian tramps, ragged and almost naked, with puffy drunkards' faces; swarthy Turks, dirty-turbaned and wearing baggy trousers that were very wide to the knees and close-fitting below; thickset, muscular Persians, their hair and nails dyed with henna to a bright carrot colour. Two- or three-masted Italian schooners were frequent callers; they were beautiful to look at from a distance, with their tiered sails, pure and white and round like the breasts of young women. And as these shapely vessels came into view round the lighthouse, they were, especially on a bright spring morning, like wonderful white visions floating, not in water, but in the air above the horizon. High-topped Anatolian *kachirmas* and Trebizond feluccas of strange colours, with carvings and grotesque ornaments, bobbed for months in the dirty green water of the harbour, amid rubbish, egg-shells, watermelon rinds, and flocks of white sea-gulls. Occasionally a strange narrow ship would run in under black paid sails, with a bit of soiled cloth for a flag; rounding the jetty and all but grazing it with her side, she would rush at full speed into harbour, heeling hard, and, amid a babel of curses and threats, come alongside a random pier, where her crew—stark naked bronzed little men jabbering gutturally—would furl the ragged sails with unaccountable rapidity, and the dingy, mysterious ship would instantly become as quiet as if she were dead. And just as mysteriously she would steal out of harbour on a dark night, without putting on her lights. At night the bay swarmed with the light boats of smugglers. Fishermen brought in their haul from far and near: in spring the tiny anchovy, of which it took millions to fill the boats, in summer the ugly plaice, in autumn mackerel, the fat grey mullet and oysters, and in winter the white sturgeon—anything from three to six hundredweights each, often caught at the risk of men's lives, many miles from the shore.

All those men—sailors from various countries, fishermen, stokers, light-hearted ship's boys, harbour thieves, engineers, workmen, dockers, boatmen, divers, smugglers—were young and robust, steeped in the tang of sea and fish; they knew what hard work was, loved the beauty and terror of daily risk, and prized above all else strength, prowess and the sting of strong language, and on shore they gave themselves up with savage relish to wild revelry, to drink and fighting. After nightfall the lights of the big city, running uphill from the harbour, would lure them like shining magic eyes, always promising something new and joyous, something they had not yet tried, and always deceiving them.

The city was linked with the harbour by narrow, steep, cranked streets where law-abiding citizens preferred not to venture at night. At every turn you came upon doss-houses with dingy latticed windows, with the dismal light of a single lamp inside. Still more numerous were the shops where you could sell your clothes down to your sailor's singlet or buy yourself any sea garb. There were also a great many beerhouses, taverns and eating-houses with expressive signs in all languages, and not a few brothels, public or illegal, from whose doorways at night coarsely painted women called to seamen in husky voices. In the Greek coffee-houses customers played dominoes or cards, and in the Turkish ones they could have night lodgings for five kopeks and smoke the narghile; there were small Oriental taverns that served snails, limpets, shrimps, mussels, large warted cuttle-fish, and other sea creatures. In garrets and cellars, behind

tightly closed shutters, were gambling haunts where a
game of faro or baccara often wound up with a ripped
belly or a broken skull and where, just round the corner,
sometimes in an adjoining cubicle, one could get rid of
any stolen article, from a diamond bracelet to a silver
cross, from a bale of Lyonese velvet to a sailor's greatcoat.

Those steep, narrow lanes, black with coal-dust, always
grew sticky and fetid towards nightfall, as if they sweat-
ed in a nightmare. They were like gutters or filthy sewers down which the big international city ejected into the
sea all its offal, all its rot and garbage and vice, which
infected strong sinewy bodies and simple souls.

The roistering inhabitants of that district seldom went
up to the elegant, trim city with its plate-glass shop
windows, proud monuments, electric lights, asphalt pave-
ments, rows of white acacias, and majestic policemen, a
city flaunting cleanliness and comfort. But before throwing away his hard-earned, greasy, ragged ruble notes
every one of them was sure to drop into the Gambrinus.
It was a time-honoured custom, though it meant making
your way, under cover of the night, to the very heart of
the city.

True, many of the customers could not have told you
the difficult name of the celebrated beer king. Someone
would simply say, "Shall we go to Sashka's?"

Someone else would reply, "Ay-ay, sir! Keep her so."

And then they would all say in chorus, "Anchors
aweigh!"

No wonder that, among the harbour and sea people,
Sashka enjoyed greater respect and fame than, say, the
local bishop or governor. And it is certain that, if not
his name, then his lively ape's face and his violin were
recalled once in a while in Sydney or Plymouth, in New
York, Vladivostok, Constantinople or Ceylon, not to speak
of all the bays and sounds of the Black Sea, where he had
many admirers among the courageous fishermen.

Usually Sashka came to the Gambrinus before anyone else had arrived, except one or two chance customers. The thick stale smell of last night's beer pervaded the two halls, and it was gloomy there because gas was burned sparingly in the daytime. It was quiet and cool down there on hot July days, while the stone-built city was deafened by the uproar in the streets, and sweltered in the sun.

Sashka would walk up to the bar, greet Mme Ivanova and drink his first mug of beer. Sometimes she begged him, "Play something, Sashka, will you?"

"What would you like me to play, Mme Ivanova?" Sashka asked obligingly. He was always exquisitely polite to her.

"Something of your own."

He sat down in his customary place, to the left of the piano, and played strange, melancholy pieces. The basement sank into a drowsy quiet, except that once in a while you heard the muffled rumbling of the city above, or the muted clatter and tinkle of plates and glasses in the kitchen behind the partition. Sashka's violin wept with the Jews' sorrow, a sorrow as ancient as the world, woven and entwined with the sad flowers of national melodies. At that twilight hour, his face with the tense chin and bowed head, with eyes gazing sternly up from beneath brows that had suddenly grown heavy, was quite different from the face which all the Gambrinus customers knew—grinning, winking, dancing. Snowdrop, the little dog, sat on his knees. She had long since learned not to howl along with the music, but the passionate sorrow, the sobbing, cursing notes, affected her in spite of herself: she would open her mouth in wide convulsive yawns and curl back her pink little tongue, and for a moment her small body and delicate, black-eyed face would tremble nervously.

Then the house began to fill, Sashka's accompanist came after finishing some daytime business at the tailor's or watch-maker's, sausages in hot water and cheese sandwiches were displayed on the bar counter, and finally all the gas-jets were lighted. Sashka drank another mug, said to his partner, " 'May Parade,' *ein, zwei, drei!*" and struck up an impetuous march. From then on he had a hard time bowing to endless new-comers, each of whom considered himself Sashka's special friend, and looked proudly at the other customers to see if they had noticed Sashka bowing to him. As he played Sashka squinted one eye, then the other, furrowed his bald, sloping skull into long wrinkles, moved his lips in a comic way, and lavished smiles all around.

By ten or eleven o'clock the Gambrinus, which could serve more than two hundred customers at a time, was packed. Nearly half the customers came with women in kerchiefs; no one minded the place being crowded, his foot being trodden on or his hat crumpled, or somebody spilling beer over his trousers; if anyone took offence it was merely because he was drunk and itching to work up a brawl. The moisture of the cellar, gleaming dimly, trickled even more abundantly from the walls covered with oil paint, and the condensed breath of the crowd fell from the ceiling like heavy, warm rain. Drinking at the Gambrinus was done thoroughly. The smart thing to do was for two or three customers sitting together to load the table with empty bottles so thickly that they could not see each other through the green forest of glass.

By the time drinking was at its height, the customers grew red and hoarse and wet. Tobacco smoke stung the eyes. If you wanted to be heard in the general din you had to bend across the table and shout. But the tireless violin of Sashka sitting on his dais held sway over the oppressive heat, the reek of tobacco, gas and beer, and the yelling of the reckless crowd.

Soon the customers, intoxicated with beer, the nearness of women and the heat, wanted each to hear a favourite song. Two or three men with dull eyes and uncertain movements hung constantly about Sashka, tugging at his sleeve and getting in his way.

"Sashka! I want a s-sad one. Please do me—*hiccup*—the favour!"

"Just a second," Sashka said again and again, with a quick nod, slipping a silver coin into his trouser pocket as noiselessly and deftly as a doctor stowing away his fee. "Just a second."

"How can you be so mean, Sashka? I've given you the money, and I'm asking you for the twentieth time to play 'I sailed to Odessa.'"

"Just a second."

"Give us 'The Nightingale,' Sashka!"

"I want 'Marusya,' Sashka!"

"'*Setz Setz*,' Sashka—let's have '*Setz Setz*'!"

"Just a second."

"'The She-e-epherd'!" a man yelled from the other end of the hall, in a voice that might have come from a horse.

And amid general laughter Sashka crowed back like a rooster, "Just a se-e-econd!"

Without pausing to rest, he played all the songs ordered. He seemed to know every single song by heart. Silver coins poured into his pockets from all sides, and mugs of beer were sent to him from every table. Whenever he came down from his dais to go to the bar he was all but torn apart.

"Sashka, my friend! Have just one."

"Here's to you, Sashka. Why don't you come over when you're called, blast you?"

"Sa-ashka, come and have some be-e-er!" the horse's voice blared.

The women who, like all women, were prone to admire men of the stage, dally with them, show off and grovel before them, called to him in cooing voices, with a playful, insistent little laugh, "Sashka dear, you must absolutely drink one from me. No, I beg you not to refuse. And please play 'Cuckoo Walk.' "

Sashka smiled, grimaced, and bowed right and left; he pressed his hand to his heart, blew kisses to the women, drank beer at every table and, getting back to the piano, on which a fresh mug of beer was waiting for him, struck up "Parting" or something like that. To amuse his audience, he sometimes made his violin whine like a puppy, grunt like a pig, or drone with grating bass notes, in time with the melody. And the audience responded with good-humoured approval and laughter.

It grew hotter. The ceiling dripped; some of the customers were already weeping and beating their chests; others, with bloodshot eyes, were wrangling over women or former offences and setting upon each other, while their more sober boon companions, spongers more often than not, tried to stop them. It was only by some miracle that the waiters managed to thread their way between barrels, kegs, feet and trunks, holding high above them their hands loaded with beer mugs. Mme Ivanova, more bloodless, impassive and mute than ever, ordered the waiters about from behind the bar, like a skipper in a gale.

Everyone was eager to sing. Sashka, softened by beer, his own kindness and the crude pleasure his music gave to others, was willing to play anything. And people bawled to the sounds of his violin in hoarse, stiff voices, sticking to the same note and staring into each other's eyes with vacant earnestness:

> Why should we part for ever,
> Why should we live apart?
> Let's marry now and never,
> Oh, never, never part.

284

Meantime another group, apparently a hostile one, tried hard to drown the voices of the first by bellowing at random a song of its own choice.

The Gambrinus was frequented by Greeks from Asia Minor, who came to Russian ports to fish. They would ask Sashka to play one of their Oriental songs—a dismal, monotonous wail that trailed along over two or three notes, which they were ready to sing for hours, their faces grim, their eyes blazing. Sashka could also play Italian folk songs, Ukrainian *dumkas*, Jewish wedding dances, and many more. One day a group of Negro sailors dropped in; as the others were singing they felt like doing the same. Sashka was quick to catch the galloping Negro melody and to pick out the accompaniment on the piano; then, to the enormous delight and amusement of habitués, the house rang with the strange, fanciful, guttural sounds of the African song.

A local newspaper reporter, an acquaintance of Sashka's, talked a music-school professor into going to the Gambrinus to hear its famous violinist. But Sashka saw through it and purposely made his violin mew and baa and bray more than usual. The customers were roaring with laughter, but the professor said contemptuously, "A clown."

And he left without finishing his beer.

IV

Quite often the elegant marquesses and carousing German sportsmen, the fat Cupids and the frogs witnessed from their walls such unbridled debauchery as could rarely be seen anywhere but at the Gambrinus.

In would tumble, say, a company of thieves on the spree after a good haul, each with a mistress, each in a cocked cap and high patent-leather boots, with refined tavern manners and a devil-may-care look. For them Sashka would play special thieves' songs: "I'm a Goner Now," "Don't You Cry, Marusya," "Spring Is Over," and others. They considered dancing beneath them, but their girl-friends—all pretty and young, and some of them still in their teens—would dance "The Shepherd" with screams and much heel-tapping. Women and men alike drank a great deal, and the only trouble was that thieves always finished their revelry with old money squabbles, and liked to sneak away without paying the bill.

Fishermen would come after a lucky catch: large companies of up to thirty men. In the late autumn there were sometimes glorious weeks when some forty thousand mackerel or grey mullet would be landed daily. During that time the smallest shareholder would make more than two hundred rubles. However, what paid even better was a good catch of beluga in winter; but that was a very hard job. The men had to toil from twenty to twenty-five miles off shore, at night, sometimes in stormy weather, when waves swept over the boats and the water froze instantly on clothes and oars, and when weather kept the men out at sea for two or three days, till they were washed ashore perhaps a hundred miles away, at Anapa or Trebizond. As many as a dozen yawls were lost every winter, and it was not until spring that the bodies of the courageous fishermen would be cast up on alien shores.

When the men came back from sea with a handsome catch, a craze for excitement would grip them. In two or three days, several thousand rubles would be squandered on the coarsest, the most deadening debauchery. The men would flock to a beerhouse or some other gay place, throw out everyone else, lock the doors and close the shutters, and for fully twenty-four hours would drink, give themselves up to love, bawl songs, smash mirrors and dishes, beat up women and often each other, until sleep overcame them on a table, on the floor, or lying across a bedstead, amid spittle, cigarette ends, bits of broken glass, spilt wine and blood stains. Thus they would go on for several days on end, sometimes moving to another place. Having drunk and eaten away all their money down to the last copper, they would go back, silent and rueful, to their boats. Their heads splitting, their faces bearing marks of fighting, their bodies weak and shaking after the bout, they would take up their beloved and accursed work, so hard and yet so exciting.

They never missed the Gambrinus. They would break into the house, huge men with husky voices, their faces lashed red by the winter nor'easter, in waterproof jackets, leather trousers and oxhide boots reaching to the thighs— the same sort of boots in which their mates went straight to the bottom on a stormy night.

Out of respect for Sashka, they would not turn out strangers, though otherwise they did as they pleased, smashing the heavy mugs on the floor. Sashka would play for them their own songs, long-winded, simple and grim as the sea, and they would all sing in unison, straining their powerful chests and wind-hardened throats. Sashka was like Orpheus taming the waves, and sometimes the hulking skipper of a fishing boat, a bearded man of forty, weather-beaten and brutal, would break into tears as he wailed in a high voice the pitiful words of a song:

> *Why was I born a fisherman?*
> *A poor and luckless boy—*

And sometimes they danced, stony-faced, crashing down their terrific boots on one spot, their bodies and clothes spreading through the house the salty smell of fish. They were very liberal towards Sashka, whom they would not let go from their tables for a long time. He knew well how hard and desperate their life was. Very often, while he was playing for them, a sort of respectful sadness would fill his heart.

But he was particularly fond of playing for British sailors from trading ships. They would come in a band, arm in arm, fine young men all, big-chested, broad-shouldered, white-toothed and ruddy-cheeked, with gay, bold blue eyes. They had muscles that threatened to burst their shirts, and straight powerful necks that rose from the low-cut collars. Some of them knew Sashka because they had put into the port before. They would recognize and greet him in Russian, flashing their white teeth in a friendly smile, "*Zdryste*!"

Without waiting for an order, Sashka would play "Rule Britannia." Probably because they were at the moment in a country crushed by slavery, they would sing that hymn to British freedom with especial pride and solemnity. They stood bare-headed, singing the wonderful closing words:

> *Britons never, never, never*
> *Shall be slaves!*

And as they did so even their most unruly neighbours would take off their caps in spite of themselves.

A thickset boatswain with an ear-ring and a beard sprouting right from his throat like a fringe would walk over to Sashka with two mugs of beer, grin broadly, give him a friendly pat on the back, and ask him to play a hornpipe. At the very first notes of the rollicking seamen's dance the Englishmen would jump up from their seats and make room by shifting the kegs and barrels to the walls. The others they would ask by gestures and cheerful smiles to get up; they would not, however, stand on ceremony with those who were slow, and would knock the kegs from under them with a deft kick. But they seldom had to resort to that, for at the Gambrinus everybody was fond of dances, and the hornpipe was a favourite. Even Sashka would climb on his chair while playing, in order to see better.

The sailors would form a circle and clap their hands in time with the quick rhythm, while two of them stepped into the middle. The dance represents the sailor's life at sea. The ship is ready to sail, it is a fine day, everything is spick and span. The dancers hold their arms crossed on their chests, their heads are thrown back and their trunks motionless, although the feet are tapping furiously. But a wind rises and the ship begins to rol. slightly. This makes it all the merrier for the seamen, and the dance figures become more and more complex and intricate. Then comes a fresh breeze—it is no longer so easy to walk on deck—and the dancers begin to sway a little. Finally a real gale sets in—the sailors are pitched from side to side, and things begin to look serious. "All hands up, take in the sails!" The expressive movements of the dancers' hands and feet show plainly that they are climbing the shrouds, furling the sails and securing the sheets, while the gale rocks the ship harder and harder. "Stop— man overboard!" A life-boat is lowered. Their heads bowed and their sinewy bare necks strained, the dancers row with swift strokes, bending and unbending their backs. But the gale passes, the roll subsides little by little, the sky clears, and once again the ship skims along before the wind, and once again the dancers are tapping the lively hornpipe, their trunks motionless and their arms crossed.

Once in a while Sashka had to play the *lezginka* for Georgian wine-makers who lived near the city. There were no dances he did not know. As one of the dancers, in sheepskin cap and Circassian coat, whirled nimbly among the barrels, throwing his hands in turn behind his head while his friends clapped in time and egged him on with shouts, Sashka could not help shouting gleefully with them: "*Khass! Khass! Khass!*" He also played sometimes the Moldavian *zhok*, the Italian tarantella, and waltzes for German sailors.

Occasionally they fought at the Gambrinus, and some of the fights were quite fierce. Old customers were fond of telling the story of a legendary battle between sailors of the Russian Navy, transferred to the reserve from some cruiser, and British seamen. They fought with fists, knuckledusters and beer mugs, and even hurled kegs at each other. It should be admitted in all fairness that the first to pick a quarrel, and the first to use their knives, were the Russians, and though they were three times superior in numbers to the English they managed to turn them out of the beerhouse only after half an hour's fighting.

Very often Sashka's intervention would stop a brawl when bloodshed seemed imminent. He would go up to the quarrelling group and joke and smile and grimace, and at once mugs would be held out to him from all sides.

"Have a mug, Sashka! Drink with me, Sashka, blast you!"

Perhaps what subdued the wild passions of those simple people was the meek, droll kindness that beamed cheerfully from his eyes under the sloping skull. Or was it a kind of respect for his gift and something like gratitude? It might also have been the fact that most Gambrinus habitués always owed him money. In the trying days of *dekokhto*, as complete lack of money was called in sea and harbour slang, people applied freely to Sashka for small sums or for a trifling loan at the bar, which he never refused.

Of course, he never got back his money, not because his debtors wanted to harm him, but merely because they forgot; in a moment of great merriment, however, the same debtors would repay him tenfold for his songs.

Sometimes the barmaid upbraided him, "It's amazing how careless you are with your money."

He would reply with conviction, "But, Mme Ivanova! I can't take it to my grave! We've got quite enough, Snowdrop and I. Come here, Snowdrop, come, my doggie."

V

The Gambrinus had its own song hits of the season.

During the Boer War the melody in vogue was the "Boer March" (it was then, it seems, that the famous fight between Russian and British seamen occurred). Sashka had to play the heroic piece about twenty times each evening, and when he had finished caps would be waved, cheers would ring out, and those who appeared indifferent would be glared at in a most unfriendly way, which was often a bad sign at the Gambrinus.

Then came the festivities in connection with the Franco-Russian alliance. Sourly the governor gave permission for the *Marseillaise* to be played. It also was asked for daily, but not so frequently as the "Boer March" had been; the cheers were thinner, and no caps were waved at all. The reason was, on the one hand, that there were no grounds for heartfelt sentiment and, on the other, that the customers of the Gambrinus did not sufficiently realize the political importance of the alliance; besides, it was always the same people who clamoured for the *Marseillaise* and cheered it.

Once the melody of the cake-walk became fashionable for a short while, and a chance customer, a carousing merchant, even danced it one night among the barrels, without taking off his raccoon overcoat, high galoshes and fox cap. But this Negro dance was soon forgotten.

The great Japanese war quickened the heartbeat of the Gambrinus customers. Newspapers began to appear on the barrels, and every evening there were discussions about the war. The most unenlightened and peaceful people turned into politicians and strategists, but each of them deep in his soul was afraid for himself or for his brother, or, more often still, for a friend: those days brought out the strong invisible bonds between people who had long shared work, danger and daily encounters with death.

At first no one doubted that Russia would win. Sashka had somewhere come by the "Kuropatkin March," which he played for about twenty nights with some success. But one night the march was ousted for ever by a song brought by Balaklava fishermen—"salty Greeks" or "Pindoses," as they were known.

> *They took me from you, Mother dear,*
> *And sent me far away—*
> *A babe-in-arms but yesterday,*
> *A man-in-arms today.*

From then on they wanted no other songs at the Gambrinus. Throughout the evening the demand would be made again and again, "Give us that sad one, Sashka! The Balaklava stuff! That soldier song, you know."

They would sing and weep, and drink double the usual amount, as did, in fact, the whole of Russia at that time. Every night someone came to say goodbye; he would strut like a rooster, dash his cap down on the floor, threatening to lick all the Japs single-handed, and tearfully finish with the heart-rending song.

One day Sashka came earlier than was his custom. After pouring him his first mug of beer, the barmaid said as she always did, "Play something of your own, Sashka, will you?"

Suddenly his lips twitched and the mug shook in his hand.

"You know what, Mme Ivanova?" he said, as if in wonder. "They're calling me up. For the war."

She wrung her hands.

"You don't say so! You must be joking."

"I'm not." Sashka shook his head in meek dejection. "I mean it."

"But aren't you over age, Sashka? How old are you?"

That was a question which somehow no one had asked till then. Everyone imagined that Sashka must be as old as the beerhouse walls, the marquesses, the Ukrainians, the frogs, and Gambrinus himself, the painted king who guarded the entrance.

"Forty-six." Sashka reflected. "Or perhaps forty-nine. I'm an orphan," he added dolefully.

"Then why don't you go and tell that to the authorities?"

"I did, Mme Ivanova."

"Wel.?"

"Well, they said to me, 'Shut up, you dirty Yid, or we'll put you in the cooler.' And they let me have it."

That evening everyone at the Gambrinus knew, and out of sympathy for Sashka they plied him with beer till he was dead drunk. He tried to show off, to grimace and squint, but his meek, droll eyes looked sad and terrified. A brawny workman, a boiler-maker by trade, suddenly volunteered to go to war instead of Sashka. Everyone saw the absurdity of the offer, but Sashka was moved to tears; he hugged the man and presented him there and then with his violin. And Snowdrop he left to the barmaid.

"Mme Ivanova, p'ease take care of the little dog. I may not come back, then you'll have her to remember me by. Snowdrop, my little dog! See how she's licking her chops. You poor dear! And there's something else I want to ask you, Mme Ivanova. The proprietor owes me some money—please get it and send it to the addresses I'll give you. I've got a cousin in Gomel—he has a family—and then there's my nephew's widow who lives in Zhmerinka. I've been sending them money every month. That's the way with us Jews—we like our relatives. I'm an orphan, and single. Goodbye, Mme Ivanova."

"Goodbye, Sashka! Let's kiss each other goodbye. We've been together for so many years. And—please don't take it amiss—I'll cross you for good luck."

Sashka's eyes were deeply sorrowful, but he could not help a final clownish joke.

"Don't you think, Mme Ivanova, that the Russian cross might strike me dead?"

VI

Now the Gambrinus had a lonely, deserted look, as though it were orphaned without Sashka and his violin. The proprietor tried to use as a decoy a quartet of strolling mandolin-players, one of whom, attired as a music-hall comedian with red whiskers and a false nose, in checked trousers and a collar rising above his ears, sang comic songs with lewd gestures. But the quartet was a complete failure; in fact, customers booed or flung bits of sausage at the musicians, and the comedian was once given a good hiding by Tendrovo fishermen for a disrespectful comment about Sashka.

Nevertheless, from habit, the house was still frequented by those young men from sea or harbour whom the war had not dragged to suffering and death. At first Sashka's name was mentioned every night.

"I wish Sashka was here! The old place is so lonely without him."

"Yes, I wonder where he is now, poor Sashka."

"*In far-away Manchurian fields*" someone would start a new season hit, then break off, embarrassed, and someone else would say all of a sudden, "There are three kinds of wounds: perforated, punctured, and incised. And there are also lacerated wounds."

> *I'm coming home with victory*
> *And you without an arm—*

"Stop whining, will you? Any news from Sashka, Mme Ivanova? A letter or a postcard?"

Mme Ivanova had got into the habit of reading the newspaper every night, holding it at arm's length, her head tipped back and her lips moving, while Snowdrop snored peacefully in her lap. The barmaid no longer looked like a cheerful skipper standing on the bridge—far from it—and her crew, listless and sleepy, wandered aimlessly about the house.

When asked about Sashka's fate she would slowly shake her head.

"I know nothing. There are no letters, and the papers don't say anything, either."

Slowly she would take off her spectacles, put them down along with the newspaper beside the warm, snug Snowdrop and, turning away, weep softly.

Sometimes, bending over the little dog, she would say in a small pathetic voice, "Well, Snowdrop my doggie? How's everything, my pet? Where's our Sashka? Hey? Where's your master?"

Snowdrop would raise her delicate little nose, blink her moist black eyes and whimper softly along with the barmaid.

But time takes the edge off everything. The mandolin-players were followed by balalaika-players, and then by a Russo-Ukrainian chorus with girls, and finally Lyoshka the accordion-player established himself at the Gambrinus —more firmly than anyone else had. He was a thief by trade, but since he got married he had decided to take the path of righteousness. He had long been known in various eating-houses, and therefore he was tolerated at the Gambrinus; indeed, he had to be tolerated, for business was very slack.

Months went by—a year passed. No one ever remembered Sashka now, except Mme Ivanova, and even she did not cry any more at the mention of his name. Another year rolled by. Sashka must have been forgotten even by the little white dog.

However, contrary to Sashka's fears, the Russian cross did not strike him dead; he was not once wounded, although he took part in three big battles and once even went into action at the head of a battalion, as member of a band in which he played the flute. At Wafangkou he was taken prisoner, and after the war a German steamship brought him to the port where his friends worked and made merry.

The news of his arrival spread like wildfire to all the harbours, piers and shipyards. That night the Gambrinus was so crowded that most people had to stand; the mugs of beer were passed overhead from hand to hand, and although many customers left without paying, business was brisker than it had ever been before. The boiler-maker brought Sashka's violin, carefully wrapped in his wife's shawl, which he there and then gave away for a couple of drinks. Sashka's last accompanist was dug up from somewhere and brought in. Lyoshka, touchy and conceited, tried to stand his ground. "I'm paid by the day, and I've got a contract!" he said doggedly again and again. But he was simply thrown out, and would have got a thrashing if Sashka had not intervened.

Probably no hero of the Russo-Japanese War was accorded so hearty and enthusiastic a welcome as Sashka. Strong, horny hands caught hold of him, lifted him from the floor and tossed him up with such force that they almost dashed him against the ceiling. And the shouts were so deafening that the tongues in the gas-jets went out, and the policeman on the beat came in several times to ask them to "take it easy, because it's too noisy outside."

That night Sashka played all the favourite Gambrinus songs and dances. He also played some Japanese songs he had picked up in captivity, but the audience did not like

296

them. Once again Mme Ivanova, who seemed to have come back to life, rose cheerfully on her captain's bridge, and Snowdrop sat on Sashka's knees and yelped with joy. At moments, when Sashka stopped playing, some simple-minded fisherman, who had just grasped the meaning of Sashka's miraculous return, would suddenly exclaim in naive and joyful amazement, "Why, it's Sashka back again!" That would bring uproarious laughter and a volley of merry oaths, and once again people would snatch up Sashka, toss him to the ceiling, shout, drink, clink mugs, and spill beer over each other.

Sashka did not seem to have changed or aged during his absence; time and misfortune had as little effect on his appearance as on that of the sculptured Gambrinus, the patron and protector of the house. But, with the sensitiveness of a kind-hearted woman, Mme Ivanova had noticed that Sashka's eyes still held the look of terror and anguish which she had seen in them before he went away, except that the look had become deeper and more significant. Sashka struck attitudes as he had always done, winked and wrinkled his forehead, but Mme Ivanova saw he was pretending.

VII

Things slipped back into their normal course, as if there had been no war at all and Sashka had not been taken prisoner in Nagasaki. A happy catch of beluga or grey mullet was celebrated as usual by fishermen in giant top-boots, thieves' girl-friends danced as usual, and as before Sashka played sailors' songs brought from all the harbours of the globe.

But unsettled and stormy times were on the way. One evening the whole city began to buzz and bustle as if an alarm-bell had rung, and the streets turned black with people at an unusual hour. Small white leaflets passed from hand to hand, and from mouth to mouth went the wonderful word "freedom," which the whole immense, credulous country repeated that evening.

There came bright, joyful days whose radiance lit up even the basement of the Gambrinus. Among those who went there now were students and workmen, and young, beautiful girls. People with shining eyes would climb on barrels, which had witnessed so much in their time, and make speeches. Some of what they said was not clear, but the fervent hope and great love ringing through the speeches would find their echo in eager, listening hearts.

"Sashka, the *Marseillaise*! Fire away! The *Marseillaise*!"

This time the *Marseillaise* was different from the one which the governor had grudgingly authorized during the week of Franco-Russian jubilations. Endless processions of people carrying red flags and singing songs moved along the streets. Women displayed scarlet ribbons and scarlet flowers. Complete strangers would meet and suddenly shake hands with a beaming smile.

But suddenly all the joy disappeared, as if it had been washed away like children's footprints on the sea-shore. One day the assistant police commissioner, a fat, puffy little man, burst into the Gambrinus, his eyes starting from their sockets, his face as red as an overripe tomato.

"What? Who's the proprietor here?" he cried hoarsely. "Get the proprietor!"

His eye fell on Sashka, who stood holding his violin.

"Are you the proprietor? Shut up! What? So you play anthems, do you? No more anthems here!"

"There'll be no more anthems, Your Excellency," Sashka replied calmly.

The assistant commissioner went purple and wagged his forefinger threateningly close to Sashka's nose:

"None what-ev-ver!"

"Yes, Your Excellency, none whatever."

"I'll show you how to start revolutions, I will!"

He popped out, leaving general despondency behind.

Darkness settled over the city. There were obscure rumours, alarming and sickening. People spoke cautiously, fearful of betraying themselves by a look, afraid of their own shadows, their own thoughts. For the first time the city thought with dread of the foul swamp stirring darkly under its feet, down by the sea, the swamp into which, over so many years, it had been ejecting its poisonous excrements. The city nailed up with boards the plate-glass windows of its splendid shops, stationed guards by the proud monuments, and set up guns in the yards of magnificent houses—just in case. And on the outskirts, in fetid hovels and leaking garrets, God's chosen people trembled, prayed and wept with terror, people long forsaken by the wrathful biblical God but still believing that they had not yet drained their cup of sufferings to the lees.

Below, by the sea, secret work was going on in the streets, which were like dark, sticky sewers. The doors of taverns, tea-rooms and doss-houses stood open all night.

Next morning came a pogrom. Those very people who, moved by the general pure joy and the light of future brotherhood, had so recently marched along the streets singing, parading the symbols of freedom won, were now out to kill. And it was not because they had been ordered to kill, or because they felt a hatred for the Jews, with whom they were often very friendly, or even because they hoped for gain, which was uncertain, but because the dirty, cunning devil that lives in every man was whispering in their ears, "Go. You'll be free to taste the forbidden curiosity of murder, the luxury of rape, or power over another's life."

During the pogrom Sashka walked about the city unmolested, with his droll, typically Jewish face. He had that unshakeable boldness of spirit, that quality of being

unafraid of fear, which protects even a weak man better
than all the guns in the world. But one day when, pressed
to the wall of a house, he was trying to keep out of the
way of a mob sweeping in an avalanche along the street,
a stone-mason in red shirt and white apron swung up his
chisel and snarled, "A Yid! Give it to him! Let's see the
colour of his blood!"

But someone caught him by the arm.

"Stop, damn you—don't you see it's Sashka? You
blasted fathead!"

The stone-mason paused. At that delirious moment of
drunken madness, he was ready to kill anybody—his
father or sister, a priest, or even the Orthodox God himself; but he was equally ready to obey like a child any
order given to him in a commanding tone.

He simpered like an idiot, spat, and wiped his nose
on his sleeve. But suddenly he noticed a nervous little
white dog that snuggled up to Sashka, trembling. He
stooped down quickly, grabbed it by the hind legs, lifted
it high, dashed its head against the paving stones, and
started to run. Sashka stared after him in silence. The
man was running along capless, his body bent forward
and arms stretched out, his mouth gaping and eyes round
and white with madness.

Snowdrop's brains were scattered over Sashka's boots.
He wiped them off with his handkerchief.

VIII

Next came a strange period that was like the sleep of
a paralyzed man. After dusk there was no light in any
window throughout the city, but the signboards of *cafés
chantants* and the windows of taverns were ablaze with
light. The victors were trying their power, for they had
not yet had their fill of licensed lawlessness. Unruly in-

dividuals, wearing Manchurian fur caps and with St George ribbons in the buttonholes of their jackets, went from one restaurant to another, truculently insisting that the "people's anthem" should be played and seeing to it that everybody got on his feet. They would even break into homes and rummage in bedsteads and chests of drawers, demanding vodka, money and the anthem, and fouling the air with their drunken belching.

Once ten of them came to the Gambrinus and took up two tables. Their manner was extremely defiant and their tone towards the waiters imperious; they would spit over the shoulders of neighbours who were complete strangers to them, put their feet on other people's seats, or pour their beer on the floor, saying that it was stale. Nobody interfered with them. Generally known as police agents, they were regarded with the same kind of secret dread and morbid curiosity which ordinary people have towards executioners. One of them was plainly the ringleader. He was Motka the Snuffler, a christened Jew with red hair, a broken nose and a twanging voice. He was said to have great physical strength; originally a thief, he had become a chucker-out in a brothel, then a pimp and police agent.

Sashka was playing the "Blizzard." Suddenly the Snuffler stepped up to him, clutched his right arm and, turning to face the hall, shouted, "The anthem! The people's anthem! In honour of our adored monarch, lads. The anthem!"

"The anthem! The anthem!" boomed the fur-capped ruffians.

"The anthem!" a solitary, uncertain voice called diffidently from the far end.

But Sashka wrenched his arm free and said calmly, "No anthems here."

"What?" roared the Snuffler. "You dare to disobey? Why, you stinking Yid!"

Sashka bent forward, very close to the Snuffler; wrinkling his face and holding the violin down by the finger-board, he said, "How about you?"

"What about me?"

"Suppose I *am* a stinking Yid. And you?"

"I'm an Orthodox Christian."

"A Christian? How much did you get for that?"

The Gambrinus rocked with laughter, while the Snuffler, white with rage, turned to his partners.

"Lads!" he said in a quavering, tearful voice, repeating somebody else's words learned by heart. "How much longer are we going to put up with the Yids' outrages against the Throne and the Holy Church?"

But Sashka rose on his dais and made the Snuffler face him again, and no Gambrinus customer would ever have believed that the droll, grimacing Sashka could speak so weightily and imperiously.

"You!" he shouted. "You son of a bitch! Show me your face, you murderer. Look at me! Well?"

Everything happened in the twinkling of an eye. Sashka's violin swung high up, flashed in the air and bang! the tall man in the fur cap swayed from the blow that caught him on the temple. The violin flew into pieces. Sashka had nothing left in his hand but the finger-board, which he now held triumphantly above the crowd.

"He-elp, lads!" yelled the Snuffler.

But it was too late. A powerful wall encircled Sashka, shutting him off. And the same wall swept out the fur-capped men.

However, an hour later, when Sashka walked out of the beerhouse after finishing his work, several men attacked him. Someone hit him in the eye, blew a whistle, and said to the policemen who came running, "Take him to the Boulevard Station. On a political charge. Here's my badge."

IX

Once again Sashka was considered lost, this time for good. Someone had witnessed the scene on the pavement by the beerhouse and reported it to others. Now those who patronized the Gambrinus were experienced people; they knew what sort of an establishment the Boulevard Station was and what a police agent's vengeance was like.

But this time Sashka's fate caused much less anxiety than the first, and he was forgotten much sooner. Two months later a new fiddler had taken his place. By the way, he was Sashka's pupil.

Some three months afterwards, on a quiet evening in spring, when the musicians were playing the waltz "Expectation," someone sang out in a thin, frightened voice, "Look, lads—Sashka!"

Everybody turned and got up from the kegs. Yes, it was Sashka, sure enough, risen from the dead for the second time, but bearded and haggard. People rushed to him, surrounding him, hugging him and thrusting mugs of beer into his hand. But suddenly the same voice cried, "Look at his arm, friends!"

There was a hush. The elbow of Sashka's left arm, twisted and seemingly crushed, was pressed to his side. Apparently he could not bend or unbend it, and his fingers stuck up near his chin.

"What's that, mate?" a hairy boatswain from the Russian Co. asked finally.

"Oh, it's nothing," replied Sashka carelessly, "a damaged tendon or something."

"Is that so!"

There was another pause.

"So 'The Shepherd' is out now?" asked the sympathetic boatswain.

"'The Shepherd'?" Sashka's eyes gleamed playfully. "Hey, you!" he shouted to the accompanist, with his habitual assurance. "Begin 'The Shepherd'! *Ein, zwei, drei!*"

The pianist started to rap out the merry dance, glancing back doubtfully. But with his right hand—the sound one—Sashka drew from his pocket a black, oblong instrument, the size of a man's palm, with a branch piece, which he put in his mouth; then, bending to the left as far as his maimed, stiff arm would let him, he suddenly started to whistle on the ocarina the gay, irresistible melody of "The Shepherd."

"Ha-ha-ha!" the audience greeted it with joyous laughter.

"Ain't he a devil!" cried the boatswain and, to his own surprise, burst into an impetuous dance. Customers—men and women—joined him. The waiters smilingly beat time with their feet, trying, however to keep up a dignified appearance. Even Mme Ivanova, forgetting the duties of a skipper on his bridge, nodded her head to the rhythm of the lively dance, and snapped her fingers slightly. It might well be that even the old, porous, time-worn Gambrinus was twitching his eyebrows, looking gaily out into the street, and it seemed as if the pitiful, unpretentious whistle in the hands of the crippled, twisted Sashka was singing in a tongue that was unfortunately still unintelligible either to the friends of the Gambrinus or to Sashka himself:

"It's all right! You can cripple a man, but art will survive and triumph over anything."

1907

EMERALD

*To the memory of Kholstomer, the peerless
skewbald trotter*

I

The four-year-old stallion Emerald, a big silver-grey
racehorse of American build, woke up in his stall about
midnight as usual. To the right and left of him, and across
the passage, the other horses were chewing hay to a
rhythm, lusti y crunching it and snorting occasionally as
the dust tickled their nostrils. The groom on duty was
snoring on a heap of straw in a corner. Emerald knew, by
the alternation of the days and the sound of that snoring,
that it was Vasily, a young chap whom the horses disliked because he smoked reeking tobacco in the stable,
often came into the stalls drunk, jabbed the horses in the
belly with his knee, shook his fist over their eyes, jerked
the halter roughly, and always shouted threateningly at
them in an unnatural, wheezy boom.

Emerald walked up to the stall door. Standing in her stall just opposite his own was Smart, a young black mare that was not yet fully grown. Emerald could not see her body in the darkness, but when she pulled away from the fodder, and turned back her head, her big eye would shine for a few seconds with a fine violet glow. Distending his delicate nostrils, Emerald took a long breath, sensed the hardly perceptible but exciting smell of her skin, and gave a short neigh. She turned swiftly and responded with a tremulous, affectionately skittish whinny.

At once Emerald heard a jealous, angry breathing close by. It was Onegin, an old, high-mettled brown stallion, who still ran sometimes in the town races. The two stallions were separated by a thin wooden partition and so could not see each other, but, putting his nose to the edge of the partition, Emerald clearly scented the warm smell of chewed hay coming from Onegin's fast-blowing nostrils. With mounting anger, they sniffed each other in the darkness for a while, their ears laid flat to their heads and their necks arched. And suddenly they both screamed and neighed and pawed the floor in fury.

"Stand still, damn you!" growled the groom sleepily, with the habitual threat in his voice.

The two horses shied back from the doors and pricked up their ears. They had been enemies for a long time, but since the graceful black mare was put up in the same stable three days before—something which normally was not done and which had happened only for lack of room during the bustle before the races—not a single day had passed without their having several big quarrels. In the stable, as at the racecourse and the pond, they used to challenge each other to fight. But secretly Emerald was a little afraid of the big, self-assured stallion, with his sharp smell of vicious horse, his Adam's apple, large as a camel's, his sombre, deep-set eyes, and above all his stone-hard frame, steeled by the years and strengthened by racing and previous fights.

Pretending to himself that he was not in the least afraid and that nothing at all had happened, Emerald turned away, lowered his head into the manger, and began to explore the hay with his soft, nimble lips. At first he just nibbled at the grass blades, but soon the taste of the cud tempted him, and he fell to in good earnest. Meanwhile slow, indifferent thoughts drifted through his mind, and swam together as memories of images, smells and sounds, before they sank for ever into the black abyss which yawned before and after the present moment.

"Hay," he thought, and recalled the head groom, Nazar, who had given him hay the night before.

Nazar was an upright old man; he always smelt so cosily of black bread and just a little of wine; his movements were unhurried and soft; the oats and hay seemed more delicious when he was in charge, and it was a pleasure to listen to him as, grooming a horse, he talked to it in undertones, fondly reproachful. But he lacked something most important to a horse, and whenever he was put through his paces he could sense that Nazar's hands were wanting in assurance and precision.

Vasily lacked that quality too, and though he used to shout at the horses and hit them, they all knew he was a coward, and were not afraid of him. He could not ride, either—he jerked and fidgeted a lot. The third groom, the one-eyed one, was better than the other two, but he did not like horses, he was cruel and impatient, and his hands were as stiff as wood. The fourth, Andriashka, was a mere boy; he would play with the horses like a suckling foal, and stealthily kiss them on the upper lip or between the nostrils, which was rather unpleasant and, moreover, silly.

But that tall, gaunt, stooping one, with the clean-shaven face and gold-rimmed glasses, was quite different.

He was altogether like a marvellous horse—wise, strong, and fearless. He never got angry, never used his whip or even threatened you with it; and when he was driving the sulky, how exhilarating, how uplifting and wonderfu ly awesome it was to obey every hint of his strong, clever fingers which knew everything. He alone could reduce Emerald to the happy, harmonious state in which every muscle of his body strained in the swift race, and he felt so light and gay.

And instantly Emerald saw in his mind's eye the short road to the racecourse and almost every single house and every stone along it; he saw the sand on the track. the grand stand, running horses, the green grass and the yellow ribbon. Suddenly he recalled that three-year-old dark bay who had sprained an ankle the other day while warming up and was now lame. And as he thought of him, he himself tried to limp a little in his mind.

One wisp of hay that got into Emerald's mouth had an unusually fine flavour. Emerald chewed it thoroughly, and for a while after he swallowed it he could feel in his mouth the fragrance of withered flowers and dry strong-scented grass. An uncertain, far-away memory flitted across his mind. It was the kind of thing a smoker experiences some-times—when an accidental pull at a cigarette out in the street conjures up for a brief moment a half-dark corridor with old-fashioned wallpaper and a lone candle on a cupboard, or a long night journey with the cadenced jingle of bells and a languid doze, or a blue wood a short way off, dazzling snow, the hubbub of a battue and a passionate eagerness that makes the knees tremble—and for an instant the forgotten feelings of that time, once so thrilling but now elusive, fleet through his heart, vaguely caressing and sad.

Meanwhile the black little window above the manger, invisible till then, had begun to turn grey and stand out dimly in the darkness. Now the horses were chewing with a lazy sluggishness, sighing heavily and softly one after another. A cock crowed outside in a familiar voice, as cheerful and sonorous as a clarion call. And for a long time afterwards, other cocks crowed far and near.

His head in the manger, Emerald was trying to keep in his mouth and enhance the strange flavour which roused in him that faint, almost physical echo of an unaccountable recollection. But it was no use and unwittingly he dozed off.

II

His legs and body were impeccably shaped, and therefore he always slept standing up, rocking slightly to and fro. Sometimes he would start and then, for a few seconds, sound sleep would give way to a half-doze; but the short minutes of sleep were so deep that they would relax and refresh his every muscle, his nerves and skin.

Just before daybreak he dreamed of an early morning in spring, the red glow of dawn above the earth, and a fragrant meadow. The grass was so thick and lush, so brightly and fascinatingly green, with a slightly pink touch of the new daylight, as man and beast see it only when they are very young, and all over it the dew glittered and sparkled. In the light, crisp air, all kinds of smells carried amazingly. Through the morning cool the smoke rising in a blue, transparent curl from a village chimney pricked your nostrils; every flower in the meadow had a scent of its own, and on the rutted damp road beyond the fence, a multitude of smells blended together—of people and tar and horse dung and dust, and the fresh milk from passing cows, and the balmy resin from the fir poles of the fence.

Emerald, a foal of seven months, scudded aimlessly about the field, with his head bent low as he kicked his hind legs. He seemed to be made of air and did not feel the weight of his body at all. The white fragrant camomile flowers raced away from under his feet. He galloped straight towards the sun. The wet grass lashing at his pasterns and knees cooled and darkened them. A blue sky, green grass, a golden sun, wonderful air, the heady ecstasy of youth, strength and swift running!

And suddenly he heard a brief, anxious, caressing neigh—a call which he knew so well that he always recognized it from afar, among thousands of other voices. He stopped in his tracks and listened for a second, his head high, his fine ears moving and his short shaggy tail thrown back like a whisk; then he responded with a long, lilting cry that shook the whole of his slim, long-legged body, and sped to his mother.

The bony, staid old mare lifted her wet nose from the grass, gave her foal a quick, careful sniff, and then fell to again, as if she had to hurry on with an urgent job. Ducking his lithe neck under her belly, the foal turned up his face, poked his lips between the hind legs with a habitual movement, and took the tepid, springy teat brimming with exquisite, slightly sour milk, which squirted into his mouth in thin, warm jets. He drank and drank, unable to stop, till the dam pulled away her rump, and made a show of snapping at the foal's groin. . . .

Now it was quite light in the stable. A long-bearded, stinking old billy-goat, a stable-mate of the horses, walked to the door, barred with a beam from inside, and started to bleat, glancing back at the groom. The barefoot Vasily, scratching his dishevelled head, went to open. It was a crisp, bluish autumn morning. The rectangle of the open door at once filled with warm steam billowing from the stable. A subtle smell of hoar-frost and dead leaves floated over the stalls.

The horses, knowing that they were going to be given oats, stood at the stall doors, snorting softly with impatience. The greedy, wilful Onegin pawed the wooden flooring, cribbed on the iron-plated edge of the manger and stretched his neck, gulping the air and belching. Emerald rubbed his face on the bars.

The other grooms—there were four of them in all—came and set about distributing oats out of feed-tins. While Nazar was pouring the heavy rustling oats into Emerald's manger the stallion tried fussily to get at the fodder over the old man's shoulder, then under his arms, his warm nostrils quivering. The groom liked the eagerness of the gentle horse, and he purposely took his time, shutting off the manger with an elbow.

"You greedy brute," he grumbled good-humouredly. "In a hurry, are you? Aw, drat you! Just try to poke your muzzle in again. I'll teach you to poke."

A gay pillar of sunlight slanted downwards from the little window above the manger, and a million specks of golden dust swirled in it, divided by the long shadows of the sash.

III

Emerald had just finished his oats when he was led out. It was warmer now, and the ground had softened a little, but the stable walls were still hoary with frost. The heaps of dung newly shovelled out of the stable sent up a dense vapour, and the sparrows pottering in the dung chirped excitedly, as if bickering among themselves. Bending his head low in the doorway as he stepped over the threshold, Emerald joyfully drew in the spicy air, then shook his head and his whole frame, and gave a loud snort. "God bless you!" said Nazar earnestly. Emerald could not stand still. He longed for vigorous motion and the tickling sensation of air rushing into his eyes and nostrils; he wanted his heart to pound hotly, wanted to breathe deeply. Tied to the picket-line, he neighed, danced on his hind legs and, twisting his neck, squinted at the black mare behind him a round dark eye streaked with red veins over the white.

Gasping with the effort, Nazar raised a pail of water above his head and dowsed the stallion's back from withers to tail. The sensation was familiar to Emerald—it was bracing but frightful because it always came so unexpectedly. Nazar fetched more water and splashed it on the horse's flanks, chest and legs, and under the tail. After each wetting he would pass his horny palm over the horse's coat, squeezing out the moisture. Looking back Emerald saw his own high, slightly sagging croup darkened and glossy in the sun.

It was a racing day. Emerald knew it by the peculiar, nervous haste of the grooms bustling round the horses; they put leather stockings on the pasterns of some horses which, on account of their short trunks, used to overreach themselves, wrapped linen bandages round the legs of others—from the hobble joint to the knee—or tied broad fur-trimmed pads across the pits of the forelegs. The light two-wheeled sulkies with the high seats were rolled out of the shed; their metal spokes glistened gaily in the sun, and their red rims and red shafts, thrown wide apart, shone with fresh varnish.

By the time the chief jockey of the stable, an Englishman, came along, Emerald had been thoroughly dried, brushed, and rubbed down with a woollen mitten. Horses and men alike respected and feared the gaunt, slightly stooping, long-armed man. He had a clean-shaven, sunburnt face and firm, thin lips set in an ironic curl. His pale blue eyes looked with a steady, calm glint through gold-rimmed spectacles. He watched the cleaning, straddling his long legs in high boots, his hands deep in his trouser pockets as he chewed a cigar, shifting it from one corner of his mouth to the other. He wore a grey jacket with a fur collar and a black cap with a long rectangular peak. Occasionally he made laconic comments in a jerky, casual tone, and at once all the grooms and workmen would turn their heads to him, and the horses would strain their ears in his direction.

He kept a particularly watchful eye on the harnessing of Emerald. He examined the horse's body from forelock to hoof, and under that scrutinizing gaze Emerald proudly raised his head, turned his lithe neck slightly, and pricked up his thin, translucent ears. The jockey himself tried the tightness of the girths by sticking his finger under them. Then the grooms put on the horses grey red-bordered linen cloths with red circles and red monograms that hung below, near the hind legs. Two grooms, Nazar and the one-eyed man, took Emerald by the bridle and led him to the racecourse along the familiar roadway, between two rows of big stone houses. It was less than a quarter of a mile to the course.

There were already many horses in the paddock, and grooms were walking them slowly round in the ring, in the direction in which the horses normally ran during the races, that is, counter-clockwise. In the inner circle of the paddock they were leading about pacers—small, strong-legged horses, with docked tails. Emerald at once recognized the little white stallion who always galloped beside him, and the two horses greeted each other with a friendly snicker.

IV

The bell rang at the course. The grooms took off Emerald's cloth. Blinking at the sun from behind his glasses and baring his long, yellow horse teeth, the Englishman came up, buttoning his gloves, a whip under his arm. One of the grooms gathered Emerald's rich tail, which reached down to the fetlocks, and carefully laid it on the seat of the sulky, so that its light-coloured end hung down. The shafts rocked under the man's weight. Emerald squinted over his shoulder and saw the jockey sitting just behind his

croup, with legs stretched out and straddling along the
shafts. Deliberately the jockey picked up the reins, uttered
a monosyllable, and the grooms at once let go the bridle.
Rejoicing at the coming race, Emerald tried to plunge forward, but as the strong hands checked him he merely
reared slightly on his hind legs, tossed up his head and
ran through the paddock gate towards the course at a
round, unhurried trot.

The broad track, strewn with yellow sand, ran along
a wooden fence, forming a mile-long ellipse; the sand was
rather damp and compact, and felt springy to the feet,
returning their pressure. The sharp imprints of the hooves
and the straight, even tracks left by the gutta-percha tires
traced a neat pattern.

Here was the grand stand, a wooden structure measuring two hundred horse lengths, with the black mass of
people seething and humming from the ground to the roof
supported by slender pillars. By a slight flick of the reins
Emerald knew that he might mend his pace, and snorted
gratefully.

He now ran at a square, sweeping trot, his back scarcely
swaying, his neck stretched forward and slightly turned
to the left-hand shaft, his face thrust up. Because his
strides were unusually long, from a distance he did not
seem to be running very fast; you had an impression that
the trotter was unhurriedly measuring the track with his
forelegs, straight as a pair of compasses, and barely touching the ground with the tips of his hooves. This was
American training, which is designed to make breathing
easy for the horse, reduce air resistance to the utmost, and
eliminate all motions useless to the race and merely
wasting strength, and which sacrifices beauty of form to
ease, spareness, long wind and vigorous pace, thus transforming the horse into a flawless machine.

Now, in the interval between two races, the trotters
were being warmed up, which is always done to condition

their breathing. There were many of them running round the outer ring, in the same direction as Emerald, or round the inner ring, in the opposite direction. A tall dapple-grey trotter of a pure Orel breed passed Emerald; with his arched neck and flying tail he was like a merry-go-round horse. His fat, broad chest, already dark with sweat, and his flabby groins shook as he ran throwing his forelegs outwards at the knees, his spleen clacking loudly at every stride.

Then a slender, long-bodied brown half-breed mare with a thin dark mane came alongside from behind. She had had an excellent training by the same American method as had been applied to Emerald. Her short, well-groomed coat glistened on her back, rippling as the muscles played under the skin. While their jockeys were discussing something, the two horses ran abreast for a while. Emerald sniffed the mare and was about to play as he ran, but the Englishman would not let him, and he had to obey.

A huge black stallion sped past them at a full trot, going the other way; he was swathed from head to tail in bandages, knee-guards and pit-pads. His left-hand shaft stuck out, being longer than the right-hand one by four-teen inches, and through a ring fastened above his head was strung the strap of a steel overcheck, which held the horse's nervous nose cruelly pinched. Emerald and the mare glanced at him simultaneously, and both instantly appreciated him as a trotter of extraordinary strength, speed and hardiness, but terribly obstinate, vicious, and touchy. The black stallion was followed by a small, smart light-grey one. Looking from the side you would have thought that he was running at an incredible speed, because he worked his feet so fast, threw them up so high at the knees, and had such an industrious and busy air about his arched neck with the small well-proportioned head. Emerald just squinted contemptuously at him and jerked one ear his way.

With a short, loud neigh-like laugh the other jockey finished talking, and gave the mare a free rein. She pulled away from Emerald's side as calmly as if it did not cost her the least effort and ran ahead at an easy trot, smoothly carrying her even, glossy back, with a hardly visible strip along the ridge.

But immediately a galloping flaming-red trotter with a large white star passed and threw back both Emerald and her. He raced on with long frequent leaps, alternately stretching out and seeming to hug the ground, and then almost joining his fore and hind legs in mid-air. His jockey was lying rather than sitting back, his whole weight thrown on the reins. Emerald got fretty and lunged aside, but imperceptibly the Englishman reined him in, and those hands, so supple and sensitive to the horse's every movement, suddenly felt as hard as iron. Near the grand stand the red stallion, who by then had galloped another lap, passed Emerald again. Although still galloping, he was already in lather and had bloodshot eyes, and his breath came with a rattle. The jockey, bent forward, was laying the whip on the horse's back with all his might. At last grooms intercepted the horse near the gate, seizing him by the reins and the bridle. He was led off dripping, gasping and trembling, having lost weight in a matter of minutes.

Emerald ran another half-lap at a full trot, then turned into a side-track that crossed the course, and walked back into the paddock.

V

The bell rang several times at the course. Now and again racing trotters would flash past the open gate at lightning speed, and the people on the stands would sud-

316

denly start shouting and clapping. In line with other trotters, Emerald walked briskly beside Nazar, waving his bowed head and moving his ears encased in linen. The exercise had sent the blood surging through his veins in a gay, warm stream, and his breathing grew deeper and easier as his body relaxed and cooled; now his every muscle craved for another run.

Half an hour or so went by. The bell rang again. This time the jockey mounted the sulky without putting on his gloves. He had white, broad, magic hands that inspired Emerald with affection and awe.

The Englishman drove at a leisurely pace to the course, from which the horses that had finished their exercise were turning one after another into the paddock. The only horses left on the track were Emerald and the huge black stallion whom he had met during the trial run. The stands were packed with people from top to bottom, a black mass with a bright, uneven sprinkling of faces and hands, mottled with parasols and ladies' bonnets, and fluttering with the little white sheets of the programmes. As he quickened his pace and ran past the grand stand Emerald felt thousands of eyes riveted on him, and he fully realized that those eyes expected him to move fast, putting out every ounce of his strength, every powerful beat of his heart—and this lent a happy ease and coquettish compactness to his muscles. The familiar white stallion, with a boy on his back, was racing alongside him on the right at a clipped gallop.

Going at a smooth, steady trot, his body tilted slightly to the left, Emerald rounded a steep curve. As he drew near the post with the red circle, the bell rang briefly at the course. The Englishman shifted just a little in his seat, and suddenly his hands hardened. "Now go, but save your strength. It's early yet." That was what his hands told Emerald, and for a second, to show that he had understood, Emerald laid back his thin, sensitive ears, and pricked them up again. The white stallion was galloping steadily beside him, lagging a little behind. Emerald could feel near his withers the other's even breathing.

The red post dropped behind, there was another steep curve, the track straightened out, and here was the second stand, black and mottled with the buzzing crowd, and growing bigger with every stride. "Faster," the jockey permitted him, "faster, faster!" A little worked up, Emerald felt an urge to strain at once all his strength. "May I?" he thought. "No, it's too early—don't get excited," the magic hands answered him, soothingly. "Later."

Both stallions passed the prize posts at the same second, except that they did so at opposite ends. The slight resistance of the taut cord and its swift snapping made Emerald move his ears for an instant, but he at once forgot about it, being intent on the wonderful hands. "A bit faster! Don't get excited! Steady!" the jockey commanded. The black swaying stand floated past. A few score yards more, and all the four of them—Emerald, the little white stallion, the Englishman and the stable boy, who stood in the short stirrups, hugging his pacer's neck, merged happily into one compact racing unit, inspired with one will, one beauty of powerful motion, one musical rhythm. "Ta-ta-ta-ta!" came the steady, cadenced clatter of Emerald's hooves. "Tra-ta, tra-ta!" the boy's horse echoed sharply. Another curve, and the other stand rushed to meet them. "Shall I go faster?" asked Emerald. "Yes," the hands told him, "but don't lose your head."

The stand swept past. The people were shouting, and that diverted Emerald. He got excited, lost the feel of the reins and, falling for a second out of the common, well-timed rhythm, made four freakish bounds, falling out of step. But the reins instantly stiffened and, tearing his mouth, twisted his neck down and turned his head to the right. Now it was hard to gallop the way he wanted. He

318

got angry and refused to change step, but the jockey pounced on the moment and with a calm, compelling movement broke the horse into a trot. The stand was already far behind. Emerald fell into step again, and again the hands became soft and friendly. Aware of his guilt, Emerald would have liked to double his trot. "No, not just yet," the jockey remarked good-humouredly. "We'll have a chance to make up for that. It's all right."

Thus, without any more slips, they made another lap and a half in compete harmony. But the black stallion was also in excellent shape that day. While Emerald was blundering he had managed to beat him by six lengths, but now Emerald was gaining on him, and as they reached the last post but one he found himself three and a quarter seconds ahead. "Now you may. Go!" commanded the jockey. Emerald laid his ears and flashed just one glance back. The Englishman's face was ablaze with keen resolution, and his clean-shaven lips were parted in a grimace of impatience, baring the large clenched yellow teeth. "Put all you can into it!" commanded the reins in the upraised hands. "More, more!" And suddenly the Englishman shouted in a vibrating voice that climbed up the scale like the sound of a siren, "O-e-e-e-ey!"

"Yes! yes! yes! yes!" the boy sang out, in time with the race.

Now the tension was at its height and held by a thin hair threatening to snap any moment. "Tra-ta-ta-ta!" Emerald's feet rapped evenly on the ground. "Trra-trra-trra!" came from ahead the gallop of the white stallion, who was drawing Emerald after him. The pliant shafts swung in time with the race, and the boy, who was all but lying on the horse's neck, bobbed up and down with the gallop.

The air rushing to meet him whistled in his ears and tickled his nostrils, which let out frequent jets of steam. Breathing was harder now, and his skin felt hot. Emerald rounded the last curve, bending inwards with the whole of his body. The approaching stand came alive, and the encouraging roar of thousands of throats frightened, excited and elated him. He could no longer run at a trot and was about to break into a gallop, but the wonderful hands behind at once entreated and commanded and soothed him, saying, "Don't gallop, dear boy! For heaven's sake don't! That's it, that's it." And as he sped past the winning-post Emerald snapped the cord without seeing it. A cascade of shouts, laughter and applause came thundering down the grand stand. Parasols, canes, hats, and the white sheets of programmes whirled and flashed among the moving faces and hands. The Englishman gently threw down the reins. "It's over. Thank you, dear boy!" said that movement to Emerald, and checking himself with an effort, he changed to a walk. The black stallion was only just approaching his post across the course, seven seconds behind.

Lifting his numbed feet with difficulty, the Englishman jumped heavily down from the sulky, took off the velvet seat, and carried it to the scales. Grooms ran up and threw a cloth over Emerald's steaming back, then led him off into the paddock. They were followed by the tumult of the crowd and a long ring from the judge's box. A light yellowish froth dripped from the horse's mouth on to the ground and the grooms' hands.

A few minutes later Emerald, unharnessed, was led back to the grand stand. A tall man in a long overcoat and a new, shining hat, whom Emerald often saw in his stable, patted his neck and shoved a lump of sugar into the horse's mouth with his palm. The Englishman was also there, in the crowd, smiling, puckering his face, and baring his long teeth. The cloth was taken off Emerald, and he was placed in front of a three-legged box covered with a black cloth, and a man in grey ducked under it and got busy doing something.

And then people came sweeping down the stands in a black straggling mass. They crowded round the horse, clamouring and waving their arms, bending their flushed, heated faces towards each other, their eyes flashing. They were resentful of something, and poked their fingers at Emerald's feet and head and flanks, rumpled his coat on the left side of the croup where he bore his brand, and shouted again, all at once. "It's a counterfeit horse! A fake trotter! It's all a swindle! Give us our money back!" Emerald heard these words without understanding them, and moved his ears restlessly. "What are they talking about?" he thought in surprise. "Didn't I run well?" And for a moment this eye fell on the Englishman's face. That hard, slightly ironical face, always so calm, was now blazing with fury. And suddenly the Englishman shouted in a throaty voice, shot up his arm, and the sound of a slap ripped drily through the uproar.

VI

Emerald was led home; three hours later they gave him oats, and in the evening, as they watered him at the well, he saw, rising from beyond the fence, a big yellow moon that filled him with vague terror.

Then came dreary days.

He was no longer taken out for exercise or for the races. But every day strangers came—many strangers—who had him led out into the yard, and there examined and felt him all over, thrusting their fingers into his mouth, scraping his coat with pumice, and shouting at each other.

Then he remembered being led, late one evening, out of his stable and along interminable deserted streets, past houses with lighted windows. After that came the railway station, a dark, shaky wagon, weariness, feet trembling from a long journey, locomotive whistles, clanking rails, the stifling reek of smoke, the dismal light of a swinging lantern. Then they took him out of the wagon and led him for a long time down an unfamiliar road, across bare autumn fields, past villages, till they brought him to an unfamiliar stable and locked him up in it apart from the other horses.

At first he kept on recalling the races, the Englishman, Vasily, Nazar and Onegin, and often saw them in his dreams, but as time went on he forgot everything. He was being hidden from somebody, and his young, splendid body languished and pined, degrading with idleness. Every now and again fresh strangers came and jostled round him, felt him over, and wrangled among themselves.

Sometimes Emerald chanced to glimpse through the open door other horses walking or running about in the open; then he would call to them, indignantly and plaintively. But the door would be shut at once, and again time would drag drearily on.

In charge of the stable was a big-headed, sleepy-looking man with small black eyes and a tiny black moustache on a fat face. He hardly took any notice of Emerald, and yet, for some unaccountable reason, the horse dreaded him.

Early one morning, when all the grooms were still sleeping, the man tiptoed noiselessly into Emerald's stable, poured some oats into the manger, and went out. Emerald was a little surprised, but meekly fell to. The oats were sweet and slightly bitter, and felt acrid to the tongue. "How strange," thought Emerald, "I never tasted such oats."

And suddenly he felt a slight colic. It came and went, then came again, stronger than before, growing in intensity from minute to minute. Finally the pain became unbearable. Emerald groaned softly. Fiery circles spun before his eyes, his body turned moist and limp with a sudden weakness, his legs shook and gave way under him, and he crashed down on the floor. He tried to rise again, but all he could do was to struggle to his forefeet, and then he fell on his side. A droning whirlwind swept through his head; the Englishman floated before his eyes, baring his long horse teeth. Onegin ran past with a loud neigh, his Adam's apple sticking out. Some unknown force was inexorably dragging Emerald down into a cold, dark pit. He could not move any more.

Cramp suddenly contracted his legs and neck, and crooked his back. Shivers raced across his skin, which gave off a pungent-smelling lather.

The swinging yellow light of the lantern stung his eyes for a moment and went out as his sight failed. His ear caught a rough shout, but he could no longer feel the heel that kicked him in the flank. Then everything was gone—for ever.

1907

THE GARNET BRACELET

Ludwig van Beethoven. 2 Son. (op. 2, No. 2)

Largo Appassionato

In mid August, before the new moon, there suddenly came a spell of bad weather, of the kind peculiar to the north coast of the Black Sea. Dense, heavy fog lay on land and sea, and the huge lighthouse siren roared like a mad bull day and night. Then a drizzle, as fine as water dust, fell steadily from morning to morning and turned the clayey roads and foot-paths into a thick mass of mud, in which carts and carriages would be bogged for a long time. And then a fierce hurricane began to blow from the steppeland in the north-west; the tree-tops rocked and heaved like waves in a gale, and at night the iron roofing of houses rattled, as if someone in heavy boots were running over it; window-frames shook, doors banged, and there was a wild howling in the chimneys. Several fishing boats lost their bearings at sea, and two of them did not come back; a week later the fishermen's corpses were washed ashore.

The inhabitants of a suburban seaside resort—mostly Greeks and Jews, life-loving and over-apprehensive like all Southerners—were hurrying back to town. On the muddy highway an endless succession of drays dragged along, overloaded with mattresses, sofas, chests, chairs, wash-stands, samovars. Through the blurred muslin of the drizzle, it was a pitiful and dismal sight—the wretched bag and baggage, which looked so shabby, so drab and beggarly; the maids and cooks sitting atop of the carts on soaked tarpaulin, holding irons, cans or baskets; the exhausted, panting horses which halted every now and again, their knees trembling, their flanks steaming; the draymen who swore huskily, wrapped in matting against the rain. An even sorrier sight were the deserted houses, now bare, empty and spacious, with their ravaged flower-beds, smashed panes, abandoned dogs and rubbish—cigarette ends, bits of paper, broken crockery, cartons, and medicine bottles.

But the weather changed abruptly in late August. There came calm, cloudless days that were sunnier and mellower than they had been in July. Autumn gossamer glinted like mica on the bristly yellow stubble in the dried fields. The trees, restored to their quietude, were meekly shedding their leaves.

Princess Vera Nikolayevna Sheyina, wife of the marshal of nobility, had been unable to leave her villa because repairs were not yet finished at the town house. And now she was overjoyed by the lovely days, the calm and solitude and pure air, the swallows twittering on the telegraph wires as they flocked together to fly south, and the caressing salty breeze that drifted gently from the sea.

II

Besides, that day—the seventeenth of September—was her birthday. She had always loved it, associating it with remote, cherished memories of her childhood, and always expected it to bring on something wonderfully happy. In the morning, before leaving for town on urgent business, her husband had put on her night-table a case with magnificent ear-rings of pear-shaped pearls, and the present added to her cheerful mood.

She was all alone in the house. Her unmarried brother Nikolai, assistant public prosecutor, who usually lived with them, had also gone to town for a court hearing. Her husband had promised to bring to dinner none but a few of their closest friends. It was fortunate that her birthday was during the summer season, for in town they would have had to spend a good deal of money on a grand festive dinner, perhaps even a ball, while here in the country the expenses could be cut to a bare minimum. Despite his prominence in society, or possibly because of it, Prince Sheyin could hardly make both ends meet. The huge family estate had been almost ruined by his ancestors, while his position obliged him to live above his means: give receptions, engage in charity, dress well, keep horses, and so on. Princess Vera, with whom the former passionate love for her husband had long ago toned down to a true, lasting friendship, spared no pains to help him ward off complete ruin. Without his suspecting it she went without many things she wanted, and ran the household as thriftily as she could.

She was now walking about the garden, carefully clipping off flowers for the dinner table. The flower-beds, stripped almost bare, looked neglected. The double carnations of various colours were past their best, and so were the stocks—half in bloom, half laden with thin green pods that smelled of cabbage; on the rose-bushes, blooming for the third time that summer, there were still a few undersized buds and flowers. But then the dahlias, peonies and asters flaunted their haughty beauty, filling the hushed air with a grassy, sad autumnal scent. The other flowers, whose season of luxurious love and over-fruitful maternity was over, were quietly dropping innumerable seeds of future life.

A three-tone motor-car horn sounded on the nearby highway, announcing that Anna Nikolayevna Friesse, Princess Vera's sister, was coming. She had telephoned that morning to say that she would come and help about the house and to receive the guests.

Vera's keen ear had not betrayed her. She went to meet the arrival. A few minutes later an elegant sedan drew up at the gate; the chauffeur jumped nimbly down and flung the door open.

The two sisters kissed joyfully. A warm affection had bound them together since early childhood. They were strangely unlike each other in appearance. The elder sister, Vera, resembled her mother, a beautiful English-woman; she had a tall, lithe figure, a delicate but cold and proud face, well-formed if rather large hands, and charmingly sloping shoulders such as you see in old miniatures. The younger sister, Anna, had the Mongol features of her father, a Tatar prince, whose grandfather had not been christened until the early nineteenth century and whose forbears were descended from Tamerlane himself, or Timur Lenk, the Tatar name by which her father proudly called the great murderer. Standing half a head shorter than her sister, she was rather broad-shouldered, lively and frivolous, and very fond of teasing people. Her face, of a markedly Mongol cast—with prominent cheek-bones, narrow eyes which she, moreover, often screwed up because she was short-sighted, and a haughty expression about her small, sensuous mouth, especially its full, slightly protruding lower lip—had, nevertheless, an elusive and unaccountable fascination which lay perhaps in her smile, in the deeply feminine quality of all her features, or in her piquant, coquettish mimicry. Her graceful lack of beauty excited and drew men's attention much more frequently and strongly than her sister's aristocratic loveliness.

She was married to a very wealthy and very stupid man, who did absolutely nothing though he was on the board of some sort of charity institution and bore the title of *Kammerjunker*. She loathed her husband, but she had borne him two children—a boy and a girl; she had made up her mind not to have any more children. As for Vera, she longed to have children, as many as possible, but for some reason she had none, and she morbidly and passionately adored her younger sister's pretty, anaemic children, always well-behaved and obedient, with pallid, mealy faces and curled doll hair of a flaxen colour.

Anna was all gay disorder and sweet, sometimes freakish contradictions. She readily gave herself up to the most reckless flirting in all the capitals and health resorts of Europe, but she was never unfaithful to her husband, whom she, however, ridiculed contemptuously both to his face and behind his back. She was extravagant and very fond of gambling, dances, new sensations and exciting spectacles, and when abroad she would frequent cafés of doubtful repute. But she was also generously kind and deeply, sincerely religious—so much so that she had secretly become a Catholic. Her back, bosom and shoulders were of rare beauty. When she went to a grand ball she would bare herself far beyond the limits allowed by decorum or fashion, but it was said that under the low-cut dress she always wore a hair shirt.

Vera, on the other hand, was rigidly plain-mannered, coldly, condescendingly amiable to all, and as aloof and composed as a queen.

III

"Oh, how nice it is here! How very nice!" said Anna as she walked with swift small steps along the path beside her sister. "Let's sit for a while on the bench above the bluff, if you don't mind. I haven't seen the sea for ages. The air is so wonderful here—it cheers your heart to breathe it. Last summer I made an amazing discovery in the Crimea, in Miskhor. Do you know what surf water smells like? Just imagine—it smells like mignonette."

Vera smiled affectionately.

"You always fancy things."

"But it does. Once everybody laughed at me, I remember, when I said that moonlight had a kind of pink shade. But a couple of days ago Boritsky—that artist who's doing my portrait—said that I was right and that artists have known about it for a long time."

"Is that artist your latest infatuation?"

"You always get queer ideas!" Anna laughed, then, stepping quickly to the edge of the bluff, which dropped in a sheer wall deep into the sea, she looked down and suddenly cried out in terror, starting back, her face pale.

"What a height!" Her voice was faint and tremulous. "When I look down from so high up it gives me a sort of sweet, nasty creeps, and my toes ache. And yet I'm drawn to it!"

She was about to look down again, but her sister held her back.

"For heaven's sake, Anna dear! I feel giddy myself when you do that. Sit down, I beg you."

"All right, all right, I will. But see how beautiful it is, how exhilarating—you just can't look enough. If you knew how thankful I am to God for all the wonders he has wrought for us!"

Both fell to thinking for a moment. The sea lay at rest far, far below. The shore could not be seen from the bench, and that enhanced the feeling of the immensity and majesty of the sea. The water was calm and friendly, and cheerfully blue, except for pale blue oblique stripes marking the currents, and on the horizon it changed to an intense blue.

Fishing boats, hardly discernible, were dozing motionless in the smooth water, not far from the shore. And farther away a three-master, draped from top to bottom in white, shapely sails bellied out by the wind, seemed to be suspended in the air, making no headway.

"I see what you mean," said the elder sister thoughtfully, "but somehow I don't feel about it the way you do. When I see the sea for the first time after a long interval, it excites and staggers me. I feel as if I were looking at an enormous, solemn wonder I'd never seen before. But afterwards, when I'm used to it, its flat emptiness begins to crush me. I feel bored as I look at it, and I try not to look any more."

Anna smiled.

"What is it?" asked her sister.

"Last summer," said Anna slyly, "we rode in a big cavalcade from Yalta to Uch Kosh. That's beyond the forester's house, above the falls. At first we wandered into some mist, it was very damp and we couldn't see well, but we climbed higher and higher, up a steep path, between pine-trees. Then the forest ended, and we were out of the mist. Imagine a narrow foothold on a cliff, and a precipice below. The villages seemed no bigger than match-boxes, the forests and gardens were like so much grass. The whole landscape lay below like a map. And farther down was the sea, stretching away for fifty or sixty miles. I fancied I was hanging in mid-air and was going to fly. It was so beautiful, and made me feel so light! I turned and said happily to the guide, 'Well, Seyid Oghlu, isn't it lovely?' But he clicked his tongue and said

'Ah, leddy, you don't know how fed up I am vid all dat. I sees it every day.'"

"Thank you for the comparison," said Vera with a laugh. "But I simply think that we Northerners can never understand the charm of the sea. I love the forest. Do you remember our woods back in Yegorovskoye? How could you ever be bored by them? The pine-trees! And the moss! And the death-cups—looking as if they were made of red satin embroidered with white beads. It's so still, so cool."

"It makes no difference to me—I love everything," answered Anna. "But I love best of all my little sister, my dear sensible Vera. There are only two of us in the world, you know."

She put her arm round her sister and snuggled against her, cheek to cheek. And suddenly she started.

"But how silly of me! We sit here like characters in a novel, talking about Nature, and I quite forgot about my present. Here, look. Only I'm afraid you may not like it."

She took from her handbag a small notebook in an unusual binding: on a background of old blue velvet, worn and grey with time, there wound a dull-golden fili-gree pattern of exquisite intricacy and beauty, apparently the diligent handiwork of a skilful and assiduous artist. The notebook was attached to a gold chain, thin as a thread, and the sheets inside it had been replaced by ivory plates.

"What a beauty! It's gorgeous!" said Vera, and kissed her sister. "Thank you. Where did you get this treasure?"

"In a curiosity shop. You know my weakness for rum-maging in old trash. That was how I came upon this prayer-book. See how the ornament here shapes into a cross. I only found the binding, and everything else—the leaves, clasps and pencil—I had to think up myself. Hard as I tried to explain my idea to Mollinet, he simply refused to see what I wanted. The clasps should have been made

331

in the same style as the whole pattern—dull in tone, of old gold, finely engraved—but he's done God knows what. However, the chain is of genuine Venetian workmanship, very old."

Admiringly Vera stroked the magnificent binding.

"What hoary antiquity! I wonder how old this note-book is," she said.

"I can only guess. It must date from the late seventeenth or mid-eighteenth century."

"How strange," said Vera, with a pensive smile. "Here I am holding an object that may have been touched by the hand of Marquise de Pompadour or Marie Antoinette herself. Oh, Anna, it's so like you, to make a lady's *carnet* out of a prayer-book. But let's go and see what's going on inside."

They went into the house across a large terrace paved with flagstone and enclosed on all sides by trellises of Isabella grape-vine. The black rich clusters smelling faintly of strawberries hung heavily amid the dark green, gilded here and there by the sun. The terrace was submerged in a green half-light, which cast a pale reflection on the faces of the two women.

"Are you going to have dinner served here?" asked Anna.

"I was at first. But the evenings are so chilly now. I prefer the dining-room. The men may come out here to smoke."

"Will you have anybody worth seeing?"

"I don't know yet. All I know is that our Grandad is coming."

"Ah, dear Grandad! How lovely!" cried Anna, clasping her hands. "I haven't seen him for ages."

"Vasya's sister is coming too, and Professor Speshnikov, I think. I was at my wits' end yesterday. You know they both like good food—Grandad and the professor. But you can't get a thing here or in town, for love or money.

Luka came by quail somewhere—ordered them from a hunter—and is now trying his skill on them. The beef isn't bad, comparatively speaking—alas! the inevitable roast beef! Then we have very nice lobsters."

"Well, it doesn't sound so bad, after all. Don't worry. Between you and me, you like good food yourself."

"But we'll also have something special. This morning a fisherman brought us a gurnard. I saw it myself. It's a monster, really. Terrible even to look at."

Anna, who was eagerly inquisitive about everything whether it concerned her or not, wanted to see the gurnard at once.

Luka, a tall man with a clean-shaven sallow face, came in carrying a white oblong basin, which he held with difficulty by the lugs, careful not to spill the water on the parquet floor.

"Twelve and a half pounds, Your Highness," he said, with the peculiar pride of a cook. "We weighed it a while back."

The fish was too big for the basin and lay with its tail curled. Its scales were shot with gold, the fins were a bright red, and two long fan-like wings, of a delicate blue, stood out from the huge rapacious head. It was still alive and vigorously worked its gills.

The younger sister cautiously touched the fish's head with her little finger. But the gurnard lashed out with its tail, and Anna with a scream snatched back her hand.

"You can depend on it, Your Highness, we'll arrange everything in the best manner," said the cook, obviously aware of Vera's anxiety. "Just now a Bulgarian brought two pine-apple melons. They're a bit like cantaloups, only they smell much nicer. And may I ask Your Highness what gravy you will have with the gurnard: *tartare* or *polonaise,* or simply rusk in butter?"

"Do as you like. You may go," said the princess.

After five o'clock the guests began to arrive. Prince Vasily Lvovich brought his widowed sister, Lyudmila Lvovna Durasova, a stout, good-natured woman who spoke very little; Vasyuchok, a wealthy young scapegrace and rake, whom everybody in town called by that familiar name, and who was very good company because he could sing and recite poetry, as well as arrange tableaux, plays and charity bazaars; the famous pianist Jennie Reiter, a friend of Princess Vera's from the Smolny Institute; and also his brother-in-law, Nikolai Nikolayevich. After them came in a motor-car Anna's husband, along with the fat, hulking Professor Speshnikov, and the vice-governor, von Seck. The last to arrive was General Anosov, who came in a fine hired landau, accompanied by two officers: Staff Colonel Ponamaryov, looking older than his age, a lean, bilious man worn out by clerical drudgery, and Guards Lieutenant Bakhtinsky of the Hussars, who was reputed to be the best dancer and master of ceremonies in Petersburg.

General Anosov, a silver-haired old man, tall and obese, stepped heavily down from the footboard, holding on to the rail of the box with one hand and to the back of the landau with the other. In his left hand he carried an ear-trumpet and in his right a rubber-tipped cane. He had a large, coarse, red face with a fleshy nose, and he looked out of narrowed eyes with the dignified, mildly contemptuous good humour typical of courageous and plain men who have often met danger and death face to face.

The two sisters, who recognized him from afar, ran up to the landau just in time to support him half-jokingly under the arms.

"You'd think I was the bishop," said the general in a friendly, husky boom.

"Grandad, dear Grandad!" said Vera, a little reproachfully. "All these days we've been expecting you, and you haven't let us get so much as a glimpse of you."

"Our Grandad's lost all shame here in the south," said Anna with a laugh. "As if you couldn't have thought of your godchild. You behave like a shameless old fop, and you've forgotten all about us."

The general, who had bared his majestic head, kissed the hands of the sisters, then he kissed both women on the cheeks and again on the hands.

"Wait, girls, don't scold me," he said, pausing for breath after each word, because of his long-standing asthma. "Upon my honour—those wretched doctors— have been treating my rheumatism all summer—with some sort of foul jelly—it smells awful— And they wouldn't let me go— You're the first—I'm calling on— Very glad—to see you— How are you getting along? You're quite the lady, Vera—you look very much like— your late mother— When'll you be inviting me to the christening?"

"I'm afraid never, Grandad."

"Don't give up hope—it'll come yet— Pray to God. And you, Anna, you haven't changed a bit— At sixty you'll be—the same fidget. But wait. Let me introduce these gentlemen to you."

"I had the honour long ago," said Colonel Ponamaryov, bowing.

"I was introduced to the princess in Petersburg," added the Hussar.

"Well, then, Anna, may I introduce to you Lieutenant Bakhtinsky. He's a dancer and brawler, but a good horseman all the same. There, my dear Bakhtinsky, take that thing from the carriage. Come along, girls. What are you going to feed us on, Vera dear? After the starvation diet—those doctors kept me on—I have the appetite of an ensign—on graduation."

General Anosov had been a companion-in-arms and devoted friend of the late Prince Mirza Bulat-Tuganovsky. After the prince's death he had passed on to his daughters all his love and affection. He had known them when they were quite small—indeed, he was Anna's godfather. At that time he had been, as he still was, governor of a big but almost abandoned fortress in the town of K., and had come to Tuganovsky's almost daily. The children literally adored him because he pampered them, gave them presents, and offered them boxes at the circus or the theatre, and also because no one could play with them so well as he could. But what they liked and remembered best was his stories of military campaigns, of battles and bivouacs, of victories and retreats, of death and wounds and severe frosts—artless unhurried stories, calm as an epic, told between evening tea and the hated hour when the children were told to go to bed.

This fragment of old times appeared as a colossal and strangely picturesque figure. He combined those simple but deep and touching traits which, even in his day, were more often to be found among the privates than among the officers, those purely Russian, muzhik traits which, taken together, form an exalted character that sometimes makes our soldier not only invincible but a martyr, almost a saint. He has a guileless, naive faith, a clear, cheerfully good-natured view of life, cool and matter-of-fact courage, humility in the face of death, pity for the vanquished, infinite patience, and amazing physical and moral stamina.

Since the Polish War Anosov had taken part in every campaign except the Japanese. He would not have hesitated to go to that war, either, but he was not called upon, and he had a maxim which was great in its modesty: "Never challenge death until you're called." Throughout his service he never struck any of his men, let alone had them flogged. During the Polish uprising he refused to

shoot a group of prisoners despite the regimental commander's personal orders. "If it's a spy, I can not only
have him shot," he said, "but am ready to kill him with
my own hand if you command me to. But these men are
prisoners, and I can't do it." And he said that simply and
respectfully, without the least hint of challenge or brava-
do, looking his superior straight in the eyes with his own
clear, steady eyes, so that instead of shooting him for
disobeying orders they let him alone.

During the war of 1877-1879, he rose very quickly to
the rank of colonel, although he lacked proper education
or, as he put it himself, had finished only a "bear's
academy." He took part in crossing the Danube and the
Balkan Mountains, camped at Shipka through the winter,
and was among those who launched the last attack on
Plevna; he was wounded five times, once seriously, and
got severe concussion from a grenade splinter. General
Radetsky and Skobelev knew him personally and had a
great respect for him. It was about him that Skobelev
had said, "I know an officer who is much braver than I
am, and that officer's Major Anosov."

He returned from the war almost deaf from the grenade
splinter; three toes on one foot had been amputated as
a result of frost-bite during the Balkan march, and he
had contracted an acute rheumatism at Shipka. After
two years of peace-time service it was deemed timely to
retire him, but he rebelled. The governor of the territory,
who had witnessed his cool courage in crossing the Danube, brought his influence to bear at the critical moment.
The Petersburg authorities decided not to hurt the feelings of the distinguished colonel and gave him for life
the governorship of K., an office which was honorary
rather than indispensable for the defence of the country.

Everyone in town knew him and good-naturedly made
fun of his foibles and habits and the way he dressed. He
never carried arms, and he went about in a long, old-

fashioned coat and a cap with a large top and an enormous straight visor, a cane in his right hand and an ear-trumpet in his left; he was always accompanied by two fat, lazy, hoarse pugs with tongues lolling between their clamped jaws. If in the course of his morning stroll he met an acquaintance, the passers-by several blocks away could hear him shouting and the pugs barking in unison.

Like many people who are hard of hearing, he was passionately fond of opera, and sometimes, during a romantic duet, his commanding boom would suddenly resound throughout the hall, "Why, that was a jolly good C, damn him! Cracked it right through like a nut." Subdued laughter would ripple across the hall, but the general would suspect nothing, being under the impression that he had merely whispered a comment in his neighbour's ear.

As part of his official duties he often visited, together with his wheezing pugs, the guard-house where officers under arrest relaxed comfortably from the hardships of military service, telling stories over tea and cards. He would carefully question each of them, "Your name? Who arrested you? For how long? What for?" Sometimes he would quite unexpectedly commend an officer for a courageous if unlawful act, or take him to task so loudly that he could be heard outside. But when he had finished shouting he would inquire almost in the same breath where the officer got his meals and how much they cost him. It sometimes happened that a lieutenant, who had erred and been sent for a prolonged detention from an out-of-the-way corner that had no guard-room of its own, would confess that, being short of funds, he had to eat with the privates. Anosov then would immediately order meals to be supplied to the poor devil from his own home, which was no more than a hundred yards from the guard-house.

It was in K. that he had grown intimate with the Tuganovsky family and established a close friendship with the children, so that with him it had become a virtual necessity to see them every evening. If it so happened that the young ladies went away somewhere or he himself was kept away by his official duties, he would feel terribly lonely and melancholy in the large rooms of the governor's mansion. Every summer he would take his leave and spend a whole month at the Tuganovsky estate, Yegorovskoye, some forty miles from K.

All his repressed tenderness and his longing for love had gone out to the children, especially the girls. Once he had been married, but that had been so long ago that he hardly remembered it. It was before the war that his wife had eloped with a strolling actor, who had fascinated her with his velvet jacket and lace cuffs. Anosov paid her an allowance as long as she lived, but did not permit her to come back to him despite all the scenes of repentance and tearful letters. They had had no children.

V

Unexpectedly, the evening was calm and warm, and the candles on the terrace and in the dining-room burned with a steady flame. At dinner Prince Vasily Lvovich amused the company. He had an extraordinary and very peculiar gift for telling stories. He would take some incident that had happened to one of the company or a common acquaintance, but would embellish it so, and use so matter-of-fact a tone, that his listeners would split their sides with laughter. That night he was telling the story of Nikolai Nikolayevich's unhappy wooing of a wealthy and beautiful lady. The only authentic detail was the husband's refusal to give her a divorce. But the prince skilfully combined fact and fancy. He made the grave, rather priggish Nikolai run down the street in his stock-

ing-feet at the dead of night, his boots under his arm
At a corner the young man was stopped by the policeman, and it was only after a long and stormy explanation
that Nikolai managed to convince him that he was an
assistant public prosecutor and not a burglar. The wedding all but came off, or so the narrator said, except that
at the crucial moment a band of false witnesses, who had
a hand in the affair, suddenly went on strike, demanding
a rise. Being a stingy man—which he actually was, to
some extent—and also being opposed on principle to all
forms of strike, Nikolai flatly refused to pay more, refer-
ring to a certain clause in the law, which was confirmed
by a ruling of the court of appeal. Then, in reply to the
customary question, "Does anyone here present know of
any impediment to the lawful joining together of these
two in matrimony?" the enraged perjurers said as one
man, "Yes, we do. All that we have testified under oath
in court is a falsehood to which the prosecutor here
forced us by intimidation and coercion. As for this lady's
husband, we can only say from personal knowledge that
he is the most respectable man in the world, chaste as
Joseph and kind as an angel."

Having begun to tell wedding stories, Prince Vasily
did not spare even Gustav Ivanovich Friesse, Anna's
husband, who, he said, had on the day following his wedding called the police to evict the young bride from her
parents' house because she had no passport of her own
and to install her in her lawful husband's home. The only
part of the tale which was true was the fact that, in the
very first days of her married life, Anna had had to be
continually with her sick mother because Vera had gone
off south, and poor Gustav Ivanovich was plunged in
despair.

Everybody laughed. Anna smiled with her narrowed
eyes. Gustav Ivanovich guffawed in delight, and his
gaunt face with the tight, shining skin, the thin, light hair

sleeked carefully down and the deep-set eyes, was like a skull mirthfully baring a set of very bad teeth. He still adored Anna as on the first day of their married life; he was always trying to sit beside her, and touch her surreptitiously, and he danced attendance on her with such smug infatuation that you often pitied him and felt embarrassed for him.

Before rising from the table Vera Nikolayevna mechanically counted the guests. There were thirteen of them. She was superstitious and she said to herself, "What a nuisance! Why didn't I think of counting them before? And Vasya's to blame too—he told me nothing on the telephone."

When friends gathered at Sheyin's or Friesse's they usually played poker after dinner, because both sisters were ridiculously fond of games of chance. In fact, certain rules had been established in both houses: all the players would be given an equal number of ivory tokens of a specific value, and the game would go on until all the tokens passed to one of the players; then it would be stopped for the evening, no matter how earnestly the others insisted on continuing it. It was strictly forbidden to take fresh tokens from the cash-box. Experience had shown that these rigid rules were indispensable to check Vera and Anna, who would grow so excited in the course of the game that there was no stopping them. The total loss seldom exceeded two hundred rubles.

This time, too, they sat down to poker. Vera, who was not playing, was about to go out on to the terrace, where the table was being set for tea, when the housemaid, looking rather mysterious, suddenly called her from the drawing-room.

"What is it, Dasha?" asked Princess Vera in annoyance, passing into her little study next to the bedroom. "Why are you staring at me so stupidly? And what are you holding there?"

Dasha put on the table a small square object, neatly wrapped in white paper and tied by a pink ribbon.

"It isn't my fault, Your Highness, honest to God," she stammered, blushing offendedly. "He came in and said—"

"Who is *he*?"

"A messenger boy, Your Highness."

"Well?"

"He came into the kitchen and put this on the table. 'Give it to your mistress,' he said. 'Only,' he says, 'be sure to hand it to her personally.' 'Who's it from?' I asked. 'It's written here,' he said. And then he ran away."

"Go and bring him back."

"Oh, but I couldn't do that, Your Highness. He came when you were in the middle of dinner, so I didn't dare to disturb you. It must have been half an hour ago."

"All right, you may go."

She cut the ribbon with scissors and threw it into the waste-basket along with the paper bearing her address. Under the wrapping she found a small jeweller's box of red plush, apparently fresh from the shop. She raised the lid, which was lined with light-blue silk, and saw, stuck into the black velvet, an oval gold bracelet, and inside it a note carefully folded into a neat octagon. Quickly she unfolded the paper. She thought she knew the handwriting, but, woman that she was, she put aside the note to take a look at the bracelet.

It was of low-standard gold, very thick but hollow and studded on the outside with small, poorly polished old garnets. But in the centre there arose, surrounding a strange small green stone, five excellent cabochon garnets, each the size of a pea. As Vera happened to turn the bracelet at a lucky angle under the electric light, beautiful crimson lights flashed suddenly, deep under the smooth egg-shaped surface of the stones.

"It's like blood!" Vera thought with apprehension.

Then she recalled the letter. It was written in an elegant hand and ran as follows:

"Your Highness, Princess Vera Nikolayevna,

"Respectfully congratulating you on your bright and happy birthday, I take the liberty of sending to you my humble offering."

"Oh, so that's who it is," Vera said to herself resentfully. But she read the letter to the end.

"I should never have dared to offer you a present of my own choice, for I have neither the right, nor the refined taste, nor, to be frank, the money to do so. Moreover, I believe there is no treasure on earth worthy of adorning you.

"But this bracelet belonged to my great-grandmother, and my late mother was the last to wear it. In the middle, among the bigger stones, you will see a green one. It is a very rare stone—a green garnet. We have an old family tradition that this stone enables the women who wear it to foresee the future, and keeps off unhappy thoughts, and protects men from violent death.

"All the stones have been carefully transferred from the old, silver bracelet, and you may rest assured that no one has worn this bracelet before you.

"You may at once throw away this absurd trinket, or present it to someone else; I shall be happy to know that your hands have touched it.

"I beseech you not to be angry with me. I blush to remember my audacity of seven years ago, when I dared write to you, a young lady, stupid and wild letters, and even had the assurance to expect an answer to them. Today I have nothing for you but awe, everlasting admiration and the humble devotion of a slave. All that I can do now is to wish you perpetual happiness and to rejoice if you are happy. In my mind I bow deeply to the chair on which you sit, the floor you tread, the trees which you touch in passing, the servants to whom you speak. I no longer presume to envy those people or things.

"Once again I beg your pardon for having bothered you with a long, useless letter.

"Your humble servant till death and after,

"G.S.Z."

"Shall I show it to Vasya or not? If so, when? Now or after the guests have left? No, I'd better do it later—now I'd look as silly as this poor man."

While debating thus with herself Princess Vera could not take her eyes off the five blood-red lights glowing inside the five garnets.

VI

It was only with great difficulty that Colonel Ponamaryov was induced to play poker. He said that he knew nothing about the game, that he did not gamble even for fun and that the only game he cared for and had any skill in was *vint*. But in the end he gave in.

At first they had to teach and prompt him, but soon he had mastered the rules of the game, and within half an hour he had all the chips piled in front of him.

"That isn't fair!" said Anna in mock reproach. "You might have allowed us a little more of the excitement."

Vera did not know how to entertain three of the guests —Speshnikov, the colonel and the vice-governor, a doltish, respectable and dull German. She got up a game of *vint* for them and invited Gustav Ivanovich to make a fourth. Anna thanked her by lowering her eyelids, and her sister at once understood. Everybody knew that unless Gustav Ivanovich was disposed of by suggesting a game of cards he would hang about his wife all evening, baring the rotten teeth in his skull-face and making a perfect nuisance of himself.

Now things went smoothly, in an easy and lively atmosphere. Vasyuchok, accompanied by Jennie Reiter, sang in an undertone Italian folk canzonets and Oriental songs by Rubinstein. He had a light but pleasant voice, responsive and true. Jennie Reiter, a very exacting musician, was always willing to accompany him; but then it was said that he was courting her.

Sitting on a couch in a corner, Anna was flirting audaciously with the Hussar. Vera walked over and listened with a smile.

"Oh, please don't laugh," said Anna gaily, narrowing her lovely, mischievous Tatar eyes at the officer. "Of course, you think it's a feat to gallop at the head of a squadron, or to clear hurdles at races. But look at *our* feats. We've just finished a lottery. Do you think that's easy? Fie! The place was so crowded and full of tobacco smoke, there were porters and cabbies and God knows who else, and they all pestered me with complaints and grievances. I didn't have a moment's rest all day. And that isn't all, either, for now there's to be a concert in aid of needy gentlewomen, and then comes a charity ball—"

"At which you will not refuse me a mazurka, I hope?" Bakhtinsky put in and, bending slightly forward, clicked his heels under the arm-chair.

"Thank you. But the saddest case is our children's home. You know what I mean—a home for vicious children."

"Oh, I see. That must be very amusing."

"Don't, you should be ashamed of laughing at things like that. But do you know what the trouble is? We'd like to give shelter to those unfortunate children, whose souls are corrupted by inherited vice and bad example, we'd like to give them warmth and comfort—"

"Humph!"

"—to improve their morality, and instil in them a sense of duty. Do you see my point? And every day hundreds and thousands of children are brought to us, but there isn't a single vicious child among them! If you ask the parents whether their child is vicious they take offence—can you imagine that? And so the home has been opened and dedicated, everything is ready and waiting, but it hasn't a single inmate! We're almost at the stage of offering a prize for every vicious child brought in."

"Anna Nikolayevna," the Hussar interrupted her, with insinuating earnestness. "Why offer a prize? Take me free. Upon my honour, you couldn't find a more vicious child than I am."

"Stop it! It's impossible to talk to you seriously." She burst out laughing, and sat back on the couch, her eyes shining.

Seated at a large round table, Prince Vasily was showing his sister, Anosov and his brother-in-law a family album of cartoons drawn by himself. All four were laughing heartily, and gradually those other guests who were not playing cards gathered round them.

The album was a sort of supplement to Prince Vasily's satirical stories—a collection of illustrations. With imperturbable calm he showed "The Story of the Amorous Adventures of the Brave General Anosov in Turkey, Bulgaria and Elsewhere," "An Adventure of Prince Nicole Boulate-Touganofski the Coxcomb in Monte Carlo," and so on.

"I'll now acquaint you, ladies and gentlemen, with a brief biography of my beloved sister, Lyudmila Lvovna," he said, with a swift teasing glance at his sister. "Part One. Childhood. The child was growing. Her name was Lima."

The album leaf displayed the figure of a little girl, purposely drawn in childish style, her face set in profile and yet showing both eyes; two broken lines sticking out from under her skirt represented her legs, and the fingers of both hands were spread out.

"Nobody ever called me Lima," said Lyudmila Lvovna with a laugh.

"Part Two. First Love. A cavalry cadet, kneeling before the damsel Lima, presents her with a poem of his own production. It contains these lines of rare beauty:

> *Your gorgeous leg, I do opine,*
> *Is a thing of love divine!*

"And here is an original likeness of the leg.

"Here the cadet induces the innocent Lima to elope from her parents' home. Here you see them in flight. And here is a critical situation: the enraged father has overtaken the fugitives. The faint-hearted cadet leaves the meek Lima in the lurch.

> *You powdered your nose in a manner so slack*
> *That now our pursuers are hot on our track;*
> *So just do your best to hold them at bay,*
> *While into the bushes I run away."*

The story of "the damsel Lima" was followed by one entitled "Princess Vera and the Infatuated Telegraphist."

"This moving poem is so far only in illustrations," Vasily Lvovich explained with a serious air. "The text is in the making."

"That's something new," said Anosov, "I haven't seen it before."

"It's the latest issue. First edition."

Vera gently touched his shoulder.

"Don't, please," she said.

But Vasily Lvovich did not hear, or perhaps he did not take it seriously.

"It dates from prehistoric times. One fine day in May a damsel by the name of Vera received a letter with kissing doves on the first page. Here's the letter, and here are the doves.

"The letter contains an ardent confession of love, written against all rules of spelling. It begins: 'O Beutiful Blonde who art—a raging sea of flames seathing in my chest. Thy gaze clings to my tormented soal like a venomus serpent,' and so on. It ends in this humble way: 'I am only a poor telegrafist, but my feelings are worthy of Milord George. I dare not reveel my full name—it is too indecent. I only sign my inicials: P.P.Z. Please send your anser to the post-office, posté restanté.' Here, ladies and gentlemen, you can see the portrait of the telegraphist himself, very skilfully executed in crayon.

"Vera's heart was pierced (here's her heart and here's the arrow). But, as beseemed a well-behaved and good-mannered damsel, she showed the letter to her honourable parents, and also to her childhood friend and fiancé, Vasya Sheyin, a handsome young man. Here's the illustration. Given time the drawings will be supplied with explanations in verse.

"Vasya Sheyin, sobbing, returned the engagement ring to Vera. 'I will not stand in the way of your happiness,' he said, 'but, I implore you, do not be hasty. Think it over before you take the final step—test his feelings and your own. Child, you know nothing about life, and you are flying like a moth to a glowing flame. But I—alas! I know the cold, hypocritical world. You should know that telegraphists are attractive but perfidious. It gives them an indescribable pleasure to deceive an innocent victim by their proud beauty and false feelings and cruelly abandon her afterwards.'

"Six months rolled by. In the whirl of life's waltz Vera forgot her admirer and married young handsome Vasya, but the telegraphist did not forget her. One day he disguised himself as a chimney-sweep and, smearing himself with soot, made his way into Princess Vera's boudoir. You can see that he left the traces of his five fingers and two lips everywhere: on the rugs and pillows and wallpaper, and even on the floor.

"Then, dressed as a countrywoman, he took up the duties of dish-washer in our kitchen. But the excessive favour which Luka the cook bestowed upon him put him to flight.

"He found himself in a mad-house. And here you see him as a monk. But every day he unfailingly sent a passionate letter to Vera. And where his tears fell on the paper the ink ran in splotches.

"At last he died, but before his death he willed to Vera two telegraph-office buttons and a perfume bottle, filled with his tears."

"How about some tea, ladies and gentlemen?" asked Vera Nikolayevna.

VII

The long autumn sunset was dying. The narrow crimson slit glowing on the edge of the horizon, between a bluish cloud and the earth, faded out. Now earth and trees and sky could no longer be seen. Overhead big stars shimmered with their eyelashes in the blackness of night, and the blue beam of the lighthouse shot upwards in a thin column that seemed to splash into a liquid, blurred circle of light as it struck the firmament. Moths fluttered against the glass hoods over the candles. In the front garden the star-shaped flowers of the tobacco-plant gave off a stronger scent in the cool darkness.

Speshnikov, the vice governor and Colonel Ponamaryov had left long ago, promising to send the horses back from the tramway terminus to pick up the general. The remaining guests sat on the terrace. Despite his protests

General Anosov was made to put on his greatcoat, and his feet were wrapped in a warm rug. He sat between the two sisters, with a bottle of his favourite Pommard claret in front of him. They waited on him eagerly, filling his thin glass with the heavy, thick wine, passing the matches, cutting cheese for him, and so on. The old general all but purred with bliss.

"Yes, autumn's coming," said the old man, gazing at the candle-light and thoughtfully shaking his head. "Autumn. And I must start packing up. What a pity! It would have been so nice to stay here at the seaside, in ease and quiet, now that the weather's so fine!"

"Why not do so, Grandad?" said Vera.

"I can't, my dear, I can't. Duty calls. My leave is over. But I certainly wish I could. How the roses smell! I can feel it from here. And in summer the flowers somehow had no scent, except the white acacias—and they smelled of sweets."

Vera took two little roses—pink and carmine—out of a small jug and stuck them into the buttonhole of the general's greatcoat.

"Thanks, Vera dear." He bent his head to smell the flowers, and smiled the friendly smile of a kind old man.

"I remember when we took up our quarters in Bucharest. One day as I was walking down the street there came a strong smell of roses. I stopped and saw two soldiers, with a fine cut-glass bottle of attar standing between them. They had already oiled their boots and riflelocks with it. 'What's that you've got?' I asked. 'It's some sort of oil, sir. We put some of it in our gruel but it's no good—rasps the tongue—but it smells all right.' I gave them a ruble and they gladly let me have it. The bottle was no more than half-full, but considering the high price of the stuff it would fetch at least two hundred rubles. The soldiers were quite content, and they said, 'Here's another thing, sir. Peas of some kind. We tried hard to boil them, but the accursed stuff won't get soft.' It was coffee-beans, so I told them, 'That's only good for the Turks—it's of no use to soldiers.' Fortunately they hadn't eaten any opium. In some places I had seen opium tablets trampled into the mud."

"Tell us frankly, Grandad," said Anna, "did you ever know fear in battle? Were you afraid?"

"How strangely you talk, Anna. Of course I was afraid. Please don't believe those who say they weren't afraid and think the whizzing of bullets the sweetest music on earth. Only cranks or braggarts can talk like that. Everybody's afraid, only some shake in their boots with fear, while others keep themselves in hand. And though fear always remains the same, the ability to keep cool improves with practice; hence all the heroes and brave men. That's how it is. But once I was frightened almost to death."

"Tell us about it, Grandad," both sisters begged in unison.

They still listened to Anosov's stories with the same rapture as in their early childhood. Anna had spread out her elbows on the table quite like a child, propping her chin on her cupped hands. There was a sort of cosy charm about his unhurried, simple narrative. The somewhat bookish words and figures of speech which he used in telling his war memories sounded strange and clumsy You would have thought he was imitating some nice ancient story-teller.

"It's a very short story," he responded. "It happened at Shipka in winter, after I was shell-shocked. There were four of us in our dug-out. That was when something terrible befell me. One morning when I rose from bed, I fancied I was Nikolai and not Yakov, and I couldn't undeceive myself, much as I tried. Sensing that my mind was becoming deranged, I shouted for some water to be brought to me, wet my head with it, and recovered my reason."

"I can imagine how many victories you won over women there, Yakov Mikhailovich," said Jennie Reiter, the pianist. "You must have been very handsome in your youth."

"Oh, but our Grandad is handsome even now!" cried Anna.

"I wasn't handsome," said Anosov, with a calm smile. "But I wasn't shunned, either. There was a moving incident in Bucharest. When we marched into the city, the people welcomed us in the main square with gunfire, which damaged many windows; but where water had been placed in glasses the windows were unharmed. This is how I learned that. Coming to the lodgings assigned to me, I saw on the window-sill a low cage and on the cage a large cut-glass bottle with clear water that had goldfish swimming in it, and a canary perched among them. A canary in water! I was greatly surprised, but inspecting it I saw that the bottle had a broad bottom with a deep hollow in it, so that the canary could easily fly in and perch there.

"I walked into the house and saw a very pretty Bulgarian girl. I showed her my admission slip and took the opportunity to ask her why the panes in the house were undamaged after the gunfire, and she told me it was because of the water. She also told me about the canary; how dull-witted I had been! While we were talking, our eyes met, a spark flew between us like electricity, and I felt that I had fallen headlong in love—passionately and irrevocably."

The old man paused and slowly sipped the black wine.

"But you confessed it to her afterwards, didn't you?" asked the pianist.

"Well, yes, of course. But I did it without words. This is how it came about—"

"I hope you won't make us blush, Grandad?" Anna remarked, smiling slyly.

"Not at all, the affair was perfectly respectable. You see, the townspeople didn't give us the same welcome everywhere, but in Bucharest the people were so easy-going with us that one day when I started playing a violin the girls at once came in their Sunday dresses and began to dance, and then it became a daily habit.

"On an evening like that, when the moon was shining, I went into the passage where my Bulgarian girl had disappeared. On seeing me she pretended to be picking dry rose petals, which, incidentally, are gathered there by the sackful. But I put my arms round her, held her close to my heart and kissed her several times.

"From then on, when the moon and stars came out in the sky, I would hurry to my beloved and forget the day's worries while I was with her. And when the time came for us to march on we swore eternal love, and parted for ever."

"Is that all?" asked Lyudmila Lvovna, disappointed.

"What else did you expect?" replied the general.

"You will pardon me for saying so, Yakov Mikhailovich, but that isn't love —it's just an army officer's camp adventure."

"I don't know, really, whether it was love or some other sentiment."

"What I mean is, have you never known genuine love? A love that—well, in short, the kind of love that is holy and pure and eternal—and unearthly— Have you never experienced love like that?"

"I can't tell, honestly," faltered the old man, rising from his arm-chair. "I suppose not. At first, when I was young, I had no time, what with merry-making and cards and war. It seemed as if life and youth and good health would last for ever. Then I looked back and saw that I was already an old wreck. And now, Vera dear, please don't keep me any longer. I'll say goodbye to you all. Hussar," he said to Bakhtinsky, "the night is warm, let's go and meet our carriage."

"I'll go with you, Grandad," said Vera.

"So will I," added Anna.

Before leaving Vera stepped up to her husband.

"There's a red case in my drawer," she said to him softly. "In it you'll find a letter. Read it."

VIII

Anna and Bakhtinsky led the way, followed at some twenty paces by the general, arm-in-arm with Vera. The night was so black that during the first few minutes, before their eyes got used to the darkness, they had to grope for the way with their feet. Anosov, who despite his age still boasted surprisingly keen eyesight, had to help his companion. From time to time his big cold hand fondly stroked Vera's hand, which lay lightly on the bend of his sleeve.

"She's a funny woman, that Lyudmila Lvovna," he said suddenly, as if continuing aloud the thoughts that had been going through his head. "I've seen it so often in my life: as soon as a lady gets past fifty, especially if she's a widow or a spinster, she longs to hang about somebody else's love. She either spies, gloats and gossips, or offers to take care of your happiness, or works up a lot of treacly talk about exalted love. But I would say that nowadays people no longer know how to love. I see no real love. Nor did I see any in my time!"

"How can that be, Grandad?" Vera objected as she squeezed his arm slightly. "What slander! You were married yourself, weren't you? Then you must have loved."

"It doesn't mean a thing, Vera. Do you know how I got married? She was a peach of a girl, young and fresh, and she would sit by my side, her bosom heaving under the blouse. She'd lower her beautiful long eyelashes, and blush suddenly. The skin of her cheeks was so delicate, her neck so white and innocent, and her hands so soft and warm. God! Her papa and mamma slunk about us, eavesdropped at the door, and looked wistfully at me— with the gaze of faithful dogs. And I'd get little swift pecks when I was leaving. At tea her foot would touch mine as if by chance. Well, they got me before I knew where I was. 'Dear Nikita Antonovich, I have come to ask you for the hand of your daughter. Believe me, this angel—' Before I had finished the papa's eyes were moist, and he started to kiss me. 'My dear boy! I guessed it long ago. May God keep you. Only take good care of our treasure!' Three months later the angelic treasure was going about the house in a shabby dressing-gown and slippers on her bare feet, her thin hair unkempt and hung with curl-papers. She wrangled with orderlies like a fish-wife and made a fool of herself with young officers, lisping, giggling, rolling her eyes. In the presence of others she for some reason called me Jacques, pronouncing it with a languid, long-drawn nasal twang, 'Oh, Ja-a-acques.' A spendthrift and a hypocrite, slovenly and greedy. And her eyes were always so insincere. It's all over now, finished and done with. I'm even grateful to that wretched actor. It was lucky we had no children."

"Did you forgive them, Grandad?"

" 'Forgive' isn't the word, Vera dear. At first I was like a madman. If I'd seen them then I'd certainly have killed them. Then the whole thing gradually wore off, and nothing was left but contempt. So much the better. God warded off useless bloodshed. Besides, I was spared the lot of most husbands. Indeed, what would have become of me if it hadn't been for that disgusting incident? A pack-camel, a despicable abettor and protector, a milch cow, a screen, some sort of household utensil. No! It's all for the best, Vera."

"No, no, Grandad, the old grievance still rankles in your heart, if you'll allow me to say so. And you extend your own unhappy experience to all mankind. Take Vasya and me. You couldn't call our marriage an unhappy one, could you?"

Anosov did not speak for a while.

"All right, let's say your case is an exception," he said at length reluctantly. "But why do people generally get married? Let's take the woman. She's ashamed of remaining single, especially after all her friends have married. It's unbearable to be a burden on the family. She wants to be mistress of the house, mother of a family, enjoy independence. Then there's the need—the outright physical need—for motherhood, and for making a nest of her own. Men's motives are different. First of all they get sick of their bachelor life, the disorder in their rooms, restaurant meals, dirt, cigarette ends, torn or unmatching linen, debts, unceremonious friends, and so on, and so forth. Secondly, they feel that it's healthier and more economical to live in a family. In the third place, they think that after they've died, a part of them will be left in their children—an illusion of immortality. In the fourth place, there's the temptation of innocence, as in my case. And sometimes there is the consideration of a nice dowry. But where does love come in? Disinterested, self-sacrificing love that expects no reward? The love said to be 'stronger than death'? I mean that kind of love for which it's not an effort but sheer joy to perform any feat, give your life, accept martyrdom. Wait, Vera, are you going to talk to me about your Vasya again? Believe me, I like him. He's all right. Who knows if the future may not show his love in a light of great beauty. But try to understand what kind of love I am talking about. Love must be a tragedy. The greatest mystery in the world! No comforts, calculations or compromises must affect it."

"Have you ever seen such love, Grandad?" Vera asked softly.

"No," the old man replied firmly. "I know of two instances that come close to it. But one of them was prompted by stupidity, and the other—it was—a kind of sour stuff—utterly idiotic. I can tell you about them if you like. It won't take long."

"Please do, Grandad."

"All right. A regimental commander in our division —but not in our regiment—had a wife. She was a regular scarecrow, I must tell you. She was bony, red-haired, long-legged, scraggy, big-mouthed. Her make-up used to peel off her face like plaster off an old Moscow house. But, for all that, she was a kind of regimental Messalina, with a lot of spirit, arrogance, contempt for people, a passion for variety, and she was a morphine addict into the bargain.

"One day in autumn a new ensign was sent to our regiment, a greenhorn fresh from military school. A month later that old jade had him under her thumb. He was her page, her slave, her eternal dance partner. He used to carry her fan and handkerchief and rush out in snow and frost to get her horses, with nothing on but his flimsy coat. It's awful when an innocent lad lays his first love at the feet of an old, experienced, ambitious debauchee. Even if he manages to get away unscathed, you must give him up for lost just the same. He's marked for life.

"By Christmas she was fed up with him. She fell back on one of her previous, tried and tested passions. But he couldn't do without her. He trailed after her like a shadow. He was worn out, and lost weight and colour.

In high-flown language, 'death had marked his brow.' He was terribly jealous of her. They said that he used to stand under her window all night long.

"One day in spring they got up a kind of picnic in the regiment. I knew the two personally, but I was not there when it happened. As usual on such occasions, a lot was drunk. They started back after nightfall, along the railway. Suddenly they saw a goods train coming. It was creeping up a rather steep incline. They heard whistles. And the moment the headlights of the engine came alongside she suddenly whispered in the ensign's ear, 'You keep telling me you love me. But if I tell you to throw yourself under this train I'm sure you won't do it.' He didn't say a word in reply, but just rushed under the train. They say he had worked it out well, and meant to drop between the front and back wheels, where he would have been neatly cut in two. But some idiot tried to keep him back and push him away. Only he wasn't strong enough. The ensign clung to the rail with both his hands and they were chopped off."

"How dreadful!" Vera exclaimed.

"He had to resign from military service. His comrades collected a little money for his journey. He couldn't very well stay in a town where he was a living reproach both to her and to the entire regiment. And that was the end of the poor chap—he became a beggar, and then froze to death somewhere on a Petersburg pier.

"The second case was quite a pitiful one. The woman was just like the other, except that she was young and pretty. Her behaviour was most reprehensible. Light as we made of domestic affairs like that, we were shocked. But her husband didn't mind. He knew and saw everything but did nothing to stop it. His friends gave him hints, but he waved them away. 'Cut it out. It's no business of mine. All I want is for Lena to be happy.' Such a fool!

"In the end she got herself seriously involved with Lieutenant Vishnyakov, a subaltern from their company. And the three of them lived in two-husband wedlock, as if it were the most lawful kind of matrimony. Then our regiment was ordered to the front. Our ladies saw us off, and so did she, but, really, it was sickening: she didn't so much as glance at her husband, at least to keep up appearances if for no other reason. Instead she hung on her lieutenant like ivy on a rotten wall, and wouldn't leave him for a second. By way of farewell, when we were settled in the train and the train started, the hussy shouted after her husband, 'See that you take good care of Volodya! If anything happens to him I'll leave the house and never come back. And I'll take the children with me.'

"Perhaps you imagine the captain was a ninny? A jelly-fish? A sissy? Not at all. He was a brave soldier. At Zeloniye Gori he led his company against a Turkish redoubt six times, and of his two hundred men only fourteen were left. He was wounded twice, but refused to go to the medical station. That's what he was like. The soldiers worshipped him.

"But *she* had told him what to do. His Lena had!

"And so, like a nurse or a mother, he took care of that coward and idler Vishnyakov, that lazy drone. At night in camp, in rain and mud, he'd wrap him in his own greatcoat. He would supervise a sapper's job for him, while he lounged in a dug-out or played faro. At night he'd inspect the outposts for Vishnyakov. And that was at a time, mark you, when the Turks used to cut down our pickets as easily as a Yaroslavl countrywoman cuts down her cabbages. It's a sin to say so, but, upon my honour, everybody was happy to learn that Vishnyakov had died of typhus in hospital."

"How about women, Grandad? Have you never met loving women?"

"Of course I have, Vera. I'll say more: I'm sure that almost every woman in love is capable of sublime heroism. Don't you see, from the moment she kisses, embraces, gives herself, she is a *mother*. Love to her, if she does love, is the whole meaning of life—the whole universe! But it is no fault of hers that love has assumed such vulgar forms and degenerated into a sort of everyday convenience, a little diversion. The ones to blame are the men, who are surfeited at twenty, who have a chicken's body and a rabbit's heart, and are incapable of strong desires, heroic deeds, the tenderness and worship of love. They say real love did exist at one time. If not, then isn't it what the best minds and souls of the world—poets, novelists, musicians, artists—have dreamt of and longed for? The other day I read the story of Manon Lescaut and Cavalier des Grieux. It brought tears to my eyes—it really did. Tell me in all honesty, doesn't every woman dream, deep in her heart, of such a love—a single-minded, all-forgiving love ready to bear anything, modest and self-sacrificing?"

"Of course she does, Grandad."

"And since it isn't there women take their revenge. In another thirty years or so from now—I shan't live to see it, Vera dear, but you may; remember what I'm telling you—some thirty years from now women will wield unprecedented power in the world. They will dress like Indian idols. They'll trample us men underfoot as contemptible, grovelling slaves. Their extravagant wishes and whims will become painful laws for us. And all because throughout the generations we've been unable to worship and revere love. It will be a vengeance. You know the law: action and reaction are equal and opposite."

He paused a while, then asked suddenly, "Tell me, Vera, if only you don't find it embarrassing, what was that story about a telegraphist which Prince Vasily told us tonight? How much of it is fact and how much his usual embellishment?"

"Do you really wish to know, Grandad?"

"Only if you care to tell me, Vera. If for some reason you'd rather not—"

"Not at all. I'll tell you with pleasure."

And she told the general in detail about a crazy man who had begun to pursue her with his love two years before her marriage.

She had never seen him, and did not know his name. He had only written to her, signing G.S.Z. Once he had mentioned that he was a clerk in some office—he had not said a word about the telegraph office. He was apparently watching her movements closely, because in his letters he always mentioned very accurately where she had spent this or that evening and in what company, and how she had been dressed. At first his letters sounded vulgar and ludicrously ardent, although they were quite proper. But once she wrote to ask him—"by the way, Grandad, don't let that out to our people: nobody knows it"—not to annoy her any more with his protestations of love. From then on he wrote no more about love. and sent her only an occasional letter—at Easter, on New Year's Eve, and on her birthday. Princess Vera also told the general about that day's parcel and gave him almost word for word the strange letter from her mysterious admirer.

"Y-es," the general drawled at last. "Perhaps he's just an addle-head, a maniac, or—who knows?—perhaps the path of your life has been crossed by the very kind of love that women dream about and men are no longer capable of. Just a moment. Do you see lights moving ahead? That must be my carriage."

At the same time they heard behind them the blare of a motor-car and the road, rutted by wheels, shone in a white acetylene light. Gustav Ivanovich drove up.

"I've taken your things with me, Anna. Get in," he said. "May I give you a lift, Your Excellency?"

"No, thank you, my friend," answered the general. "I don't like that engine. All it does is shake and stink—there's no pleasure in it. Well, good night, Vera dear. I'll be coming often now," he said, kissing Vera's forehead and hands.

There were goodbyes all round. Friesse drove Vera Nikolayevna to the gate of her villa and, swiftly describing a circle, shot off into the darkness in his roaring, puffing motor-car.

IX

With a disagreeable feeling Princess Vera stepped on to the terrace and walked into the house. From a distance she heard the loud voice of her brother Nikolai and saw his gaunt figure darting back and forth across the room. Vasily Lvovich sat at the card table, his large head with the cropped tow hair bent low as he traced lines on the green cloth with a piece of chalk.

"It should have been done long ago!" said Nikolai irritably, making a gesture with his right hand as if he were throwing down some invisible burden. "I was convinced long ago that an end should have been put to those foolish letters. Vera wasn't yet your wife when I told you that you and she ought not to make fun of them like children, seeing only what was laughable in them. Here's Vera herself, by the way. Vasily Lvovich and I were talking about that madman of yours, P.P.Z. I consider the correspondence insolent and vulgar."

"There was no correspondence," Sheyin interrupted him coldly. "He was the only one who wrote."

Vera blushed at that, and sat down on the sofa, in the shade of a large fan-palm.

"I'm sorry," said Nikolai Nikolayevich, and threw down the invisible heavy object, as if he had torn it from his chest.

"I wonder why you call him mine," Vera put in, heartened by her husband's support. "He's mine as much as he's yours."

"All right, I'm sorry again. In short, what I mean is that we must put an end to his foolishness. I think this matter is getting beyond the stage where we may just laugh and draw funny pictures. Believe me that what I'm concerned about is Vera's reputation and yours, Vasily Lvovich."

"I think you're exaggerating, Kolya," replied Sheyin.

"Perhaps I am. But you risk finding yourself quite easily in a ridiculous position."

"I don't see how," said the prince.

"Suppose this idiotic bracelet"—Nikolai lifted the red case from the table and at once threw it down again with disgust—"this monstrous thing remains in our house, or we throw it out or present it to Dasha. Then, first of all, P.P.Z. will be able to brag to his acquaintances or friends that Princess Vera Nikolayevna Sheyina accepts his gifts, and, secondly, the first opportunity will encourage him to further exploits. Tomorrow he may send her a diamond ring, the day after a pearl necklace, and then, for all we knew, he may land in the dock for embezzlement or fraud and Prince and Princess Sheyin will be summoned to testify as witnesses. A nice prospect, eh?"

"The bracelet must certainly be sent back!" cried Vasily Lvovich.

"I think so too," Vera assented, "and the sooner the better. But how are we to do it? We don't know the name or address."

"Oh, that's child's play," Nikolai Nikolayevich replied carelessly. "We know the initials of this P.P.Z. Is that what they are, Vera?"

"G.S.Z."

"Very good. Besides, we know that he's employed somewhere. That's quite enough. Tomorrow I'll take the town directory and look up an official or clerk with those initials. If I don't find him for some reason, I'll simply call a detective and get him to trace the man for me. In case of difficulty I'll have this paper here with his handwriting. In short, by two o'clock tomorrow I'll know the exact name and address of the fellow and even the hours when he's in. And then we'll not only give him back his treasure tomorrow but will also see that he never reminds us of his existence again."

"What are you going to do?" asked Prince Vasily.

"What? I'm going to call on the governor."

"Not the governor—please! You know what terms we're on with him. We'd only make ourselves ridiculous."

"All right. I'll go to the chief of police. He's a club-mate of mine. Let him summon that Romeo and shake his finger under the man's nose. Do you know how he does it? He brings his finger close to your nose but doesn't move his hand—he just wags his finger and bawls, 'I won't stand for this, sir!' "

"Fie! Fancy dealing with the police!" said Vera, pulling a wry face.

"You're right, Vera," the prince agreed. "We'd better not drag any outsiders into this. There'd be rumours and gossip. We all know what our town is like. One might as well live in a glass jar. I think I had better go to that —er—young man myself; God knows he may be sixty. I'll hand him the bracelet and give him a talking to."

"Then I'll go with you," Nikolai Nikolayevich cut in. "You're too soft. Leave it to me to talk with him

364

And now, my friends"—he pulled out his watch and glanced at it—"you'll excuse me if I go to my room. I can hardly stand on my feet, and I have two files to look through."

"Somehow I feel sorry for that unfortunate man," said Vera hesitantly.

"No reason to feel sorry for him!" Nikolai retorted, turning in the doorway. "If anyone of our own class had played that trick with the bracelet and letter Prince Vasily would have sent him a challenge. Or if he hadn't, I would. In the old days I'd simply have had him flogged in the stable. You'll wait for me in your office tomorrow, Vasily Lvovich. I'll telephone you."

X

The filthy staircase smelled of mice, cats, paraffin-oil, and washing. Before they had reached the fifth floor Prince Vasily Lvovich halted.

"Wait a bit," he said to his brother-in-law. "Let me catch my breath. Oh, Kolya, we shouldn't have come here."

They climbed another two flights. It was so dark on the stairs that Nikolai Nikolayevich had to strike two matches before he made out the number of the flat.

He rang and was answered by a stout, white-haired, grey-eyed woman wearing spectacles, and slightly bent forward, apparently as a result of some disease.

"Is Mr. Zheltkov in?" asked Nikolai Nikolayevich.

The woman's eyes looked in alarm from one to the other and back. The two men's respectable appearance seemed to reassure her.

"Yes, won't you come in?" she said, stepping back. "First door on your left."

Bulat-Tuganovsky knocked three times, briefly and firmly.

"Come in," a faint voice responded.

The room had a very low ceiling, but it was very wide —almost square in shape. Its two round windows, which looked very much like port-holes, let in little light. In fact, it was rather like the mess-room of a cargo ship. Against one of the walls stood a narrow bedstead, against another was a broad sofa covered with an excellent but worn Tekke rug, and in the middle stood a table spread with a coloured Ukrainian cloth.

At first the visitors could not see the occupant's face, for he stood with his back to the light, rubbing his hands in perplexity. He was tall and thin, with long, silky hair.

"Mr. Zheltkov, if I'm not mistaken?" Nikolai Nikolayevich asked haughtily.

"Yes, that's my name. Very glad to meet you."

Holding out his hand, he took two paces towards Tuganovsky. But Nikolai Nikolayevich turned to Sheyin as if he had not noticed the gesture of welcome.

"I told you we weren't mistaken."

Zheltkov's slim, nervous fingers ran up and down the front of his short brown jacket, buttoning and unbuttoning it. At last he said with an effort, pointing to the sofa and bowing awkwardly, "Pray be seated."

He had now come into full view, a man with a very pallid, delicate girl's face, blue eyes and a cleft chin like a wilful child's; he looked somewhere between thirty and thirty-five.

"Thank you," said Prince Sheyin, who had been scanning him with keen interest.

"*Merci*," Nikolai Nikolayevich answered briefly. And both remained standing. "It'll only take us a few minutes. This is Prince Vasily Lvovich Sheyin, the marshal of nobility in this province. My name is Mirza Bulat-Tuganovsky. I'm assistant public prosecutor. The business which we shall have the honour to discuss with you concerns in equal measure the prince and myself, or, to be exact, concerns the prince's wife, who is my sister."

Completely dazed, Zheltkov sank down on the sofa and stammered through blanched lips, "Please, sit down, gentlemen." But, apparently recalling that he had already suggested that, he jumped up, rushed to the window, tousling his hair, and came back again. And once more his trembling hands ran up and down, tugging at his buttons, plucking his light-coloured, reddish moustache, and touching his face.

"I am at your service, Your Highness," he said in a hollow voice, with an entreating gaze at Vasily Lvovich.

But Sheyin made no reply. It was Nikolai Nikolayevich who spoke.

"First of all, may I return something that belongs to you," he said, and, taking the red case from his pocket, he carefully put it down on the table. "To be sure, it does credit to your taste, but we earnestly request that no further surprises of this kind shall be sprung on us."

"Please forgive me. I know I'm very much at fault," whispered Zheltkov, flushing, his eyes on the floor. "Wouldn't you like a glass of tea?"

"You see, Mr. Zheltkov," Nikolai Nikolayevich went on, as if he had not heard Zheltkov's last words. "I'm very glad to see you are a gentleman, who can take a hint. I believe we shall reach agreement promptly. If I'm not mistaken, you have been pursuing Princess Vera Nikolayevna for the last seven or eight years?"

"Yes," answered Zheltkov softly, and lowered his eyelashes in awe.

"But so far we haven't taken any action against you, although you'll concede that we could and, indeed, *should* have done so. Don't you agree?"

"Yes."

"Yes. But by your last act, namely, by sending this garnet bracelet, you overstepped the limit of our forbearance. Do you understand? the limit. I shall not conceal from you that our first thought was to refer the matter to the authorities, but we didn't do so, and I'm glad we didn't, because—I'll say it again—I saw at once that you are an honourable man."

"I beg your pardon. What was that you said?" Zheltkov asked suddenly, and laughed. "You were about to refer the matter to the authorities? Did I understand you rightly?"

He put his hands in his pockets, made himself comfortable in a corner of the sofa, took out his cigarette-case and matches, and lighted a cigarette.

"So you said you were about to refer the matter to the authorities? You will pardon my sitting, Prince?" he said to Sheyin. "Well, go on."

The prince pulled a chair up to the table and sat down. Mystified and eager, he gazed fixedly at the face of the strange man.

"It's open to us to take that step at any time, my good man," Nikolai Nikolayevich continued, with some insolence. "Butting into a stranger's family—"

"I beg to interrupt you—"

"No, I beg to interrupt *you*," all but shouted the assistant prosecutor.

"As you wish. Go on. I'm listening. But I want a word with Prince Vasily Lvovich."

And paying no more attention to Tuganovsky, he said, "This is the most difficult moment of my life. And I must speak without any regard for convention. Will you listen to me?"

"I'm listening," said Sheyin. "Be quiet, Kolya, please!" he said impatiently as he saw Tuganovsky make an angry gesture. "Yes?"

For a few seconds Zheltkov's breathing came in choking gasps, and suddenly he burst out in a torrent of words. He spoke with only his jaws; his lips were a ghastly white, and rigid like a dead man's.

"It's hard to utter those words—to say that I love your wife. But seven years of hopeless and unassuming love give me some right to it. I'll own that at first, while Vera Nikolayevna was still unmarried, I wrote her foolish letters and even expected her to answer them. I agree that my last step, namely, sending the bracelet, was an even more foolish thing to do. But—I look you straight in the eyes and I feel that you'll understand me. I know it's beyond my power ever to stop loving her. Tell me, Prince—supposing you resent the whole thing—tell me what you would do to break off that feeling? Would you have me transported to some other town, as Nikolai Nikolayevich suggested? But there I would go on loving Vera Nikolayevna as much as I do here. Put me in jail? But there, too, I'd find means to remind her of my existence. So the only solution is death. If you so desire I'll accept death in any form."

"Instead of talking business, here we are up to our necks in melodrama," said Nikolai Nikolayevich, putting on his hat. "The point is quite clear: either you cease completely persecuting Princess Vera Nikolayevna or, if you don't, we shall take such measures as are available to men of our standing, our influence, and so on."

But Zheltkov did not so much as glance at him, although he had heard him. Instead he asked Prince Vasily Lvovich, "Would you mind my leaving you for ten minutes? I'll admit that I'm going to speak to Princess Vera Nikolayevna on the telephone. I assure you I will report to you as much of the conversation as I can."

"All right," said Sheyin.

Left alone with his brother-in-law, Nikolai Nikolaye-vich set upon him at once.

"This won't do," he shouted, his right hand as usual throwing down some invisible object from his chest. "This just won't do. I warned you I would take care of the matter. But you turned sloppy and gave him a chance to enlarge on his feelings. I'd have put everything in two words."

"Wait," said Prince Vasily Lvovich, "everything will be cleared up in a moment. The important thing is, I think he has the face of a man who is unable to deceive or lie deliberately. But is it his fault that he's in love? And how can you control a feeling like love, which people still can't account for?" He paused thoughtfully, and added, "I feel sorry for the man. Moreover, I feel as if I'm looking at a tremendous tragedy of the soul, and I can't behave like a clown."

"I call that decadence," said Nikolai Nikolayevich.

Ten minutes later Zheltkov came back. His eyes were shining and deep, as if they were filled with unshed tears. And it was obvious that he had quite forgotten about his good manners, about who should sit where, and had stopped behaving like a gentleman. And once again Prince Sheyin understood the reason with great sensitiveness.

"I'm ready," he said. "From tomorrow you'll hear nothing more of me. For you, I'm as good as dead. But there's one condition—I say this to *you,* Prince Vasily Lvovich—I've embezzled money and I must fly from this town anyway. Will you permit me to write a last letter to Princess Vera Nikolayevna?"

"No. If it's finished, it's finished. No letters!" shouted Nikolai Nikolayevich.

"All right, you may," said Sheyin.

"That's all," said Zheltkov, smiling haughtily. "You'll hear no more of me, let alone see me. Princess Vera Nikolayevna didn't want to speak to me at all. When I asked her if I might remain in town so as to see her at least occasionally—without being seen by her, of course—she said, 'If only you knew how tired I am of the whole business! Please stop it as soon as you can.' And so I'm stopping the whole business. I think I've done all I could, haven't I?"

Coming back to the villa that evening, Vasily Lvovich told his wife in detail about his interview with Zheltkov. He seemed to feel it was his duty to do that.

Vera was worried, but not surprised or bewildered. Later that night, when her husband came into her bed, she suddenly turned away to the wall and said, "Leave me alone—I know that man is going to kill himself."

XI

Princess Vera Nikolayevna never read the newspapers because, firstly, they dirtied her hands, and, secondly, she could never make head or tail of the language which they use nowadays.

But fate willed it that she should open the page and come upon the column which carried this news:

"A Mysterious Death. G. S. Zheltkov, an employee of the Board of Control, committed suicide about seven o'clock last night. According to evidence given at the inquest, his death was prompted by an embezzlement He left a note to that effect. Since testimony furnished by witnesses has established that he died by his own hand, it has been decided not to order a post-mortem."

Vera thought, "Why did I feel it was coming? Precisely this tragic finale? And what was it: love or madness?"

All day long she wandered about the flower-garden and the orchard. The anxiety growing in her from minute to minute made her restless. And all her thoughts were riveted on the unknown man whom she had never seen, and would hardly ever see—that ridiculous "P.P.Z."

"Who knows? Perhaps a real, self-sacrificing, true love has crossed the path of your life," she recalled what Anosov had said.

At six o'clock the postman came. This time Vera Nikolayevna recognized Zheltkov's handwriting, and she unfolded the letter with greater tenderness than she would have expected of herself.

This was what Zheltkov wrote:

"It is not my fault, Vera Nikolayevna, that God willed to send to me, as an enormous happiness, love for you. I happen not to be interested in anything like politics, science, philosophy, or man's future happiness; to me life is centred in you alone. Now I realize that I have thrust myself into your life like an embarrassing wedge. Please forgive me for that if you can. I am leaving today and shall never come back, and there will be nothing to remind you of me.

"I am immensely grateful to you just because you exist. I have examined myself, and I know it is not a disease, not the obsession of a maniac—it is love with which God has chosen to reward me for some reason.

"I may have appeared ridiculous to you and your brother, Nikolai Nikolayevich. As I depart I say in ecstasy, 'Hallowed be thy name.'

"Eight years ago I saw you in a circus box, and from the very first second I said to myself: I love her because there is nothing on earth like her, nothing better, no animal, no plant, no star, because no human being is more beautiful than she, or more delicate. The whole beauty of the earth seemed to be embodied in you.

"What was I to do? Fly to some other town? But my heart was always beside you, at your feet, at every moment it was filled with you, with thoughts of you, with dreams of you, with a sweet madness. I am very much ashamed of, and blush in my mind for, that foolish bracelet—well, it cannot be helped; it was a mistake. I can imagine the impression it made on your guests.

"I shall be gone in ten minutes from now. I shall just have time to stick a postage stamp on this letter and drop it into a box, so as not to ask anyone else to do it. Please burn this letter. I have just heated the stove and am burning all that was precious to me in life: your handkerchief which, I confess, I stole. You left it on a chair at a ball in the Noblemen's Assembly. Your note —oh, how I kissed it!—in which you forbade me to write to you. A programme of an art exhibition, which you once held in your hand and left forgotten on a chair by the entrance. It is finished. I have cut off everything, but still I believe, and even feel confident, that you will think of me. If you do—I know you are very musical, for I saw you mostly at performances of the Beethoven quartets— if you do think of me, please play, or get someone else to play, the Sonata in D-dur No. 2, op. 2.

"I wonder how I shall close my letter. I thank you from the bottom of my heart because you have been my only joy in life, my only comfort, my sole thought. May God give you happiness, and may nothing transient or commonplace disturb your wonderful soul. I kiss your hands.

"G.S.Z."

She went to her husband, her eyes red with crying and her lips swollen, and, showing him the letter, she said, "I don't want to conceal anything from you, but I have a feeling that something terrible has come into our life.

You and Nikolai Nikolayevich probably didn't handle the matter properly."

Prince Sheyin read the letter with deep attention, folded it carefully, and said after a long pause, "I don't doubt this man's sincerity, and what's more, I don't think I have a right to analyze his feelings towards you."

"Is he dead?" asked Vera.

"Yes, he's dead. I think he loved you and wasn't mad at all. I watched him all the time and saw his every movement, every change in his face. There was no life for him without you. I felt as if I were witnessing a tremendous agony, and I almost realized that I was dealing with a dead man. You see, Vera, I didn't know how to behave or what to do."

"Look here, Vasya," she interrupted him. "Would it pain you if I went to town to take a look at him?"

"No, no, Vera, please go. I'd like to go myself, but Nikolai's bungled the whole thing. I'm afraid I should feel awkward."

XII

Vera Nikolayevna left her carriage two blocks off Luteranskaya Street. She found Zheltkov's flat without much difficulty. She was met by the same grey-eyed old woman, very stout and wearing silver-rimmed spectacles, who asked as she had done the day before, "Who do you wish to see?"

"Mr. Zheltkov," said the princess.

Her costume—her hat and gloves—and her rather peremptory tone apparently impressed the landlady. She began to talk.

"Please step in, it's the first door on your left, and there—he is— He left us so soon. Well, suppose he did embezzle money. He should have told me about it. You

374

know we don't make much by letting rooms to bachelors. But if it was a matter of six or seven hundred rubles I could have scraped it together to pay for him. If only you knew, madam, what a wonderful man he was. He had been my lodger for eight years, but he was more like a son to me."

There was a chair in the passage, and Vera sank down upon it.

"I'm a friend of your late lodger," she said, carefully choosing her words. "Please tell me something about his last minutes, about what he said and did."

"Two gentlemen came to see him, madam, and had a very long talk with him. Then he told me they'd offered him the position of bailiff on an estate. Then Mr. George ran out to telephone and came back so happy. And then the two gentlemen left, but he sat down and began writing a letter. Then he went out to post the letter, and then we heard something like a shot from a toy pistol. We paid no attention to it. He always had tea at seven o'clock. Lukerya, the maid, went to knock at his door, but he didn't answer, and she knocked again and again. We had to force the door, and there he lay dead."

"Tell me something about the bracelet," Vera Nikolayevna commanded.

"Ah, the bracelet—I quite forgot. How do you know about it? Before writing the letter he came to me and said, 'Are you a Catholic?' 'Yes,' I said. Then he says, 'You have a nice custom'—that was what he said—'a nice custom of hanging rings, necklaces, and gifts on the image of the Holy Virgin. So won't you please hang this bracelet on your icon?' I promised."

"Will you let me see him?" asked Vera.

"Of course, madam. There's his door, the first on the left. They were going to take him to the dissecting-room today, but he has a brother who asked permission to give him a Christian burial. Please come."

Vera braced herself and opened the door. The room smelled of incense, and three wax candles were burning in it. Zheltkov was lying on the table, placed diagonally. His head rested on a very low support—a small soft cushion that someone seemed to have pushed under it purposely, because that did not make any difference to a corpse. His closed eyes suggested deep gravity, and his lips were set in a blissful, serene smile, as if before parting with life he had learned some deep, sweet mystery that had solved the whole riddle of his life. She remembered having seen the same peaceful expression on the death-masks of two great martyrs, Pushkin and Napoleon.

"Would you like me to leave you alone, madam?" asked the old woman, a very intimate note in her voice.

"Yes, I'll call you later," said Vera, and she at once took a big red rose from the side pocket of her jacket, slightly raised the head of the corpse with her left hand, and with her right hand put the flower under his neck. At that moment she realized that that love of which every woman dreams had gone past her. She recalled what General Anosov had said, almost prophetically, about everlasting, exclusive love. And, pushing aside the hair on the dead man's forehead, she clutched his temples with her hands and put her lips to his cold, moist forehead in a long, affectionate kiss.

When she was leaving the landlady spoke to her in her ingratiating accent.

"I can see, madam, that you're not like others, who come out of mere curiosity. Before his death Mr. Zheltkov said to me, 'If I happen to die and a lady comes to look at me tell her that Beethoven's best work is—' He wrote it down for me. Here, look."

"Let me see it," said Vera Nikolayevna, and suddenly she broke into tears. "Please excuse me—this death shocked me so I couldn't help myself."

She read the words, written in the familiar hand: "*L. van Beethoven. Son. No. 2, op. 2. Largo Appassionato.*"

XIII

Vera Nikolayevna came home late in the evening and was glad not to find either her husband or her brother in.

However, Jennie Reiter was waiting for her; troubled by what she had seen and heard, Vera rushed to her and cried as she kissed her large beautiful hands, "Please play something for me, Jennie dear, I beg of you." And at once she went out of the room and sat on a bench in the flower-garden.

She scarcely doubted for a moment that Jennie would play the passage from the sonata asked for by that dead man with the odd name of Zheltkov.*

And so it happened. From the very first chords Vera recognized that extraordinary work, unique in depth. And her soul seemed to split in two. She thought that a great love, of the kind which comes but once in a thousand years, had passed her by. She recalled General Anosov's words, wondering why Zheltkov had made her listen, of all Beethoven, to this particular work. Words strung themselves together in her mind. They fell in with the music to such an extent that they were like the verses of a hymn, each ending with the words: *"Hallowed be thy name."*

"I shall now show you in tender sounds a life that meekly and joyfully doomed itself to torture, suffering,

* Derived from *zheltok*, yolk.—*Tr.*

377

and death. I knew nothing like complaint, reproach, or the pain of love scorned. To you I pray: *'Hallowed be thy name.'*

"Yes, I foresee suffering, blood, and death. And I think that it is hard for the body to part with the soul, but I give you praise, beautiful one, passionate praise, and a gentle love. *'Hallowed be thy name.'*

"I recall your every step, every smile, every look, the sound of your footsteps. My last memories are enwrapped in sweet sadness—in gentle, beautiful sadness. But I shall cause you no sorrow. I shall go alone, silently, for such is the will of God and fate. *'Hallowed be thy name.'*

"In my sorrowful dying hour I pray to you alone. Life might have been beautiful for me too. Do not murmur, my poor heart, do not. In my soul I call death, but my heart is full of praise for you: *'Hallowed be thy name.'*

"You do not know—neither you nor those around you —how beautiful you are. The clock is striking. It is time. And, dying, in the mournful hour of parting with life I still sing—glory to you.

"Here it comes, all-subduing death, but I say— glory to you!'

With her arms round the slender trunk of an acacia and her body pressed to it, Princess Vera was weeping. The tree shook gently. A wind came on a light wing to rustle in the leaves, as if in sympathy. The smell of the tobacco-plant was more pungent. Meanwhile the marvellous music continued, responding to her grief:

"Be at peace, my dearest, be at peace. Do you remember me? Do you? You are my last, my only love. Be at peace, I am with you. Think of me, and I shall be with you, because you and I loved each other only an instant, but for ever. Do you remember me? Do you? Here, I can feel your tears. Be at peace. Sleep is so sweet, so sweet to me."

Having finished the piece, Jennie Reiter came out of the room and saw Princess Vera, bathed in tears, sitting on the bench.

"What's the matter?" asked the pianist.

Her eyes glistening, Vera, restless and agitated, kissed Jennie's face and lips and eyes as she said, "It's all right, he has forgiven me now. All is well."

1911

ABOUT THE AUTHOR

Alexander Ivanovich Kuprin was born in 1870, in the small provincial town of Narovchata. His father, an official of modest means,
died when the boy was about a year old. Soon the family moved
to Moscow. Kuprin's mother was compelled to send him at the age
of seven to an orphans' school; three years later he entered a
military school.

In 1889 the eighteen-year-old Kuprin, then a military cadet, had
published in a newspaper a short story, "The Last Début," and
was placed under arrest, because cadets were not allowed to write
anything for the press. In 1893, after an unsuccessful attempt to
enter the General Staff Academy, he gave up his military career
and became a "free man."

Penniless he arrived in Kiev. There came years of "unemploy-
ment, wandering, dire poverty." In his "Autobiography" he says:
"I found myself in a strange city without money, without relatives or acquaintances. Worst of all, I had no special training, or
any real knowledge of life."

He wrote short stories and poetry, which were published in
newspapers and magazines, and worked as a reporter, clerk, estate
bailiff, actor in a provincial company, land surveyor, and porter.

In 1896 his first major work, *Moloch*, was published.

A year later his short stories appeared in a collection.

That was when he met Maxim Gorky. Gorky invited him to
contribute to the Znanye Company literary collections, in which
many progressive Russian authors published their works. After the
publication of *The Duel,* a story dedicated to Gorky, Kuprin wrote
to him· "I owe to you all that is bold and impetuous in my story
If you only knew how much I have learned from you and how
grateful I am for it."

In the years preceding the first Russian revolution (1905), Kuprin became increasingly popular as a writer. His literary work, his humane sentiments, and his improving artistic skill earned him high praise from progressive critics

But in the years of reaction, which set in after the defeat of the revolution of 1905, Kuprin drifted away from Gorky and associated with decadent writers, who tried to discredit the democratic tradition in literature and advocated art for art's sake

Kuprin's reaction to the Great October Socialist Revolution was sympathetic, but he did not grasp its significance. He was afraid of what seemed to him "elemental" in the movement of the people, and he doubted whether he would be able to work as a writer in the new, Soviet Russia.

From 1920 to 1937 he lived in Paris While abroad he hardly wrote anything, except a few chapters of *The Cadet*, an autobiographical novel. Throughout those years he was aware of the mistake he had made, and longed to go back to his country "My heart aches and yearns for my homeland, unabatingly..
It is only in Russia that I can work for her...." he said.

In 1937 Kuprin came back to his country "I am happy," he said," "to hear at last my own Russian language spoken all around me.... During the last years ... I have keenly felt and realized my heavy guilt towards the Russian people, who are doing a wonderful job—building a new life " He planned to write new books about the Soviet people, about their creative effort, but illness prevented him from doing so He died in 1938

Printed in the United States
1459200001B/4